THE HUNGER ARTIST

A Novel

Jeffrey N. Johnson

MEDDLER PRESS
Alexandria, Virginia

MEDDLER PRESS
Alexandria, Virginia 22308

ISBN: 978-0-692-27122-3

Printed in the United States of America

Acknowledgments

The author would like to thank the Virginia Center for the Creative Arts and the Mid-Atlantic Arts Foundation for providing much needed solitude. Praise to my first readers, Sally Hazard, Joan Pryde and Jill Sanderson for their insights and for not pulling any punches. And thanks to the mighty and motley crew of writers and provocateurs at Scrawl for their critiques of my early work, as well as their literary and not so literary comradery over the years. Above all I thank my toughest reader and greatest friend, my wife and my life – Heather.

To the memory of my mother and father.

THE HUNGER ARTIST

A Novel

Prologue

Carl Rittenhaur hadn't thought of the consequences of throwing the first punch. As a boy of thirteen, when fisticuff challenges were a rite of passage in the locker rooms and hallways of junior high, he managed to avoid the brawls and bruises through luck, timing and a pedestrian gaze that made his classmates forget he was there. Petrified of the more riotous boys in school, he hid his fear behind a face of passive indifference, though the face was a lie. His mind raged at the injustices witnessed and the humiliations of every boy who succumbed to the casual and unchecked bullying. It wasn't until his friend, Mick Coates, was slammed against a locker by a member of the wrestling team that Carl's mask dissolved. Perhaps being unfamiliar with the combat ritual aided his courage and blinded his common sense. The instant he threw the punch, an uncontrolled blow at best, he felt euphoric, the smack of flesh and the pounding of bone being justice too long denied. He had no way of knowing that four hours after his fist made contact with the thug's right jaw his parents would lose their lives.

After the wrestler regrouped, which didn't take long, he released his own barrage of merciless overhands, and things went grey for Carl. His euphoria passed. His face felt like it was being beaten with a bowling pin, but instead of covering up or backing away, he stood there taking it blow-by-blow. This was his first fight and on some nebulous level, whether in defense of his friend or not, he knew he was receiving his penance for starting it. The repeated blows to the brain frightened and fascinated him as he tongued his lip and tasted both blood and rebellion. He was soon beyond the point of making decisions, though there were few choices left when he was hoisted off the floor by the strong arm of the assistant principal.

"Turn the other cheek," his mother, Anna, lectured him the week before the incident. She would frequently recite homegrown platitudes and verses from the Bible, not in some fire-and-brimstone sermon, but in an affirmative prose that made her son feel as if he'd been taken into the confidence of God himself, or at least God's secretary. Carl sat at the kitchen table in the old stone farmhouse eating the breakfast she'd prepared for him. He mixed the last of the cold eggs into the grease from the sausages. He didn't looked up once from his plate during her entire address.

"But they're beating on Mick now," Carl said.

Her son's comment proved none of her homily had sunk in. "That's Mick's business," Anna said, slipping over the edge of impatience. She turned and snapped a finger at him. "He needs to tell the principal. It's the principal's job to deal with bullying. You keep to yourself, else your choices will come home and nip you in the butt." Anna Rittenhaur's rare bouts of wrath were biting and swift, making her ideally placed as the disciplinarian of the family. She countered any of her son's dubious behavior with a dictatorial tone that shamed him into submission. Carl was always on his best behavior in her presence and regarded her like a disciple would his savior – he both loved and feared her.

"Take the son-of-a-bitch out," his father countered the next day as he heaved a bale of fresh cut clover into the hay loft at Carl's feet. The sun lit a churning storm of hay dust where it poured into the barn, but the cloud was invisible in the dark corners where Carl and his grandfather were dragging and stacking the bales. Grandfather Rittenhaur needed only one arm and a steel baling hook to do the work, but Carl had to throw his whole body at the task. Jack Rittenhaur stood below them on a half loaded trailer with gloved hands and a sweat soaked shirt. He must have had some memory of school-life at Carl's age and remembered the limits of adolescent tolerance. "If it's as bad as you say, I'm surprised you haven't already taken a swing."

Malcolm Rittenhaur, Carl's grandfather, stepped to the loft door. The baling hook was a gross extension of his arm, and he shook it at his son. "You ain't taught this boy nothing about fighting."

Jack dropped a bale and paused for a moment. He touched the brim of his hat and squinted. "Anna would frown on it, I suppose."

"Don't be sending him into no fight until you teach him something about it. I ain't seen him so much as kill a lightning bug."

Jack Rittenhaur was a quiet man who deferred all but the major family decisions to his wife, but this time he was at an impasse. He called to his son, and Carl stepped by the old man into the light. "Well alright then," Jack said, sizing up his boy. "You at least need to learn some defensive moves. Your mother can't object to that."

The same evening behind one of the outbuildings surrounding the farmhouse, Jack Rittenhaur gave his youngest son his first and last instruction on boxing while his own father watched from his seat on a tree stump. Carl had developed little in muscle tone and was excited at the attention as if given a car and a license to drive. Though he didn't realize it at the time, this was to be one of his fondest memories of time spent with his father. They worked a half hour on the basics, his stance and balance and a few basic punches. Carl flailed his arms wildly and was out-of-sync with anything resembling rhythm. His grandfather looked on, shaking his head. After the session Jack took his son by the arm and spoke to him in grave tones, calmed him down and told him how wrong it was to fight and how nothing good ever comes from violence. He concluded by giving Carl blessing to kick some ass, if ass-kicking was indeed called for. But only when he had seen enough. Only when he had no other options.

The day Carl decided his options were spent, he wasted a perfectly good afternoon in detention and suffered the indignity of waiting on the school house steps to be picked up by his angry parents. After speaking to the principal over the phone, Anna Rittenhaur went into a tirade and made it clear this would not happen again. No son of hers was going to be known for picking fights. Late in the afternoon the last teacher to leave for home, and even the principal, failed to notice Carl still loitering by the flagpole. He stood there in the waning daylight licking his swollen lip, his face still numb from the hammering it had taken. Night came on and he huddled by the door under the canopy. When a police cruiser eventually pulled up, he was sitting alone on the steps under a spot light, shivering, though not from the cold. He knew something was wrong.

Jack and Anna Rittenhaur were on the way to retrieve their delinquent son when their sedan was torn in half by a tractor-trailer on the bypass. Carl's birthday gifts were found in the wreckage, but due to an oversight the police didn't turn over the shopping bags that had been cut from the trunk until a month after the accident. His grandparents, still shaken from the loss of their only son and daughter-in-law, never wrapped the belated gifts, but left them on Carl's bed where he discovered them one day after school. The soft plastic body-bag cover did little to protect his new guitar. The A, D & E machine bolts had ripped off the splintered neck in the accident. Carl strummed his fingers over the three remaining strings, all flat and out of tune, and promptly laid the ruined instrument to rest in the back of his closet. His new timepiece, a Swatch with a face of minimalist red dots, was undamaged, but he examined it for no more than a breath before placing it in a drawer.

For two years after his parents' deaths, which happened a week before his fourteenth birthday — a day left vacant by his mourning grandparents — Carl grieved in a silent wonder of fog and regret. There was a new seriousness about the boy as if he were always reading the front page of the newspaper, digesting the latest rape, murder, or far-off genocide. His grandparents weren't sure what to make of him. The generation gap doubled the second the sheriff informed them of the accident, and it didn't help that this tragedy coincided with the normal bout of teenage apathy. His grandfather, whose only philosophy was "hard work makes the man," was fed up with the dinner table silence and reacted by expanding Carl's farm chores, which only made Carl suspicious of the old man's motives. Since his older brother was already married and on his own, he felt like a replacement for lost labor, or worse — all the extra work was punishment for having a hand in his parents' fates.

For lack of a better outlet for his pain, Carl began to draw. He had shown artistic merit in grade school, but lacked the attention span necessary to nurture it. So in the absence of parental guidance and the presence of overwhelming guilt, the ink pen came easily to his hand and in less than a year he became proficient at drawing scenes of brutality, senseless decay and remorse. Notebooks were ritually filled with hate-vision and discord, as he was convinced that nothing was real and nothing was permanent, except penance. All of this caused him to arrive late to the awkward social square dance of dating.

∞

Miriam Boyd's first appearance turned every head on Carl's bus route. When she boarded the bus and walked its gum-stained aisle, her face was cold and anxious. Without speaking a word, she gave every impression she didn't belong there, that she didn't belong anywhere. There was a hesitancy to sit down, nervous glances over each shoulder, arms wrapped modestly around her young breasts, a sense of shame for being at a party she wasn't invited to. Her auburn hair fell plainly over her shoulders, and her fair skin gave her a vulnerable beauty that made every boy on the bus want to save her, or worse. Carl, who had never taken much of an interest in anyone, took an immediate and hypnotic interest in her. The next day he seated himself near where she had sat the day before, where he hoped she would sit again. He was drawn to her at first sight, but not on the same level as the other boys. A great wave of curiosity washed him up from the depths and he found himself wondering, not of adolescent lust, but of how one person could cause him to feel this way.

Whatever pain Miriam held within, Carl perceived it as parallel to his own and imagined a kind of unspoken fellowship with the girl. He couldn't bring himself to speak to her, paralyzed as he was in social settings, so he first approached her the only way he knew. After wallowing for two years in a void of shame and ugliness, the pendulum swung – Carl began drawing images of Miriam. There was a fascination with her proportions, the line of her nose, the dimpled curve of her ear, the reddish curl at her temple. He wanted to find her essence so as to understand what she did to him, how she filled him. He asked himself questions that would have brought outright ridicule from his classmates, and he discovered a whole new level of adolescent confusion. He didn't show his sketches to anyone, quickly destroying each, lest he be found out and accused of being obsessive. It took several months before he befriended her, and she took to him as a kind, if not demur, brooding soul in a strange crowd. He didn't ask her out for another year.

For Miriam, whose mother had moved her from Knoxville to Pittsburgh to Ithaca, the town of Compton in the Virginia Piedmont was just another scratch on the map, though it did have the benefit of being the closest to the beach she had ever lived. It was at the beach where she last saw her father when she was seven years old. On his insistence, they went for a week-long vacation to Rehoboth Beach, which by chance was only thirty-five miles from the harness racing at Harrington. On their last day at the shore, after having breakfast with his family, Miriam's father went alone to bet on the ponies and that was the last they ever saw of him.

Miriam's mother didn't appear surprised. The police were called and shoulders were shrugged, so she laid out a beach towel, oiled herself and extended their stay another week on the off chance her wayward husband might return. She would have known the volatility of her marriage far better than her seven-year-old daughter, but apparently saw no point in explaining what she had likely expected for some time.

Adjusting to being a single mom, the newly Ms. Boyd took a stab at selling Tupperware out of her basement and soon discovered her knack for sales, or at least entertaining. She cultivated her skills by selling everything from window blinds to batteries to cases of wine by the hundred. By the time she hooked up with a New York winery, she was proficient at the art of sales through seduction, and her income rose in proportion to the number of men she brought home. Young Miriam quickly lost interest in the names and faces of those who passed in and out of her mother's bedroom door, and the sounds and squeals passing through the door made her lose interest in most everything else.

The one thing that didn't escape Miriam's interest was the whereabouts of her father and why he had left. During the initial separation, her anxiety multiplied with each lie she was told. The first was he'd been called away on a business trip. Later there were sick relatives to which he was tending. She was even told her father was working on the Trans-Alaska Pipeline – a particularly tired excuse since the pipeline had long been completed. Each time

Miriam uncovered a lie, and after each inevitable fight with her mother, something in her would shut down, something related to trust.

When the reality of the situation finally set in, that she had been willfully abandoned, she still wouldn't let go. Rarely a week passed by that Miriam didn't ask her mother about some trivial aspect of her father. Whether he was right-handed or left, what were his favorite sports teams, and what section of the newspaper he would read first. She began secretly rummaging through her mother's closets and drawers, confiscating anything that might have belonged to her father. Among the prizes hoarded were a broken Timex watch, a porcelain ashtray, a cribbage board, a two-headed quarter and a soap on a rope. This was Miriam's way of staying close to him, as if the accumulation of all the useless tidbits of his life might one day help her find him. It wasn't until she was a teenager that she learned her father's greatest love was a blackjack table.

∞

High school friends are accidents of geography. Though Carl and Miriam shared little in common, they were fortunate enough to find solace in each other's company and discovered a few parallel dreams neither thought possible to fulfill. But while Miriam was able to lift Carl from the depths, there was a limit to what Carl could do for her. There was always something troubling her left unsaid, poisonous things she kept hidden from even herself.

Carl believed all her troubles stemmed from her father skipping town, but his perceptions forever changed the evening in late March of their senior year when Miriam showed up on the Rittenhaur back porch. Carl's grandmother, Adria, was rinsing dishes in the kitchen, struggling against her arthritis, when she heard three faint knocks. It sounded like it came from the furnace, as the old house was full of pangs and creaks, but when it repeated she flipped on the back porch light and pulled the lace curtain aside. Miriam was standing there all curled into herself with a hand latched onto her opposite arm and a book-bag at her feet.

"Miriam?" the old woman rang out. "You come in here right now. You look near frozen." She called upstairs to her grandson who was finishing his homework. By the time Carl came down his grandparents were flanking his girlfriend at the kitchen table. Adria was chatting away while Malcolm sat there mute and observing. Miriam looked as scared and stiff as the first day Carl watched her step onto the school bus. Her hair was matted down and several new pimples were erupting on her forehead. She looked like something inside her was painfully bent.

"What's wrong?" Carl asked.

"Nothing, really," she said, with everyone's eyes bearing down on her. Her voice was barely audible. "I don't want to put you out." She slid her chair back, but Malcolm Rittenhaur stood tall and looked on her kindly.

"Can't rightly put us out of our own house. Now you just sit on down and warm up." He caught his wife's eyes before lumbering off through the house. Adria went about fixing something for Miriam to eat.

"What happened?" Carl asked, taking his grandfather's seat.

"Just another fight with my mother. I can't be there right now."

"You can be with us as long as you like," Adria said, her shrunken frame making a fuss at the linoleum counter. "I had a friend once that you remind me of. Her mother had her fit to be tied." After she set up Miriam with a sandwich, she left the kids alone in the kitchen. The elderly Rittenhaurs' low voices could be heard in the next room. Doors opened and closed. Carl sat by his girlfriend while she nibbled on a tuna sandwich and warmed her hands on a mug of hot chocolate. They changed the subject to avoid any talk of her mother, speaking only of a mutually despised math teacher and a movie they wanted to see.

Malcolm Rittenhaur stepped into the doorway. "Got you all set up," he said.

The teenagers followed him, but stopped cold on seeing the open door to Carl's parents' bedroom. The door had been locked for four years and the light shining from inside was strange to them all. The air was stale and the wallpaper yellowed, though it had already been faded for a generation. It was a small room. A tarnished brass bed frame held a full size mattress enshrouded by a quilt sewn by Adria's mother. A tall dark walnut dresser stood on the opposite wall with untouched trinkets and spare change still scattered on top. Silhouettes of great great and long dead Rittenhaurs hung in plain wood frames on the walls.

A darkness came over Carl. He had no intention of going in. Miriam stepped closer, as if to see for herself where Carl's parents once slept. "No," she said, raising a hand to block the suggestion. She shook her head and looked to Adria. "The sofa would be fine."

"The room's not gotten much use in a while. Come along, now. It could use some warming up."

Miriam glanced back to Carl, who was sitting on a bruised ottoman at the foot of his grandfather's favorite chair. He felt sick. "Go ahead," he said, staring at the floor. Malcolm already set her book-bag, which was stuffed with clothes, on the floor by the dresser. She stepped inside and sat on the edge of the bed, torn between intrusion and exhaustion.

Adria sat by her and took her hand. "A long time ago this bed was mine. It's been years, but I remember it was a good bed." Malcolm adjusted a knob on the radiator, made sure it was making heat, and showed the girl the extra blankets stowed in the closet. When they left Miriam alone to get settled, Carl was nowhere in sight.

His bedroom was in the low eaves of the attic, the sloped ceilings giving the sense of confinement and deflection. He paced the room once and turned back, staring across the triangular space, feeling the dampness of it. The opening of the door opened a wound. He wanted to break free of this place, to run away from it all. Though Miriam had lifted Carl from his isolation, the burden of his parents' deaths hadn't lessened with her companionship. It had merely been shelved in favor of the illusion of a normal life and his courtship with a pretty girl. His guilt was fresh as the last gusts of winter leaking through the old house. At that moment he hated his life and his family, and for a brief moment even Miriam, though the anger quickly dissolved at the remembrance of her face.

Once the lights were out downstairs, Carl felt his way down the bannister and paused on seeing the glowing gap under the bedroom door. He tapped three times and a sleepy voice answered.

He pushed the door wide and was taken with the memories, the print of the curtains, the sunflower wallpaper and the long mirrored closet door. Miriam was her under the covers on his mother's side of the bed, paging through a trashy celebrity magazine. Her long sleeve tee-shirt read 'Rehoboth Beach' with a sequined dolphin diving across her breasts. Her untouched homework sat at her feet. Carl stood there staring at her until she dropped the magazine and admired the quilt with her palms, gently smoothing it out along the seams. Each square was composed of swaths of drapery, clips of upholstery and old flannel shirts, whatever scraps of fabric were laying around the Rittenhaur farm during The Depression. The texture was varied and the colors clashed, though not in an unpleasant way.

"I love this quilt," she said, caressing the squares.

Carl sat on the edge of the bed, his father's side, facing mostly away.

Miriam must have sensed his awkwardness. "Guess this is kinda strange."

Words came hard for Carl. "What were you fighting about that was so bad?"

"It was nothing. She's just such a bitch."

"But it's never been so bad that you left."

"Don't question me about this," she snapped. "I'm here, so it must have been bad, don't you think?"

"That's why I want to know. If you tell me, then maybe I can help."

"Sometimes you don't have to explain yourself. Sometimes it just is. We had a fight and it just is."

"Okay," he said, looking at her for the first time. The soft flesh of her face tensed at the mere thought of her mother. Best to let her be.

"Are your grandparents asleep yet?" she whispered.

"Yeah."

She tugged his sleeve, but Carl pulled back. The bed of his grandfather's truck was one thing, but he couldn't think of fooling around in his parent's bedroom.

"No, that's not what I meant," she said. "I just want you to hold me." When Miriam took his arm, her shirt sleeve slid back and unveiled the bruises on her wrist.

Carl studied the bluish marks. "What's this? he asked.

"Don't," she said, pulling away. She grabbed both shirt cuffs and squeezed them in her fists. "It is. It just is." She held herself the same way as when Adria found her on the porch, shivering like some wayward traveler.

"What did she do to you?" he insisted.

"Shush" she said. Miriam slid under the covers and rolled onto her side, settling in the old depression in the mattress.

"What did she do?"

He could hear her crying. "*She* didn't do anything."

Carl studied the formless mound under the quilt. He put a hand on her side and spooned into her, waited for her warmth to pass through pattern, but there was too much material separating them. He felt only her outline, a rough sketch of his old obsession, and he knew he loved her and always would. And though he accepted that some things could not be saved, he wanted to save her. He just didn't know what to save her from.

She cried a little more, let out a small gasp and settled down. A minute passed. "She didn't do anything to me," she said again in a sleepy whisper. "She didn't do a damn thing."

∞

They never spoke again of the ugly marks on her wrists, though Carl remembered them long after the soft tissue had healed. He vowed not to let anything bad happen to her again. Since the elderly Rittenhaurs could trace Carl's renewed spirit to the day she moved to town, they took her in as another grandchild and were themselves protective of her, having likely seen the same bruises.

Over the next four years, Carl lived across the Blue Ridge working toward his art degree, but dutifully came home every weekend to be with Miriam. Since she was cut off from her mother's money, college was not an option, so in a strange nod to her father she took jobs working horses on various equestrian estates in the Piedmont. When she wasn't spending large periods of time living in caretaker's quarters, she stayed near the warm hearth of the Rittenhaurs.

Carl's graduation brought a job doing layout work for an ad agency in town, which he condemned as drudgery. It paid little in money or reward, but was enough for him to get off the farm and take an apartment in town with Miriam. Despite his degree, a new job and Miriam's presence, the deaths of Carl's parents still hampered his drive. Though a part of him felt he'd paid his penance to his family in manual labor, his guilt never fully waned, the spiritual displacement never healed. He felt undeserving of a place in his forebears' line and the future he would have in it. He longed for a fresh start, to leave the old ways behind and build a new life and a new family. And he was ready to start from nothing.

∞

It was to be a spring wedding on a Friday evening. The sun was setting over the Blue Ridge, lighting the final hour of day with orange-red strands of cloud arcing over from the south and igniting the steeple of the Compton Lutheran Church in celebration, but inside the stain glass was quickly dimming. Carl waited for her in the vestry behind the altar with his old friend, Mick Coates. They wore matching black suits and neck ties, which they straightened and loosened several times over. Carl cracked open the heavy wooden door and spied the sanctuary. The handful of invited guests were spread unevenly about the pews, as if they'd gathered there by chance. The mother of the bride, Elaine Boyd, sat in the front row. Miriam told her if she had the gumption to make an appearance, not to sit in front, but there she was. Her face was a kind of mask, red with too much makeup, and her hair was teased into some unnatural concoction. She gushed for attention, laughing loudly and jabbering with a couple sitting behind her.

"Her mother actually showed up," Carl said.

"Did she bring anything to drink?" Mick quipped.

"Miriam wouldn't skip out because of her, would she?"

"She's probably caught in traffic."

"There is no traffic."

The reverend was in the center aisle talking to Carl's grandfather. They nodded hopefully to each other before parting. The reverend's cream colored robes, all crossed and layered, made him larger than he appeared in street clothes. He filled the arched doorway to the vestry.

"Carl, the organist is willing to stay for another half hour, but then she has other plans."

"I'll pay her whatever she wants."

"She has to leave at eight o'clock."

"Plenty of time," Mick said, stepping between them.

There was a kind of knowing dread in the reverend's voice. "I'm sure she'll be here." He gripped Carl's shoulder and squeezed before making his way to a back office.

Staring into the hallow space of the sanctuary, Carl remembered how little comfort he'd received from the church following the deaths of his parents. All the trite platitudes laid before him about faith and healing and fate. He felt none of it. What composed his feelings was the great weight of time both past and future, but void of a present to heal and mourn. The past was regret, and the future was leaden with the fear of more regret, while in between was too thin a slice to compose a new life. There had been nothing in the current of time to cleanse him until Miriam arrived in his life. And even then, still, the guilt was always present.

So Carl waited. He waited into the evening the way he had waited on the steps of the school house nine years before. In another half hour the church windows lost their color and the smattering of guests were beginning to leave. Carl was laying on a tabletop used for preparing the chalice and other sacraments for communion. Mick paced the room, making excuses, expanding on hypotheticals. When the great wooden front doors of the church creaked open and echoed through the nave, everyone still present turned to see Carl's grandfather lumbering up the aisle. He wore a string tie and an old black suit, one rarely taken from the closet. Its lines were tailored sometime after the Second World War, and the material had a strange sheen to it. He stepped onto the altar like the last exhausted step after a full day of work in the fields. Carl sat up as the old man stood in the doorway.

"It's not going to happen today, Carl. Maybe some other time, but not today."

Carl's hands were damp and cold, an old but new pain coming over him. The organist found the end notes of "Sleepers Awake" for about the seventh time.

"Tell her to keep playing," he said. "Tell her I'll pay double."

"I tracked down Miriam's maid of honor," Malcolm said, looking weary and less than his usual stoic self. "You need to come on home now." His wife of fifty-six years nudged him aside and took his place under the arched doorway. Her hands were crippled with arthritis, all shiny knobs of knuckles and near bone, and a turquoise cross lay over her sunken chest. She presented her arm to her grandson as if he were the one needing physical aid. He said not a word and entwined her crimped up fingers in his own. Together they passed under the arch onto the altar, the same altar where Carl's parents had lain at their funeral. His breath seized a little. The guests had already filed out. Miriam's mother was the first to leave. While they made their way down the aisle, someone was snapping off the lights section by section, letting the darkness gather behind them.

The cool evening air did little to revive the groom as they all stepped onto the sidewalk. He looked up and down the street, as if an explanation might present itself. When none appeared, he said, "Just take me back to my apartment."

"I don't think that's the place for you tonight," his grandmother said.

Grandfather Rittenhaur added, "You don't want to go there, Carl. She's packed her bags and gone. Where to, I don't know, but that don't matter much right now."

Mick paced off to one side, stiff lipped and shaking his head as if he expected so much. He walked back to his friend. "You can crash at my place tonight."

"I can't go there either."

"Then let's get a drink." Mick was surprised when the grandparents were open to the suggestion. They looked like they could use a belt too.

"No," Carl said. "I want to sleep." His eyes followed the street lamps to somewhere beyond his vision. "I just want to sleep."

After promising to meet with Mick the next evening, Carl climbed into his grandfather's Impala, and within a winding half hour drive he was back in the stone farmhouse of his ancestors.

The attic bedroom smelled of damp plaster, and the softwood floor was buckled and full of creaks. The room's musty air was ever-present. Carl lay in his old twin bed and stared at the strange angles of moonlight reflecting on the sloped ceilings. It might have been cold feet, he lamented, or perhaps another man. And her mother was forever poisoning her spirit. Miriam once said, unrealistically, that her father should be there to give her away on her wedding day, this so-called father she probably wouldn't recognize if she bumped into him on the street. Carl cursed the man before placing blame on himself, something he was good at. What had he done wrong? Had he pushed her into this, or had he somehow pushed her away? A light push might do it. She was forever going off on tangents, rarely staying at any job or farm quarters for too long. Always changing her situation, never satisfied. Then it occurred to him maybe Miriam just had a little of her father in her.

PART ONE

Chapter 1

Carl stood high on the ladder under the roof of his front porch and considered the weight of things around him. After much planning, careful calculations and some trial and error, he swung his hammer and struck the old wood column holding up a corner of the porch, sending it plunging into the fine spring grasses. When the column cleared, the porch roof still projected from the house, levitating above with the help of several two-by-four stilts angling from the ground. Balanced above his modest plot of land, shoulders thrown back in defiance to the awkward mass above him, he tapped its underside with the hammer as if daring it to fall.

The rapid click of a camera shutter sounded behind him. He turned to see a mid-size four-door idling across the street, the same car that had passed three times in the last hour. Out the driver's window flashed a barrel shaded camera lens focused on the back of his head. Carl jumped the last three steps off the ladder and bent deep in the knees. "Hey you!" he shouted, trotting toward the street, but the driver fired off two more shots before speeding off. He stood there on the curb scratching his three-day-old growth. He missed the license tag. He was used to tourists snapping photos of cavalry battlefields and other barren tracts in the Piedmont where some obscure Civil War skirmish had taken place, but there was no history on this street worth recording. After the first pass, he was afraid it might have been the county building inspector – he hadn't bothered with a permit for the new porch – but a civil servant would have simply stopped and questioned him. In uncertainty, he felt rushed to finish the project.

A mess of plans and sketches were sprawled over his workbench, and he hovered over them, trying to rededicate himself to the job. At thirty years of age he was putting on weight and felt the sluggishness that came with the added pounds. There was a harshness about his body as if he'd been sketched from a model of wooden blocks – face square and benign, skin pale as birch, knees and elbows like knots in a rope. The lengths of muscle in his arms were taut, while other parts of his body sagged and atrophied. But beyond the severe features were delicate hands that were always moving, exploring whatever was within reach and possessing a certain gentleness, a slow silken handling of small things between the fingers.

He lumbered back to the ruin hanging from his house, set a crowbar to the old floor boards and applied leverage. His arms turned to stone as the nails screamed. Another piece of the old house severed, another piece of the past unburdened and retired. Straining to lift several boards at once, he launched them into the scrap heap, sending a hollow crack echoing down the street. Carl paused to wipe the sweat from his brow, again aware of being watched.

Next door held an audience of one, a curiosity bred of idle time. Lester Kilgore, motionless as a lawn ornament, leaned over the chain link fence clutching a half-burnt cigarette between a short thumb and one crooked finger. His forearms were toasted like a burn victim, and he was rarely seen wearing anything but his sweat-stained shop clothes. A rectangular patch on his shirt pocket said "Lester Kilgore," which came in handy since he couldn't read or write. It appeared each toke on his cigarette aided in the collection of thought – words accumulated in his mouth until they were expelled in a whither of smoke.

"Bring her down, eh?"

Carl didn't face the old man, responded with only a grunt. His knuckles turned white as he laid into another floor board. Kilgore filled his mouth several more times.

"Don't get no help?"

"Don't need no help." Carl always spoke to Kilgore in his own language. The old man cinched one eye tight and scratched the grey wire hair on his neck.

"Strange be doin' all that by yourself."

Carl lowered the crowbar and rested a foot on the framing. "You seen that guy taking pictures?"

"What picture you talkin' about?"

Based on the few times he tried to engage the old man in conversation, Carl knew better. "Never mind," he said, turning back to his sketches. Measure twice, cut once, he thought. Ignore him.

"Ought to get some help. A friend would come in handy on a job like this," he persisted, flicking a smoldering butt into Carl's yard. Looking winded and rueful, he limped off and sat a few feet away on his own decrepit porch where he thumped another Salem from its pack.

The house was a semi-detached brick shoe box. Only an eight-inch party wall separated Carl from the sordid lives of the Kilgores, which amounted to daily screaming, the constant blare of a television and an unexplained thump in the plumbing. But Carl bought the house cheap, and at the time cheap was a virtue. Six years before, on the morning of his real estate closing, Lester Kilgore felt his house rumble in a series of violent concussions, sending him blundering into his front yard. The front door of the twin house had been boarded for years, but on this day Carl stepped out cradling a rusty kitchen cabinet in his arms. In one swift motion, he heaved the old box into the front yard before disappearing inside to the sound of more hammering, never once acknowledging his new neighbor. He had owned the house for less than an hour, and Lester had been leaning on the fence ever since.

When he sat on his stoop, Kilgore's two grandsons, ages three and five, bounced by him into their grassless yard. Clothed in their underwear, they rolled plastic trucks in the dirt and occasionally explored under their briefs with roving hands. While Carl measured a new floor joist, a plastic ball sailed over his head, bounced off the rubble and came to a rest at his feet. The older child pointed at the younger.

"Kyle did it!"

Carl grabbed the ball, annoyed as if he'd dropped a tool. He ran his fingers over the little fake baseball stitches and teeth marks. The boys stared uncertainly. Carl wanted nothing to do with them, but there was also a chivalrous yearning to get those boys the hell out of there, to help them escape to someplace where they might have a chance at a normal life. Where they were now was a dead end. While he stood watching them, a truck with a ladder rack on top rumbled to a stop on the street. Dale Kilgore, the old man's son, climbed from the passenger seat and slammed the door. Leaning in the window, he drank from a paper bag and mumbled something to the driver. He slapped the truck goodbye and swaggered through the front gate. His cheeks were red and swollen under each eye, looking a decade older than his forty years. Carl threw the ball back over the fence so Dale's children might catch it.

"Dammit," Dale yelled at his boys. "I told you two not to throw your shit into Carl's yard." He kicked the ball across the root-fractured earth and grabbed his elder son by the arm.

"I didn't do —"

"I don't give a damn who did what. Get on inside." Dale released him and kicked again, this time at the kids without effect as they scurried up the steps and squealed into the house. He stumbled to the fence and held on with both hands. "Sorry for that. I told'em before."

"Don't worry about it," Carl said. Having lost his confidence, he measured a third time. Dale's stomach made a diamond-patterned impression in the fence. He stood there shaking his head.

"They don't listen," he said.

"They're just kids."

The neighbor leaned back and sucked in his gut, making himself a worthy helper. "Place looks good," he said.

"Place is a wreck."

"You want, I can help. We'll get that framing plumb."

"I can manage."

Dale released into his usual droopy posture. He stepped around his father like he was avoiding a potted plant and pushed into the house. Carl glanced over, seeking proof he was gone, and returned to his therapy — something needing his attention, something he couldn't hurt and that certainly couldn't hurt him.

In two hours he'd reduced the porch to a pile of boards and splinters smothering half his front yard. His spine ached like someone had placed a cold quarter between each vertebra. He arched his back, feeling the additional twenty pounds he'd recently put on, and rested in the stillness. It was mid-April and the lawns were bushy and uncut. The crab apple and azalea were in full glory, but the red tip buds of the maples had nearly fallen away, replaced by the first pale green leaves jittering in the high breeze. This small grid of streets was legally recorded in the land records of Compton, Virginia as *The Villages*, but most folks in town referred to it as *The Village Jizz*. Obscured by overgrown hedges and tangles of wisteria were paired identical houses facing the street like a row of children's' blocks. The scarred texture of the bricks was like someone had attacked them with an ice pick, and the mortar joints rubbed into sand with the application of a firm thumb. The street trees were planted in odd increments and impaled by utility lines, and the sidewalks heaved and slumped from the roots, sinking below the pavement in places and allowing for minor flooding of neighbors' yards. Across the street, supported by a tall bank of still-dormant honeysuckle, the railroad made a dull dusty streak into town.

Up the street were children playing, balls bouncing, their laughter and cries something foreign to him. Kilgore the elder was releasing grunts and wheezes, perhaps recalling an old conversation, and in the distance a whining Briggs and Stratton was being prepped for the season. A wind rose and flushed the sparrows from the electric lines. The sound of Carl's telephone blended in with the rest.

He ran under the porch roof and climbed the three feet off the ground through the front door. Everything inside was covered with the chalky dust of continual reconstruction. The phone sat on the end-table by an uncovered futon, its beige mattress spotted with food stains. One end of the futon bore an impression where one man usually sat alone. He grabbed the receiver.

"Half the herd got out this morning," came his grandfather's winded voice. "I patched the fence in two places, but we gotta check the whole north tract."

Carl sat heavy, ready to give up on the day. "You want me there now?" He pictured his grandfather leaning a dirty hand on the woodwork where fingerprints collected by the phone.

"Tomorrow. I'm worn out. I suppose you got your own goings on anyway," he said.

Carl shook his head. "Fine."

"And I got some news you might be interested in."

"What news?"

The old man was slow to respond, at first offering only his labored breath. "I don't figure to get into that just yet."

"Well then, why —"

"You be here at seven in the morning?"

Carl jumped up and paced the room. "Fine," he said, before dropping the phone in its cradle.

Though loyal to his grandfather, Carl's mood still soured when confronted with that part of his life. He stepped to the door and stood high above the latest mess he had created. Now with fresh eyes, he saw his property as a ruin. Every project ran on like this, over and over, repeating the pattern of demolition and reconstruction. Whenever a project was near completion, he would lose interest and abandon it, until months later, in a fit of restlessness, he would take a sledgehammer to the next room and begin again. He loved the process to distraction, but what he ended up with was never enough. What he wanted he couldn't seem to finish or define.

The front yard was in shade and the air cool, reminding him winter was not long past. Tools, lumber and debris were scattered across the trampled grass, and a variety of rusty nails were hidden among the fresh blades of fescue. The chill and the self-imposed devastation depressed him. He felt the weight of the porch roof suspended overhead and felt certain his neighbors were waiting for the fall.

He locked the door and wandered through the house. A rack of half painted canvases leaned against a living room wall and tools covered the dining room table. Carl pushed through the back door where the sun was still there to warm him and entered his own private quarry. Several chunks of marble were strewn about like fallen meteors, and under the stoop were wooden crates of white alabaster. Soft, luminous and powdery, it was the easiest to work and what he knew best. Each stone felt cool in the hand and emitted a prayerful glow when carved thin and held to the sun, yet would slowly dissolve if left to the elements.

Carl grabbed his tools and stood at his bench, an old butcher block covered with sandbags. A piece of red rose marble with a dusted ash hue nestled between the bags, waiting. Carl raised his hammer, a two pounder, and struck the chisel, grazing the rock —

too hard. He shifted his spine and searched for control. Chisel reset, he struck again, repeat in rhythm, chips flying. A small valley opened in the stone. Reset again, a parallel cut, the chisel plowing its furrow with each blow. He lay down the tools and felt the stone, his gentle hands rolling over the clefts, searching for the soft places until he was satisfied. The tools came back to his hands. Chisel set, he raised the hammer.

Chapter 2

Where Carl's street and the railroad parted, a long brick train station stretched between, its deep overhangs and tracery made all the more intricate by fingernail-size chips of alligatored paint. He aimed his pickup down Albemarle Street, which ran west from the station to the courthouse and sprouted a grid of proper streets. The first block was sparsely populated. The few shaky businesses that hadn't been bankrupted by the strip shopping centers mingled with boarded storefronts and vacant lots. Only on the west side of town did Compton show any sign of prosperity. The first new restaurant in a dozen years, The Parsley Sage, welcomed the equestrian set back to town, and the storefronts around the courthouse were always stocked with attorneys and bail bondsmen, as it's rare to find the law in recession.

Carl turned his truck, an old Chevy S-10, onto the northbound artery and within two blocks the town's intimate scale receded into a desperate strip of fast food, parking lots and traffic lights. Superstores in their macadam fields were bankrupting the smaller strip centers the same way the strip centers had wiped out the old town businesses decades before in an endless cycle of retail displacement. For a mile the commercial gauntlet passed like a slow burn in Carl's chest, and he cursed each missed traffic light until splaying onto a familiar two-lane road to the northwest. At the corner a billboard sponsored by the Cavalry Baptist Church said, "Don't give up. Even Moses was once a Basket Case."

The road sliced through forest and dipped into valleys where ancient stone walls marked the oldest estates, penning in freshly plowed fields, grids of budding apple trees and pale vineyards with their virgin spring vines. A dewy morning breeze flailed his hair, cooling his face and waking him from his slumber. Ten miles out he drove by a roadside stand where people were unloading antiques, handmade quilts, bric-a-brac and jugs of cider for a morning market. Carl waved to a familiar face, but didn't stop. The narrower lane had no lines or name, only a state route number and a general direction, and though the road was a passage of surprises, Carl leaned into the winding turns from memory as the landscape expanded and contracted, rounding blind corners and bridging over and over the same crooked creek. The land was rumpled like a messed up bed sheet – the surrounding formations too large to be hills, but not up to the authority of a mountain.

The truck emerged into a long valley with a patch of fog in its palm. Farther down the basin were farms whose pastures had been converted into vineyards to support the growing wine industry, but the north point of the valley was still graced with the familiar smell of manure. Carl veered off at the first mailbox, rumbling over bluestone and splashing brown water from the pot-holed drive. In a hundred yards he circled the stone farmhouse with porches front and back. Out-buildings surrounded the old structure like wayward children and were painted dried-blood red and capped with rust-streaked metal roofs. Lean-to sheds pushed against the large barn and skewed its proportions, if not aided in propping it up. To the rear of the property a four-board paddock held thirty Black Angus bellowing in the mud.

Carl circled to the rear porch and landed heavy on the brakes. Two ancient white oaks shading the yard in summer only added a chill to the air as they were still bare and lifeless from their winter dormancy. A man was leaning against the porch rail holding a mug of coffee. He was prematurely grey, stocky in build, and looked planted and growing where he stood.

"I see you're glad to be back," his brother said.

Carl grabbed his gloves, hopped from the cab and cut a trail across the dew-tipped grass. "Where's granddad?"

"Inside. What's your hurry?"

"Maybe I *am* glad to be back."

"Like you look it."

Carl regarded his older brother, Vince, as the younger often does, wavering between awe and suspicion. While he considered punching him, their grandfather stepped outside with his own steaming cup at his lips. He steadied himself on the porch railing, considered his kin and said, "Let's go."

Once a giant, Malcolm Rittenhaur had settled into a thin shadow of a man. He stood erect to the shoulders, but his head lurched forward as if his neck might have once snapped and healed without being properly set. His brow was deep and his corneas were tin-can grey between the folds. What little flesh that was exposed was an uneven shade of brown. Malcolm clung to the old and the known, with a special fondness for the 1948 vintage tractor parked under a shaky barn. Like the old man's skin, the tractor's body had developed a rust-brown patina – not a trace of color but for the fresh pollen covering everything like a sprinkle of curry powder. The engine was caked in lubricous chaff, and more oil had soaked into the ground under the pan than was lubricating the engine block. And the hydraulics were shot, so it was a one-dimensional tractor – it pulled things and made for a nice ride.

The patriarch mounted the old implement, cocked his head to one side and felt for the starter button – the machine groaned. With another crank, the tailpipe hemorrhaged and he eased up on the choke, nursing the engine to life. He stood on the clutch, slipped it in gear and rode the contraption alongside his two grandsons as they emerged from a shed, armed with tools and buckets of nails. A flatbed trailer was hitched and loaded with spools of wire, stretchers, couples and cutters. The two younger men sat on the splintery boards and rode to the far end of the paddock where they hopped off like a couple of hitch-hikers.

The north fifty was leaking steer. The old wire fence was woven with countless generations of barb spaced just tight enough to stop a cow's head, but now the wires sagged and some sprang loose and flailed from their posts. Carl and Vince took long steps down the line and pulled each strand with heavy gloved hands, post by post, each gap scrutinized like the review of a life broken down into bite-size pieces. They re-stretched the wire in places, replaced it in others, the slack drawn with the stretcher, crimped behind a barb for leverage, braced and nailed. They didn't measure, just eyed each section and walked the line. At each segment, being sensitive to the fine angles he was creating, Carl imagined a linear composition and studied each division of fence as if it were an endless sectional painting. He often gave too much thought where to nail the next strand of wire, and either his grandfather or his brother would let him know by yelling, "Just nail the damn thing." Vince was more efficient – not a smidgen of nonsense in his hands as he worked the line.

Mr. Rittenhaur never left the saddle except to add oil to the crankcase. His eyes were failing him and he didn't spot problems in the fence until long after his grandsons were aware of them. Most of the time he rubbed his knees and raised his head to the sky.

Carl said to his grandfather, "You ever thought about starting over? Just replacing the whole fence?"

Malcolm looked down from the heavens and balanced a hand on the stick-shift. "Do you have any idea how much two thousand yards of fence is gonna cost? You got problems being realistic. You always have." The old man's hands were trembling. "I suppose you'll own it all soon enough. Then you can do whatever you want." He shifted into gear and the tractor lurched forward. Vince finished nailing a line and eyed his little brother.

They worked the perimeter all morning, running first along the pine ridge where everything was dry and sharp and stubbornly green before coming to the soft grasses along the valley road as they cut their gloves and talked of little more than the weather. The last run of fence was in good shape, so the two brothers bounced on the trailer with their legs dangling, rolling over the clover field toward home.

The fence they mended encircled Carl's childhood and returned to his origin, the rough stone farmhouse that gave their end of the valley a center. Between the house and the wooded ridge was an isolated rise where an iron fence penned in a clutter of stones. The old marble slabs were leaning and chafed, the names and dates eaten away by time, while the granite stones stood sharp, erect and strangely modern. Carl's eye caught the hill and its inhabitants before turning away.

When they returned to the paddock, Carl jumped down and swung open the gate. Through the vertical slits of the barn, he watched the old machine sputter into its stall as several chirping swallows blew out the other end. Malcolm told Vince to get on with lunch while he put away the tools. He asked nothing of Carl, who joined his brother on the way to the house. Vince, always sure of himself, kept one step ahead. The brothers walked as though each were alone.

"You sticking around for once?" Vince asked.

"Yeah. I want to hear what Granddad has to say."

"He hasn't said a damn thing all day."

"Did he say anything to you about news?"

They climbed the porch and Vince pulled open the screen door. "He said we got meat in the crisper."

Vince washed up in the kitchen sink as the whistling faucet broke the quietness of the house. Carl pushed through the swing door to the dining room and entered a silence that manifests itself only when one is alone in a familiar place. He stepped lightly, as if the creaking floor might disturb a memory. Over the past six years his visits to the farm were only by necessity, helping his grandparents with farming chores, but he rarely summoned the spirit to venture inside. Sunlight filtered into the room from the south window and lit the threaded shears like some half devoured ghost. The heavy curtains that once hung there were gone, disintegrated from sun-rot and recently thrown away by his grandfather. Carl felt a pang of regret when he remembered his mother had sewn them. She picked out the pattern to complement the wallpaper, which had faded to a sickly green image on a beige field, a toile pattern wrapping the room with a young couple in colonial garb holding hands, and they held hands over and over in eighteen-inch increments. Where the wallpaper came full circle, across from Carl's seat at the dinner table, the cut didn't line up properly and the young man faced his own back, his hands fingering his own pockets as though he were mugging himself.

Family photos were clustered on the china cabinet in frames of brass, wood, and pewter, doing their best to make the living relevant and the dead greater than life. His grandmother's photo had faded to a ghostly sepia, which saddened him. She died of a stroke a year before and the pain of her loss was still fresh. She had wrapped her crippled hands in a scarf for the picture, which reminded Carl of his grandfather's advanced years. At the heart of this cross-generational gathering were his father and mother encased in an elaborate brass spectacle his father hadn't approved of – he considered himself a simple man, and he was – but his mother took pride in the family photos and always strove for the grand gesture. His father wore a simple sport jacket and open collar, looking like he'd been held there at gunpoint, but Carl's mother shone brightest while the other photos, from Civil War tintypes to Carl's and Vince's elementary school pictures, orbited around her. She wore an intricate paisley dress she'd sewn herself, and her hands were folded on the family bible. He imagined them lying there together on the hill under the cool granite slab. Five generations of Rittenhaurs were buried around them and were also resided in the sloping floors and mildewy air of the house. He couldn't imagine taking possession of such a thing.

A scabbed porcelain sink hung off the bathroom wall like an ancient baptismal font. He waited for the water to warm and raised a pool to his face. It felt like a minor blessing and his spirit rose. He dabbed off with a towel, but not enough to dry as the coolness gave comfort and made him more accepting of being there again.

In the kitchen, Vince sliced smoked ham off a bone with an electric knife. Malcolm pushed through the screen door and contemplated the fat slices of ham meat piled high on the tray. "We'll eat outside," he said, rolling his sleeves to his elbows and washing in the kitchen sink like a surgeon. His hands dripped across the floor. "Vince, you know what I want. Biscuits are on top of the freezer."

The three men sat at a picnic table on the back porch and planted their elbows on either side of their plates. Malcolm gripped a biscuit in both hands and sunk his false teeth into it. He chewed and admired his tract and watched his newly released herd of Black Angus trample the buttercups. He looked tired but, for the first time all day, appeared to be at peace. He took another bite and mumbled to Carl, "Miriam stopped by last week."

Carl chilled and the old house regressed into the shell of memories it had been before he washed up. "Granddad –" He lowered his food to the plate.

"Now don't go off all half-cocked," the old man said with his mouth full. "It's time you faced her and said your piece."

"I don't want a damn thing to do with her. You know that."

"I gave her your number. Told her you were living in town."

"Ever heard of privacy, Granddad?"

"She had a baby with her," he said to Vince as much as to Carl. "Well – not a baby. More like a small child. She was asleep in the car-seat."

Carl couldn't swallow what he had bitten off. His chest tightened from either the smoked ham or something rising from his stomach. He didn't want to hear any more. He couldn't take another bite. Another section of fence to mend would have been a relief. Vince checked back and forth between the old man and the younger.

With an odd and sudden bout of curiosity, Carl asked, "Did she look like her?"

"She looked like a baby."

"I mean she looked like Miriam, right?"

"She looked like a baby asleep in a car-seat."

Carl broke from his shock, though he knew there was nothing to be shocked about. He suspected, assumed, even hoped for Miriam to have settled down, or so he told himself in his better spirits. He wanted her to be happy, though this charitable mood often had sour undertones – a mood not to be completely trusted. She has a baby, he told himself again, as if he hadn't believed it the first time. He sank into the slats of the bench as questions rifled through his head.

"I don't want to talk to her," he said, pushing his plate aside.

"You gotta start talking to someone about this or you're going to waste away."

"I'm living my life as I see fit."

Malcolm lifted a hard finger and pointed. "You're still hammering on those rocks like it was the altar she left you standing on."

Carl gazed past the two men across from him, the remains of his family, into the green fields beyond, but his mind only grazed aimlessly across the pasture and didn't care for fence or composition of wire in his endless sectional painting. He didn't remember his last bite of ham, but the salt still lined his mouth. He licked the tang between his gum and cheeks.

"I don't need this," he said.

Vince dropped his hands to the table and lit up. "You don't need what? It was six years ago."

"Seven."

"Better yet. Seven. I got how you took it bad at first, but man."

"Don't you worry about it."

Malcolm began assembling a second sandwich. "Vince, you're all settled and satisfied. You weren't left in the lurch like he was. You don't know," he said, waving the same boney finger between his grandsons. "Now with that said, it might be a good idea for y'all to talk things out. Put things to rest."

Carl considered it for a moment and, bereft of anything to hold onto, wanted details. The questions passed in a frenzy, questions that didn't matter.

"What was she driving?"

"Some rental car. She was heading up to Dulles. Flying home to Florida, she said."

"See there?" Vince exclaimed. "She don't even live up here to bother you. She's got a husband and a child and lives in another world. She probably just wanted to see how you're doing."

Carl cringed at the mention of a husband, and something in his chest twisted like a wire barb. In his shock, the baby hadn't implied a husband, and this news came as a second wave of pain. Even though he swore never to see her again, there was still the fantasy in his head. This woman who had stepped into the void in his life, this woman to whom he'd attached himself like a man nailed to a cross, even in absence had been elevated to an ideal, or perhaps idol, and the thought of her child conceived by another man sickened him.

Carl lurched from the table and marched to his truck. He slammed the door and fired her up.

Chapter 3

It was the spring of avoidance. Carl kept the shades drawn and screened his calls, what few there were, but despite the self-imposed calm he developed a case of insomnia and spent long brooding hours in bed wrestling with Miriam's image and composing imaginary pictures of her on his bedroom ceiling. He treated Miriam's disappearance on their wedding day the same as his parents' deaths – he believed the trail of blame could be traced back to some indiscretion on his part, some wayward poor choice his mother had warned him about. Late at night he fixated on the imaginary paintings on his ceiling of Miriam in whatever phase he could remember – long hair and short, from high school to college breaks to wedding planning. The last year they spent together he teased her about a premature grey hair spinning from her brow, and she replied with some offense that it must have been from all the wedding preparations. He often wondered if there was something more to her flip reply. In truth, he found a grey hair or two becoming, as he liked the idea they'd been together long enough for time to reflect on them.

When sleep did come for Carl, he began to dream again, and he hadn't dreamed in years. Miriam appeared in these visions like the spotting of a great fish, its scales glittering like some miraculous creature from another world before vanishing under the flowing blackness. You know something extraordinary is lurking, but not when it will appear or how long it will stay.

Carl dreamed his dreams and painted his paintings, occasionally rising in his weaker moments to stomp on his bed and shake his fists. He thought of little else and prayed to forget her and to never see her again, only to chill and feel ashamed during the moments when he couldn't picture her at all. Those moments were the loneliest and the most unforgivable, as he sensed the damage done to him and to not have an image of a beautiful woman to blame was unpardonable.

On a weekend escape to Charlottesville, Carl met up with Mick Coates, his last remaining friend from high school, the same boy he had defended from the wrestler on the day of his parents' deaths. Mick was freckled and built like a horse jockey, with enough muscle now to defend himself if the need ever arose. Like Carl, he taught in the public schools, so they often commiserated together over a case of cold beer. They sat in Adirondack chairs on Mick's porch with their feet propped on a cooler. Carl was slow to open up.

"Is she coming back up here?" Mick asked.

"I don't have any idea. All I know is she's supposed to call and I don't want to talk to her."

"So don't. Her leaving was the best thing for you."

"She didn't have a great family."

Mick sat up in his chair and dangled the bottle between his legs. "Can I level with you?" he asked, but his friend just stared away. "Miriam was a basket case. Remember when she ran off for two weeks senior year? Then just turned up like nothing happened."

"She went to Atlantic City. For some reason she got the notion that's where her father ran off to. What made everything worse was her mother didn't seem to care she was even gone."

"You said she took off again when you were in college."

"She was too embarrassed to talk much about those trips."

"I know her mother was a mess," Mick conceded, sinking back in his chair, "but weren't you worried she would turn out the same way?"

"Never. Miriam was nothing like her."

"She dumped you at the altar. She left town without a trace. Who does that?"

"She was your friend too."

"She was, but I knew better than to fall in love with her."

"Well, I didn't." Carl thought about storming out of there. He didn't like being told his feelings weren't valid. He didn't see love as something controllable, but as something organic, a natural outgrowth that can spring up anywhere at any time.

"You need to get her out of your head. You need to be past her now."

"I know that," Carl said.

On his way home under the influence of a Sunday afternoon hangover, he stopped at a 7-11 and bought a six-pack of micro-brew in long menacing bottles. He drank them one-by-one and spiraled into a deep melancholy, and by the time he pulled into his street all six bottles rattled on the passenger seat floor. The street light popped on as he staggered across the lawn and climbed onto his newly minted porch. He fell heavily against the door and jiggled the key in the cylinder, but it was like someone changed the lock. He yanked the key and made for the back yard where he kept a spare. It was supposed to be under a box of alabaster, so he turned one over and then another, flipping every crate in sight before raising one unfortunate stone over his head and smashing it onto the patio where it fractured into a dozen pieces, leaving a white powder explosion mark on the concrete. In the dimming light, he sank to his knees and studied the point of impact as if examining a masterpiece, tracing his finger along each line of powdery residue. He picked up a piece of the shattered stone and held it like it was a sick bird.

He woke a few hours later from the evening chill, lying on his side with his hands between his knees and his cheek pressed against the cold patio. A fine silvery sheen covered his workspace under a high round moon, and chunks of alabaster lay around him like wads of tissue that had missed the trash can. When he lifted his head he looked as if he'd been wounded on one side by white buckshot. His head pounded. Stone chips pierced his back as he rolled over and the pain brought him home, though he didn't want to be home – he didn't want to be anywhere.

He forced himself back to the front door and pushed the same key into the lock-set, and this time it turned in one twist. The sudden light was painful, so he flipped the switch off, leaving a blinding flash-bulb impression of the room – a dozen canvasses abandoned in the corner, a new kitchen sink on the floor and dripping paint cans stacked against a wall that was skim-coated several months before. The odd pulsing image faded from his eyelids, and he thought it's never done, his home will never be finished.

He crossed the house with one hand in front of him, though he knew where everything was. At the kitchen sink, he shook out four ibuprofen and chased them with a glass of water. Faced with the silence of his own home, he flipped the faucet back on. The sound of flowing water calmed him and he lowered his head to the drain and listened. The surge from the tap sounded like a raging fire, but the high pitched gurgling coming from the drain was something of an escape. He hovered there over the endless pipe, listening and wishing he could go in such a way.

After collapsing on the futon, the room spun a little clockwise in a stutter-step whirlpool. The moon threw a grid of pale light across the hardwood floor and the ambient glow lit the ceiling enough for Carl to make out the sloppy plaster work. Strangely aware of his breathing, he wondered if he could shut down his body by thought, an act of concentration so intense he might stop his heart and save the beats for another day. He tried, realized it was silly, and tried again. Though he couldn't shake the impulse, there was no shutting down. His mind whimsically absorbed the idea and took him out of place, and for a moment he happily played with breath and time.

The sharp angular ring of the telephone sliced through the room and shattered his play. He sat up and hoped it would go away, but the ringing made his head pound harder. On the third ring he grabbed the receiver.

"What?" he said.

"Carl?"

"Who is this?" He knew who it was the instant he heard her voice. The question was more of a stalling tactic.

"Oh my gosh, Carl. It's you." The first thing he noticed was her voice contained no guilt. This was nothing more than a simple call from an old friend on a spring evening, and it annoyed him. He rubbed his face to get the blood circulating.

"Who?"

"It's Miriam," she said with rising uncertainty in her voice. "Miriam Boyd. I hope I'm not calling too late."

"No, it's not too late," Carl said, closing his eyes.

"I was in your neck of the woods last month and ran into your granddad."

"You just happened to drive past my granddad's farm? On your way to what?"

"Is this a bad time? I don't want to walk in on anything if you're with someone. It's not bad is it?"

Here was his chance to cut her off and be done with it. She even gave him the out, but he couldn't bring himself to use it. The questions he had stored over the years gathered in his head – too many questions. Too many "what ifs," and Carl hated "what ifs."

"No, Miriam. It's not bad." The phone gained weight in his hand, and he propped an elbow on one knee to help hold it to his ear.

"It's been too long," she said. "Almost six years."

"Seven."

"Seven? Has it? My Gosh, that never should have happened."

"Seven."

His tone seemed to have finally connected, reminding Miriam of how she parted and how she likely tried to forget.

"I'm sorry, Carl. I'm sorry for everything."

"Are you?"

"I am. I handled it all wrong. I've handled a lot of things wrong."

"So did you find your father?" He knew the answer and that the question would sting.

"No, I didn't. I ended up in Florida. I bummed around for a while." Between each sentence she paused, as if giving Carl time to respond. "Then I sort of found myself pregnant." Miriam's voice regained some of its loft. "I have the most beautiful baby girl, Carl. I can't wait for you to meet her."

Though this was nothing he didn't already know, hearing it come from her feathery voice made him fold over.

"Did you manage to *find yourself* a husband?" He knew he sounded curt, but didn't care.

"Well – yeah. That's another story." She spoke with a sudden and unexpected bitterness, though seemingly not from the tone of Carl's question. "I'm in the process of getting rid of him. That's partly why I was up there. The whole thing was just a bad idea. I'll explain it all later." Her voice could go from dark to bright in an instant. "So where are you? What are you doing?"

"I bought a house in town. A year after you left."

"You bought a house," she said quietly, as both a question and a fact.

"It was a dump, but was all I could afford. I'm sure you remember that."

"The next time I'm up there I want the grand tour. We have a lot to catch up on."

"Do we?"

Her tone turned serious again. "I have some issues you need to know about." A child whimpered in the background, a disturbing cry from someone small. "Look," she said. "I have to go. My little one's fussing and I have to put her down. I need to see you the next time I'm in town – a few weeks?"

"That's fine, Miriam."

They exchanged goodbyes and Carl was left with the static buzzing dial tone merging with the buzzing in his head. He knew the call would come and had planned several speeches that were hard and gallant, all under the guise of putting her in her place once and for all. But this was better, more dignified. He hadn't insulted her, and he would simply avoid her calls or put her off until she lost interest. He was sure she would. She had before.

He climbed the steps to wash the powder and beer sweat off his body. He lingered under the shower head, somewhere between drunkenness and a hangover, and grew enraged. So now Miriam's divorcing the father and comes home looking up old flames. Well it won't go anywhere, he told himself. Dammit all. He shut off the water and almost ripped the shower curtain off the rod as he grabbed the towel. His naked body dripped in front of the mirror. Pouched belly, farmer tan lines on his arms and neck, looking more like his dead father every day.

Chapter 4

Miriam called again and the ground rules were set. She would come to see Carl at his house, but not with her daughter. He wasn't ready for that and wasn't sure he ever would be. His generosity was stretched taut as it was, but he conceded his Grandfather was right, he needed to talk it out and be done with it.

The morning of Miriam's visit, he vacuumed the floor and wiped down every surface in the house, put away all the dripping paint cans and stored the new kitchen sink in the hall closet. He stacked the stones he had thrown around the lawn in their boxes and spread a canvas tarp over the workbench and the block of marble sitting on it. All the while, he tried to get his mind off his nervousness by thinking benign thoughts. How did she look? What had seven years of Florida sun done to her? Perhaps the tropics pushed her age, in fact he hoped it had – a few wrinkles might help him cope. He found some high school photos in a drawer and studied them, examined the faces, their pink cheeks and smooth and childish grins. It occurred to him he didn't know these people anymore.

The designated hour passed and he paced the house, quick-stepping to the window at the sound of every passing car. He grabbed a beer from the refrigerator and stared aimlessly into his back yard, feeling cold and resentful from being kept waiting. The knock on the door drained the blood from his fingertips and made his knuckles ache. He rushed to the front window and pinched the blind. On the street sat a twenty-year-old BMW with rusted quarter-panels and age spots. Two voices bandied outside the door; the first one light and lyrical and painfully familiar, the other as raspy as a turkey call. His hand felt weak as he opened the door.

She stood on the porch in profile, fair in complexion and a knowing smile, the placid face of a rose cameo. Her jeans and white blouse showed off her slimness, slimmer than he remembered, and her hair was fastened up in some mystery. With her hands folded in repose, she faced the recent bride of Kilgore the younger next door. Millie Kilgore, a bulwark of a woman – who had recently justified her marriage to Dale on the grounds that their eldest child was about to enter kindergarten – sat on her stoop with her ham legs spread wide, jowls grinning, mouth jabbering.

"He don't get many visitors," she squawked loud enough for the whole neighborhood to hear. "Just be nice to him and he won't bite." She jerked her head toward him. "Say Carl, you got one hot lady there on your porch."

So long as Miriam was looking away, Carl couldn't take his eyes off her, and when she turned to face him they were both astonished. He suffered her gaze for only a second before lowering his head. "Come on –," he said, stepping back.

"That won't do." Miriam threw her slender arms around his neck. She held him tight, while Carl floated a hand behind her back, making an effort to hold her only to signal an end to their awkward embrace. Millie Kilgore extended her fat frame over the fence for a better look. Still grinning, she gave Carl a thumb up. With his free hand, he pushed the door shut.

"Some neighbors there," Miriam shrugged.

"You can't pick your neighbors."

He took a hard swallow of beer and crossed the room. With his back turned, he offered her a drink. Miriam's grey eyes panned the room and slowed whenever they crossed anything telling about Carl's life. His rack of waiting canvasses, a rented Tarantino film, an Art Now magazine.

"So this is it," she said.

"What?" he responded, turning toward her. "The final confrontation?"

"Your house."

Carl took another swig. "Have a seat," he said, going to the kitchen for another beer. He leaned on the cased opening to the dining room like one might do in an earthquake. Miriam planted herself on the edge of the futon, her carriage prim and erect, balancing her bottle on one knee as if pleased with herself for gaining entry into some exclusive club. Here she was in his house, drinking his beer, her soft cheeks sinking nicely into his futon, and he wasn't sure anymore what he needed from this visit. His resentment grew. Neither spoke for a moment until he grew impatient.

"So how have you been for the past seven god damn years?"

"I'm not going to do this if you're going to be this way."

"Fine," he said, shying away.

"What do you want to know?"

"I have no idea," he said. "I don't know what I want. I do know that I don't want to hear about why you left. I can't do that right now. Just tell me what you've been doing. Just talk. I don't want to talk. You talk."

"That was one of the problems."

"I said I'm not ready."

"Okay," she said with finality. "So I ended up in Florida. You probably heard my mother moved there." She paused again, giving Carl time to respond, but he didn't. "I actually stayed with her for a while. She wanted to reconcile and I was stupid enough to try." Miriam quickly added, "I didn't date anyone for almost a year," as if this might make him feel better.

"I got you beat there."

"You said you didn't want to talk." Carl waved her on with his bottle. "I didn't know it hurt you this much. I'm sorry. I could never tell what was going on inside you."

"You were living with your mother –"

"I was living with my mother, but of course it didn't last. She told me she was going to meetings, but there were bottles stashed all over the house. She started bringing home all these creepy men and I couldn't take that again. I swear I'll never ask that woman for anything again."

"You're lucky to have a mother."

"You want her? She's yours."

Carl was tempted to push the negative until she walked out, but what held him back was a growing desire to know what she'd done with her life, right down to the last minute, though he knew whatever he learned would have no value beyond therapy. He wanted to construct a day-by-day comparison of their whereabouts. Where was she working when he was closing on the house? Who was she screwing when he was renovating the bathroom? And it occurred to him that where you are working and who you are screwing accounts for most of an average life.

He stared at her, not from the attentiveness of a polite host, but out of amazement, his gaze bordering on being rude. She was thinner in the arms and cheeks, and the slightest creases fanned from the corners of her eyes, complimenting the thin lips of her smile. Her hair had gone from a gentle auburn to a harder reddish tone, so he knew it was dyed. The early grey strays were gone – by now there would have been too many to pluck. She wasn't young anymore, but she wasn't old either.

"So I moved around," she continued. "Got into a few situations. Most of the guys down there, well . . . I was engaged a few times and it just never worked out."

"Exactly how many men did you almost marry? Not counting myself."

"Three," she said plainly. "I married the last one, and he turned out to be the worst. I didn't want to, but I had the baby and couldn't move back with my mother again." There was a pleading in her voice, a plea for understanding. "And he was the perfect gentleman – for a while. He said he wanted to be in the child's life. Of course that only came after I refused to abort her. He was ready to drive me to the clinic."

"So he knocked you up. How well did you know this guy?"

"Not well enough." She swirled her beer and stared into the bottle. "Don't you have any Kahlua?"

"What do you want?"

"You don't remember?"

Carl welcomed the distraction. In the kitchen he took bottles of Kahlua and vodka from the cabinet, measured the jiggers into a rock glass and topped it off with cream. He exchanged the glass for her bottle and again braced himself between the two rooms.

"At first I was attracted to him because he reminded me of you," she said.

Carl slouched, felt he might slide to the floor. In a kind of retreat, he crossed the room and settled into a beaten leather recliner, resting his head on one shoulder. "Exactly what traits did this man possess that reminded you of me?"

"He had your face. Same lines. Same clenched jaw. I stopped in my tracks the first time I saw him. He was into construction too."

"I'm not into construction. I'm into creation."

"I don't know what that means, Carl. All I'm saying is he reminded me of you." She watched him lying there, perhaps noticing his weight gain. "That part of him made me feel safe. I think it's why I trusted him at first."

Carl perked up his head. "Why didn't you trust me?"

"I did. I don't know. Things were tight then."

"I know I didn't have a pot to piss in, but it's not supposed to be about money."

"You didn't know what you wanted. You hated your job. I thought you looked at marriage as some sort of magic fix-all."

"Bull. I looked at marriage as being married. It was never an escapist fantasy."

"How was I supposed to know what you were thinking? You never talked."

"The words 'I love you' didn't tell you anything?"

"That's not what it all boils down to. There's more to marriage than that."

Carl scooted to the edge of the chair. "So it was all about money?"

"It was about what you wanted. You weren't happy. You wanted to do your artist stuff and I never understood any of that. I knew you wanted to leave town, go to New York or something. You talked about that once."

"Yeah – talked. I never said I wanted to leave you behind and move into a loft in Soho."

"Where's Soho?"

"Never mind. I'm happy in the country. I always have been. You never figured that out?"

She paused for a moment and stared at the floor. "I thought I was holding you back."

"Christ, weren't we going for the clichéd American dream? Get married dirt poor, live in a one bedroom apartment and fuck five times a day?" He dropped back into his chair. "Whatever was in front of us, we'd have worked through it."

"I thought you needed something more."

Carl shook his head, refusing to accept her excuse. "You were it, Miriam. You were it for me."

Her face flushed with astonishment. "I made some mistakes," she said. "I didn't know you felt that strongly."

A quiet settled over the room like a leaden shroud, weighing down the furniture and its occupants. Their thoughts, dreams, and conclusions separated them.

"What are you doing now?" she asked.

"I teach future stock brokers, auto mechanics, and convicts how to draw old shoes." Miriam raised her brow. "I teach art at the middle school," he said, thinking how unimpressive it must sound. "It's steady and I get the summers off. You?"

"Right now I'm waiting tables at a rib house. I'll get something better when the divorce is final and I can get back up here with my daughter." She spied the stack of canvasses facing the wall. "Are you still sculpting too?"

"That's all I work on anymore. You should see the back yard."

She rested her eyes on him as he lay helpless in the chair, looking wounded though more relaxed.

"I want you to meet her, Carl. I want her to meet you."

"She's with her father this weekend?"

Miriam drew in her shoulders and said that she was.

"We'll see."

The two entered a silence void of any awkwardness, the silence enjoyed by two people who are naturally comfortable in each other's presence. Miriam asked to see the house, so he took her upstairs where it showed like a model home that hadn't been completed. The walls had been skim coated, but only primed, and the oak hardwoods refinished, but the baseboard trim and crown moldings had never been fully installed. The bathroom, though gutted and retiled, had areas left without grout.

"Could use a woman's touch," she said with a finger on her chin. "Drapes would be nice."

He led her to the back yard where the trees had leafed out lush and full against a blue sky marked by the winnowing stripes of contrails. The few remaining stalks of daffodils along the fence line had collapsed and a fat robin rustled in the leaves beside them.

Miriam lifted the edge of the tarp on his workbench and peeked underneath.

"You're carving marble now?"

Shocked at her interest, he pulled back the canvas and brushed aside the few rotting whirly-wheels dropped from the maples.

"It's harder to work, but more rewarding."

"I still like your alabaster."

"It sells well, but Alabaster is too easy. I can't compete with the material. The stone is so beautiful, it makes what I'm trying to create seem secondary."

"What are you trying to create, Carl?"

He didn't have an answer for her, though he was sensing a break in his exile. He recognized there were desires in life he couldn't generate by himself, and now here she was again strangely filling a void. Her presence was effortless. They stood together in the grass surrounded by stones, each mesmerized at the sudden presence of the other. He felt as if he'd stumbled upon something precious lying in a drawer, something he had long ago forgotten.

Chapter 5

It didn't rain that spring, it only stormed. There were no multi-day soakings to muddy the ground, drive you inside and make you long for the sun. Instead the rain came one punch at a time, each a violent downpour replete with lightning and power outages, the kind of rain that bounces off the sun scorched earth in flash floods and carries away anything dumb enough to stand in its way.

The clouds had just broken after a Memorial Day storm as Carl examined his face in the bathroom mirror. He pushed his nose from side-to-side and examined the pores, massaged the two wilting crescents beneath each eye. Under the shower he let the water batter him to life, numbing his memory and washing away the day. He scrubbed his body hard enough to kill any virus and lingered under the cascade until he drained the hot water from the tank. He was dressed in time to hear the knock on the door.

Miriam stood on the porch with a pink sweater draped over one arm. She wore a flowery dress tied at the waist that showed off her figure as well as any dress could. Her hair flowed in red curls and settled on her shoulders like feathers fallen from the sky. She bounced on her heels and waved through the glass as Carl answered the door. He took in as much as he could without staring too long.

"You look good," he said, avoiding her eyes.

The storm cooled the evening, and the sidewalks were dark and wet with clods of leaves and cigarette butts clumped at the edges. Together they strolled toward town following the raised railroad, its bank smelling of creosote and blooming honeysuckle. Carl scuffed his feet as they strolled and was careful not to touch her, though Miriam brushed his side several times on the way.

"Not the best side of town," she said, sauntering beside him. "But some of the houses aren't so bad. At least you own yours."

"When I'm done, I'll have the best house in the worst neighborhood."

The setting sun struck the tops of the old warehouses behind the train station where the ghostly images of Sanitary Grocery & Co., Purina, and Grosen & Son were flaking off the abandoned brick ruins like fading clues of some extinct way of life, a way Carl knew his ancestors must have played a part.

On the far end of town under the flicker of newly installed gas lamps, The Parsley Sage had opened to rave reviews, though no critic dared say anything to undermine a new business in town. The owners brought their riches, refined taste and personal chef from Manhattan with the idea of catering to the region's old-money equestrian culture. Together they stared into the glowing box displaying an elegantly scripted menu.

"We're not eating here," Miriam said.

"Why not? I've been wanting to try it." Miriam appeared uncertain. "I've got it covered."

Miriam bounced on her heels as Carl held the door. The dining area was decorated in renaissance hues of burgundy and ochre, and at each place setting was a red cloth napkin folded into a rose. She requested a table by the window where they could soak up the old familiar street.

The waiter, an overconfident young man who claimed to have prepared the food himself, made an uncomfortable production of uncorking the wine, a local *Cabernet Sauvignon*. He checked the glass for spots, dribbled some red into its bottom and presented it to Carl. Not versed in wine etiquette, he faked his way along by raising the glass to his nose and sloshing around his first sip like a shot of mouthwash. It tasted fine, but he had no idea why. He held the glass to the candlelight as if he knew something about color or legs. Miriam and the waiter were poised as if he were removing a delicate soufflé from the oven. He lowered his glass.

"This will do," he said.

They shook out the red rose napkins when the bread arrived. Carl ordered a steak, rare, and Miriam a pink salmon that went with her dress. Their conversation wandered among trivial matters of their shared history; of the time something horrible happened to a classmate, something that hadn't been funny at the time but could now be revived with great hilarity over an overpriced bottle of wine. For a time, heavier subjects were avoided, but halfway through the main course Miriam picked at the tender flakes of salmon, summoning her nerve.

"I can bring Annaliese up in a few weeks," she said.

He knew it was coming, but the mention of her daughter was still a jolt to the conversation. This was the first time she'd mentioned the child's name, and he felt self-conscious, as if realizing he was missing several buttons from his shirt.

"I'm not ready to see her, Miriam."

"I'm going to be raising her by myself. She needs all the positive influences I can find."

"You're not raising her by yourself. She has a father."

She straightened up and pinched her lips together, gave her hair a little shake. "He's not going to be good for her – not from what I've learned about the man. She needs a positive role-model."

Carl cracked a smile, as if for the first time seeing himself clearly. "You haven't been around lately, have you?"

"What's so funny?"

He sliced into his baked potato. "*Positive* wouldn't be the best word to describe me."

"I still want her to know you."

"What will I be to her? Crazy Uncle Carl?"

"Yeah," Miriam said, giggling. "I'll tell her wild stories about you. Everyone needs an eccentric uncle."

He tried to ignore the comment, but there was too much truth in it. Unsure how to deal with this new role, he sipped his wine and stared into the street. He wanted to change the subject. "You're staying with Naomi?"

"Yeah, but she's got a small place. Guys are in and out all the time, so it's a little uncomfortable."

Carl's mind went black. He wanted to say she should be used to that, but held himself. This dinner was his olive branch and he didn't want to sprinkle it with the powdery bitterness he still ground daily, albeit in lesser portions. He forced a smile and asked the waiter for the dessert menu.

By the end of dinner the evening had cooled. The gas lamps gave a warm glow to peoples' faces, but when they crossed to the east side of town the old sodium lamps threw off a sick yellow pallor and weakened their pace. Miriam bumped into him more than before, and Carl attributed her brushing flirts to the bottle of wine. He gave her a little nudge back.

When they approached his house a car motored toward them, shut off its headlights and rolled to a stop in front of the Kilgore's house. A kid in a baggy windbreaker hopped out of the passenger seat and quick-stepped to the front door where he knocked two times. The door creaked open, but the visitor wasn't welcomed inside. On the way back to his car he adjusted something in his pocket. Miriam said hello and the kid said, "Hey," and picked up his pace. He was barely in the car before it sped off, the tires chirping in second gear before the headlights were lit.

"Not too friendly," she said, as Carl fumbled with the keys. She pushed in behind him as though she'd lived there all along. A damp breeze filtered through the windows and freshened the room, though it also chilled the space and made the house feel ancient. While Carl lowered a sash, she collapsed on the futon and put her hands on her belly. "My God, I'm stuffed." She wriggled around until she was content. Carl settled into the recliner and regarded her, watched her breasts rise and fall, her lips pursed in a sigh. If there were any small creases near her eyes they didn't show – her cheeks were full and smooth, the color of cream with a little grenadine.

Watching over her, Carl said, "The next time you bring her up, I'll see her."

Miriam reached over and put a hand on his knee like nothing else mattered. "Thank you," she said, and lay back down. In a monotone voice that hung in the air, she said, "Ed is fighting for custody."

For some reason, Carl wasn't surprised. "He'll never get her," he said.

"You haven't seen the hearings so far. This judge is a piece of work. He has a history of giving custody to the father. He has a history of a lot of other crap too. I think he's already made up his mind."

"You have a good attorney?"

"The judge fell asleep last week when my attorney cross-examined. He closed his eyes."

"Maybe he was concentrating."

Miriam sat up and hugged herself. "This wasn't concentration." The space around her turned tense and a kind of coldness emanated from her.

"When's the next hearing?"

"Another week or two. Maybe longer. It depends on the whims of Judge Hawkins and the crap Ed's attorney pulls." She sat motionless as she spoke. "Things are different down there."

"Unless they can prove you're either insane, incompetent or on drugs, there's no way you'll lose her. That just won't happen."

"I don't share your confidence," she said, rubbing her face hard.

"Don't be upset."

"You don't know what this is like. You don't have a child."

"No, I don't have a child. I wanted one with you, but you had other ideas. How long did you know this guy?"

"We dated about a month. I had no idea he was like this."

"Like what? You said he was like me."

"He wasn't. Not like I thought." She rested her hands on her cheeks. "He's been stalking me ever since I threw him out."

"Then you have to use it against him. Does Florida have anti-stalking laws?"

"No. We brought it up in the last hearing and the judge slammed me for it. I couldn't prove it."

"If you keep a log of every time –."

"They're already using it against me, Carl. Ed's attorney twists everything around. The judge thinks I'm making it all up. Now he thinks I'm a liar."

"Your attorney should be preventing that."

"He's not. He's not doing a damn thing. He won't even meet me except for ten minutes before each hearing. He doesn't object to their shit. He doesn't even know *when* to object. I could represent myself better."

"I don't know, Miriam. Relax," he said, trying to calm her growing rage. He remembered how quickly her mood could shift. He scooted to the edge of his chair. "Can I get you anything?"

"No. Yes. I don't know."

Carl took a fleece blanket off the back of his recliner and draped it over her, but she sat cold and rigid, not caring to shape the blanket to her contours. He longed for something useful to do, but just stood there absently.

"You don't have to go back to Naomi's tonight," he said. "You can crash here."

"Thank you," she murmured.

After laying out the futon and fitting it with linen, Carl climbed the stairway to his bedroom and stripped off his clothes. He stared into the mirror and threw water over his face, ran his fingers through his thinning hair.

In bed he grew angry. He rolled in the cold sheets and found no comfort. After all that had happened, she was downstairs, asleep in his own home, and he couldn't bring himself to touch her. She was damaged too, but in a different way – in an ever growing way if what she said was true.

He drifted into a half sleep and dreamed of footsteps. Closer still and his mind wandered, dreaming of loneliness. The holiest of tapping sounded on the door, too quiet to answer, and it opened without invitation. Miriam stepped in from the blackness into the silvery moon-lit room. Her dress was missing the tie at the waist, flowing free.

"It's too cold down there," she said, folding back the covers. Carl lay on his back and watched her pull the dress over her head. She sat next to him and he studied her with the concentration of a scholar. Her bare shoulders stirred and stretched, the pale bone rolling under her skin. His eyes examined her in the same way as when he made his secret drawings years before. She unhooked her bra and dropped it to the floor. The line of her breast drooped more than he remembered, but she'd given birth and nursed a child. She slid between the sheets and lay on her side, facing away, hands between her knees as in prayer, radiating a warmth that had become foreign to him.

"That won't do," he whispered. He rolled her over and kissed her and worked his way down.

55

Chapter 6

He sat on a three-legged stool on his patio, arms and legs dusted white, regressing on this cloudless afternoon out of a fear of failure. His mind wasn't focused on the stone, but instead wandered like a child lost in the forest, a child who hadn't yet realized his dilemma. Despite his muddled and drifting mind, he needed to carve, if only to purge the jitters. All morning he guided his chisel over the stone, looking like an impassioned artist to any impressionable dilettante, but he lacked any trace of inner confidence. The slightest mistake, a single blow too heavy or slip of the point would not only alter the process but change the entire outcome. He had the sense to set aside the marble he'd been working, knowing it was too far along to chance ruin. Instead he spent the time beating on a small chunk of expendable alabaster, something he could savage and still salvage the beauty.

The three-point chisel ran rough and uncertain, peppering the ground with dust and chips and tiny flints, making it look like an isolated snow storm had passed overhead. He maintained his effort, waiting for the moment when his instincts would take over, the moment when he forgets his isolation and his abysmal heart, the moment when he would be swept away in the all-consuming process. A car door slammed and he rested his tools and listened. A minute later another slam and a voice fluttering from the front yard. He chipped at the stone again, though he knew the moment of inspiration would never come.

"Do you hear that sound?" a voice asked. "What could that be?"

In timid steps, the child revealed herself. The hem of her dress bobbed into view followed by her whole cherub figure. She wore a white cotton dress strapped over her bare shoulders, patterned with a wandering strawberry patch. Hands clasped and held to the heart, fingers awkwardly entwined, she stopped and fidgeted at the sight of the dusty and uncertain man.

The girl's mother stepped behind her in a surf shop tee-shirt, sunglasses and cutoff jeans bunched up at the crotch. A canvas tote bag hung from one arm like it had been hanging there for several days. Her face was lined and drawn, mouth crimped with stress, her hair wind-whipped from the ten hour drive. Despite her obvious fatigue, she somehow filled her words with the buoyant inflection of a proud and encouraging mother.

"It's okay, sweetie. He won't bite."

"Well," Carl said, resting the chisel on the butcher block. "Hi there."

His heart lightened on seeing the girl and he felt stupid for having been so nervous and reluctant. Annaliese was cautious and looked to her mother. After a little coaxing, she stepped forward like a heron on the prowl, more taken by what was happening under Carl's hands than with Carl himself. Without warning, as if several recently ingested sugar cubes were kicking in, she hopped forward and stopped just short of kissing distance. Standing opposite the workbench, her hands were still clasped, but her fingers were wagging to the left and right as if conducting a little imaginary orchestra. If her fingers were an indicator of brain activity, she was surely busy processing the scene. She was close enough for Carl to notice her eyes, the same blue-grey galaxy sparkle as her mother's, and they were intent on the stone.

"Dirty," she said.

Carl, for lack of anything better to say, repeated, "Dirty," and they rolled their lower lips and nodded. After pondering her for a moment, he asked if she wanted to touch the alabaster. Annaliese seized the invitation, reaching out and patting the stone like it was a puppy.

"I guess it's time for proper introductions," Miriam said. "Annaliese, this is Carl. Carl is an old friend of mommy's. He's an artist." Annaliese put a finger in the powdery white dust. "Please don't get that all over your pretty dress."

Like a cleverly timed act of defiance, the girl spread her palm and slapped the butcher block, sending an explosion of white talc into the air.

"No!" Carl shouted as Miriam pulled her away from the gypsum cloud. "Don't let her breath it in!"

A deep welling came from her lungs, a drowning gasp before Annaliese let out a wail that made Carl stand and take a step back.

"It's okay, it's okay." Miriam brushed off her dress and glared at Carl. "Don't yell at her."

"I didn't mean to yell."

"She's only two-and-a-half."

Carl wondered why he couldn't yell at a two-and-a-half year old if it was justified, but he wasn't about to argue the point. It was then he remembered Miriam's temper. Since she was obviously tired from the long trip, it was best to let it go.

Miriam turned her full attention to her daughter. "Let's get you changed," she said, leading her into the back door through the kitchen. Annaliese cried and hung her head like a prisoner guilty of some great infraction. Carl noticed her profile as she passed. Her stub nose hadn't taken its full shape, but the wisp of hair off her brow again reminded him of her mother.

Wanting to make amends, he called to her, "It's okay, Annaliese," though he wasn't sure if this was true. She didn't respond beyond her monotone groaning. While he listened to water running in the upstairs bathroom, he stood there wondering if he'd somehow encouraged her misbehavior.

When he picked up his hammer and chisel, they felt foreign in his hands. Though it had been a half-hearted attempt, his stone no better for the effort, the session had at least soaked up any creative drive for the day. He balanced his tools on one knee and wrapped them in a leather pouch, tied them with a cord and knotted it. He left the stone nestled in its own powder and covered it with the tarp, weighing it down with smaller stones at the four corners. After he finished spraying the dust off the patio with the garden hose, the two women in his life, one old and one new, pushed through the screen door. Annaliese bounced outside in her play clothes with no apparent short-term memory. She knelt by Carl's boxes of alabaster and began touching the tops of them. Miriam took off around the house and just as when she was out of sight, Annaliese lurched up. A sharp cough broke from her throat – a piercing terror as if she were about to be left alone in a place without light or sound. She screamed, "No," and ran to her mother.

"I'm just going to the car to get your things," Miriam said, but Annaliese wailed and wrapped herself around her mother's leg like a wild vine.

"I'm not going to leave you." Miriam placed her palms on her daughter's head. "Mommy will never leave you." She bent down and received her in open arms, but the girl's eyes were still shut tight, her fists squeezing knots in her mother's shirt. "Okay. Let's go get your toys."

"I go too," she said, choking and uncertain.

"Yes, you go too."

Miriam picked her up and carried her to the car. A few minutes later they returned lugging a small blue suitcase and dragging a fishnet bag full of bulbous plastic toys designed with less concern for fun than for lawsuits. Carl took in the colorful masses with trepidation. The toys were too clean, too sanitized. He recalled the toys from his youth – the steel trucks and rusty sheet metal farm sets. Not once did he ever need a tetanus shot.

Annaliese emptied the bag in the yard and staked claim on the land, but quickly lost interest as she again made for the boxes of alabaster. Using both hands, she picked up a stone weighing about two pounds and placed it upright on the patio. She heaved up another and grunted, proclaiming it heavy, and slid it next to the first one. Carl approved.

"I thought you wanted her to stay away from your rocks," Miriam said.

"She can play with the rocks all she wants. I just don't want her in the powder. You don't want that stuff in her lungs." Annaliese picked up each stone and examined it as if she might discover a sparkling quartz on its underside. He'd never had a two-year-old in his house and considered himself ill equipped to entertain one, but as he watched her play with the stones it occurred to him most of what he did was in the realm of a child. Ink pens and paper, paint and clay, even rocks. He dashed inside and reemerged moments later with a small wooden box, a large pad of paper and a mason jar topped off with water.

Miriam shriveled into a lawn chair with her arms splayed out and legs parted. She had no more presence than a post or a bush, and looked like she might have been starving. "Don't you want to play with your toys?" she said, trying to nudge Annaliese along, but the girl responded with a firm "no" and never slowed from the dream city she was building.

Carl sat in the grass and watched her for a time, before telling Annaliese he had something for her. When he said this it came out in an unexpected way, not unusual to anyone in earshot, but unexpected to his own ear. Having years before gone over to oils, his water colors had been left idle and forgotten in a closet, but on retrieving them for use by a child the tray of colors was as full of optimism as the day he bought them. He tore a page from the tablet and wetted it down with a wide brush. Annaliese was absorbed in her alabaster towers and regarded Carl with suspicion, but on seeing the blots of paint her interest grew. Balancing a wobbly stone with one hand, she let it topple over and stepped into the grass. She dropped to her knees opposite the paper, while he laid out the palette and wetted a brush in the Mason jar. She pressed a finger on each hard oval of pigment.

"She's only finger-painted," said Miriam, sounding relieved her daughter hadn't pinched a finger between the rocks.

"Like this," Carl said. He dabbed a wet brush on the red tablet, worked up the pigment and stroked the brush across the page. A brilliant wisp of color expanded into a tropical sunrise. Annaliese looked like she'd just seen a flower open. Carl handed her the brush, but instead she took his hand, clasping two of his fingers, and together they made swaths of color like blood brothers, both bound and enchanted with the moment. Annaliese was elated. Having bled together in solemn ritual, Carl handed over the brush and watched her with a wonder he had never known. The closest feeling he could recall was his initial contact with the girl's mother so many years before, at how something in her had touched him and filled his heart. He wetted a few more pages and showed her how to wash the brush between each color, but she commingled them anyway, adding streaks of green, orange, purple, and eventually muddy brown to her compositions. Wanting her to find her own way, he left her in the grass with her explosions of color.

Miriam moved behind the screen door to the kitchen sink, still within her daughter's sight, and busied herself with the dirty dishes.

"You don't have to do that," he said, coming inside.

"I know," she said, mousy and tired, holding something back. He wrapped around her from behind.

"You're not here."

"I'm fine. It was just the drive." She scrubbed a plate hard, trying to rid something stubbornly dried to it. "It was a long drive."

"I was the one who was uncertain about this."

"I'm sorry. There are other things on my mind."

∞

Early that evening, Miriam lowered the blinds and flattened the futon in preparation of Annaliese's bed. The sheets and blankets in the house were all drab solid colors, more for a man than a child, but she'd packed a blanket patterned with cackling Disney characters and spread it over the mattress. Annaliese was wound up and more interested in burrowing under the pillows than sleeping.

"You know what time it is," her mother said, with dark crescents under each eye. She put her daughter down and tucked the sheets, though Annaliese was still restless and wiggling underneath. Miriam cut the lights and climbed the stair, but before she reached the landing a small cry sounded from below, followed by a long wavering groan.

"Annaliese, you go to sleep. Go to sleep now."

The sound of her wailing rose. Carl sat in the second bedroom he used for an office, relaxing in an Eames chair in the pinkish glow of waning daylight, lost in the strange new sounds in his house. He watched Miriam come out of the bedroom in her nightgown and rush back downstairs.

"I'll light a candle for you," she said. Rummaging through Carl's kitchen gadget drawer, she found a nicked up votive, which she lit and put on the dining room table within glimmer of the distressed child. "That's better." She leaned over and brushed the hair from the girl's eyes and kissed her salty cheek. "I'll be right upstairs."

The girl raised her arms, her little fingers making gestures of want. "No go," she whimpered.

Miriam was gaunt and delivered to defeat. She lay down and enveloped the small bundle into her arms like it was all she possessed. The girl quieted down and a new calm blanketed the house. "That's my girl," her mother said, holding her tight. "You'll always be mommy's girl." Her voice cracked and she didn't speak again.

Carl busied himself with a newspaper and noticed the silence had a different quality than when he was alone. After an hour he tiptoed down the stairs, being careful not to step on any of the known squeaks in the floor boards, and saw them laying there together deep in sleep, Miriam in her nightgown bear-hugging the hairy warm lump under the covers. He poured a glass of milk and came back and stood there staring at them. Miriam's nightgown had slipped up to her hips, and in the sacred din of the candlelight her full vagina lay inviting like some exotic flower whose petals were about to open. It was part tease and part beauty, where the sadness of loss and the rekindling of desire came awkwardly together. The whole room made him want to break down.

Late that evening he woke as she came to bed.

"I have to leave early Sunday morning," she said, her voice curt.

The wood blinds were drawn tight and the room clad in black. Carl, still in a dream state, dreaming of recent sightings, rolled toward her dim silhouette.

"You said you were taking the week."

"I have to get back."

"What's going on? You were all excited about this trip. This is what you wanted."

She rummaged inside her bag for a brush and began raking it over her head, struggling through the windblown tangles. "Everything's fine," she said.

"Obviously not." He rolled back toward the wall and pulled the covers over his shoulder. "And you accuse me of not talking."

"You scared her this afternoon. You have a gruff voice."

"I can't change my voice," he said. "And I was trying to protect her. I said 'no' when I thought 'no' was a reasonable thing to say."

"You were gruff."

"I know you have more experience with these things, you actually having a child and all, but I don't see where disciplining her would be a problem."

"She's going through hell right now. She cries whenever I drop her off with her father. She won't go to sleep if I'm not in the room. Christ – she even cries when I get out of the car to pump gas."

"You still have to discipline her."

Miriam lowered the brush and jerked her head toward him. A silent rage passed through the room, mirroring the screams that had earlier passed through the house. He sensed her eyes in the dark. "Don't tell me how to raise my daughter."

"Oh God," Carl said, rocking his head. He wanted to say he expected that, but held back. Miriam shushed him and whipped the brush over her head so hard he expected to see tufts of hair all over the sheets in the morning.

"Look," she said, "I don't want to fight with you. I admit I might be a bit defensive with her."

"I can see why you would be," Carl said, softening his tone. "Given the hearings, sure."

Miriam stuffed the brush back in her bag. She spoke in a clear, controlled voice. "I want you to understand. I really do. I can't –." She broke off and gathered herself. "I just want her to be happy."

Carl sensed she needed something from him, though he didn't know what. He knew her mood swings could go in any direction at any time.

"She seems like a happy child," he said. "She's very interested in things. Very animated."

Miriam turned eagerly to face him in the dark. "She's so smart, Carl. I know I must sound like a typical proud mother, but she is." She pressed her fingers on Carl's arm. "She's an artist, like you."

"I think so. Did you see her watercolors?"

"She was happy."

Miriam dragged herself into the bathroom, and the ambient light poured through the hall and flooded the bedroom. She came back with a bottle of aloe lotion and rubbed it over her legs in long strokes, though it was more mechanical than sensual. She was still tight and distant, something untouchable about her.

The momentum of the conversation was lost. Carl rolled again toward the wall and settled in for the night. Miriam tossed the bottle into her bag, crawled under the covers and spooned into him. She pressed her breast into his back and laid an arm over his side. He felt behind and clasped her thigh.

"He has her," she said.

"Huh?" Carl groaned, not moving.

"Last week. He won."

"He what?" Carl propped up on one elbow and placed a hand behind her ear.

"Ed won. That man has custody of my child."

Chapter 7

The next morning Miriam rose early. She tied on Carl's robe and went to the kitchen where she poured silver dollar pancakes, fried bacon and sliced strawberries into a bowl, making a commotion unfamiliar to the house. Annaliese was still knotted in the sheets with a pacifier pulsing between her cheeks, watching through her tangled hair the oddly phallic Yo Gabba Gabba characters mindlessly dance and poke each other. In the bedroom the blinds were still drawn shut and Carl lay in bed unmoving and listening, unaccustomed to the sound of morning cartoons and the smell of sizzling bacon. He felt ill with anticipation, as if he was due to take an exam he hadn't studied for. The moment would have suited him better if it weren't for Miriam's revelation the night before. His eyes fixed on the whirling ceiling fan until she called to him in her sing-song voice.

They sat across from each other at the breakfast table, though Miriam did little actual sitting. She doted over every detail, refusing to rest for more than a few seconds at a time. Annaliese sat next to her mother's plate with a checkered kitchen hand towel tucked into her shirt and a ready fork in hand. The toast popped up, the tea kettle whistled and Miriam ran back and forth fetching sugar and jams and butter and napkins as her hair fell into her face. She slid the pancakes right from the frying pan onto their plates and shuffled back to pour more batter.

Carl stirred his coffee and stared into the whirlpool. "How about you sitting down and eating something," he said.

"I'm fine," she responded, as if any pause in activity might leave her open to unfair judgment. Only when she exhausted the last detail of the perfect breakfast did she sit down and nibble a cold pancake that had been laying on her plate since the start of the meal. She ate like someone at a wake, not from hunger, but from an awkward lack of anything to do with her hands.

After they finished breakfast, Miriam commented on Carl's construction-pocked yard. She acknowledged his house was better than most in the neighborhood, with its new porch of fresh grey floorboards and white trim, but the front lawn was an eyesore, still blighted from the spring demolition. The dead zone around the porch would grow nothing more than weed, she said, unless they put some life in the ground.

Annaliese bounced up and down on the bench seat of the truck in a joyous surge of energy. "There's no middle seat belt," Carl said, climbing into the cab. "You'll have to strap her in with you."

"Then let's take my car."

"If we're buying things to plant then we'll need the truck."

"Oh no. It's bad enough there's no car-seat."

"It's only a five minute drive. She'll be fine."

Miriam wavered. "If my ex-husband sees this or if we get a ticket –.

"He's in Florida."

"Is he?" Miriam stretched out the seat belt and it wrapped around the two of them easily, though the confinement didn't mesh well with Annaliese's giddiness. Carl had been flirting with her all morning and once they were on the road he reached over and squeezed her knee. The girl squealed in delight and shook her legs. "Don't do that again," Annaliese dared, so they repeated the ritual until Annaliese kicked on the radio and the speakers blared a commercial for a used car dealer.

"No, no," Miriam scolded. "We don't do that." She pushed her leg down and flicked off the radio.

"She's fine," Carl said, with Annaliese nestled between them. "Just fine."

At the nursery along an avenue of sweet gum trees, Annaliese joined her mother's and Carl's hands, this after seeing them hold hands the night before – something she had likely never witnessed her mother do with her father. The girl ran ahead and found secret passages through the maze of dogwood and witch hazel. When she came to a narrow path through the tubs of rose bushes, Carl bent down beside her and held a royal red to her nose. He told her to sniff, and she did so excitedly. They wandered down the path and stopped at every color, searching for the perfect scent, though she was never satisfied until she mashed the petals to his nose. "How's this one?" she would ask, and Carl would answer "too sweet" or "too salty" and twisted his face in either sweet ecstasy or wild grimacing distaste, eliciting from Annaliese a giggle with each rosy encounter.

"Look at these, Annaliese," Carl said. At the end of the row they came into a patch of lavender snapdragons. "Pinch one, like this." With two fingers, he clasped one from behind and opened and closed its fiery mouth.

"Lemme," she said, grabbing the one from his hand. She took it between her fingers and squashed it in half.

"Gently," he said. He showed her again and she squashed the next one too, though not as badly. He held her hand and worked her fingers for her, manipulating the dragon's delicate cheeks.

"Mommy, come see!" she called, but her excitement quickly froze as a black thought entered her head. Her face contorted, working up from the mouth until her eyes cinched shut and she bawled. Her mother was nowhere in sight.

Carl tried to console her as he looked in vain for Miriam. "Hey now. She's here," he said. Red faced and inconsolable, the child chewed on one of her hands. "She was right here. She must have gone into the greenhouse. Let's go to the greenhouse." The girl wouldn't budge. She was planted there, arms hanging like the branches of a willow, her open mouth howling for her mother.

Miriam burst from the greenhouse carrying a box of raspberry impatiens, the dirt in the tray trembling in a mini-earthquake. Once in sight, Annaliese swallowed her scream. She ran over and clung to her mother's leg. Miriam handed the tray to Carl and pulled a pacifier from her pocket.

"Mommy's not going to leave you," she said, sighing. "I promise." She bent down and stretched the elastic waistband of her pants and winced. "Oh no, Annaliese. What did we already learn?" She led the girl into the greenhouse to find a restroom, leaving Carl staring into the shaken grid of impatiens.

When they arrived home, the sun arced high overhead and beat down through the dead-still humidity. Carl opened the truck camper, dropped the tailgate and retrieved two buckets of azaleas as Miriam took the tray of perennials. Annaliese wandered across the yard and stopped short of the porch, where she considered the two boys across the fence.

The Kilgore kids were expelled from their house for the afternoon. Clothed only in underwear, covered with dirt and confined to their pen, they were more caged animals than little boys. Russell, the oldest and nearly ready for kindergarten – though only in age – pedaled a plastic car in circles around a bark-battered elm tree. His face was plump like his mother's, with hair mopped over his brow in sweaty streaks, though he carried his weight like his father, all in the stomach – the bloated belly of a starving child, though it was not likely food he was starving for. In contrast to the rest of the family, his younger brother Kyle was a stick. His pale freckled face was hard for being only three, but he revealed more thought than his brother, a certain attentiveness as if planning his eventual escape. He was standing on the sidewalk and, with a girlish overhand, throwing rocks at an abandoned shoe sitting a few yards away.

The longer Annaliese watched them, the faster Russell pedaled his car around the tree, his neck twisting, his eyes never leaving her, but she took more of an interest in his brother. When Carl and Miriam reached the porch, Russell rolled out of his spiral and slammed into Kyle, sending him hard to the concrete where he howled in pain.

"Russell, why in the world did you do that?" Carl said. Miriam froze, her mouth shaped in disbelief. "Kyle, are you okay?"

Millie Kilgore tromped onto the front porch and yelled at her youngest, who got up whimpering and limped toward her, holding out two scratched and bloodied palms. There was a red mark on the back of his leg where the plastic car struck him. His mother said it probably served him right and scolded both boys for playing too hard. She told Carl not to worry, they're just boys, and waddled back inside where shouts and sirens could be heard from a television.

All the while, Annaliese examined the boys in their pen, standing just shy of grabbing distance.

"Daddy says boys don't cry," Annaliese said to Kyle. "Why you crying?"

Kyle stopped his heaving and froze for his first awkward moment with a girl. Muddy tears trailed down his cheeks and mixed with a wet brown crust under his nose. He wiped his mouth with his naked arm and mumbled something, but it didn't come out right. Russell climbed from his car and strode over with the confidence of a cowboy.

"He fell down," Russell said. "Like this." He pushed Kyle hard to the ground, and this time the boy let out a scream that rattled even his brother. Millie burst through the screen door and stomped onto the porch.

"Kyle, you get up here right now. Russell, I don't know what you're doing, but knock it off or I'll lay into you something good."

Kyle lay contorted on the concrete, wailing at the injustice until his mother took hold of him. He was a limp rope over her arm as she carried him inside. Before they disappeared, Millie stuck her head back out the door. She flashed a smile at Annaliese and gave Miriam a mischievous gaze. "Glad to see you come back," she said. "Your little one's a real cutie."

Miriam was mortified. "Yeah," she said.

Russell's attention was still focused on Annaliese. In a rough emulation of his father, he sucked in his stomach and puffed out his chest. Carl stared the young man down.

"That wasn't a nice thing to do to your brother, Russell." The boy twisted his feet and glared at the ground.

"Not nice," Annaliese echoed with an authoritative nod.

"Annaliese, look," Miriam said, as if desperate to divide the two properties by more than a wire fence. "Let's go plant the pretty flowers." But the box of perennials had been forgotten – the girl found a new interest.

Miriam gave Carl a look telling him to do something, perhaps a first test of surrogate fatherhood. He dropped the tubs of azaleas and took Annaliese's hand, but ended up having to carry her inside while she strained to see over his shoulder, hypnotized at the sight of this filthy, burly boy with a streak of violence in his eyes. Miriam followed with the tray in hand and shut the door with her foot.

"My God," she said. "I don't want her involved with those kids."

Carl knelt down to Annaliese. "You can go play out back if you want."

"Wanna go there," she said, pointing to the front door.

"No," her mother said. "We don't play in front yards because of the cars."

"Wanna go there. You go too." She grabbed her mother's hand and tugged toward the front door.

"No, we don't play there."

Miriam led Annaliese to the back door and shooed her outside. The little one protested until her mother assured her she would be right inside the screen door where she could see her. Carl climbed the steps and sat at his desk, reclining under the ceiling fan to let his body cool. He heard the screen door slam and the scrape of little footsteps across the patio rise through the open window. Heavier steps sounded in the stairwell and he waited for the familiar squeak of the top tread. Miriam stood in the doorway with her arms folded.

"I can't have her playing with them."

"So we won't let her."

"If Ed comes around and sees her with them, I'll never hear the end of it."

"Why are you so worried about him being up here?"

"You know those people are dealing drugs, don't you?" she asked. Carl shrugged in response. "At least three cars stopped by last night. Don't tell me you've never noticed."

He sat up in his chair. "Look, I figured so much, but I have to live next to them."

"If Ed sees that I'm keeping her next to a crack house –."

"It's not a crack house. They're probably just selling weed. Do you really think your ex would drive all the way up here to spy on you?"

Miriam shook her head and sat on the edge of his desk. "You'd be amazed." The light was flashing on the land-line answering machine and she punched the button. It beeped once.

"So Carl, it's Liz. You've been hard to get a hold of lately. I didn't have anything going on this weekend. I was wondering if you wanted to hook up. Catch a movie? The usual? Give me a call."

Carl tried to restrain an embarrassed smile.

"I know what that was," she said, staring down at him.

"It's nothing, Miriam."

"You asked me about my fiancés'. So how many friends with benefits do you have?"

"I said I hadn't been in any serious relationships since you left. I never said I was celibate."

"So are you going to call *Liz*?"

"Yes, I am. I'm going to tell her not to call again." Miriam approved, and they let the air from the fan sweep down and cool them.

"Hey," Carl said. "She's quiet. You're up here and she's quiet."

Miriam's face was crossed with both relief and dread that she'd somehow lost significance. She called out, "Mommy's right here, Annaliese," but there was no answer.

"We'll keep them apart," he said, hoping that might settle the issue of the Kilgores.

∞

A six-foot tall wood privacy fence divided Carl's back yard from his neighbors. The bottom of the wood slats were rotten and chipped, making passages large enough for squirrels to pass. Half way down the yard an eight foot section of the fence broke away from its post and leaned into Carl's property, making a "v" shaped wedge just wide enough for two children to have a conversation.

Russell stuck his bloody arm through the gap in the fence.

"I'm bleeding," he said.

Annaliese twisted on one leg, inching closer. "What you do that for?"

"I didn't do it on purpose."

"Mommy fixes my cuts."

Russell, perhaps thinking of his own mother's lack of attention in such matters, lost some of his swagger. "Your mommy's skinny," he shot back.

Miriam threw up the screen in the bathroom window and thrust her head out. "Annaliese! You come inside. It's time for your nap." The girl kicked the grass and stared at the boy's muddy legs. "Come inside now," her mother insisted.

Millie stuck her head out the matching window next door. "Hey Miriam. I'm gonna take the kids to a water park tomorrow afternoon. We'd love to take your cutie-pie daughter along."

"We're going back to Florida tomorrow," she gutted out, before adding a quick thank you.

"Maybe we still got time today?"

"We have plans. We have to plant all these flowers, don't we Annaliese?" Miriam's voice went from loving to rigid and back again with the ease of a fly-cast. The girl trudged back to the house, dragging her feet.

Carl sidled up behind Miriam. "I can prop the fence back up," he whispered.

"Don't bother," she said without hope. "We're leaving tomorrow."

"I'll take care of it," he said, but she broke away and trotted down the stairwell to intercept her daughter.

∞

The evening production of putting Annaliese down was the same as before, the cries of separation lining the walls with sadness like a mourning for someone who had not yet died. Carl lay in bed in his boxers and pretended to read a book, his eyes skimming the lines but comprehending only the sounds beneath him, the pampering, the cajoling, the constant reassuring. An hour later, in a silence enhanced by a sleeping child, Miriam climbed the cold steps with two accordion files bulging with paper and sat them on the bed.

"You're not going to like what you see," she said. She went into the bathroom and ran the faucet, while Carl opened the first file and perused the tabs. She came back jiggling a toothbrush in her mouth. "I marked the ones you'll want to read with yellow stickies," she mumbled before drifting back into the bathroom.

He pulled out the first stapled pages. It was a court transcript – all legalese, pomp and decorum. It made Carl nervous to hold, as if read by the wrong person it might burst into flames. The opening verbiage looked ready to carve into an important building, and the margins and format were so precise from page to page that if even one line were out of place the entire document might be invalidated.

He heard her spit and rinse, and a minute later she was sitting cross-legged at the foot of the bed. "Your name is mentioned a few times," she said, "but that comes later."

"Where the hell did my name come from?"

"As part of their strategy, they claimed we've been having an affair for the past year."

"I only just saw you again a few weeks ago. I sure as hell hope your attorney struck that down."

"This is how they operate. The judge let them present their case first. After they've bloodied me, I have to spend my allotted time defending myself from their allegations. They can allege anything they want, even if they know it's a pile of lies." She reached into a file and pulled out a tuft of documents. "Before I even got to all my counterclaims, the judge called equal time and ended the hearing. He said he'd heard enough. The bastard made up his mind before I even presented my side."

"But how'd they get my name?"

She unclipped the papers and fingered through them. "I came up here a few times over the past year to see Naomi. Things weren't good with Ed, so I made excuses to get away. I told the Judge I wanted to move back to Virginia with Annaliese, since I had old friends here and better job prospects." Carl waited for her to make a point. "Then the judge asked about my family." She lowered the papers she was holding. "You and your grandparents were the only family I could think of."

"You brought me into this before you'd even seen me again? And not to mention, we're suddenly related?"

"They know I don't have any family except for my mother, and they know she's a drunk. I had to tell them I had someone. Ed has family and family money – I don't have anything." She sniffled and swung one of her legs into a half lotus, the pain showing in her face. "Your grandparents were always so good to me. Y'all were the only family I had."

"At one point that was the idea."

"I'm sorry, Carl, but this is where I am now." She picked up the papers and straightened them. "I don't have any energy to rehash that. I just don't."

"So how were we having an affair when I hadn't seen you for seven years?"

"It was in the last hearing," she said. "Ed knows someone up here. I don't know who. Maybe he hired someone. Maybe he drove up here himself." She stared out the darkened window. "He did have access to my old address book. We were married for over a year, so he had plenty of time to copy it."

"That still doesn't lead them to an affair."

"At the last hearing his attorney presented photographs of my car in front of your house and a few more of us in town from Memorial Day weekend. They had a nice shot of you in the window of that restaurant. I'd like to get a copy."

"I'm not laughing here."

"There were also photos of you working on your porch. They subpoenaed my long-distance bills and asserted that my calls to Naomi were a cover, that I was really contacting you through a mutual friend."

"That's crazy."

"That's what they claimed."

"But we weren't together until after your legal separation. You can sleep with anyone you want."

"But my trips over the last year, Carl. Don't you see? They already had proof I was coming up here. Then they just asserted we'd been having an affair all along."

"But we weren't," he said exasperated, the whole of the situation still not fully registering.

"It doesn't matter. They said it, the judge believed it and it's done." Miriam untangled her legs and shoved the papers back into the file. "It's done."

Carl sat up in the sheets, mute and stunned.

"There's more," she sighed, too tired to go on. "You can read it now or the next time I come up."

"I think I have enough to chew on."

She leaned over and set the alarm clock. "I have to get up by six and be gone by seven if I'm going to get her to her father's by dinner."

The night was black and moonless, and they lay together neither touching or seeing, waiting for a rare breeze to cross the room and cool them, waiting for sleep that wouldn't come.

"You were grinding your teeth last night," he whispered.

"My friend Shayla said I need to find a way to unload all the stress."

He rolled against her and one of his hands wandered over her belly. "You know what's good for sleep?"

"That has nothing to do with sleep," she said, smiling weakly as his hand roamed.

He hovered over her and whispered in her ear, "You mean we could have been doing this for the past twelve months?"

She smiled and opened herself to him.

Chapter 8

The next Saturday morning, Carl and Miriam drove southwest of Compton under a receding bank of clouds. The landscape was swollen from thunderstorms that had lingered through the evening, and now the sun was slicing through in intervals, breaking to the ground and splashing the trees and fields in patches of bright wet viridescence. The mountain creeks spilled over their banks and bubbled over their rock beds, while the valley river swirled in a rich brown stew, its root and vine tangled banks holding the torrent shy of reclaiming any of the rich bottom land.

They were a half hour out of town on a no-name back-road. Miriam fidgeted in her seat and jutted her head forward, trying to better see what was to come.

"How far is this place?" she asked.

"We're almost there," Carl said. He took a scribbled note from his breast pocket, read it and placed it on the dash. In another mile they turned onto a gravel road snaking around one of the raging creeks. The hard-pack shoulder was washed away in places, and at one low hairpin turn the road was partially submerged in a back-flow eddy. Carl kept two wheels on the high side and ran the puddle. Miriam stared at him uncertainly.

"Are you sure about this?"

The road rose and separated from the creek, finding safe ground at the point of a valley opening before them. They followed the tree line to the right while a grid of ripening apple trees opened to the left. Carl counted the miles on his odometer until they saw the "for sale" sign tacked to a tree. He slowed down and idled. The driveway ran straight up the mountain.

"Up that?" Miriam said.

"The agent said not to worry about the first rise." He pointed. "Look. It levels off right there." They drifted back into the road, found first gear and popped the clutch, running the truck up the hill. Miriam pressed her feet into the floor board and held on for the rocket launch. Though it appeared dangerous from the road, the slope topped at a twenty foot rise and broke to the left along a gradual cut and fill ascent along the side of the mountain. "That wasn't so bad," Carl said, secretly relieved it hadn't been worse.

"You said this was a foreclosure?"

"Bank owned," he explained. "They're looking to get it off their balance sheet and they just put it on the market. I might have first dibs."

The access road hadn't been used in years. It was overgrown with weed and fallen branches, but they plowed ahead, climbing higher into the forest as saplings struck the bottom of the S-10. The rolling underbellies of the front were breaking and the sky was brightening through the treetops. When they rolled by a blighted patch of dead hickory, they grasped how high they had come.

"Oh my," Miriam whispered.

They stared wide-eyed across the valley as if they'd stepped into some great gilded palace. The clouds dispersed into fast moving gatherings that cast their shadows across the valley floor like ghosts of old forests come and gone. They were two hundred feet above the fertile floor, suspended in place between the last loitering clouds and the bubbling currents they fed in a divine placement in nature.

"Look," Miriam said.

"Yeah."

"No, look ahead!"

Carl slammed on the brakes. The front wheels stopped a few feet shy of a crevice where a ten foot section of road had washed out. Below them, halfway down the muddy landslide, was a corrugated drain pipe straddling two trees. Carl let the truck roll back and yanked the emergency brake.

"Wanna go for a hike?" he said.

They stepped to the edge of the divide where they could see the old house farther up the trail. Carl headed up the mountain, grabbing small trees and branches for support. They crossed the spring that had caused the damage and descended to the far side of the chasm. In another fifty yards the trees parted at a small perch of flat land where some god had leveled a sliver of the mountain rise with his finger. The farmhouse had been built at the first level opportunity, and Carl pondered the effort in getting the building materials up there. It had surely been no easier fifty years before when the home was constructed.

The two-story clapboard house hadn't been lived in for years, but the real estate agent who gave Carl the keys said it was habitable. It had fallen into an estate and been abandoned for several years before an heir was found; an uninterested second cousin who rented the property for a time before walking away, as unpaid back taxes accumulated.

Carl took long strides, excited like he was approaching some ancient jungle ruin. A tangle of Virginia creeper smothered one side of the house with little invading tentacles tucking under the siding. The shingles curled badly, but the roof plane was flat, a hopeful sign there might be no water damage. The gutters and fascia boards had fallen to the ground and were choked in vine like stones caught in the grip of tree roots. The house hadn't been painted in decades. Carl took stock of the ruin with a longing that it was already his.

He high-stepped through the weeds to the concrete stoop and took a key from the envelope the agent had given him. When he jiggled the lock, two squirrels scurried from the attic where the fascia board had fallen and disappeared into the underbrush.

"They have pets," Miriam said.

The door was swollen, so Carl gave it a bump with his hip and popped it open. The interior smelled of moldy upholstery and moth eaten suits. The floor was covered with slime green carpet, and the plaster walls, draped with cob web and sealed in lead-base paint, were smooth but for a few minor stress cracks and an assortment of rectangular shadows where a family's pictures once hung.

Carl hopped up and down in the middle of the room. The house rumbled, but it wasn't as rickety as he feared – nothing that couldn't be shored up. He tested each room the same way, curious how the years of isolation had affected the old structure.

Miriam rubbed a dirty window pane with her wrist and peeked through the hole. Most of the windows faced the wooded mountain rise only yards away, but there were few facing the majesty of the valley.

"It needs more windows," she complained, reading Carl's mind. He was thinking long-term of a bulldozer, but in the meantime, yes, more windows to the valley were a given. Every room would have a view. It was all coming together. This was where he could make a fresh start, a place without memory.

They left the house and continued along the fading driveway treads to the first barn, an ancient mass of timbers with a gambrel roof that was much older than the house. The cavernous space was full of busted stalls and cobwebs, and the vertical boards let in ripples of light so the walls moved as they passed through. Abandoned hay was still stored in the loft, but the smell of fresh cut clover had given way to the stink of rotting flesh of some animal that had recently wandered inside to die.

The back opening framed a second barn. It was smaller but much newer, with a low pitch roof and sheathed in plywood. The slider bay doors were padlocked. Carl found the right key and shoved the doors aside. Within they found three stalls, a wash bay, and a tack room. In the rear was a door to a field feathering back down to the valley floor like the train of a wedding dress.

Miriam inspected the tack room and checked the latches and the feed bins. She looked like she might start shoveling the stalls.

"This is wonderful," she said, her eyes bright with possibilities.

Miriam had loved working at the boarding farms after high school, but she'd never owned a horse of her own. It was far more than she could afford, so she'd contented herself with working out other people's Thoroughbreds. She made no secret of wanting her own.

"I'll use the first barn for my studio," Carl said, and turned to her. "This one will be yours."

She looked skeptical. "You're serious about this?"

"I've been saving." He entered one of the stalls.

"I'm not talking about the property."

"School lets out next week. I can renovate the house over the summer." He opened the top half of a Dutch door and the daylight streamed inside. The sun filled the valley with light as the rain had filled it with green. "I'd like to plant a vineyard on that slope," he said, pointing. "You think I could make a decent red?"

"You don't know a thing about wine."

He shrugged. "We could sell the grapes to the vintners. You wouldn't believe how many wineries have opened in the last few years."

"Won't you inherit half your grandfather's farm? His land would be perfect for a winery."

He shook his head and shied away. "I can't live there again," he said. She slid under his arm and gave him a little squeeze. He regrouped and responded to her question. "Yes, I'm serious. If we're married, we can get her back."

She pulled away. "Who said anything about marriage?"

"Where did you think I was going with this?"

"I'm sorry, but I haven't had much luck with the institution."

"This is what we used to talk about. A place of our own." He studied her reaction, which was neither cold nor warm. "You won't get custody if we're just shacking up on the weekends."

Her quick response sounded with a touch of paranoia. "We can't let them know we've been sleeping together. It would just validate all their accusations."

"But if we were engaged it might make a difference in an appeal."

"My God, I'm just coming out of a divorce."

"You admitted you made a mistake about leaving. And this place is exactly what we talked about seven years ago."

She warmed to his side and watched the last of the clouds breaking up. "I was thinking of something a little flatter," she said, "but this would do nicely. Annaliese would love it here." They stood for a while, gazing into the light bathed valley. She tugged on his shirt sleeve. "I have to talk to you about something. It might make a difference on whether you make an offer."

"I'm making an offer with or without you."

"But this may affect things."

"How so?"

"We weren't real careful that first weekend."

Carl stepped back and searched for something in her face. He slumped back over the door. "Then we'll have to make it work, won't we?" he said, staring away from her.

"It's not a sure thing. I'm just late. I've missed my period before."

"If you're pregnant, there sure as hell won't be any hiding of our relationship. Can you take one of those stick tests?"

"I don't trust them. I want to wait and go to my clinic in Florida."

"Then let's not worry about it until we know for sure."

"I don't have health insurance right now, Carl. I'm only a part-timer at that shitty rib shack, so they won't give me any coverage. And no one's going to insure me while I'm pregnant. Not until after the baby comes. This is going to cost a lot of money."

"What does it cost to have a kid nowadays?"

"A lot. And if there are complications . . . do you have any idea how expensive neonatal ICU can be?"

"So we won't have any complications."

Miriam regarded him sternly. "You can't say that."

"Well I'm tired of expecting the worst. I've done enough of that. I'll put money aside to handle the pregnancy and write the offer with whatever's left."

"It sounds reckless."

"You'd prefer we stay in town next to the Kilgores? Look, this is what we used to talk about, at least in the other life we had together. What do you want now?"

She said without hesitation, "I want my daughter back."

"So do I."

Miriam folded her arms and paced the stall. "If you can do it, then fine. I don't know how much money you have anyway." She headed toward the house in a fluster. He studied her, tried to figure her out. He followed her down the path not knowing what to say, but knowing he wanted the three of them right there on that piece of land.

She reached the house ahead of him and this time they explored upstairs, each choosing a different bedroom. Carl tested the floor and the window sashes, and when he stepped back into the hall he heard a sound – a faint controlled gasp. He stepped into the next room and said her name.

Miriam was in the smallest bedroom where the teddy bear pattern wallpaper was brown with age. She opened the closet door and peeked inside where it ran for a length into darkness. In the shadow was an abandoned toy box gathering dust. She dragged it into the light and knelt beside it. She hovered over its contents and wept.

"Bastard," she said.

"What?"

"That bastard." She huddled over the box like it contained a vision of an uncertain future. Carl knelt beside her and held her. "You have no idea," she said. She shuddered and rocked in his arms. "You have no idea what it's like. You don't."

PART TWO

Chapter 9

He had flown only twice before, to New York City and quickly back to Virginia during the post-Miriam melt-down. He had searched the brownstones of the Lower East Side in search of a cheap apartment and kindred spirits and perhaps a sign he belonged there, but after living for a week in the Pioneer Hotel, an old Bowery relic where the smallest rooms were mere cells, each with a urinal-like sink hanging next to the bed, he knew he was just running away. Part of his disillusionment was the presence of so many people trying to outdo each another. The art scene had less to do with art, than appearance and grandstanding and activism. Carl missed the class in design school on being hip, and he felt the whole urban existence was clichéd and tragic. He knew he could live just as tragically in a small town and do his work.

There were other reasons why he didn't stay, though he wouldn't admit to them. To run off to New York and live some Bohemian lifestyle might have been exactly what Miriam expected of him, and he didn't want to validate her suspicions. There was also the possibility that Carl, from a dark place called denial, wanted to be found by her again. He might have gone looking for her if he knew where she'd run off to, but she had no reliable family and their mutual friends just shook their heads and encouraged him to let her go.

On his flights to New York and back there was no one to meet him at the gates, which caused intense bursts of melancholy since he found it anti-climactic to survive the unnatural ascent and descent of seventy tons of metal over hundreds of miles, only to find there is no one there to see your safe landing. To land without welcome or acknowledgment left him feeling like a piece of unclaimed baggage circling around and around on the carousel long after everyone had left the terminal.

THE HUNGER ARTIST

On his arrival at Jacksonville International, the girl he'd met at sixteen was there to meet him and now she wasn't a girl at all. At thirty and a mother of one, Miriam carried her whole being differently and on seeing her in the terminal as he passed by security Carl questioned if he knew her at all. She stood erect like a caryatid, handling a great weight with ease, though there was a hint of grimace on her face indicating she might collapse at any moment. Again, he noticed she was thinner – too thin. The flesh in her arms held less mass, and her hair no longer followed the same lush curves it used to, but stayed close to her scalp with lesser strands breaking away to form curls of their own. Her smile appeared less natural, more calculating, though by most standards it was still a pretty smile.

He went to her and they embraced. I'm found, he thought, thankful someone was there to meet his safe arrival. But the moment was short.

"We have to pick up Annaliese," she said, and charged down the terminal. She turned and gave him a kiss. "Welcome to Florida," she said, before taking off again.

"I thought you'd already have her by now."

"It got put off. Ed's being an ass. We're doing the exchange at a McDonalds across the street from the police station. He can't pull any of his shit there."

The exchanges she'd described sounded like covert operations at the border on a moonless night. Miriam marched down the terminal and the crowd parted before her, as if they knew she were on some noble pursuit. The temperature in the terminal was frigid, more hospitable to Northern Spruce than the potted palm trees dotting the way. He stood there shivering while they waited for his luggage. The blast of cold air in the vestibule heightened the shock when for the first time Carl swam into the Florida muck. His sunglasses immediately steamed over. It wasn't the watery humidity of the Piedmont, but the air was thick and acidic, as if cleverly brewed to rot the fibers of his clothing. He was sure he felt his skin burning under the porous fabric of his shirt. Miriam flipped on her seven dollar sunglasses and led him to the farthest parking lot. Halfway there he wanted to stop and hyperventilate, and wondered if it was climate that had changed Miriam's hair.

The odometer on her BMW had broken 210,000 miles, and the car looked it. The windows were rolled down since there was nothing of value to steal, including the car. Each quarter panel was peppered with rust spots and the paint shriveled back from the windshield in a boiling plume that was devouring the entire cab. Carl pictured the top peeling away as they motored down the highway.

He slid in and perched on his toes to keep his bare thighs from touching the leather seat, which was torn along the seams with pasty food stuff accumulating in the crevices. The interior was cluttered with napkins, wet wipes, pouches of soy sauce, fashion magazines and cheap plastic toys from fast food promotions. Miriam folded the windshield sun screen emblazoned with a giant pair of sunglasses and stuffed it in the back seat. She maneuvered through the airport traffic, cursed the parking fee, paid it, and slipped onto the interstate. A southwest exit put them on a two-lane road cutting into the inland flats. Carl's postcard image of palm lined art deco avenues, high surf and colorful drinks washed away as they plunged into the bowels of the state. There were no manicured lawns or sexy surf shops where they were going. On either side of the road were second growth forest and the occasional dirt farm, and it went on like the plains. The road floated over a never-ending bog, reminding Carl there are flat landers and there are mountain dwellers – he was a mountain dweller. The smell wasn't of fresh cut hay and manure and sweet honeysuckle of the country he knew, but was of burnt and rotting wood piled high and decaying under a rancid sun. Heaps of toasted timber and brush from recent wildfires were piled high on the side of the road, and beyond them were the charred and blighted fields of their origin. Carl was hypnotized by it all, his vision stretching ahead to a one-point perspective where the road and its line of crucifix electric poles merged to infinity. They drove on in silence as if the mournful scenery demanded it. He couldn't bear to ask why she'd ever come to such a place.

A billboard counted one mile to Barrett's Antique Auction, and another said "Come to Colonel Jones Grill." Seagulls circled above the county landfill, and several boarded-up motels littered the final approach to town. In one of the sandy parking lots, women busied themselves behind tables for a market, but it wasn't the Saturday morning markets Carl knew. These people weren't selling produce, flowers or handicraft, but they were selling their own belongings and memories. They were hawking their children's outgrown clothing and toys from their closets, portable televisions and stacks of romance novels – anything to pay the rent.

Miriam slowed as they rolled into downtown Dixon. "I want to see if his car's here," she said. The red and yellow plastic-like McDonalds sat on the one corner in town with a traffic light, blinking amber. She drove through the light and spotted Ed's car on the first pass. "He's already here." Carl threw an arm over the seat and tried to spot the guy, but Miriam snapped at him. "Turn around," she said. He examined the hardened line of her jaw as she turned at the next street where bungalows were scattered among vacant and overgrown lots and the sidewalk competed with the crabgrass. She circled the block and pulled over when she came back to the secondary road.

"Hop out and meet me there," she said. "Pretend you're nobody. He's not expecting you. He might not recognize you."

"What if he does?"

"Then we're just friends. That's all, just friends." She gripped the steering wheel like she was twisting her ex-husband's neck. "I'd rather not spring you on him yet. Right now all I want is my daughter." Carl caressed her arm and tried to settle her down. "I'm glad you're here," she added.

He climbed out in the shade of a crepe myrtle and watched her drive down the smoldering macadam before disappearing into the parking lot. He loitered there for a minute like a man up to no good before walking the shoulder. The sun was roasting his exposed skin as he spotted Miriam's BMW wedged between two oversize pickups. He cut between the idling cars in the drive-through and stepped inside where he was greeted by another rush of cold air. He scanned the restaurant, but there was no sign of them, so he ordered fries and a coke from a plump and pimply girl who might have milked a cow that morning. She smiled and called him "honey" and said she'd bring the fries out when they were done. He took the cup and empty tray to the fountain, and it was from there he saw them. Miriam stepped back from behind the jungle gym in the indoor playroom, and through the squares and triangles of the gym was the shape of a man in grey slacks and a pea green shirt. He picked up a bag and thrust it at Miriam, before grabbing her arm and backing her into full view. Carl fixated on his face as soda fizzed over the edge of the cup and dribbled through his fingers. He shook the sugar water off his hand, but never stopped staring. Ed Groeper shared his profile, the lines hard and chiseled with no sign of a smile. His hair was smooth and combed back the same as Carl's, but there the similarities ended. What extra weight Carl carried on his belt, Miriam's ex-husband carried in his pecs, and he wore a tight Polo shirt to show them off. But by their facial features alone they could have passed for brothers, though Carl would have been the dumpy awkward one.

Ed clutched Miriam's arm and talked down to her, made her smaller than she was. Her submission rattled his instincts, so Carl did not go to her. The idea of a fight sickened him, as he'd paid for fighting in the past. Tinged with fear and the shame of that fear, he made excuses. She'd told him to stay out of it, so he retreated to a plastic booth on the far side of the restaurant and shredded a napkin with his sticky hand. The cashier wandered over and sat the fries on the tray.

"Here you go, honey," she said. "Anything else I can get you?"

He waved her off. A few minutes later Miriam tapped his shoulder, startling him.

"He's gone," she said.

Carl gathered his food and followed her to the playroom where several bob-haired mothers were watching their children clamor through the tubes. He was scanning the room as if Ed might have left some vestige of himself when he spotted a pair of familiar eyes peering through a plastic slot in the gym. The eyes belonged to the only child who wasn't screaming and carrying on. She barricaded herself in the castle tower.

"Annaliese, it's time to go home," her mother called to her. She was rubbing the wrist Ed had grabbed, and Carl felt ashamed at his inaction.

"She's been in there the whole time?"

"She hugged me when I got here, but Ed started lecturing and she ran back inside." Miriam tapped the underside of the tube where her daughter was hiding. "Guess who's here?" she said, her voice rising like a singing bird. The girl crawled onto a rope bridge with her hair dangling in her face. She glanced at Carl before sheepishly vanishing into the maze. "She's not right."

Carl knelt at one of the openings with a pouch of fries. "Annaliese, are you hungry?" he called to her.

"Please don't give her any of that crap. That's all Ed feeds her." Miriam looked pained, like she'd been waiting in line for several hours. "Annaliese please, we have to go." The girl popped out of an adjacent tube, chomping on her own supersize order of fries. Miriam sighed. "He wasn't supposed to feed you." With dirty hands and socks, the girl toddled into her mother's arms, though with some reluctance, as if into the arms of an amiable stranger.

∞

Twenty minutes out of town they entered a grid of gravely roads lined up on base lines and meridians. To either side were deep trenches and endless wilderness of yellow pine. Each turn lead deeper into the interior, and Carl wondered if they might eventually emerge from the darkness onto the white sands of the gulf.

"Why did you move so far out?" he asked.

"We wanted to raise her in the country."

By a clearing of burnt grasses were two houses sitting side-by-side and a fallow field to the rear. Miriam and Ed had rented a house on ten acres of flat scrub land, where it wasn't unusual to find armadillos rummaging through trash cans or watch horses die slowly of sand colic. Their house was reminiscent of an old cavalry barracks, a long low rancher with lap siding and uniform double hung windows standing at attention along the length. A porch and railing you might expect to see a saddled horse tied to ran the length of the back of the house, and off the porch, offering shade from the south, was a lone oak tree dripping with Spanish moss.

The house next door was a double-wide with hail-dented siding and blue shutters. The foundation blocks were hidden by a skirt of weeds, and over the front stoop hung a flag with a lobster on it. In back was a prefab metal barn with a painted white trim "x" on the door.

They veered off the shared driveway and parked in the shade, the sound of the tires softening as they rolled into the grass. Annaliese had nearly fallen asleep, and her head bobbed when her mother unbuckled her.

"You can't sleep yet," she said. "We have to eat soon and then we'll put you down."

A forty-year-old man with a crew-cut stepped off the deck of the neighboring double-wide. His skin was pink and spotted, and his eyes lost beneath the brim of his baseball cap. He smiled and scratched his bearded chin, maybe cooking up something clever to say, while his three young daughters clamored out of the house and scrambled around him. The eldest was nine and each sister two years apart, and they all ran to Annaliese and squealed her name. Still flush with sleep, the girl was shy and wobbly, but the older girls surrounded her and led her off to the barn where secret childhood things were happening.

The sky was cloudless and the sun descending. A streak of sweat ran down Carl's back, and a pearly film of moisture shrouded Miriam. She said, "Hey there," at her neighbor, who scuffed through grass and said "hey" back at her. His wife walked bow-legged onto the deck as if she'd been with child for most of her life. She was built like a prize fighter, and her long hair was tied off at the neck making a swinging bullwhip. They all stood there smiling at each other.

"Oh gosh," Miriam said. "I'm sorry. Lyle, Shayla, this is Carl." He shook Lyle's hand as hard as he could, as the moment seemed to demand it. He gave Shayla an awkward wave.

Shayla barked at her husband and pointed at the smoke bellowing from the grill. Lyle ran over to roll sausages and flip burgers, while the women went chattering inside to get on with supper. The children sat in a circle in the barn where two rabbits wandered lethargically between them.

There were no chairs on the deck, so Carl hopped on the rail. No time was wasted before he was handed a beer. Lyle hovered over the grill with a spatula in one hand and a sweating aluminum can in the other.

"So how long you known Miriam?" Lyle asked.

"We go back a ways."

"She said high school."

"If you knew, then why'd you ask?"

Lyle opened the grill and let out a plume of smoke. The burgers were sizzling and dripping, making an orange fire under the grate. "I like to follow up on Miriam's stories," he said, rolling a sausage a quarter turn. "Let's just say she's known for exaggeration."

Carl thought about it and couldn't help asking, "Did she tell you we were almost married?"

"She said y'all both made some mistakes, but shrugged it off like water under the bridge."

"She didn't by chance mention what those mistakes were?"

"I don't imagine you'd agree with them. Shayla and me got our share of mistakes too, but we never agree on what they are."

The sun was behind the house and the shade gave some relief. Carl was feeling more comfortable, thinking this guy might know something worth knowing. "So what's Ed like?"

Lyle scratched his nose with the back of his mitt. "A real sourpuss. Ain't never seen the man smile."

"Does Annaliese smile when she's with him?"

"She's a kid. She smiles when there's something to smile about." He closed the lid to the grill and reconsidered. "No, she don't smile much around her dad."

"What do you figure about Miriam losing custody?"

"Can't say anything surprises me down here. I'm from Georgia and we don't do things like they do down here."

"She said her ex got the attorney with the right connections."

"That may be, but he also got the money. All he did was odd construction jobs until the divorce, but then he finally took up his daddy's offer to come into the family HVAC business. Now he's got good money coming. On top of that, he cleaned out the bank accounts the day she threw him out. Poor planning on her part."

"I still don't get how she lost custody. It's not like she's a drug addict or a prostitute."

"Connections is all it takes down here." Lyle seemed to be approaching his words carefully. "You must know her temper."

"She's been pretty level since I've been back with her."

"She pissed off the wrong person." Carl was engrossed and waved a hand to bring it on. Lyle pointed the spatula at him. "She told you about the hearings?"

"Some."

"To hear her describe it, it sounds like she went off on the judge. Complained about the fairness of the hearing and tried to sound all righteous." He shook his head. "I think she came off real bad."

Shayla stuck her head out the door and called in the girls while Lyle tonged the burgers and links onto a Pyrex plate. The trailer had the feel of a carpeted meat locker, with shiny melamine walls and blasts of stifling cold air drafting from the window units. The floor was strewn with toys, all kicked aside from the traffic patterns, and the walls were covered with photos of the three girls at every age. The children were seated at the built-in breakfast bar in the kitchen, and the adults gathered at the dining room table, which was covered with a coral pattern table cloth pocked with cigarette burns. It was set with paper plates, a heaping bowl of potato salad, a multi-cheese casserole, a pot of baked beans and Lyle's simmering plate of meat and grease. It was more food than they could possibly eat.

Shayla sat across from Carl and inspected him with discerning eyes. Her nose was bulbous and her cheeks pocked from acne scars. He sensed her gaze but didn't look back.

"So Carl," she said. "Miriam tells me you two were high school sweethearts."

His eyes flirted with Miriam's. "I guess you could call it that."

"Yes, we were," Miriam said, validating him. "And are." Squabbling broke out from the children's table and she strode over to settle them down. Shayla just sat there, likely used to it.

"You don't got no kids of your own?" Shayla asked.

He shook his head and swallowed hard before answering. "Never married."

"That don't have much to do with it anymore," Lyle said.

"If I have any kids, I don't know about them."

Miriam perked up her head. "If I hadn't told Ed about the pregnancy, I wouldn't be in this mess." She rattled around in a kitchen drawer for one of the girl's special spoons.

"Miriam, will you come on and eat something," Carl said.

Lyle cut in with no uncertainty in his voice. "I don't blame Ed none for going after her." He watched his wife, who stared back with concern. "If we ever split, I'd fight like hell for those kids."

"You would, would you?"

"I would."

"You'd take my babies away from me?"

"What are you complaining about? I'd probably get them going into their teens. I figure you'd be appreciative."

Shayla crinkled her nose. "Let's not go there." She scooped a spoon-full of potato salad onto her plate. "What about you, Carl? Would you fight for custody of your child?"

Miriam whisked back to the table, and Carl knew she was listening intently.

"Like I say, I don't have any kids."

"But what if you did?" she pressed. "What if you had a little one just like her," Shayla said, motioning toward Annaliese.

"I don't know. I guess it would all depend on the situation."

Miriam's jaw tightened. She took a small taste of baked beans and looked unsatisfied, as if uncertain of the recipe.

∞

After dinner they said their goodbyes, Miriam giving each of her neighbors a hug while Carl stood there with his hands in his pockets. They crossed the lawn in the growing dusk to Miriam's rental, where she'd lived with her ex-husband for the past two years. The crickets had woken and a whip-poor-will sounded from the tree-line behind the barn. Annaliese trailed behind the adults, finding things to see in the grass, taking her time.

"Did you take that stick test?" Carl asked.

"I don't trust those things. I have an appointment at the clinic next Tuesday."

"What are you waiting for?"

"My favorite nurse practitioner was on vacation this week. She'll be back Tuesday. What difference does it make? Either I am or I'm not."

He stared at her belly and resisted an urge to help her onto the porch. She bounded ahead of him two steps at a time. They lingered there by the rail taking in the heavy stillness that came with evening and watched Annaliese scurry around the yard trying to cup fire-flies in her palms.

"Any word on the farmhouse?" Miriam asked.

Carl rested a foot on the rail. "The agent said he was waiting on two more contracts this weekend. He'll sit down with the bank next week and go over the offers."

"Did you set some money aside?"

Carl took the question with reserve. "I came in where I thought was appropriate."

"That doesn't answer my question."

"The answer you're looking for is yes, I sat money aside." He was disgusted with himself and harbored a tinge of resentment for Miriam. "I didn't know there would be this much competition. I'm afraid I came in too low."

"I'm sorry Carl, but I just don't have any money."

"That's not what I was getting at. And you don't need to apologize. I'm taking care of things." He told himself he was making decisions, moving forward.

She said thank you and gave him an uncertain kiss on the cheek. When she stepped inside, Annaliese lost interest in the fire-flies and ran after her, leaving Carl to watch the southern stars reveal themselves.

Chapter 10

The next morning Miriam strapped Annaliese into her car-seat, rolled down the windows and drove them south in the sun-scabbed Beemer to what she billed as their "surprise weekend." She reclined the driver's seat an extra notch and spread her legs to gather the breeze. Had she been in the passenger seat she might have stuck one leg out the window. They met the interstate south of Jacksonville where the pavement ran flat and straight, bleached white with black stripes pointing south toward lands end. Billboards lauded coastal living in luxury condos, with pictures of smiling families and doting elderly who were fortunate enough to have found their way there. Carl clenched his armrest every time they passed a rumbling tractor-trailer. He never tempered his hatred of them. Through a blur of trees they passed one of the many gated communities with their low slope rooftops like giant penned in mammoths lumbering behind high brick walls.

"That's where we need to live," Miriam said. "Ed couldn't get in to bother us."

"Couldn't he jump the fence?"

"He's too underhanded for that. He'd be more likely to pass himself off as a delivery man."

"Didn't you say your mother lived in a development like this?"

She didn't answer right away and drove on a few miles as if to digest the question and keep her temper in check. Miriam's mother was making good money in Miami as a sales rep for a liquor distributor, and she kept her clients, and her cupboard, well stocked.

"She might if she hasn't lost her job. I have no idea where she lives now. She was talking about moving up to be closer to Annaliese. For all I know, she might have moved in with Ed." Miriam took the next exit hard, and Carl braced himself on the door. "It doesn't matter," she said, laying into the curve. "I could never afford to live in a place like that."

Daytona International Speedway barricaded one side of the strip and killed the breeze just when the sun and heat were coming on hard. They missed every traffic light as they motored by a shopping mall, Krystal burgers, a Hooters and more fast food. Occasionally Carl reached back and pinched Annaliese's knee, but she brushed his hand away and smiled only shyly, not yet acclimated to his presence. Past the track they stopped at a stucco office building with black tinted windows sheltered deep in the facade. Miriam led them to a small office suite where the first room was more for storage than reception, with legal files stacked high on every surface. Through an open door behind a government surplus metal desk was a man with horn-rimmed glasses and a pony tail. His wrinkled blue oxford was buttoned to the collar, but his necktie was laying on a stack of documents as if worn only for court. On seeing Miriam, he dropped the text he was studying and leaned back in his chair.

"Hey cat," he said.

Miriam pranced around the desk and kissed his bearded cheek. She introduced him to Carl, but the attorney never rose from his seat. "Carl, this is Gary Kolanchek. He helped me beat a DWI a few years ago." Miriam and her friend chatted about old times, abandoning Carl and Annaliese to their uncomfortable selves. Given no better entertainment, the girl began warming up to Carl by playing a hand slapping game in semi-violent fashion. Carl was content to be her target as he zoned out of the conversation. Through his jealousies, he couldn't help wondering if this attorney had been one of Miriam's fiancées'. He was pulled back when Miriam's voice dipped.

"That's what I thought," she said, turning to Carl. "Are you listening?"

"He said we have to get a local attorney," he responded, while yanking a palm away from Annaliese's wild overhand. He already knew that much and wondered why she was bothering with this guy.

Kolanchek said, "If you can get the venue moved down here, I can help, but as long as you're in the boonies, I can't do anything."

"It's that or get it changed to Virginia," Miriam said.

He gave her a bleak eye. "It's next to impossible to move venue out-of-state. It would be hard enough moving it down here."

"My last attorney said it could happen."

Kolanchek let her down delicately. "It's unlikely to happen, Miriam. To move any future hearings out-of-state, both parties typically have to agree. Ed will never do it because he has a sympathetic judge. As long as he lives in that county and has that judge, it will never be moved."

She reached over and stroked her daughter's hair. "He also mentioned something about getting the judge recused."

"Fail and you piss off the judge for life."

"He's already pissed off," she grumbled, before brightening to a playful pitch. "Sure you don't want to move upstate? You can live with me."

This bothered Carl, and Kolanchek appeared to sense it.

"No, Miriam." He gave her a distant, sympathetic smile. "You can see I'm already working weekends. It's too far for me to go up there." Miriam looked jilted, turned down for the dance, but she gave him a hug anyway before turning to leave. Carl caught Gary's eyes and they were filled with pity, implying there was nothing to be done to help her.

On the road again, Miriam was her lighthearted self, wandering carefree in the sun-splashed world she'd originally gone to Florida for. They crossed Route 1, passing the slender Channel 2 radio tower, and found the old commercial district along the Intracoastal where Miriam drove up and down the avenue to show off her idea of paradise. Brilliant bursts of palmetto trees lined the median and a dazzling strip of stucco buildings painted turquoise, yellow and pink lined one side of the drag. Opposite was a green strip of parkland along the Intracoastal where yachts, pleasure boats and jet-skis stirred the water, sending their rolling wakes ashore. When they crossed the bridge to the barrier island, Miriam tapped Annaliese's knee, telling her to look. Beyond the outer banks was the line where the ocean turned to sky and the world glimmered in some electrified oil painting. The high arc of the bridge was like a threshold to something hopeful, but the feeling sank when they turned south down A1A, away from the more expensive resorts and into a run of tee-shirt shops, cheap hotels and biker bars.

After a few miles, Miriam said, "Now for the surprise."

She wound into a crushed shell parking lot in front of a village of little downtrodden bungalows. Each unit was twelve feet square with a small appendage stuck to the side where pipes and vents penetrated the roof. Miriam led the way to the office and rang the bell on the counter. A woman from a back room hollered for them to hold on. After the television shifted from the local weather to an elderly man selling life insurance, a sun-scarred old woman hobbled through the door and stared them up and down. Her hair was wired from a perm gone bad, and her sun damaged face, still moist from recently applied lotion, wore the pained look of a smoker who'd waited too long for a cigarette. She felt under the counter for the register and dropped it in front of them.

Miriam said, "We have a reservation for Rittenhaur."

The woman ran a finger down the ledger and stopped on a name. "Ritten–," she said, and paused. "house."

"Rittenhaur. R. I. T. T. –."

"Fine, fine." She began writing something in small shaky print. "Only one night?" she lamented, likely used to one-night stands.

"Yes. And we'll need an extra bed. A child's bed."

The woman eyed Annaliese, who was twisting the dull metal handle on a bubble gum machine. Miriam handed over a credit card and the old woman studied it before running it through the scanner. "Says here Boyd. Not Rittenhaur."

"I'm Rittenhaur," Carl said. The woman glowered at him, sized him up.

"You two ain't married?"

"We don't have to be *married*," Miriam said. "And we don't have to put up with –."

"We're engaged," Carl cut in. "This one's mine." He motioned to Annaliese who stared at her wide-eyed.

The woman swiped the card, wrote the receipt and pushed the paper across the counter. After Miriam signed it and slapped the pen down, she was handed a wooden baton with B-2 routed into one side and a key dangling on the end.

"Y'all ought to make it legal," the old woman chimed in before they were out the door. "That girl ain't got no name 'til she got a father."

They ignored her and went back to the car for their bags. A boardwalk of warped planks, burnished like driftwood, was half sunken into the sand and ran between the bungalows to the beach. Each unit was built of concrete block painted a different pastel color, and their Spanish mission tile roofs were chipped and weathered.

"Why did you give in to that old bitch?" Miriam asked, as they carried their bags down the boardwalk.

"Why did you want to fight her?"

Unit B-2 was painted a pale pinkish hue and its front door acid green. This was the first room in Florida where Carl wasn't freezing – it was hotter inside than out with a stale air of nicotine, carpet cleaner and sandy sheets. A queen bed sat against the far wall, flanked by a wardrobe and chest of drawers that didn't match. The carpet was ground with sand, and the walls and ceiling were paneled with a heavy textured pulp board coated with so much gloss paint it looked hand molded with spent chewing gum. The bathroom was off to one corner and might have been added at the invention of indoor plumbing.

"This was your surprise?" Carl asked.

Miriam dropped her purse and planted a hand on her boney hip. "They looked so cute from the ad."

She inspected the bathroom, while Carl turned on the AC unit hanging out of the wall. Sand blew around in its guts as it hemorrhaged to life and coughed hot air over his hand. When it cooled, he sat on the bed and bounced a few times, reminiscent of how he had checked out the old farmhouse in the Piedmont. Annaliese searched her mother's purse for the pacifier and popped it in her mouth.

Miriam stepped back into the room. "I need to put her down," she said.

"Let her nap on the beach."

"It's too hot out."

"This is any better?" he said, motioning around the room.

She held her hand in front of the wall unit and adjusted a knob. "Okay, we'll go out until it cools off."

They followed the embedded planks between the last two bungalows to the beach where Annaliese ran past them onto the wet hard-pack, stopping quickly at the edge of the surf as her mother called for her to slow down. Distant piers flanked the shore to the north and south, and boats dotted the horizon, trolling up and down the coast with fishing lines taut. Carl kicked off his sandals and stepped into the Gulf Stream. The girl pranced on her toes into the water and grabbed his leg as the first wave crashed around them, leaving arcs of popping foam at their feet.

"How about I take you swimming?" he said to the girl.

She squeezed the hem of his shorts and looked uncertain.

"How about I throw you in right now?" He tried to grab her and she squealed and ran off, but slowly, tempting him to chase her, which he did. Annaliese's curls bounced off her shoulders as they splashed through the surf with Carl intentionally stumbling and recovering, always giving her a step.

"Don't you dare throw her in," Miriam protested, still standing by a trash can where the boardwalk petered to sand. She was more guardian than parent, her arms folded and weight planted on one leg.

Carl dropped into the dry sand winded but happy, happy for the first time in a long while. Annaliese ran to him. "Don't you get me," she giggled, before backing off. He pretended to be uninterested and then took off after her and the two howled together, digging their feet in the sand as they ran. He grabbed her by the waist, and when he raised her to the sky she hollered, "Daddy!" Carl brought Annaliese in close, cradling her high in his arms. The open beach made a stage with the spotlight sun trained on these two bit part players. At that moment, he swore he would never let anything bad happen to her.

Miriam checked her watch and called out to her daughter, "It's time for your nap."

"We just got here," Carl said, letting her go. He squinted into the sky and caught his breath.

"She's tired, Carl. We've been traveling all morning and she didn't get her nap."

"This is tired?" He motioned to the girl, who was scooping up soggy lumps of sand and tossing them into the air.

"Annaliese, please don't throw the sand." Miriam brushed off her clothes and led her back to the boardwalk as the girl whined and protested. "I'm sorry sweetie, but you'll be a terror tonight if I don't get you down. The room should be cooler by now." She called back to Carl, "You can stay if you want."

He wanted to stay. He wanted them all to stay. The problems of his world, past and present, were on hold and for the first time he was allowed to feel normal, surrounded by a normal family, the family he wanted all along. Why Miriam would have no part of it, he couldn't understand. He stepped into his sandals and jogged after them.

When they reached the bungalow there was a man at the door who was out of place for the climate, the only person they'd seen wearing long pants and a long sleeve shirt. His face was raw and blemished under his hat, which he tipped as he stepped out.

"Got your extra bed set up, Ma'am," he said. He tipped his hat again and left.

The room cooled enough so breathing was no longer an effort. The large bed was pushed over so the dresser drawers would open only halfway, and a roll-away bed unfolded, leaving a one-foot passage to the bathroom door. A blood-stained pillow and a square of folded sheets sat at its foot.

"He didn't even make it up," Miriam said, going straight to work shaking out the fitted sheet.

"Will you come back down?" Carl asked.

She said she would, and Carl left with a blanket under his arm. Annaliese watched him through the window with her fingers pinching the sill, likely expectant of something more than a nap after arriving at the sea shore. Close to an hour passed before Miriam's feet brushed through the sand and woke Carl from his own nap. She still wore her shorts, but had changed into a pink bikini top where her breasts swayed in the hollow cups. She held a baby monitor to her ear and fiddled with a knob before setting it on the blanket.

"We should still be in range," she said. She also brought a cheap bottle of Zinfandel in a tall paper bag, a corkscrew and two paper cups.

"Thank God," Carl said, brushing sand from his arm. He took the bottle and raised its cork.

She pressed a finger on his arm. "You're getting burnt." He'd lain there in his tee-shirt, making his farmer tan more ridiculous. He poured the first cup and handed it to her. She sat on the far edge of the blanket, gazing alone into the indifferent sea.

"You don't seem to be here," he said to her.

The sky to the north was uneven and a breeze was picking up, dusting the blanket with sand. She tried to brush it off, but only made it worse. "I just want everything to be right."

"We'll get you moved this week. We'll get a new attorney too."

"I'm dreading it."

"One step at a time."

"I want it all to go away." She took a long sip of wine, letting her lips dwell in the tannins. High tide was cresting, breaking closer to their feet. "I know this sounds terrible, but sometimes I wish I didn't have her. That I'd listened to Ed and aborted her."

"Miriam."

"Does that make me awful? Am I an awful mother?"

"No, it doesn't make you awful. You've been through hell."

"Or if I could just leave," she said, her eyes intent on the water. "Sail away somewhere, only take her with me. That's what I really want." She pointed southeast toward a tiny white triangle on the horizon. "See that sailboat? That's where I want to go. Wherever the hell he's going would be just fine. Someplace warm. Someplace without lawyers and judges and asshole ex-husbands."

"That would be nice," Carl said, and he meant it. "But you can't run away."

"Well, I can wish. He can't take that away." She finished her cup and set it in the sand. "Maybe I should start going back to church," she said shaking her head. "Maybe God can help. I need a guardian angel, or better yet an archangel. One with a spear who'll kick some ass and deliver me from this crap." She lay back on the blanket. He rolled against her and put his hand on her belly, but she only lay there stiff and corpse-like, hypnotized by the clouds. Over the crashing waves they heard a murmur. A cry rose from the static and Miriam rolled out from under him. "Dammit," she said. "I can't be away from her." She grabbed the monitor and ran back to the bungalow.

Inside the heavy curtains were drawn and the room was black. When she opened the door, light fell across the bed where Annaliese lay bawling in a tangle of sheets. The girl held out her arms and her mother received her like it might have stopped the onslaught of a turbulent life. She held her tight to her breast and whispered into her ear.

Carl stayed on the beach and finished the bottle alone. Under the lightness of the wine, the hypnotic sky and the percussive pounding of the surf, he slipped into a dreamless slumber that spent the day, waking only from the mild hangover taking over his head. When the sun dipped low and the sky dimmed to a deep ultramarine, he left the empty wine bottle on the blanket and stumbled back to the bungalow where he found them curled together in the sheets. The room was freezing. He turned off the air conditioner and it wheezed and gurgled like the death rattle of a dying man.

"We slept the whole day away," he said, clearly annoyed.

Annaliese sat up first. "Hungry," she said. Her mother's eyes darted around the room, bewildered as if wondering how she came to be in such a place.

∞

Though the last hour of sun still shone from the west, the sky was dark and heavy with storm clouds to the north, where distant branches of lightning tracked to land and sea. Carl and Miriam kept an eye on the ominous sky as they quick-stepped down the street with the child hand-in-hand between them. In two blocks they found a restaurant with an awning-covered terrace open to the beach. Opposite the fiery sliver of sunset, the sky and ocean merged to black and the wind came up strong, rattling the awnings and blowing napkins across the tables and onto the beach. The waitresses unrolled heavy walls of clear plastic and tied them down with laundry cord, but it wasn't enough to keep out the horizontal weather. The three of them sat away from the rail and ordered the catch of the day, coconut shrimp, coleslaw and two baskets of hush puppies. A light salty spray settled on their arms and plates as they ate.

They made it back to the cottage during a lull with the wind and a few large rain drops hurrying them on. Carl ran with Annaliese's arms tight around his neck, holding on for life, her cheeks plump and full of excitement. The next band of the storm hit as they crashed into the bungalow shouting and laughing as the squall blew in right behind them. Miriam slammed the door, leaving the howling of the wind and rain drowning the measure of the surf.

Carl grabbed his duffel and went to the bathroom where he showered the salt and grime from his body. His arms, legs and face were badly sunburnt, and it stung most where Annaliese had clutched him around the neck. When he stepped from the shower the lights failed, followed by a nearby crack of thunder. He felt for his boxers and wrestled them on, nosed back into the room where Miriam was opening the curtains to let the glow from a security light filter inside. In the dimness she rustled in her purse and found a tiny key-chain flashlight. She shined it around the room.

"Are you ready to find a *real* hotel now?" Carl asked.

"No. We'll make a good time of it, won't we?" she said to her daughter, who was bouncing in the middle of the bed, wide-eyed and wired. After getting Annaliese into her pjs, the two huddled together on the roll-a-way bed and played a matching card game, though the girl was more interested in the flashlight, jiggling it around the room and placing it to her palm to examine the outlines of her finger bones. Carl watched them for a while, the woman he still loved but did not understand and the little girl who once called him *Daddy*, but at that moment he no longer felt a part of them. Either the wine or the storm had altered the fabric of their time together on the beach, and he was now a stranger in their presence. Wiped out from the sun-burnt hangover and too much greasy beach food, he slipped into the far side of the bed and listened to their play until fading off into an uneasy slumber.

Hours later, when the girl settled into sleep, Miriam cut their umbilical link and crawled into the larger bed, backing into Carl. He wrapped a drowsy arm around her and took her breast and, like in a dream, he felt the length of her body and plowed his hand under her shirt. He nudged in closer as she cocked one leg forward and arched back to receive him. He stretched her wadded rope of panties aside and they moved together slowly and silently, as if exploring each other for the first time, searching for the right repose and the right angle. With building force they strained to hold their voices. Just shy of release, the headboard made a thunderous clap against the wall.

Annaliese stirred and rubbed the balls of her eyes.

"Mommy come," she said, holding her arms out in the dark.

"No. You go to sleep now." Miriam said with labored breath.

"I come over there." She began bridging from her bed to the queen.

"No, Annaliese. You have your very own bed. We got that bed especially for you." Carl was frozen in place, embedded at full thrust, holding her still as if the slightest movement might send them crashing through the wall.

"Sleep with mommy," the girl insisted. When the child crawled onto their bed, Miriam lurched forward and Carl slid out the other side and sank to the floor. He felt under the covers and found his shorts where he'd kicked them off.

Outside the rain had passed, but the wind still howled steady from the northeast. Carl walked down to the beach and stood on a high-tide break facing the sea with a thirty-knot gale sandblasting his ankles and legs. Clods of sea foam, glowing as if lit by a black light, raced from the surf between his legs and disintegrated over the dunes. The sky was a dense blue-black veil shrouding the distant boats anchored in the murk, their white lights unmoving from shore but tossed unseen in the ten foot seas. Hovering over him, the low rolling underbellies of storm clouds caught the lights of the coastal resorts, giving the sky high drama like some chapel ceiling painted in renaissance fury.

He regarded the distant points of light marking each boat anchored off shore, and he thought what a hell of a place to be. Why didn't they come into the Intracoastal where they'd be safe? He noticed even without a weather warning the Florida sky reveals itself. It's not above you the way it is in Virginia. In Florida the sky is around you, allowing for easy anticipation of a near miss or pending disaster. Didn't they see the storm coming? Were they too drunk or too stoned to notice? Did their radio batteries die? Perhaps they just like a good fight. More likely, it was man's blind spot for the inevitable.

Chapter 11

A thin line of morning light made a pictureless frame on either side of the door, and Carl squinted mindlessly into the space within the glow as he stretched and arched his back. The mattress sagged deeper through the night, and he found himself in the depression of a cold bed, the sheets worn and granular as if used for a beach picnic. His joints were stiff and head was clogged from too much sleep. Over the sound of the shower were the murmurings of familiar voices, though he couldn't piece together the words. One was from a complaining child, all whiny and muffled, the other a maternal voice of reassurance. For a brief moment, before the sleep drained from his being, Carl thought he was eavesdropping on an adjacent hotel room and felt a tinge of shame when he broke through the fog and realized the voices did not belong to strangers.

Miriam blew through the bathroom door in a two piece bathing suit, her breasts raking from side to side as she ransacked one of her bags. The shower was still running and the bulb over the sink sprayed the room with a pale light.

"What time is it?" Carl said, squinting at her figure.

"Almost ten. Look," she said, jiggling a plastic zip-lock bag. "We combed the beach for shells."

"Christ." He opened his eyes wide and blinked.

"We already ate breakfast."

"Why didn't you wake me?"

"You were so out of it, we couldn't see disturbing you."

She threw a wadded shirt at him. "Put some clothes on. It's bad enough she was in the same bed last night." She didn't find what she was searching for, so she hauled the whole bag into the bathroom where she went about fussing over her child. "We need to go soon," she said, pushing the door to.

"We just got here." Carl knew she didn't hear him as the water was still running. "We're spending the afternoon on the beach, right?" he called louder.

"We need to start packing the house," she said, whisking back into the room and grabbing her beach bag. "I have to get her back to her moron father by seven o'clock. I'm not giving him any chance to beat me up over visitation."

"We can pack the house tomorrow."

She paused her manic pampering and stood over him. "You said we could look for an attorney tomorrow."

"Right," he groaned, thinking they'd come all these miles for this?

After Carl finished his shower, he found the heavy curtains drawn aside and the room transformed by the glaring sun into a window display in a department store, spot-lit and exposed for the world to see and measure. His open duffel spilled onto the floor, but Miriam's and Annaliese's were gone. He stepped outside where little shards of sea glass and shell stung his feet. The air was warm but still blustery from the storm as a few high clouds tracked to the northeast. He stood there alone, listening to the tireless surf batter the shore until an old fear welled up inside. In a slowly swelling panic, he ran down the boardwalk to the parking lot. The Beemer was gone. He burst into the office where the same frazzle-haired old woman was gripping a cup of black coffee, playing solitaire.

"B-2. Did they check out?"

She never looked up from her cards. "You mean that woman and *your* daughter?"

"Yes."

"You don't check out. Just leave the key in the room."

He pushed out the door and winced as if the air was toxic. The heavy taste of salt in his mouth rose with the sun, a nauseous taste making him want to rinse. Not since his parents' deaths had he let himself be dependent on anyone, but here he was again, abandoned and waiting. He was about to make for the street when Miriam's BMW whipped into the lot.

"Aren't you ready yet?" she asked from behind her shades.

Carl's mouth gaped open. "Where did you go?"

"To get a coke." She raised an old scarred bottle and twirled it from the neck. Annaliese was strapped in her child seat, and she did the same as caramel sugar water dribbled down her chin. "There's a store down the road that still sells the old fashioned bottles." She flipped it back and took a long gulp, making a bubbling cauldron inside the glass.

Embarrassed and slightly confused at his paranoia, Carl lugged himself back to the bungalow to pack his bag. He took a last look at the beach, where couples and families were staking their claims in the sand. Women in floppy hats and men in baseball caps were spreading blankets, unfolding chairs, and setting out baskets, coolers and towels. A toddler was bobbing toward the sea with a distressed mother running after him, and a pack of teenagers were making for a distant pier, anxious to lose their parents and find themselves. Red-armed fishermen with green tattoos sat in chairs by PVC tubes, each holding a rod bending hard from the undertow. A part of Carl longed for convention, but convention was something he'd never allowed himself. But now he believed a normal life was being denied by forces beyond his control, and there was a welling urge to fight for it. He hoped his sudden family, now waiting impatiently in a German car with no air-conditioning, simply wasn't broken in yet.

Carl took the wheel and they motored north on A1A, staying away from the big truck routes. They passed the hotels and Harley shops of Daytona, and sailed by Ormond Beach and Flagler, at times skirting the Intracoastal where men parked their trucks and SUVs on the flat sand inlets to launch their boats and fish. On passing the concrete ruins of Marineland, Carl pondered the concept of abandonment until they crossed the Intracoastal into Saint Augustine. Miriam faced backward the whole trip to tend her child, giving her cereal and stickers and picking up toys the girl repeatedly threw to the floor. It was far more attention than Miriam ever received from her own mother.

By mid-afternoon a few miles shy of the house, the wind and weather calmed to its usual swelter and the open windows offered little relief from the rising smell of fresh shit swirling in the cab. Miriam whipped around like a referee about to call a foul. "Oh no, Annaliese." Carl was thankful it hadn't happened earlier. The second they pulled up to the porch, Miriam jumped out and rushed the girl inside. "Do you remember what we talked about? About having to go?" Annaliese was flush and wind-whipped as she toddled off to the toilet, the pacifier making a little red mark under her nose.

"Where do you want me to start?" Carl called after them.

"The bedroom. Grab a box off the porch."

Carl entered through the kitchen, where the counters were cluttered with stacks of plates and cans of food already set out for packing. Though the living room was orderly and would make a good impression to any guest, the bedrooms were a disaster, as if a hurricane had ripped off the roof and swirled all its domestic contents. Miriam's clothes, some folded, some balled up for the wash were evenly scattered over the bed, floor and open drawers. On the dresser and side tables were countless trinkets; porcelain ashtrays filled with *Mardi Gras* beads and junk jewelry, plastic bracelets and drugstore sunglasses with colorful neck straps, sand dollar earrings and sea shell pendants. On the night stand, crowning a stack of mothering magazines was a copy of Tales from Margaritaville, book-marked at something called "Boomerang Love." To Carl, who led a fairly Spartan life, this was more crap than he'd ever seen.

He dropped to the floor by the dresser and began separating the clothes from the debris. In the bottom of one drawer under several rarely worn old sweaters was a flat white box. He lifted the lid and found a photo album with a pillow pad cover and a strand of fake pearls framing its perimeter. He sat there and considered it. He knew what it was and had no desire to see it, but he opened it anyway. The blood drained from his fingertips and he felt robbed.

They posed in front of a contemporary style church of fake stucco with strained smiles on their faces. She was heavier then, but she'd birthed the child only months before. Her cheeks were plump and full, but she looked tired, as if wrestling with postpartum depression or straining to be happy about marrying a man she barely knew. Her dress was snug, and the frilly lace at the neck and wrists ended with a flourish, making her look like an expensive vase where something might take water and grow. All the same, she was as beautiful as he'd ever remembered seeing her and was precisely what he had expected to see coming down the aisle of the Lutheran Church in Compton on his own wedding day.

The groom wore a five-button tuxedo with a blue ascot bubbling from the chest – something worn to attract attention and quickly returned to the rental store. His grin was thin-lipped and forced, lasting no longer than the snap of the shutter. Carl didn't doubt the man rarely smiled. There was also a meddlesome excitement in his eyes, the severe gaze of a warrior who'd just conquered or captured something, something he might have even loved, but for all the wrong reasons. Carl flipped the pages and let the staged shots burn into his head. Her hand was always consumed in his, curled into his fist with his smile saying, "You belong to me now." In the back of the album were a few loose photographs. He flipped through them and found one of Ed fondling Miriam's ass as she looked over her shoulder in both shock and appreciation of being pursued. Carl closed the album. He wanted to go home, away from all of this.

He reset the lid and tossed the album in the packing box. In the same drawer, he uncovered two felt ring boxes. He checked over his shoulder to see if he was being watched, but heard only a child's cartoon playing in the next room. With one thumb, he flipped open the first box. It was her wedding band, white gold and unadorned, without markings, engravings or any sign of endearment. He set it down and opened the second box. Inside was a folded slip of paper with a handwritten note.

The quality of this ring pales in comparison
to the quality of my commitment.
My love for you is greater than any symbol.

Carl removed the ring from its little felt notch and held it to the light. It was a hand-mashed band of aluminum foil. He slipped it over his pinky finger and studied its dull crumbly sheen with amazement. Bullshit, he thought. Cheap bastard. Phony son-of-a-bitch. He took it off and pinched it in half, crumbled it into a useless tid-bit and flicked it across the room where it was lost in the rubble of Miriam's life. He stuffed the ring boxes and the wedding album into a plastic trash bag and covered them with old magazines. The wedding band he slipped into his pocket.

Miriam stuck her head in the door. "How's it coming?"

"Making progress," he said.

Carl worked the bedroom the rest of the afternoon, filling two boxes with her junk, four trash bags of loose clothing and one lawn bag, the largest, full of garbage. He took the trash to a plastic bin next to the house and dropped it in with great satisfaction.

Miriam was working the kitchen where Annaliese was busy waving a pan over her head like some crazed chef on too much sherry. She pulled as many things from the packed boxes as from the cabinets, and by the time Carl walked in nearly every square inch of the floor was covered.

"Oh man," he said, rubbing his neck.

"She's mommy's little helper." Miriam checked her watch. "We need to get going. Can you grab that box of books and put them in the trunk? We can make a first run to the apartment while we're out."

The largest box in the room sat in the corner with its flaps up, filled with self-help books and romance novels. Bending deep, Carl slipped his hands under and heaved. "God damn," he said, as one of his knees popped. His arms strained as he leaned back to counter the weight.

Annaliese ran to him. "I help," she said.

"No, Annaliese." Carl said. "Stand back."

She put a hand on the box. "I help."

"Miriam, get her out of the way." The girl whimpered as Carl swept past her.

"Let her help," Miriam said, taking her daughter's hand. "You can help too." Carl was stuck at the screen door, using his elbow to feel for the latch, while Miriam placed Annaliese's hand on the box where it sat uncertainly. "Don't talk to her like that. She's only two."

"Yeah, she's only two. She can't help."

"It's important for her psychology."

"Where did you read that? Cosmo?" Carl kicked open the screen door and it bounced back into his shoulder. He stomped across the porch and down the steps into the grass, with Miriam rushing her daughter along with her hand touching the edge of the box. "Open the trunk," Carl commanded, resting the box on the bumper. Miriam popped the latch while Annaliese stood by, helping. Carl heaved the books inside. "Let's get out of here," he said.

"I have to get her bag." She went inside and Annaliese ran after her, chewing the tips of her fingers. Carl clasped his hands behind his head and cracked his neck, wondering where she came up with this stuff. The sun was low in the sky, no longer a threat, but the air was still full of menacing insects. After a few minutes, Miriam stepped out with a small blue suitcase and a day-bag, but Annaliese wasn't with her. "Come'on sweetie," her mother called.

Through a window sounded a defiant, "no."

"It's time to see daddy."

"No!"

Exhaustion weighted on Miriam as she climbed the porch and disappeared inside. Carl stood by the window and listened to them negotiating, Miriam promising things would be better, that she would come back and never leave her again.

Carl hoisted the baggage in the trunk and scanned the car. He swept the Cheerios and Gummy Bears from the child seat into the yard, pushed the empty juice boxes and dried clods of wet wipes under the seat and picked up a stuffed manatee from the floorboard and set it within the child's reach.

Miriam stepped outside with Annaliese tight in her arms, cheek to breast. The girl was quiet now, sucking on her pacifier and gazing into the distance like some lost voyager. The car-seat was a tight fit. She hadn't just grown in the past few weeks, but she'd gotten chunky in her arms and legs. Once her mother strapped her in, Annaliese reached for the manatee, yanked its nose a few times and threw it on the floor.

"You really want me going along?" Carl asked.

Miriam's face gave way to apathy. "Why not," she said. "He has to meet you sooner or later."

Though the sun was behind them, they hid behind their sunglasses driving east on the crown of the road, moving over only to avoid oncoming traffic. Thin lines of gnats and grime collected in their fleshy joints, and their hair whipped in the wind. The heat of the day had settled on the land and emanated from every surface, even the grass and trees, back to the sky where the heat collided with itself.

In town they rolled under Dixon's lone traffic light, passed the police station, which looked strangely abandoned, and turned into the same fast food parking lot as before. Ed Grouper's square head rose from behind a new Toyota sedan parked two spaces away. He looked like he'd spotted an animal in his gun sight.

"You're late," he said, slamming the car door.

Miriam unbuckled Annaliese. "Five minutes," she said.

"Ten."

The girl slid onto the tar-puddled lot where she clung to her mother's leg. Her father swept forward and held out his hand, but his eyes followed Carl, who was popping the trunk. "Who is this?" he said, though by his tone it was evident he already knew.

Carl's chest tightened. Like two combatants in an uneasy truce, the men sized each other up. Each was known to the other only through a camera lens; one through surveillance, the other through old wedding photos. Though they weighed about the same, the distribution was uneven. Ed had an inch on Carl, maybe two, and his reach was farther. His biceps stretched the hem of his shirt sleeves, whereas the only thing stretched on Carl was his waistline. In a sudden wave of insecurity, Carl felt out of shape and lethargic. He was glad the car was there to separate them.

"This is my friend, Carl," Miriam said. "He came down from Virginia to help us move."

Ed turned to face Miriam, but didn't take his eyes off Carl. "Annie's already moved," he said.

"He's moving *me*," she retorted.

Ed extended a firm hand. "Ed Groeper. Nice of you to come down and help."

Carl took his hand and they both squeezed hard, pumped once and let go. He didn't say a word. Ed swaggered toward his daughter.

"Where's my little girl?" Ed said, taking a forced turn at being charming.

Miriam coaxed her daughter forward. "Time to go to daddy," she said, but the girl pressed back into her mother and pondered her feet. Her arms hung limp at her sides.

Ed wasted no time heaving her into his arms, and she let out a whine. "You can tell me all about your weekend," he said, carrying her to his car. When he opened the rear door, Annaliese pushed at her father's chest and reached out for her mother, fingers pulsing to draw her near. Miriam rushed to her.

"It's okay, sweetie. It's okay," she assured her. "Mommy will see you Wednesday."

Ed nudged the door open with his leg and put a hand on his daughter's head. "Stop it, Annie. It's time to go."

"Don't force her. Let me put her in."

"Stand back from the car, Miriam." The girl howled and wouldn't be put down. She tried to crawl over her father's shoulder to safety, but he caught her before she slipped over his back and forced her inside where she cried like an innocent imprisoned.

"I'm right here, Annaliese," Miriam cried back. "Let me put her in the car-seat. Just let me –."

Ed backed out with his body blocking Annaliese, who was in full tantrum, still trying to crawl past him. "Stand back from the car," he commanded. He seized Miriam by the wrist and raised her arm to his chest. "She has to get used to this. You don't understand that now, but you're going to."

"You're hurting my arm," she said, her voice wavering.

Something drained from Carl's defensive front like an old memory awoken. He'd had enough. He dropped Annaliese's suitcase behind Ed's car and came at them, his heart pounding. "Let go of her."

"This is none of your business," Ed said.

"I said let go of her." His blood was pumping hard and he felt his pulse in the tips of his fingers. His hands shook and he was close to throwing up.

Ed held on a few more seconds, taunting him, daring him to make the first move before letting go as though he planned to all along. Miriam backed into Carl, rubbing her wrist as Ed caught hold of his daughter. Annaliese was curled into a ball in the back seat, her cries morphed into a constant whimper, the groans of starvation and mourning.

"I've had enough of your tantrum," Ed said. "Into your seat now." She didn't resist, nor did she cooperate as he stuffed her into the car-seat and buckled her in with no more trouble than handling a stuffed animal. Ed bumped Carl as he grabbed the suitcase. "Excuse me," he said, tossing it in the trunk. Carl braced for him to come again, but this time Ed gave a clear berth before commanding the driver's seat and turning over the engine. He backed out and swung the car around, and Carl stepped to the window.

"Don't ever touch her again," he said.

"You're a nosy son-of-a-bitch, aren't you?"

"Don't do it."

Ed raised a finger. "This is none of your damn business. You remember that."

He punched the gas and the car jolted to the curb before easing slowly onto the empty street. Carl watched him drive off until he was out of sight. Miriam was already in the passenger seat with her head in her hands. She was shaking, not making a sound.

"You drive," she gasped.

Chapter 12

Carl sat on the living room floor in his boxer shorts surrounded by half-packed boxes, wads of bubble wrap and stacks of videos. The Jacksonville Yellow Pages lay open to "attorneys" where several firms were highlighted in fluorescent marker. He was scribbling a note in a three-ring binder when Miriam walked in wearing a tee-shirt hanging to her knees. Her hair was still wet and stringy from the shower. She cocked her head to one side and screwed a Q-tip in one ear.

"Any luck?" she asked.

"I've got you an appointment at noon."

"Today?" She spread her legs and dropped into his lap, kissing him hard on the lips. "Thank you," she said, her eyes meaning it.

"It was one of the ads we looked at last night. Divorce, custody and appeals – thirty-five years experience."

"I'll need thirty-five years just to get past this," she said, rocking in his lap before kissing him again. She grabbed his shirt and gave him a shake. "Did you call the realtor?"

"I left another message. He's probably tired of hearing from me."

"Keep calling him."

Carl burrowed his face in her chest and breathed her in. The shirt was hiked up to her waist and he slid his hands under her. There was something about her when she was fresh from the shower.

"Oh no you don't. We have work to do." She pushed herself up, but then lingered over him. Her smile morphed into a seductive gaze as she slowly raised her shirt and rolled her body in a long sensual wave beginning at her toes and rippling to the top of her head. She danced her hypnotic lap dance like a pro, her bush swaying a sweet breath from his nose before dropping the curtain and ending her little act. "More for you later," she said. "I have to get ready." She trotted away, leaving Carl alone on the hardwood floor.

∞

Carl took the wheel and Miriam sat with an open accordion file in her lap. She removed several small bundles of legal papers and placed them all over the cab, covering the dash, the console and floorboards, trying to organize. Though the sun was intense, they cracked the windows only an inch so the papers wouldn't blow all to hell.

"He needs to know about the stalking," she said, coaching herself.

"I'd be more concerned with Ed grabbing you yesterday. Has he done that before?"

"Yes, almost every time. That's how he is."

Carl thought about it. "Did he ever hit you?"

"He would have eventually, if I'd hadn't thrown him out."

"Did the judge hear about his manhandling?"

"He was asleep."

"All I'm saying is stick to what you can prove," he warned. Little anger dimples formed around Miriam's mouth. Carl felt her growing away from him. "You got burned on the stalking charges because you didn't have any witnesses. Well now you have a witness."

"This attorney needs to know *everything* this man has done," she said.

"You should forget about what you can't prove."

"I can't prove anything," she cried, slapping one stack of papers on top of another. "The stalking, the verbal abuse, his throwing our fucking wine glasses across the room, his – *preferences*." She drifted off with an air of shame.

Carl wanted to probe, but she was getting too worked up. He was afraid to push any further. A garbage truck was lumbering in their lane, so he flipped the turn signal hard and whipped passed it. "I still can't figure out why you married this asshole."

"He was different before." She let out an exasperated gasp, as if just realizing she'd been fooled. "He sure could sweet talk.

Smooth as silk. And he *was* her father. I sure as hell couldn't raise her with my mother."

"You considered him a better influence than your mother?"

"You don't know. Her drinking had gotten worse. Ed said he didn't drink."

"And does he?"

"Not much. He was more fond of the stash of pot he kept hidden in his fishing gear. That was another reason I threw him out."

"And the judge slept through that too?"

"My attorney refused to bring it up. He said it was hearsay and not pertinent. It would only make the judge uncomfortable."

"It's *supposed* to make him uncomfortable."

"Well it never came up."

They stopped talking as if worn down by the conversation, listening instead to the hiss of passing cars.

"What did you mean by *preferences*?" Carl asked, and was immediately sorry he did. She didn't answer right away. Her hands fidgeted, tried to straighten the documents.

"He wanted me to pee on him." She sniffed and wiped her nose. "Did you know in over a year of marriage I can count on one hand the number of times I saw the man smile?" She raised the wad of papers and slung them over her shoulder where they exploded in a white accordion burst. "Fuck it. Just fuck it!"

"Calm down."

"You calm down. You don't fucking believe me either."

"I never said any such thing."

"You don't know what it's like. Have you ever had someone hold you by your hair and piss in your face?"

"I believe you, Miriam."

"It doesn't matter. I've been alone from the start. I don't know why the hell I thought you could help."

"I'm here. I'm right here. I flew six hundred miles to be here for you. Don't tell me I'm not here to help. Don't give me that crap."

Carl realized they'd been weaving in traffic and he gripped the wheel tight and brought them between the lines. All the other cars and trucks were giving them a wide berth. He'd put her temper out of his mind since they'd reconciled, but now he remembered it vividly. It was the one thing about her that rattled him and gave him second thoughts about being with her again. He was never sure what might set her off, though he wasn't surprised at this conversation doing some damage.

"Why don't you turn around," she said. "Go home."

"I'm going to help you, Miriam. No matter what happens between us."

"Why are we bothering with all this?"

"So you'll get your child back."

She leaned on the door as if exhausted of all willingness to fight. "I just want this to be over."

"We'll get you a good attorney, okay? I have a good feeling about this guy."

"I don't."

"Well I do. Now get your map out. I need a navigator."

The steel blue skyline of Jacksonville rose beyond a maze of bridges and overpasses like blunt knives needling the sky. Carl and Miriam were soon under the shadows of Bell South and Modis and Mercantile Bank, circling the central blocks in vain for a parking space. Miriam was still upset and insisted they give up, the city had no space for them, but he ignored her pleas and pulled into a garage where he handed the keys to a Cuban attendant in an orange vest. The man adjusted the driver's seat and plunged the car into the bowels of the city.

The office of Marshall Coulton, Esquire, filled a corner of the tenth floor in the old limestone Dickerson building a block east of the courthouse. The lobby was clad in polished pink marble and art deco accents, and Miriam ran a finger down the stainless steel framed register, noting all the attorneys in the building.

"How do we know if we found the right one?" she asked meekly. "With all these lawyers, how do we know?"

Carl came up behind her. "I talked to him. He said he does divorce," he said obviously, hoping a simple assurance would set her at ease.

She lifted her finger from the glass case and watched the little oval of condensation evaporate. "But how do we know?"

They took timid steps from the elevator down to a suite at the end of the hall, each carrying one of the bulging accordion files. They looked at each other before going inside. The waiting room was windowless with plastic ferns gathering dust in the corners. The far side of the room bled into a secretarial area with desks crammed together and file cabinets lining the perimeter. Every surface was covered with paper, files, computers and commotion. A lone secretary sat at the far desk typing mechanically, her cropped hair framing a boyish face. She wasn't old, but grey hair was taking over and it appeared she'd given up on appearances.

Miriam rested her file on the reception counter. "We have a twelve o'clock with Mr. Coulton."

The secretary checked a ledger on her desk. "Boyd?" she said, and Miriam nodded anxiously. "Have a seat. He's with another client."

Carl expected a long wait and he'd already found a seat across from a young Hispanic couple whose dark faces were filled with hopelessness. They held hands for a while until she let go to fiddle in her purse. The man moved his hand to the armrest, to his knee, and back to the armrest. His eyes were gloomy and knowing, expecting the worst. Carl wondered what they were going through that was so awful, and whether it was worse than what Miriam was enduring.

Miriam rummaged through her file and asked Carl to find something in the papers he was carrying. They reorganized all the documents left in shambles from her fit in the car and still sat there another forty-five minutes. She stormed to the counter.

"Excuse me. It's almost one o'clock. This isn't acceptable."

The secretary regarded Miriam as if she'd been asked to change the month from June to October. "He's still with a client, Ma'am."

"We've been waiting for an hour. I expect better – "

She was interrupted by an office door opening wide and the voices coming out of it. An anemic looking teenager with a pot-damaged physique lumbered out the door without a care, followed by his mother whose wrinkles curled around her eyes in deference to some magnetic field. She was shaking the hand of a man still hidden. Another secretary slipped out of the office with an armload of papers and busied herself in the file cabinets.

"He'll see you now," the greying boyish secretary said without looking up from her typing.

When the mother and son left the office, Marshall Coulton stepped forward and filled the doorway.

"Come in, come in," he said, coaxing the timid into his den. His large frame took its shape from eating all of his meals in restaurants, and though his age was not obvious, the years of experience listed in his ad told them he must have been at least sixty. His hair was still jet black, too black to be natural, but what also defied his years was his energy, confident posture and a dancing foot that never stopped moving. His face was pock-marked from childhood, but was still soft and kind, having somehow never been scorched from either the tropical rays or the years of practicing law.

Carl and Miriam sat in chairs opposite a glass topped mahogany desk. Coulton closed the door behind them and circled the office, studying the two as if waiting for an opening to break the ice. Carl was staring at a beaded Indian breastplate and tomahawk hanging on a wall between the framed degrees.

"Seminole," the attorney said, with both pride and a little defiance. "One eighth blood. My great-grandmother was said to be from Creek extraction. She must have been where I got my bullheadedness." Carl curled his lip and nodded. Miriam said it was all very interesting, but she said that about anything she didn't understand. "The government tried to run them out of her country, but she wouldn't have any part of it. She stood her ground."

"Weren't they driven into the swamps?" Carl said.

"A lot of them are still down there on the reservations. Some of us didn't do too well, but some of us did all right." He took his seat, leaned forward and peered at Miriam over his glasses. "So you lost custody of your child?"

"Yes, sir," she said earnestly.

"Over in Dixon County?"

She nodded.

"Why are you in Jacksonville? Why aren't you using a local attorney?"

"There aren't that many there to choose from. It's a backwards area."

Carl cut in. "Your ad said you go there."

"Well, I do. But to be honest, I don't like making the trip. I charge extra for that. I told you that on the phone."

"Yes, I know."

Coulton adjusted his glasses, as if indicating an eagerness to get to the bottom of things. "Who was your last attorney?"

"Walt Skinner," Miriam said.

"Never heard of him."

"It's no wonder. He lost my child."

"You should have used Gabe Appleby."

Miriam looked down at her papers, looked ready to drop them on the floor. "I did. At first."

"Gabe's a fine attorney. What happened?"

"He kept coming at me wanting more retainer fees," she said, her voice rising. "I gave him money and he kept coming at me for more, saying what I gave him wasn't enough."

"All right now. This is an expensive situation. I can't speak for Gabe, I don't know how he runs his business, but dissolving a marriage, even in an amicable way, is an expensive endeavor."

"I know. I know that now."

Coulton motioned at the papers she was holding. "What do you have there for me?"

Miriam handed him one paper-clipped bunch at a time. First, a typed chronology from the day she threw Ed out of the house, the story of how he kept showing up at her job at the rib house to charm her manager and bad-mouth her. And of the times he cased her house late at night, and the incident at the daycare and the tug-of war with the child in the parking lot over a disputed visitation. She handed over copies of bank statements showing the account being cleaned out the same afternoon she threw him out of the house, leaving her eight dollars and fifty-seven cents in the checking account. The last thing she presented was the court reporter transcripts of the hearings and all of the judge's orders throughout the separation and final decree.

Coulton leaned back in his chair and studied one of the documents. "As you know, this is a lot to digest. I intend to go over all of this in detail, but not just yet. Right now I need to ask you some questions, some you probably won't like." He waited for any sign of objection, but got none. "Have you ever been in trouble with the law?"

"No," Miriam answered.

"No arrests? No drunk driving convictions?"

She paused, as if considering the word *conviction*. "No, sir."

"Drug possession?"

"She's never done drugs," Carl said.

"Do you have any history of mental illness?

"No."

"Any medical conditions I should be aware of? Something that might put your daughter at risk? Asthma attacks? Seizures of any kind?"

"No. Nothing."

Marshall shook his head, lifted the papers and dropped them back on the desk. "I don't see how you lost custody. If what you're saying is true, I don't see how this happened."

Miriam pulled three photos of Annaliese from her purse and handed them to Coulton. "Here she is. She was a happy child, and she isn't happy anymore." Miriam wasn't crying, but she snatched a tissue from her purse and balled it in her hand. "And there's this." She handed him one more stapled batch of papers from her file. "This is the court ordered report from the family therapist. Judge Hawkins let Ed's attorney choose the doctor."

Marshall read the first page, leafed through the rest and read the summation. "This isn't proper," he said. "The formatting is all wrong for its purposes." He reread the last page. "Here, listen here. It says both parents are considered stable and fit – then he goes on to recommend custody to the father, but there's no basis." He held the report out, as if weighing its value. "No basis." He dropped the report on the desk. "You've got to have a good reason to separate a child from her mother in this state. This doctor was drawing straws."

"You never showed me that," Carl said.

Miriam stared at the report and its damning decision. "It's not something I'm proud of," she said.

Coulton scanned another page. "You say the judge let your ex-husband's attorney choose the doctor?" Miriam nodded eagerly. "Well I ought to be able to do something about this," he said. "I ought to be able to help you. I assume you have standard visitation?"

"Every other weekend and Wednesday evenings." Miriam sat up in her chair. "We're still within the thirty days for an appeal. The deadline is Friday."

"Friday?" Marshall waved her off. "I run a small shop here. I'm already in court every day this week. There's no way I can drop everything and go to Tallahassee. And an appeal is a costly thing. I have to travel to Tallahassee and file the papers, then again for the hearing and probably put up in a hotel. Then hope the docket doesn't run over and strand me there another day. You have to pay for all that. If you thought Gabe's bills were high, just wait."

"So what you're telling me is only the rich can appeal?"

"An appeal is an expensive proposition for any client. The larger law firms have branch offices in Tallahassee that can handle these on less notice, but their fees are higher than mine. I have a small practice, just me and my two nephews." He sat back and regrouped. "You can go one of two ways. You can appeal this decision, but you're going to have to get another attorney. I can't do it this week. You came to see me too late. The only other option is to let this decision stand and petition for a change in custody. I may not have time to go to Tallahassee, but I can handle Dixon County. I've gone before Judge Hawkins and he's a reasonable man. Not the friendliest, mind you, but I've always found him to be fair. A new petition would be based on how your ex-husband has been raising your daughter since the decision was handed down. Now has he done anything wrong or detrimental to Annaliese since the divorce? Anything at all that hasn't already been presented in court."

Miriam pointed to the papers on his desk. "He stalked me for six months during the separation."

"I see that, but it's already been considered. The judge made his decision based on what was presented. If we go with a new hearing we have to concentrate on how he's doing with the child right now."

"But it *wasn't* considered."

"The stalking wasn't presented in the initial hearings?"

"Yes, it was presented, but he didn't care." She rested her fingers on the edge of his desk. Her voice was shrill. "The judge didn't care."

"Now hold on. It's all right now."

"It's not all right."

Coulton offered her a box of tissues, but she waved it off with the crumpled one in her hand. "Miriam," he said, putting on a kinder face, "If it was presented in the last hearing, then we can't use it. The judge's decision was based on all the evidence presented. What impact the alleged stalking had on the judge will never be known, though I grant you, it doesn't look like it swayed him much."

"He physically grabbed Annaliese from my arms at the day care. He was violent," she said.

"Was that discussed at the hearing?"

The words squeezed out of her. "Yes."

"That might be material to an appeal, but we can't use it in a new hearing. To petition for a reversal of custody we need new evidence."

"Well, dammit then."

Marshall Coulton rubbed his leather armrests. "You have to give me something that's happened since you turned over custody. You need to keep an eye out for any kind of abnormal behavior – from him or your daughter."

Carl touched Miriam's arm. "She's gaining a lot of weight. You said he only feeds her fast food. There should be a law against that."

"Annaliese is in terrible shape," Miriam said emphatically. "She's withdrawn and never happy when I pick her up, and by the time she finally opens up, it's time to take her back. She's terrified of her father. She's suffering from separation anxiety. She cries in fits whenever I leave the room – especially when I drop her off with her father."

"Now you see, we might have something here. We could first petition to get her seen by a child psychologist, one that wasn't chosen by your ex-husband's attorney, or possibly a nutritionist.

Someone I know who can follow Florida law. If a professional can determine the child's mental or physical condition has deteriorated since she's been in the father's care, then we can petition to reverse custody. We may have a shot."

"Oh God." Miriam said. "Please."

Carl cut in again. "And he grabbed her yesterday."

"He grabbed her, you say? How so?"

"He grabs me every time I pick up Annaliese or drop her off," Miriam said.

"Well, he can't do that. He can't touch you if you don't want to be touched. That's called battery. Has this come up before?"

It did, but the judge yelled at me for it. Said I couldn't prove it and insinuated I was a liar."

"I saw him do it," Carl said. "Last Friday and again yesterday. I could be a witness."

"Well then, there's something else for us to consider. Now I have another question," he said, eyeing the two of them together, before centering on Miriam. "What is your relationship to this gentleman by your side?"

She acted like this was his most unexpected question. "We've known each other since high school."

"You seem close. Do you have plans to get married?" He raised a hand, apologizing for prying. "I ask this because if you do, this will be a major advantage in reversing custody. The child will have both a mother and a father in a stable home. A bachelor father won't have near as much leverage."

The earlier fight in the car and the flare of Miriam's temper was fresh in Carl's memory. In his hesitation to answer, he noticed Miriam's own hesitation.

"We're considering it." Carl said. "Marriage."

Miriam took his hand for second and let go. "But they accused us of having an affair. It's all in the papers I gave you."

"Well then, we'll get to that later. What about your parents? Family comes in handy at a time like this."

Miriam winced at the suggestion. "My mother is not reliable," she said. "She's a drunk."

"And your father?"

"He's dead," she said. Carl regarded her strangely. Miriam gazed into Coulton's concerned eyes, as if he were the only one who understood her. "I want to go with the new hearing. I want to use you."

"We need to talk about fees." He turned to Carl. "On the phone we spoke about a payment plan, but I'll still need a retainer to start reading up on the case."

"How much are we talking?" Carl asked.

He sized up the stack papers in front of him, as though he charged by the inch. "Given what I need to catch up on . . . the first petition . . . the first hearing . . . I'd say $2,000. Hopefully we won't double it before we get this mess straightened out."

Miriam snapped her purse shut and stood.

"That's fine," Carl said, pulling out his wallet. "Who do I write it out to?"

"Carl, no," Miriam said.

"We're doing this, aren't we?"

She turned to Coulton. "But what about your payment plan?"

"That doesn't apply to the retainer. I need this to get started. I do take credit cards, but I wouldn't advise it. Damned interest rates."

She dropped back into the chair and looked helpless as Carl wrote the check and handed it to Coulton. "It's okay, Miriam."

"I have your numbers," Coulton said. They all stood and shook hands. "I'll call you by the end of the week, after I've reviewed all this in more detail. Then we'll discuss the best way to go forward."

"We'll be in town for the next two weeks," Miriam said. "Then we're going up to Virginia for the first two-week summer visitation."

"I have one more question. This attorney you used – Skinner? Is he still in any way involved with this case? I assume he's not still under retainer?"

"No way. A week after he lost my daughter, he sent me another bill for office expenses. Staples and paper clips. He may have been cheap, but I'm not paying him another dime for the damage he did."

Coulton opened the door. "I don't mean to be nosey, but I guess that's part of my job. Do you mind me asking what he charged to represent you?"

"Five hundred dollars," she said plainly.

"You mean for the retainer?"

"No. Five hundred for the whole divorce."

"God almighty." He stood there and rolled his head back. "No damn wonder." He checked himself and gave Miriam a fatherly touch on the shoulder. "I'm sorry. I really am, but five hundred dollars is barely enough to settle an amicable divorce. You have a bloody mess on your hands." Miriam lowered her head in shame with Marshall standing by her. "Now I know what happened. This is all starting to make sense."

"Skinner said I would have no problem keeping custody. He said it would be easy." Knowingly or not, she leaned against her new attorney's side. "He said good mothers don't lose their babies."

"You're not going to lose her. Even if custody is never reversed, you'll never lose your child. That just won't happen."

"But it is happening."

"I know it's not right," he said. She looked to him for reassurance, like he was the father she'd been waiting for. "I believe I can help you." Miriam cried a little and said thank you, awkwardly shook his hand a second time before parting.

They left the lobby and lugged their burden of documents down the sidewalk in the broiling sun. The attendant brought the car from the abyss and when they buckled up Miriam was calm and refreshed, as if transported back to the days before the baby and life was just the carefree beach she'd gone down there for.

"Why did you tell him your father was dead?" Carl asked.

"He is, as far as I'm concerned. He's had twenty-three years to come back and be a father." She rolled down her window, searching for a breeze to pick up as they pulled into traffic. "If I could have a real father, I'd pick Coulton. I really like him."

"That's important. It's important you feel comfortable with your attorney."

"I do." At the first traffic light she put a hand on his knee as if that might stop the world. "Thank you."

"Don't mention it."

"I don't know what I'd do –." she trailed off. "Do you have enough money for all this?"

"Don't worry about the money. Don't worry about anything right now." Knowing she was on the verge of being happy and not wanting to jeopardize it, he drove her to a restaurant overlooking the St. John's River. He wanted to broach the subject of marriage again, but decided it wasn't the time. They sat on a deck with thick ship rope guardrails, and ordered tropical cocktails and watched the pleasure boats and barges pass by.

Chapter 13

The sign in front of the apartment complex read: *BURGUNDY GARDENS, A Concerned Community*. The buildings were two-story walk-ups with stucco veneer failing at the corners, revealing the concrete block at its core. Useless balconies sized for a lone chair hung from every apartment like deep fry baskets ready to be dipped into the boiling parking lot. On the second floor of the first building, above a broken section of stucco where someone's car had jumped the curb, was Miriam's new one bedroom unit.

They rented a small trailer, the only one the BMW was powerful enough to pull, and shuttled five times between the house Miriam once shared with Ed and her new refuge. The furniture was hastily shoved into place and towers of boxes were stacked along the walls. One box of odds and ends that passed for family heirlooms, including her father's trinkets, was left in the trunk to be taken back to Virginia. Miriam requested this box be left in Carl's care, and he didn't question her.

Their muscles sore and too tired to unpack, they slept that first night on the mattress in the middle of the bedroom floor and covered themselves with a comforter pulled from a trash bag full of linen. In the early hours, Miriam ran a fever and dampened the bed sheets, but by first light it broke and she felt well enough to eat a little cereal. Carl was standing on the balcony with a cup of coffee squinting into the parking lot when a groan sounded from inside. She was scrubbing the kitchen, insisting it was too filthy to use, when she stopped and bent over. With both hands on her stomach, she crouched off to the sofa and curled up in a ball. She groaned again and that's when Carl reached her.

"Can you get me some ibuprofen?" she asked.

By the time he brought the pills and a glass of water, Miriam's color had gone. She pushed herself up and Carl put a hand on her side to guide her.

"What's wrong?" he asked. "Where does it hurt?"

"So you're a doctor now?"

"The best."

"Help me to the bathroom."

He motioned to carry her but she waved him off, accepting only his hand on her back, which did nothing. She slipped inside and shut the door. He expected to hear her vomit or heave, but heard only a series of long deep groans timed with each breath.

"Are you sure you're okay?" Carl called to her, pressing his forehead on the door.

"I don't know."

Carl paced the apartment like an expectant father from the old school, brimming with anxiety but effectively useless. After pondering the mattress still laying on the floor, he grabbed the cheap tool kit Miriam had probably bought at a drug store and assembled the bed frame. She spent the next hour on the toilet bleeding, but refusing to go to the hospital. It wasn't bad enough, she claimed, and an appointment at the clinic was already scheduled for the next morning. Carl finished the bed just as she came out, all pale and grimacing. Her hair was matted with sweat.

"Will you let me take you to the ER?" he asked.

"It's easing up." She curled on the mattress and Carl draped the comforter over her. He sat by her, and after a few minutes, with a tone that scared him, she said, "Take me now."

∞

In its twenty years of operation the Gatreauex Women's Clinic had been the scene of thirty-seven acts of vandalism, two stink bombs, a drive-by shooting and weekly protests. Sandblasted graffiti could still be seen on the textured block walls. Though there was nothing to memorialize its sordid past, the broken glass having long been swept away, the building's depressing history was a weight on anyone entering the building.

Carl waited in an orange plastic chair and fingered a pamphlet some woman shoved in his face when he ushered Miriam inside. He unfolded it and read the title: "A Child is not a Choice." The political intent was not lost to him, but at the moment he didn't give a damned for anyone's political intent.

After an hour Miriam stepped carefully from the hall of examination rooms and sat at the cashier's desk to finish the paperwork. When they left the building, her arms were folded under her breasts and Carl steadied her. She was drawn in, holding it together.

"Well?" he said, holding the door, where they squinted from the sunlight.

"I miscarried."

All Carl could muster was, "Okay." Given everything going on, he knew this was for the best. He was indifferent. So long as she was okay, this was no real loss. They didn't even want a child, at least not yet. There was already enough to worry about, and he assumed she felt the same way. "Do you need bed-rest or anything?"

Before she could answer, the woman who accosted them with the pamphlet rushed up and blocked their way. She focused on Miriam.

"Did you just murder your baby?"

Carl locked his jaw and felt his anger welling up. "What?"

"Did she murder your baby?" She pointed accusingly. "Shame on you. Shame!"

"Get the hell out of our way." Carl kept himself between Miriam and this woman as they tried to slip around her, but she side-stepped and held her ground.

"You'll atone for this."

Carl erupted in a rage suppressed for over half his life. In one swift and violent motion, he pumped his fists on her boney chest and sent her and her wad of pamphlets flying into the bushes. The woman's male companion saw it from his car, and he sprinted up the sidewalk.

"You! Stop right there!" he yelled.

Carl stepped out of himself in a blind rage, an animal-like lashing-out where his normal self was no more than a spectator. To some inner part of him it was like watching a violent act on television. For the first time since his fight in high school, the fight that had cost him so much, he threw a blind and crazy right cross in the man's general direction. His knuckles popped in a flash of pain, and all he could recall seeing was a twirling dumbbell of saliva bounding through the air. The man went down hard, but in his good fortune his head fell into the grass and not on the concrete sidewalk where Carl fantasized seeing his skull split in half. The woman climbed from the bushes, screaming. She crawled over and knelt by her friend.

"Sons of bitches," Carl spat at them. He wanted another piece of the guy, but Miriam took him by the arm.

"Go. Just go," she said. She kept a hand on her belly as they trotted off to the car. He fired up the engine and never took his eyes off them, both still on the ground consoling each other. "Fucking bastards." He drove off fast and didn't care if it looked like they were running from something. He didn't think they caught the tag number. His hand hurt and he began squeezing an imaginary ball with his fist. When they were clear and he'd settled down, he checked over Miriam.

"Sorry about that," he said, but he didn't mean it. It felt good and he was glad he did it.

"Sorry? You should have belted her too." She handed him a crumpled slip of paper. "I need to go to the pharmacy." She pressed her fingers into her eyes. "I don't have any money for the prescription."

"If I was going to pay for the pregnancy, then I think I can handle a bottle of pills."

"You've done enough."

"You need to rest."

"The attorney, the apartment. Now the house, the land." She was sobbing.

Carl worked the joints on his sore hand, tried to figure her. "Did you want this child? In the middle of all this?"

"I already lost one. What if I can't have another?"

"Did you ask the doctor about that?"

She fiddled with the hem of her shirt. "Yes."

"And?"

She didn't answer right away, as if recalling the conversation. "She said there's no reason I can't."

"So there's no long term problem," he said, examining his knuckles.

Carl filled the prescription while Miriam waited in the car. She was pale and weak, but composed. Back at the sad little apartment she spent another twenty minutes on the toilet before crawling into bed. Carl lumbered around absently until she was deep asleep, drugged and snoring through the afternoon. He was afraid to unpack the kitchen as it would make too much racket, so he worked until twilight on the endless boxes of crap she'd managed to accumulate. He was sitting on the floor assembling her stereo components when the cell phone rang. He checked the number on the screen and answered.

"What's the news?" Carl asked.

"It was real close," the man said apologetically.

"You're not telling me what I want to hear."

"You missed it by less than a grand." Carl lowered the phone, but could still hear the broker's voice. "The third bid wasn't even close. It was just the two of you. Damn close."

"Less than a thousand bucks? Is that all they based it on?"

"Highest bidder."

"You said one of the offers came from another real estate agent. Was that agent the high bidder?"

The broker paused long enough for Carl to know the answer. "I'm sure that doesn't have anything to do with it, Carl."

"God damn you people. You Realtors protect your own, don't you? Dammit, I gave a clean contract. Good credit, no contingencies. What did this agent offer? What were the terms?"

The bedroom door opened and Miriam stepped out wearing a lavender sweat-suit. She looked cold and kept her arms tight to her sides. "What's wrong?" she asked, sitting down on the edge of the sofa. "Who's that?"

Carl gave her a petrified stare and listened.

"I can't reveal the details of an active contract," the broker said. "And I don't appreciate what you're insinuating. An individual seller might have been more interested in a clean contract, but this was a foreclosure situation. The holding company for the bank just looked at the bottom line."

"By less than a grand," Carl said, making a sore fist.

"Yes, by less than a grand. I'm sorry, Carl."

"Is by any chance the winning bidder an agent in your brokerage? If so, I guess you just magically doubled your commission."

"You can either pick up your earnest money check or I can – ."

Carl turned off the phone and threw it onto a chair. He went back to untangling the wad of speaker wire in his lap.

"What was that? What's wrong?" Miriam asked.

"The house. We lost the house."

She bent over and squeezed her eyes tight. "That property could have helped us get her back. It would have shown the judge we had a good home for her."

Carl's mind was black with rejection. "I bid lower than I wanted to so we could afford the pregnancy." He realized there was an accusation in his tone, but it was too late to take it back.

"You're more upset about the house than my miscarriage."

"We're ready for a house, Miriam. We're not ready for another kid. I don't think that's unreasonable."

"Fine," she said, and left the room. Carl could make no sense of the tangled mess of wire, but he kept working it obsessively, refusing to give up.

Chapter 14

On the second Friday in July they walked into the Palm Kids Daycare Center, housed in one wing of a retired brick elementary school. In the classroom at the end of the hall Annaliese and her teacher, a black woman of fifty with orange freckled skin, sat across from each other at a low table covered with flash cards. The teacher whispered something to the child, who turned to see her mother squat and bounce at the knees, smiling and extending her arms. Annaliese walked sheepishly toward her, submitting her plump body to her mother's embrace.

"Come here, you." Miriam squeezed her daughter, but only after continually smooching her on the cheek did she meekly return the affection.

Carl stood to one side, examining the room like he might an art gallery, seeing if anything spoke to him. The walls, painted by high school art students, were swimming with sting rays and manatees in a deep sea mural. Bins of toys and bright foam blocks lined the walls, and in the far corner was a stack of sleeping mats and folded blankets.

The teacher, Ms. Janine Haygood, met them with her hands folded. "She's all ready for her trip," she said. "That's all she wanted to talk about all day. Isn't that right, Annaliese?"

"Did he bring her luggage?" Miriam asked.

"It's right over there." Ms. Haygood motioned toward a small blue suitcase sitting by itself against the wall.

"He did something right for once." She said to her daughter, "Can you go get your suitcase and stay with Carl for a minute? I need to talk to Ms. Haygood." Miriam stepped into the hall with the teacher, but framed herself within the rectangular window in the door so she was still within sight of her little girl. "Has she been the same since Wednesday?"

Ms. Haygood shook her head and spoke in a whisper. "She hasn't said a word all day. I tried to get my assistant to engage her this morning, she has such a good way with kids, but Annaliese just wouldn't open up. She played some, but she was in her own world. She's barely acknowledged the other kids all week. Even the ones who picked on her."

"You saw what she was like before all this. You know that's not the same child."

"I know, I know." Janine touched Miriam's arm. "At least she's eating. I've seen some troubled little girls who won't even eat."

"But look at her," she said, staring through the window pane. "She's getting fat. He doesn't cook for her. All she gets is pizza and junk food."

"She gets a fruit and a vegetable here every day. And milk too. We do our best."

"I know you do."

"You should also know she's had some real bad diaper rash the past few days. I changed her a few minutes ago and put on some ointment, so she should be fine to start your trip."

Carl was sitting in a tiny chair next to Annaliese flipping through a deck of flash cards, though she watched with little interest. "I had her potty trained last spring," Miriam said, watching them. "She's regressing. God damn him."

"Y'all get on out of town and forget this for a while. Spend some time with her in your arms."

The court order did not restrict where Miriam could take the child for summer visitation, but Ed still warned her not to leave the state. Miriam insisted she could take Annaliese wherever she wanted and proved it by crossing the Georgia state line within an hour of stowing the girl's suitcase in the trunk of her car. By six o'clock they crossed the St. Mary's bridge into the coastal flats of Georgia where it felt like an escape. With each mile of interstate, past Kingston and Woodbine and Darien, through the occasional lingering stench of the paper mills, they grew lighter and more hopeful as they put miles between themselves and the raging fire of Miriam's life. Carl couldn't wait to be back in his house, in his own bed, the place of his self-imposed purgatory. Oddly, he even found himself missing his grandfather's farm and briefly thought he might have taken it and the old man for granted. He puzzled over how the space of two weeks could have altered his perceptions.

All week Miriam had talked about leaving Florida for good. She detested the state. Even if she couldn't wrestle back custody, she said she would move back to Virginia and travel twice a month to be with her daughter. Carl argued she needed a place to live with her, a real home, not a hotel room on a weekend visit, but she didn't want to hear this and accused him of not only being unsupportive, but of somehow undermining her. Carl was learning to not say anything.

Shy of the South Carolina line, Carl was the first to notice the smell of warm shit whirling through the car. He groaned and Miriam bent the rear view mirror to meet her daughter's eyes. The child sat there tugging the ribbons in her hair.

"We have to stop," Miriam said.

"You'll get no objection from me."

The next exit didn't have any signs for gas or food, no reason to stop at all, which gave Carl the impression this might be a good place to live. They drove on for another ten miles before taking a long exit ramp down into a glut of truck-stops. He pulled up to the pumps and Miriam led Annaliese across the lot into the station. Carl leaned against the car while the gas flowed, listening to the roar of interstate traffic overhead.

On the opposite side of the pump was a man whose face was scarred to a purplish red powder, the tint of an old Bordeaux with too much sediment. His arms were the same color, but his hands were scaled with soft patches of pink. He pumped gas into his F-250 and held a cigarette with his free hand, watching the dollar count rise. Carl studied him before turning away. The man sucked on his cigarette and nodded to him.

"Hot evening, ain't it," he said.

"Sure is." Carl fidgeted and fingered the linings of his pockets. "Bum a cigarette off you?" The man's pump clicked off and he topped the tank before hanging up the handle. He took a green and white pack from his shirt pocket and thumped it in his palm, extending a stick to Carl. He lit it and inhaled long and deep like a man who'd long been denied some essential nutrient. The pump spit out a receipt and the man tore it off and threw it away. He rolled down his window and spat before firing up the engine.

"Fertilizer burn. When I was a boy," he said, giving a painful smile. "I get lots of stares."

"I didn't mean to."

"Most people don't mean no harm. I'm beyond teasing."

When he drove off, Carl hollered thanks, but the scar-faced man was too far off to hear. The handle clicked off and he took one last drag on the cigarette and set the stub on top of the pump. When he reached the counter with a couple of drinks and handed the money to the cashier, Miriam called to him from across the store, her voice shrill and urgent. She was standing in the little alcove by the rest rooms, and she motioned with both hands for him to come.

Carl took his change and hurried down the aisle. "What's wrong?"

"Come in here. I need you to witness this."

He heard Annaliese crying in the womens room. "What the hell?"

"Come here."

"I can't go in there."

She stormed inside, unwilling to argue. "Stop being such a baby."

He checked over his shoulder and followed her. Annaliese was bawling and chewing her hand, sprawled out naked below the waist on a plastic changing table folded down from the wall. Her loaded diaper was wadded up and smoldering to one side. Between her legs was a pimpled rash expanding outward like a burst of toxic red dye.

"Good God," he said, turning away as if shielding himself from some malignancy. "I don't want to see this."

"I need you to see this. *He* did this to her. In *two days* Ed did *this*."

Carl backed up to the door. "Okay, I've seen it."

"Go get your camera."

"Use your cell phone."

"I don't know how to get the photos off of it."

"Can't this wait until we get home?"

Miriam's face grew harder, her lips crimped up. "You don't care." She pulled Annaliese's hand out of her mouth and inserted a pacifier. The girl quieted a little, but was still mumbling.

"This isn't going to go away over the next eight hours. Let's get her to the house, then you can document it. Your video camera is in Virginia anyway." He peeked through the door. "Get her in a clean diaper and put some ointment on her. I'll have the car running."

He stepped out of the restroom like he was sneaking out of a bar without paying. It was getting on toward dusk. The sky was bluish-black with Saturn shining high to the west and the waning moon rising through the trees to the east. He turned over the engine and slipped back out to pick up the cigarette he left on top of the pump. Most of it burned off, but a small stub of tobacco still rested there. He relit it with the dash lighter, closed his eyes and inhaled the last quarter inch of tobacco, releasing the tension in his neck and shoulders. When he heard Miriam's footsteps, he flicked the butt out the window and popped open her door. After Annaliese was strapped in, Miriam collapsed into her seat.

"Were you smoking?" she asked.

"Gas stations stink." He shifted a button on the door and lowered the rear windows.

"I thought you stopped."

"I did."

Northbound again in the long line of red tail lights, Carl drove faster, pushing past the screaming rigs with a renewed urgency. Miriam and Annaliese were soon asleep as the thick twilight wind blew through the cab. They rode into Compton at four in the morning, their necks stiff and worn from the miles. Carl gathered Annaliese into his arms and carried her in, while Miriam laid out the futon and made her bed. She whipped out the sheets in one motion and topped them with an old blanket she'd found balled up in the linen closet. The air conditioning was off while they were gone and the house was hot and muggy.

Miriam took a bag from the hall closet and pulled out her old video camera. While she checked its batteries and tested its features, Carl set the thermostat and paced back to the kitchen where he rinsed a glass sitting on the counter. He let the water run over his hands for a while. When he came back to the living room, Annaliese's diaper was off and Miriam was pointing the video recorder between her legs, zooming in and out, scanning the delicate and neglected tissue and, like a doctor recording a transcript of an examination, giving a voice-over narrative of what she was seeing, including the date and time of her last visitation to prove this happened on Ed Grouper's watch. Carl was amazed at how the child slept through such an invasion. After Miriam finished, she applied more cream, diapered the child and tucked her in.

Carl and Miriam trudged upstairs, peeled off their clothes and slipped into bed, but they didn't fade to sleep as easily as the child. Carl's left arm and cheek still tingled from the drive. His skin was sticky and hair frazzled. He was too tired to either shower or sleep. Miriam lay on her back, arms at her side, cold to the touch.

"He's abusing my baby," she said.

"I'd say it's at least negligence."

"It was abuse."

"It looked like he hadn't changed her all week."

"That's not abuse?"

Carl knew to be careful with his words when Miriam was floundering in anger. "I'm trying to think how a judge would look at it."

"This judge doesn't know shit about children."

"This judge is in charge. This judge is God. We know he's an asshole. We just have to figure out the best way to present this."

"How to present it? I'll show him the damn tape. I'll show him what that man did to my child."

"Let Coulton deal with it. Show him the tape and let him decide how to proceed."

Carl lay there all knotted up, one leg crossed over the other, arms folded, but Miriam was prostrate and unblinking.

"I'm showing this tape to the judge," she insisted.

"Fine. But that's just part of what we'll show him. We'll see if Coulton can get his child psychiatrist approved. And the nutritionist. If we can show enough trauma and neglect, we should be able to reverse this."

"This is abuse," Miriam said defiantly.

Her attitude worried Carl, especially after what he'd learned from reading the transcripts of the initial hearings. The judge was stiff on false accusations, at least false accusations coming from the mother. "You have to be careful saying something like that. Neglect, incompetence, sure. Abuse is another matter."

"You don't know."

"Know what?" He rolled toward her. "What aren't you telling me?"

She turned away from him. "He's not right."

"How so?"

She sniffed and fidgeted, drew the sheets to her chin. "Ed used to call me 'his little girl' when we had sex. He called *me* that."

Though taken aback, Carl tried to downplay it. "That's a little weird, but not the weirdest I've heard."

"You don't understand. It was the tone of his voice." She rolled to her side and drew up her knees. "When he would go down on me he would say, 'here's my little girl.'"

Carl lost his gentleness and sat up in a rush. "Why in the hell didn't you mention any of this before?"

"I've been trying to forget."

"Did you mention any of this to Coulton over the phone?"

She shook her head repeatedly. "I can't tell anyone about this." She was crying, and Carl couldn't bring himself to touch her. "I can't tell *anyone*."

"Did you ever see him abuse her?"

"I never let him get close enough. Not as long as I had her. As long as I had her I could protect her." Her voice grew weaker. "I can't protect her now. I can't protect my own baby anymore."

Carl sat there in a black daze with Miriam lying dead next to him. Sleep was far away. He wanted to put his fist through the wall.

Chapter 15

They woke when the child climbed into bed between them. Her spirit magically returned as she snuggled wide-eyed against her mother, who egged her on to torment Carl until he opened his eyes. He played along in a half slumber until he squinted long enough to see the clock. It was 7:30am – three hours of sleep.

"It's a little early," Carl mumbled. "We're on vacation, you know."

"Time to get *up*!" Annaliese shouted, throwing her chubby arms in the air and letting them fall like bouncing sausages. Those were the first words she'd spoken since they picked her up at the daycare, and they marveled at her sudden change. Carl again saw Miriam in the child, the same sweep of hair at the temple, and he also saw the child in Miriam as she wrestled with her girl before getting up to make breakfast. Annaliese rolled into the warm place where her mother had slept and came onto her knees. Hovering over him, she again flung her arms over her head. "Time to get *up*!"

∞

Carl walked barefoot to the mailbox where he found a Penny Trader, a flyer for new windows and a notice to pick-up his held mail. His grass hadn't been cut for three weeks and was bushy and overgrown with tentacles of weed sprouting high and going to seed. While he stood there rubbing the sleep from his eyes, Millie Kilgore pulled to the curb in her grey Impala. Her two boys were wedged next to her in the front seat, and they tumbled out of the car and went hollering into the house. Millie hefted her sacks of groceries from the trunk and carried them like pails of water.

"I see your lady-friend is back," she said, motioning toward Miriam's BMW. "She bring that cutie-pie daughter of hers with her?"

"For a while."

She sat the bags down, but her legs still strained under her own weight. "Judge gave her to the father, didn't he?"

Carl studied her, wondered how she knew. "Looks that way," he said.

"I seen it before. He musta done something not right to get her."

"He's a piece of work."

"If her ex needs an attitude adjustment, you just let me know."

"You'll take care of him, eh?" Carl said, amused he wasn't the only one who wouldn't mind beating Miriam's ex-husband.

"I won't, but I have friends who will. You don't know my crowd. Two of my ex-lovers served time in Jarrett. They don't need much reason for a fight. If this guy's an asshole, they'll do it for sport."

"I'll keep that in mind, Millie." When he lumbered back to his house he was slow to realize there was a part of him that took the offer seriously.

Annaliese was still in their bed watching cartoons. Her picked-over scrambled eggs sat cold on the night-stand. In the next room her mother was at Carl's desk with a white lined notepad and the Yellow Pages. Carl walked in and dropped the mail in the trash.

"What are you doing?" he asked.

"I want her to see a child psychiatrist. A real MD."

"I thought that's what the first petition was about. We're going to let Coulton find someone down there."

"I can't wait for a hearing," she said. "That man is abusing her and I want her seen by a professional right now."

"You told me she's on Ed's insurance plan. How are you going to hide this from him?"

She went over her notes. "I'm just looking for a consultation. Just one hour. I can afford one hour." With a finger on a listing, she picked up the phone and began dialing.

"Miriam, it's Saturday."

"I'll get something in writing. Something to prove what he's doing."

"Miriam."

She hung up the phone and slammed the yellow pages shut. "Dammit," she said, but not loud enough for her daughter to hear.

"Get her dressed," Carl said. "Let's get your mind off things."

∞

"Don't tell him I lost her," she said. They were driving out of town along the familiar two lane byway to the northwest with the spine of the Blue Ridge rising before them.

"What difference does it make?"

"When a mother loses custody, everyone thinks there's something wrong with her."

"He won't think that about you."

"He will. Everyone does. Have you already told him?"

"No. I avoided him before I left for Florida. I didn't want him to know about the other property."

They turned onto the narrow lane that wound its way to his grandfather's farm. Malcolm Rittenhaur was waiting in a rocker on his back porch, his head cocked forward and a mason jar of milk in one hand. His shirt sleeves were rolled above the elbows and his forearms were tarnished with moles, age spots and old wounds. He rose wearily and stepped off the porch into the grass in his burnished leather work boots. Every joint in his body strained to bend. Annaliese sprang from the car and ran to the wire fence where the herd of Black Angus were loitering near the salt lick. One of them bellowed, but the girl approached without fear and offered her hand for licking.

"She has a way with livestock," Malcolm said, focusing on the child as if recalling a memory.

Miriam strolled toward him. "They're just pets to her." She reached her arms around the old man's neck. "You look so good."

"I'm uglier than when you last saw me," he said. His green flannel shirt was buttoned to the neck – always flannel, no matter the weather. He called out to Annaliese, "You look to be a fine cowhand."

"She needs a lot of looking after, herself," her mother said, and gave Carl a severe glance. "I suppose you could use some help out here."

"Y'all back for a while?"

"We have two weeks," Carl said, staring across the fields. "Then we'll see."

"I'm trying to get up here with her permanently," Miriam confirmed.

They took a few steps toward the fence and Malcolm kept an eye on the girl. "You want, we can go on a hay ride. Would you like that?" Annaliese clutched the wire fence and contorted herself so she looked at the old man upside down.

"She would love that," Miriam said.

"This young lady has grown something since I seen her last spring. Hardly looks like the same child."

"She's not the same child, but she will be if I have anything to do with it."

Malcolm contemplated the sky for a moment before pinching Miriam's elbow. "I have something for you."

"What are you up to?"

Carl joined Annaliese at the fence where together they scratched a white spot on the head of a curious cow.

With Annaliese occupied, Malcolm led Miriam through the kitchen and into a small alcove off the parlor, a one-story addition just big enough for a desk and a wall of shelves. This was the first time she'd set foot in the house in seven years. Malcolm lowered himself into a chair behind the walnut desk covered with pink Southern States receipts, a farmer's almanac, electric co-op magazines and Department of Agriculture bulletins. It was all sprinkled with layer of ancient dust. He pulled open the top drawer.

"Been a while since I looked at this," he said, removing a slender box. "With y'all back together, I figured this might be of interest." He opened the box and under a mash of tissue was a thin gold necklace. From an eyelet hung a cross inlayed with brilliant turquoise. "My wife was always fond of you. Took to you like another grandchild," he said, draping the chain through his trembling fingers. "She never understood what happened between you two, but she never said a cross word about you. Even after you left him there."

Miriam parted her lips and stepped back. "I can't take this."

"It shouldn't even be here for you to take. She wanted to be buried with it, but for the life of me I couldn't find the damn thing."

"I can't. I never saw her without it."

"It was in the barn the whole time. Right where she fell."

"I miss her," Miriam said.

"Musta come off and got kicked under the hay." He held it before her, his hand in motion like a gesture in parting. "Go on. Take it."

Miriam wiped her nose and took the necklace, let it drape over her palm.

"Thank you," she whispered.

"She'd approve, I imagine. Whatever happened, she knew you did that boy some good when he needed it."

"Thank you." She brought the end clasps behind her neck and fastened them together. She flipped her hair outside the chain and admired the cross in her hands, touched it to her chin.

"Can I get you anything?" she asked.

"I have all I want."

"I mean lunch. Let me make you lunch."

He slid the drawer shut. "I suppose you can put something together."

∞

The sun was high and the air still and collected, laying there on the land like a warm breath. Flies were swarming the cattle, and Annaliese lost interest. She headed toward a scattering of caged rocks on the hill.

"Annaliese," Carl said with some urgency. "Let's feed the cows. Do you want to feed the cows?" She ignored him and charged up the hill. Carl jogged to catch her, his heart beating faster, though only in part from being out of shape. "Here sweetie. Watch this." He plucked a wide blade of grass, framed it between his thumbs and blew, sending a loud cawing screech across the fields. She wasn't impressed and marched ahead.

The old iron gate wouldn't budge under her small hands, so Carl lifted hard and broke its rusty grip. Together they entered the garden of stones. Annaliese ran her hand over one of the mossy names on a piece of marble. "What's this say?" she asked. Carl recited the names and dates on the stone. They wandered down each row and did the same at each lonely slab of marble and granite. The oldest marble stones worried Carl – the inscriptions were nearly indecipherable, eaten away by time and pressure, and he wondered if anyone in his family had written them down. They came to a clean granite stone, a man and woman whose names were sharp and whose dates of death were the same. Carl hadn't seen it close in years, and he read their names aloud to Annaliese and recited the dates of their lives.

Annaliese traced her fingers over the elaborately carved flowers and tracery in the monument. She made a cold hammer with her fist and brought it down hard. "Did you make this one?" she asked.

From the cemetery hill Carl could see up and down the entire tract. There wasn't an inch of the property he didn't know, and he reminisced about how he learned the terrain. Once when he was a boy, he wandered into the woods and lost his way. Though he spent only an hour wandering in circles, bawling ferociously while trying to find his way home, it felt like days and rattled him badly. When his father found him, he said if he ever got lost again to go in one direction, any direction, until he came to a fence. Follow the fence, don't cross it, and it would always take him home. With that advice, Carl conquered his first childhood fear and learned to explore his little corner of the valley. Until his parents' deaths, he always found his way home.

He stared down at his parent's tombstone and was afraid to answer Annaliese's question.

"I wanna try," Annaliese said, pounding away with her imaginary hammer.

"We can't change these stones," he said. "These stones are already done."

Chapter 16

The same evening they gathered in Carl's office to satisfy a commitment. The windows were open and a fan was pushing the relentlessly muggy air through the room. Carl was sprawled out in his Eames chair, while Miriam fiddled with a tape recorder by the phone on the desk. The girl lay on the floor between them, lured there with crayons and a pad of paper.

"Are you ready to talk to daddy?" Miriam asked. The girl ground the crayon deep into the paper and didn't answer. "Sure you are. I'm going to call him and you can tell him about your day."

"No," she said, flipping over the box of crayons and scattering busted sticks of color all over the floor. Miriam dialed the number and pushed the speaker button on the tape recorder. Ed answered on the first ring.

"It's us," Miriam said, her voice soft and measured for her daughter's benefit. "Annaliese wants to talk to daddy, don't you?"

"Where are you?" Ed demanded.

"We'll get to that in a minute." Miriam held out her arms to her daughter and made little star-bursts with her fingers. "Sweetie, do you hear daddy? Daddy wants to talk to you." The child rose reluctantly and wiggled into her lap, though it could have been the severity of her father's voice that drove her there.

"Annaliese," her father said. "Where did your mommy take you today?"

The child plowed her head under her mother's arm. "We saw moo-cows," she mumbled. "And rocks."

"Cows and rocks. Your mother knows how to show a girl a good time."

"We took her to a farm, Ed."

"Who is *we*?"

"Ed, this is your time to talk to her. I'm following the court order."

"I need to know where you are. The order says that too."

She closed her eyes. "We're in Virginia. We're staying at Carl Rittenhaur's house." She quickly added, "As guests."

"I told you I didn't want her out-of-state."

"There's nothing in the order that says I can't. You have no say."

Ed paused, perhaps calculating his response. The child burrowed deeper into her mother's bosom, though she didn't fit so well when all Miriam's muscles were taut. Her mother spoke to her as if in prayer, seemed to breathe her in. "Can you please just talk some more to him?"

Annaliese blurted out, "He licked me."

"He what?" Miriam was aghast and Carl sat up in his chair.

"The moo-cow," the girl said. Carl and Miriam stared at each other as they settled back into their seats. Annaliese spotted her pacifier at the back of the desk and strained to reach it.

"She's tired, Ed. I have to put her to bed."

"You're keeping her up too late."

"No, Ed. I'm not."

"I'll give you a half hour to put her down. Then I'm calling back." Annaliese found the binky and popped it in her mouth.

"I'll call you in three nights, as per the order."

"I need a check from you." There was pride in Ed's voice for catching her off-guard, and she hesitated in responding.

"I don't have it right now."

"If you're so concerned with the court order, then you should pay the child support."

"I'm not going to talk about this right now, Ed."

"I have your number," he said, and hung up. Miriam punched a button and the phone went dead. She turned off the recorder and glared at it.

"He has caller ID." She shook her head. "He knew all along where we were."

"He wanted to hear it from you," Carl said.

Annaliese broke from her mother's grasp and ran to the next room. Miriam dropped her hands into her lap. "I can't do this for the rest of my life. I can't."

"You want me to put her down?" Carl offered.

"She won't let you. I have to do it."

She squeezed Carl's hand before leaving him splayed back in his chair, head cocked to one side. He listened to Miriam having a time getting Annaliese into pjs, and to the maternal scolding and sweet-talk necessary to prod her onto the futon bed. Their voices merged with an approaching freight train loaded with lumber, empty flat beds and oil stained tankers rumbling its way north. The house was close enough to the embankment to feel the vibration, but it was an intrusion he didn't mind. Carl loved the railroad as it gave him an illusion of escape. The billowing flight of a dozen Norfolk and Southern freight trains a day brought most of his neighbors to curse, not to mention it kept the property values down, but Carl always stopped whatever he was doing to watch or listen, and fantasized about jumping aboard and running off to some other life he couldn't imagine. At night the trains blended into his sleep, the cars clanging between the rails and pulsing through his subconscious.

He was snoring when the phone rang, but he managed to emerge from the depths and grab the receiver before the second ring.

"Put Miriam on," Ed said.

Carl pushed the door shut and ran his fingers through his hair.

"She's busy right now. She said she'd call you in a few days."

"What kind of crap are you pulling?"

"What kind of crap *am I* pulling?" Carl paced the room and knotted the phone cord. "How the hell do you tear a baby away from her mother?"

"That's none of your damn business."

Miriam ran up the stair and came in angry. "Don't," she said. "Give me the phone." She punched the phone's speaker button and the recorder. "What do you want, Ed?"

"You have no business taking her to Virginia. You're breaking the court order."

"I am not. It says nothing about taking her out-of-state."

"It says we have to agree on where you take her, and I never agreed to this."

"No, Ed. The court order says no such thing. My attorney said so and you have no say in the matter. I grew up here and I have friends here. I want Annaliese to know those friends."

"You didn't tell me where you were taking her. The order does say you have to keep me informed where she will be at all times."

"I told you three times of my intentions to bring her to Virginia, and I'm telling you again on the first evening we're here."

"I want to know where you take her every day."

"I'll call you every three days per the order."

"You tell me right now where you're going tomorrow and I want updates every night."

"Oh for Christ's sake," Carl belted out. He couldn't hold his anger any longer. He wished the guy was in the same room. He wished him dead. "You want to know what subversive acts we have planned, Ed? Tomorrow we're going to pick strawberries. Miriam mentioned something about baking a pie." She tried to shush him, pumping her hand up and down.

Ed said, "Okay smart ass –."

"The next day we're going to take her to the zoo in DC. Do you feel threatened by that?"

"Are you planning on marrying her?" Ed asked.

Carl stopped cold, his eyes locked on Miriam. "We're not dating, Ed. We never were. Your testimony was bullshit."

"Butt out. This is none of your business."

"It is my business when my guests are getting harassing phone calls."

"Ed," Miriam said. "We're staying here the whole two weeks. I'm not reporting to you every day. You don't need an hourly itinerary."

"We'll see what the judge says about that."

"I guess we will."

"And when can I expect a check?"

Miriam seethed, gritted her teeth. "I'm not working these two weeks."

"So you've blown off work?"

"I haven't blown off anything. I'm taking time to be with my daughter."

"You're already a month behind. Are you going to pay me my money?"

"I'll pay you."

"I want my money."

"I'll pay your damn money."

"If you can keep a job."

"Damn you."

"This is why you lost custody, Miriam."

"Don't get used to having her."

"The judge said I'm a better parent."

"You're an idiot."

"If you were a better mother –."

Carl lunged for the phone. "This conversation is over." He picked up the receiver and slammed it back down, knocking the recorder across the desk. Annaliese had been downstairs crying the whole time, but no one noticed until now. Miriam stormed out of the room. Carl examined the recorder and pushed rewind, doubting this was a call she wanted to keep.

Chapter 17

The doctor brought him in at the end of the session. Carl assumed, after the cursory look given him in the waiting room that the doctor was sizing him up, as if he were the one doing the abusing. Doctor Cecilia Ainsberg's handshake was cold and deliberate. She'd reached the age where she'd given up on her femininity, but compensated by buying expensive clothing to drape her widening body. She could fluctuate with ease from a dimpled approving smile to a deep penetrating stare that left no doubt of her seriousness or intelligence. She was completely sure of herself.

One side of her office was a glass wall facing a forest where the leaves formed shafts of sunlight making the room warm and inviting. A desk and computer were built into the far wall solid with books, though she appeared to do most of her work in a chair by the windows. The doctor motioned for Carl to sit. Miriam and Annaliese hovered over a low table in an anteroom, each with intent hands guiding fat crayons over a coloring book. Miriam looked hopeful as she rose to join them.

"Honey, I'm going to be right here," she said, but the girl dropped her crayon and ran to her, tearing at her dress as she sprung into her lap. "Careful," her mother winced, rubbing her breast where the girl had grabbed. The doctor watched them knowingly, as if she expected their every move. Miriam spoke before the doctor could sit down. "Carl's witnessed the whole thing," she said. "He saw her before all this and he knows what it's done to her." She turned to him. "Tell her how she was last spring."

The doctor interrupted. "Ms. Boyd, I asked him to come in since we're about to wrap up. The last thing I want to ask is what do you want from me?"

"I need you to write maybe a report or something about what this separation is doing to her. That it's harmful to her."

The doctor seemed to sense Miriam's frailty. "You're looking for something you can use in court." Miriam nodded as the doctor carefully chose her words. "I'm walking a fine line here. You said you have joint custody. I should be speaking to both parents."

"How can anyone determine if there's been abuse if the abusing parent will obviously never consent to an examination?"

"Abuse is hard to prove, and unfortunately it's not typically stopped until the child ends up hurt."

"But that's what I'm trying to avoid!"

"Ms. Boyd, I can see she's having separation anxiety, but there are no obvious signs of neglect here. And even if there was something tangible to report, I'm not licensed in the state of Florida. My conclusions may not be admissible in Florida court."

Miriam's eyes lit up. "I haven't shown you the video yet!" She grabbed her day-bag off the floor. "I have a video." Dr. Ainsberg looked like she was ready to put this one to rest, but relented when Miriam thrust the key-chain drive toward her. "Please let me show it to you. You'll see."

"Okay," she said, checking her watch. "Let's look at the video."

The doctor plugged it into her laptop with Miriam close behind, ready to give the play-by-play. Carl steered Annaliese away from the show, doing his best to occupy her. He glanced up once and caught the shaking camera hovering between the child's legs, zooming in on her red and swollen tissue.

"A bad rash," the doctor said.

"What I'm telling you is *he* caused it. It happened in *his* care. Annaliese is too old to be getting diaper rash. And she was out of diapers last spring. If it weren't for him –"

"Did you take her to a hospital?"

Miriam shook her head, her anger turning on herself.

"If you were that concerned – after all, you went to the trouble to record it – then why didn't you take her to the ER?" The doctor's professional demeanor was tinged with an air of scolding. "If you ever suspect child abuse, you need to report it immediately."

Miriam hung her head. "We were on the road."

"If the ER doctor suspects any wrongdoing, he can bring in child protective services. That will get you your day in court without having to worry about joint custody notification. How many days ago did this happen?"

"Five," Miriam said, diminished as a presence.

"And how is she now?"

They stared at Annaliese, whose hands were busy wrestling with Carl's upturned thumb. "Better," she said, "now that I have her."

"No doctor can make an accurate diagnosis from a video. Especially given what you're alleging. If any of this happens again and you suspect abuse, you need to report it immediately to the proper authorities. Do you understand?"

"Yes," she whispered.

Dr. Ainsberg sat at her writing desk and scribbled something on a piece of paper. "I'm only going to charge for a half hour," she said in Carl's direction.

"That's nice of you, but what are you going to do for me?"

"I can't do anything," the doctor said. "I suspect what you're saying has some truth in it, but the only thing I can do is treat her anxieties, and that requires a commitment. Right now you can't provide that commitment. If you get full custody, then I can help her with the transition, but right now I can't help you."

"You can't even write an opinion I can take back to the judge?"

"I'm afraid it would have no standing in Florida, not to mention I could be in ethical violation. I have no permission to examine her from the custodial parent."

"This isn't right."

"I'm sorry Ms. Boyd, but this is all I can do." She stood to signify the finality of the meeting.

Carl suspected as much. He knew this was a mistake, but Miriam had insisted. He pulled out his wallet.

"How much do we owe you?"

Chapter 18

Candlelight softened the walls and reflected in the windows from the votives she had lit. The flames danced as Miriam whisked by and burrowed under the blanket, joining them on the futon with a fresh bowl of popcorn. Carl grabbed the first handful as they watched an old Disney animation, the three of them nestled together as one family.

Halfway through the movie the house shuddered in two violent blows. Deep voiced men began screaming over the rush and rumble of footsteps like a platoon sent on some domestic liberation. A blazing light penetrated the blinds and there was crying through the walls, more shouts, someone barking orders.

Carl sprang up and ran barefoot to the front door, crouching low like he was taking fire. Miriam covered her daughter.

"Jesus," Carl uttered.

"What? What is it?"

At least a dozen cars formed a fan patterned barricade around the house, their headlights bearing down on the Kilgore's side like it was a Broadway stage. Some cars were unmarked, others were state troopers and at least half were county cruisers with their blue lights flashing, sending dance light flickers against the houses and into the trees. A swarm of men commandeered the street and the neighbor's yard, most in uniform, but others wearing blue wind breakers with a DEA patch on the breast. A select group of men wearing all black, their faces hidden under ski masks, were rushing in and out of the Kilgore's house.

"The whole cavalry is here," Carl said.

Annaliese wiggled from her mother's hold. "Lemee see," she said, trotting to Carl's side.

"Well me too," Miriam said. They all scrunched up together and glimpsed through the wood blinds at the comings and goings of gloved men with guns and flashing lights. "Holy shit," she whispered.

With an authoritative nod, Annaliese concurred. "Holy shit," the two-year-old said.

"Oh no." Her mother was mortified. "No, no, no," she pleaded. "Don't say that. Don't listen to mommy." She turned the girl around and squeezed both of her hands. "Please don't ever say that again. That was a bad word and mommy never should have said that." Carl couldn't help grinning, and Miriam caught it. "It's not funny. If she repeats it in front of Ed, it'll come back to burn me. Or you," she added.

"Listen to your mother," Carl said, without turning from the spectacle outside.

Miriam stroked her daughter's hair. "You don't need to see any of this. Let's put you to bed."

"Put her in our room," Carl said, before standing and opening the front door. "No use in hiding. We didn't do anything wrong." Miriam scooped up Annaliese and carried her upstairs, while Carl stepped onto the porch where he could better see and hear the application of law.

There were men converging on the Kilgore house with plastic boxes, clear rubber gloves and forensic kits. In a patch of dirt in the front yard sat Dale Kilgore with his arms cinched behind his back. He was shirtless, and blood from his lower lip was splattered on his chest.

"I ain't got nothing on me," Dale cried. A DEA agent in a blue windbreaker motioned for him to stand. "Not out here, man. Come'on," he pleaded, as if he'd suffered this indignity before.

"Stand up," the agent said. Dale stood and a second agent lowered his frayed jean shorts to his ankles. "Step out." He did so and the agent picked up the shorts and examined them, running his hand along the in-seam, feeling his way along while the first agent held a flashlight that doubled as a billy club. He removed a small seed from the front pocket and held it up so both could examine it. One nodded and the other put the shorts into a plastic evidence bag. Dale was ready for the public stocks, stripped to his briefs, glancing around at imagined neighbors in the shadows. "Now sit down," the agent told him.

"Come'on man," Dale repeated. The officer with the flashlight took one of his arms and forced him to the ground, where he sat among his children's battered toys. Though it was a warm evening, he hunched over and shivered, looked like he might throw his head back and howl.

The agent in charge of the operation was pacing across the Kilgore's porch, barking orders over his cell phone and flexing his pecs through his tee-shirt. "I've never seen anything like this," he said in disgust. "Knee-high garbage in every room and the whole place smells like feces. We could condemn it from the kitchen alone. No, she wasn't here. Yes, send them down. Two boys . . . preschool. We're not taking in the old man. He's in there rubbing his chest. The ambulance is on the way."

When he was off the phone, Carl faced him at the edge of the porch. "Mind sharing what y'all all are doing?"

The agent turned as if being challenged. "This is none of your concern, sir."

"My house shook like an earthquake when you rammed in their front door. You could say I'm a little concerned."

A hooded agent carrying a cardboard box marched out of the house toward an unmarked car, while another man went in to replace him. The agent in charge let them pass before replying. "I can't comment on an ongoing investigation." He kicked aside a last splinter of the front door into the yard with the rest of it. "You should go back inside until this is over."

Carl wasn't used to being told what to do, so he settled into the wooden rocker on his porch. For once it was Carl staring into the Kilgore's yard for entertainment. Miriam stood inside the screen door.

"You put her down already?" he asked her.

"She was easy this time," Miriam answered in a puzzled tone. "What about those kids?" she said from the shadows.

"I think someone's coming for them."

Miriam pumped her fist. "Yes," she whispered.

Several cameras flashed, and it was evident the local papers were getting the story. Two squad cars backed out so an approaching ambulance could get close to the house. Dale's lips were parted and he rocked a bit, but made no visible sign when the paramedics rushed past carrying their white boxes. A few minutes later a sedan with black lettering on the side from Compton Social Services pulled up behind the cruisers. A lanky gentleman with a spidery carriage slipped out of the driver's side, and a younger brown-haired woman charged ahead of him. They wore baby-blue collared shirts and the woman carried two stuffed bears. She marched with such purpose that all the uniformed men in her path stepped aside.

"Look," Miriam said, as if watching angels about to perform miracles.

They cut across the Kilgore's yard, showing no regard for the naked handcuffed man sitting in the dirt. Dale twisted and spat at them. "What you gonna to do with them? Them's my boys!"

A man in Dale's position didn't require acknowledgment, so the case workers said nothing and met the lead officer on the porch where he was conducting the operation. "We have them upstairs" he said as they all stepped inside.

Dale shook his head and stamped his heel in the dirt. "God damn'em," he cried.

An odd assortment of things began coming out of the house, men carrying plastic evidence bags full of unassuming objects; plastic Tupperware bowls and a woman's make-up kit, a clock radio with its back hanging off and old tin canisters that might have once held flower or sugar. They stowed it all in the trunks of unmarked cars and slammed the lids shut.

When the lead agent came back out, he motioned to his second, who took Dale's arm and forced him to stand.

"Time to take you in," he said, as if fed up seeing him there in the dirt.

"What you gonna to do with my boys?"

"They're the last thing you need to worry about right now."

Two county officers met him at the squad car, and one put a hand on Dale's head and pushed him in the back seat. The officer wiped his hand on his pants leg before revving the cruiser. He backed out and roared off toward town with Dale staring pathetically out the back window.

The lead agent nodded once to his team and stepped off the porch. They all converged on the far side of the yard where they spoke to each other in hushed tones and folded their arms. They were completely silent when the children appeared. Each boy was led by a social worker and each clutched a brown bear to his chest, though neither appeared aware of it. The eldest boy, Russell, was being led by the hand of the lanky gentleman who was chronically stooped over. The boy strutted out like a man in control and forever would be. No stuffed animal would bring either influence or solace. Behind them the woman was guiding Kyle, though much more slowly. He'd been crying and crying hard, his face bent from its normal shape. When he wouldn't step off the porch, the woman drew the boy near and whispered something to him. She lifted him into her arms and he laid his head on her shoulder. When she stepped off the porch, he raised his head and bit her ear. The woman screamed, almost dropping the child, but held on as she yanked her head back and twisted him away. Two agents ran toward her, but she waved them off.

"No, no, no," she said, grimacing. "You're not what he needs." She pressed her ear to her shoulder and eased the boy to the ground. "They're not what you need, are they?" Kyle stood there frozen, face bent, squinting through wet eyes. The caseworker massaged her ear matted with blood, while the other hand combed the boy's hair back. She managed a smile. "So does this mean you're hungry? How about we get you something good to eat?"

The boy went easily now, like he'd released something caged and tormenting inside him. The woman led him to the car. Carl watched the scene from his rocker, Miriam peered from behind the screen door and the little girl who had made such an impression on the boys stood in silhouette in an upper window. More flash-bulbs caught the scene.

In another hour the authorities were clearing out. Having found what they wanted, the police, deputies and DEA agents were climbing into their cruisers and fanning into the night. The paramedics were the last to leave the house, and they shook their heads while they spoke to the lead agent.

"The old man won't come," one of them said. "Doesn't like hospitals."

"He looked pretty bad."

"His vitals are stable. We gave him a tranquilizer and left him in bed."

The street eventually cleared and the invaded block went back to normal, though the moonless night seemed blacker and quieter than usual. A crazy bat whirled in loops around the street light and the insects sang their piercing songs. By the time Carl retired from the rocker on the porch, the movie had run out. Upstairs he found Annaliese in his own bed, wrapped safely in her mother's arms.

Chapter 19

Hard oak chairs lined the corridor in the Dixon County Courthouse, where citizens could sit and admire oil paintings of the seminal events in Florida history, including the vanquishing of the Spanish, the Seminole Wars and the forced exodus of the indigenous peoples. The vinyl floor was polished to an institutional grey glow that reflected citizens gathered outside each closed chamber door, many of whom appeared to be there against their will. Carl sat alone with one leg crossed over the other and arms folded. His hands were sweating and he stared with great concentration at the pressed fold in his slacks where it disappeared at the knee. Like a tethered dog, he wanted to chew through the leash holding him there and run, but he just sat and tried to cleanse his mind.

The door across from him opened and a freckled women in a brown business suit stuck her head into the corridor. Cold and dour, she said his name and slipped from sight. Before Carl stood, she opened a second door into the chamber. He stepped cautiously as if there were something to sign or a toll to pay. When he passed through the second door, she said, "You'll sit there," and pointed. The hearing was being held in a conference room lined with walnut paneling, the longest wall so solid with law books, so rank and uniform he wondered if they were real or had ever been opened. There was an artificial calm in the room, one imposed rather than formed out of consideration. He wouldn't have been surprised to see any one of those present pipe up and start hurling accusations across the table.

He took his seat at the far end of a ten foot conference table, opposite Judge Hawkins, who was staring off to one side with his chin resting on a bent thumb. His deep bronze skin might have been applied in a booth, which only heightened the effect of his white shock of hair. Combed back and full of body, it looked bleached, if not powdered, and Carl imagined him lifting it off his head each evening and storing it in a box. His fingernails were manicured to an unnatural sheen and the deep frown lines around his mouth made his smile unimaginable. He was outrageous, attractive and stern. He looked like he'd gone through many wives, or at least many other men's wives.

To Carl's left sat Marshall Coulton, the man to whom he'd recently sent an additional five hundred dollar retainer. His face was plump, the red of Virginia clay and ready to pop from the pressure of his neck tie. His open briefcase was filled with manila folders bounded with rubber bands. He lowered a handkerchief from his nose and poured over the mess of notes before him. Miriam sat next to him, closest to the judge, though she was turned away is if in physical aversion to the man. She'd spent all morning obsessing in her closet for whatever said modest and motherly. She chose a yellow dress tied off at the waist, with a high neckline that left her breasts to the imagination.

Opposite Coulton rested Elizabeth Shanks, Esquire. She was no more than thirty, with jet black hair pulled tight and fastened in a ball with two sticks. She wore a loose jacket the shade of kiwi over a white blouse exposing her pale and powdery neck. She had looks and pluck and a charmed approach that could either seduce or crucify. The three folders in front of her were precisely aligned, making Carl believe they were doomed. To her right, across from Miriam, sat the defendant, Ed Groeper, sitting at attention, so still and proper a well-dressed mannequin could have taken his place.

The secretary followed Carl to his seat where she told him to swear an oath on a book he had little confidence in. When he said, "I do," to the promise of speaking the truth, the truth in a place where so many lies had been told, the irony of that same simple vow used to confirm a marriage was not lost to him.

Judge Hawkins, chin still firmly planted on thumb, raised his hand toward Coulton and closed his eyes. To this understated gesture, Coulton cleared his throat.

"Mr. Rittenhaur, will you give your full name and address for the record." After he did so, Coulton adjusted himself and faced Carl like talking to an old friend. "Now Carl, how long have you known Miriam?"

"Fourteen years, give or take." Carl was sitting straight and alert, but weary as if the simplest question might pose a threat.

"Almost half your lives."

"Yes." He had never thought of it that way.

"And how would you describe her as a mother?"

"She's a wonderful mother. She's always nearby, she cooks for Annaliese, she reads to her, she tucks her in every night. She's very good with her." He realized he was rattling on.

"So you can attest to the bond between Miriam Boyd and Annaliese."

"Absolutely."

Marshall shifted the glasses on his nose. "Have you seen any change in the child since before the divorce?"

"Yes. She's gained a lot of weight –."

"Objection," Shanks cut in. "The witness never knew the child prior to the divorce. This was the period when he was having an affair with the mother."

"I was not having an affair –."

Judge Hawkins broke in, but kept his eyes shut. "Sustained. The witness will confine himself to answering the question."

"Judge," Coulton continued. "He met the child at or about the time of the divorce. I'm sure the precise date is in my papers here, but let me rephrase the question." He raised his handkerchief and blew his nose again. "Have you seen any change in the child since you met her?"

"As I was saying, yes. She's gained all sorts of weight. She's never happy anymore. When we pick her up for visitation she doesn't talk. She's always depressed."

"Objection. The witness is not an expert in child psychology."

"Sustained."

"Skip the diagnosis, Carl." Marshall regarded him kindly, trying to settle him down. "Just give us your observations."

"You can't get the pacifier away from her. She's having accidents, so she's back in diapers again. Miriam can't leave the room without the child screaming. The girl won't even go to sleep without lying in her mother's arms."

Coulton shuffled the papers in front of him. "Carl, have you ever witnessed a physical altercation between Miriam and her ex-husband."

"Yes. I saw him grab her twice."

"He grabbed her in what way?"

"By the arm both times. Once when she was picking up Annaliese, and again when she dropped her off."

"And he did this violently?"

"I would say so." Carl detailed how Ed grabbed Miriam in the restaurant and the altercation in the parking lot. By the time he finished, his throat was dry.

"Judge, we're ready for the video."

Judge Hawkins showed little interest. "Do you think this is necessary, counselor?"

"Yes, Judge, I do. Mr. Rittenhaur was there and can testify to its veracity."

The secretary took the thumb drive from Marshall Coulton and plugged it into a monitor in the corner of the room. After a few seconds the screen brightened to Annaliese's sleeping face, her lips pursed open in a kiss. The frame panned down her body, over her pj tops to her naked and spread legs and the burning rash between.

"Objection! This is outrageous!" said Elizabeth Shanks.

"Turn the tape off," the judge snapped, and the secretary did so.

"Judge, this was six weeks ago at the beginning of her summer visitation. This was the condition the child was in when the defendant turned her over to the mother. Mr. Rittenhaur was present at the time this video was shot."

"Yes, I was," Carl said meekly.

"Carl, precisely where and when was this video shot and what were the circumstances that led to it?"

"Miriam and I picked up Annaliese for the two-week visitation last month. We spent those weeks up in Virginia. On the way up Miriam had to change her at a rest stop." His voice cracked. For as careful as he was trying to be, something about Miriam's stern unblinking profile unnerved him. "That's when we discovered the abuse."

"Objection. There has been no *abuse*. This is a simple case of diaper rash."

"Miriam filmed it as soon as we got to my house."

"Your honor," Shanks protested. "I object to these inflammatory tactics. This is nothing but a cheap attempt to smear my client."

"Sustained." The judge pointed down the table. "Mr. Coulton, I had my own children and I remember what diaper rash looks like. This proves nothing and the court is offended at having been presented this video. Do you have anything of substance to ask this witness?"

Miriam sank in her chair. Coulton fingered through his papers, trying to regain some dignity. "I have no further questions for this witness, judge."

"We would like to cross-examine, your honor." Shanks looked seasoned and ready for the game. Though her build was attractive, her cheeks and fingers were plump, and Carl knew she would be fat one day and took comfort in the thought. Judge Hawkins settled back into his usual posture, angled across the room, eyes closed.

"Yes or no, Mr. Rittenhaur. Every time you've seen the child with the mother she's been worse than before."

"It's not because of the mother."

The judge slapped his hand on the table. "You will answer the question as asked, either yes or no." Carl hesitated and sought out Marshall for help, but he didn't even raise a brow.

"Yes," he said.

"What is your relationship with the mother?"

"We're friends," Carl said. Against his wishes, Miriam had decided not to reveal their relationship in the hearing so as not to validate the alleged affair.

"But you have been romantically involved with the plaintiff?"

"That was a long time ago."

"Yes or no will do. Have you ever been romantically involved with the plaintiff?"

Carl watched the judge raise his hand, though he answered the question before he brought it down. "Yes," he said.

Miriam made no visible reaction.

Ms. Shanks opened another folder, took out a photo and slid it across the table to Carl. "Is this your house in Virginia, the one where you and the plaintiff kept Annaliese?" The photo showed Carl's house with most of the front porch demolished and a pile of scrap wood devouring the yard.

"That was last spring. I was rebuilding the porch."

She handed him a second photo at a wider angle, showing Carl's and the Kilgore's attached houses. The Kilgore's porch sagged to the right, the asbestos tile siding was cracked and peeling, and a front window was stuffed with a pillow where a pane was missing. "And is this your house on the left?"

"Yes."

"Your honor, please note the house on the right in this photo." She passed out extra copies to the judge and to Marshall Coulton. "Four weeks ago today this house was the scene of a major drug arrest involving the local authorities, the Virginia State Troopers and the DEA. One arrest was made and there's an outstanding warrant on a second inhabitant of that property." She passed out a third photo, this one a night shot of the raid showing Carl in the rocker on his porch, Miriam's silhouette in the screen door, and above them Annaliese's unmistakable face pressed to the bedroom window. For the first time ever, Miriam cringed at the sight of her daughter. "Mr. Rittenhaur, is this you and Ms. Boyd and Annaliese in this photograph?"

He studied the image and tried to remember the photographers he assumed were from the newspaper that night. "Looks that way."

"And you find it appropriate to have a child this age exposed to a drug bust?"

"With all the police, I'd say it was the safest place in town."

"Do you find it appropriate to raise a child in this drug-infested neighborhood?" Before he answered, she added, "Next to a crack house?"

"That's only one bad house."

"Mr. Rittenhaur, were you present when the plaintiff took Annaliese to see Dr. Cecilia Ainsberg?"

Marshall Coulton looked on his client with shock, clearly taken off guard. Carl also focused on Miriam and hesitated. What did they know? his eyes asked.

"Your honor," Shanks said. "The witness is being coached by the plaintiff."

"I am not." Carl straightened his posture. "Miriam was concerned after she discovered the rash. She wanted Annaliese seen by a doctor."

"But wouldn't it have been more appropriate to see a medical doctor than a child psychologist?"

"I'm not a medical expert. You already declared me unfit to answer such questions."

The judge tapped his fingers on the table, ready to come down hard again. "The witness will keep his attitude in check."

Shanks persisted. "I'm asking for your layman's opinion."

"She did the right thing."

"Did the plaintiff say anything to you about informing her ex-husband of her decision to seek medical advice?"

"No."

"In fact, the doctor refused to write a report when she found out this was a joint custody situation, and that the mother was trying to hide information from the father."

"Is that a question?"

"Your honor, this goes to show how the plaintiff will stop at nothing to smear and defame her ex-husband. Ms. Boyd petitions the court to have another psychological evaluation, then thumbs her nose at the legal process by taking her daughter to a psychologist before we've even had the hearing. And now these unnecessary trips to the doctor may have long-term repercussions on the child." Carl leaned back and shook his head, though there was no surprise on Miriam's face. "Mr. Rittenhaur, you mentioned the child's weight several times. Did you weigh the child when you met her?"

"No."

"And do you know her current weight?"

"No."

"Are you familiar with height and weight growth charts for infants?"

"No."

"Are you currently in a sexual relationship with the plaintiff?"

"Objection," Coulton said, but Carl countered anyway.

"I don't see where that's anyone's business."

The judge lurched in his chair and his voice ripped across the room. "The witness will answer the question."

Carl's eyes fixed on the glassy conference table that captured the judge's reflection. At this point he didn't care how bad it all sounded.

"No. We're just friends."

"Do you really expect us to believe that?"

"I'm just helping my friend."

Ms. Shanks turned over a page and examined a new one before presenting the next question. She tipped her head and asked, "Is Ms. Boyd still working at the Holidaze Gentleman's Club in Daytona Beach?"

Carl's face drained of blood and spirit. "What?" he said, but *what the fuck* was what he meant.

"Judge, I object," Coulton cut in. "This has nothing to do with the purpose of this hearing or the well-being of the child."

"Is she still stripping for tips?" Shanks persisted.

"Objection, Judge," Coulton tried again.

Carl filled with anger. "She's a waitress at the Rib House in Dixon County." He glared at Miriam, not believing, but also believing fully. Like the judge, her eyes were closed, but her mouth hung open like she was recovering from a blow to the gut. Across from her, Ed Groeper formed one of his rare thin-lipped smiles.

"Are the two of you living together out-of-state in a drug-ridden neighborhood?"

"Judge, this is badgering. The witness has answered the questions."

Judge Hawkins checked his watch. "Is that all for this witness?" Both attorneys rested and the judge waved his hand.

Back in the corridor, Carl paced in a tight oval with his shoes sliding on the glossy floor tile. Hands on hips, jacket thrown back, he cleared a path that no one dared to cross. Ten minutes later, Marshall stepped out with Miriam under one arm. Her eyes were closed and she was sobbing. Marshall led her down the hall, away from the judge's chambers and sat her down. She drew her arms around her breasts. Marshall sat by her as Carl approached them.

"What the fuck was that?"

"Come now," Marshall said to him, still comforting Miriam.

"Who's suing who here?"

Coulton was sympathetic, exasperated and shaking his head. "I've never seen anything like that. In all my years, I've never seen a judge not respond to my objections."

"He doesn't care," Miriam piped up. "He'll never reverse his decision. He's more concerned with being right than with the welfare of my child."

Coulton got firm with her. "Miriam, now why in God's name did you take your child to a psychologist when that's what we were petitioning to have done legitimately?"

"I couldn't wait for that. She was suffering too much."

"Don't you see how you've undermined our case? The judge won't be inclined to authorize anything of the kind now."

Carl cut in and demanded, "Why the hell didn't you do something when I was getting grilled?"

"Look, young man. This is a small jurisdiction and I do have other cases out here. When I feel a judge is on edge, I have to lay back. Any good attorney has to, else the next time I go to Judge Hawkins bar he's sure to rule against me."

"So it's not about the credibility of the case, it's about the judge's mood? It's about not getting on the judge's shit list?"

"Get on a judge's bad side and you'll never win a case. Then everyone loses. That's just the way it is. What I don't get is why he's being this way on this particular case. I've stood before Judge Hawkins before and he's always been straight and fair."

"Well this is bullshit. We have a judge who's biased and an attorney who's afraid to do his job." Carl scuffed by him.

Marshall checked the time, angrily tapping his wrist. "That's not fair of you. Not fair at all." He rose and faced him down. "You have to be realistic. You have to understand how things work and you don't. I take winnable cases. Clients who've been genuinely wronged. I don't make frivolous charges on my clients' behalf. If I cross the line with a judge, then I stand to harm every client I'll ever have. Good clients. Good people. I have a fine line to walk."

Miriam stood and collected herself. "When will we know?"

Coulton grabbed his briefcase and tried to put on a positive front. "We didn't even have all our witnesses, but we might still have a chance. Stranger things have happened. The judge should have a decision in a few days. Now I have to be in court in Jacksonville in an hour and I barely have time. I have your numbers. I'll let you know as soon as I hear anything." Before he left, Marshall gave Carl a look saying he was sorry for the whole damn thing, sorry even for leaving him there alone with Miriam. Carl let him pass from sight before turning to her.

"Where was Janine Haygood? I thought she was supposed to testify."

"She didn't show up."

"What else happened in there? What about the battery?"

"The judge didn't do anything about it. Ed's attorney brought up the child support. I'm already $825 behind. And they had more photos of the drug bust."

"That bastard probably *called in* the drug bust. I'd like to know who he knows up there."

"I called it in."

"You what?"

"They were dealing right off the front porch, Carl. I couldn't have Annaliese near that."

Carl had a punch list of questions for her, but didn't know how to ask them, nor was he ready for the answers. He studied Miriam, trying to picture a different side of her, a side he never imagined. The assemblage of all he knew about her didn't add up to the woman in front of him.

There was more chatter from inside chambers, and Carl took Miriam's hand and led her down the hall. Elizabeth Shanks and Ed Groeper stepped out looking confident, as if a secret deal had been struck. When they slipped through the double doors, Ed dropped a hand to his attorney's ass and squeezed.

Chapter 20

Miriam did little to settle into her apartment in the intermittent weeks she spent in Florida. Unpacked boxes outnumbered empty ones and were piled high against bare walls, giving the rooms the feel of an abandoned storeroom. The kitchen counters were littered with carry-out menus, Chinese food cartons, and leaking pouches of ketchup and soy sauce. Only on weekends with Annaliese would Miriam cook full meals. So long as she was alone, there was only energy for the same fast-food crap that was fattening her daughter.

Carl woke from a nap on the couch and didn't recognize the room at first. He sat there rubbing his eyes. The place smelled of disinfectant and nicotine. On the television the Marlins were playing some team he didn't recognize, and the announcers, even in their more animated calls, made only a static white noise that numbed the room. He stumbled off to take a leak, and over the sound of his stream he heard Miriam clicking furiously on the computer keyboard. The weekend was restless and scarcely a word exchanged. When he opened the bedroom door, Miriam diminished one window after another on the monitor.

"I got an e-mail from Janine Haygood," she said. "The daycare center wouldn't give her the afternoon off. They apparently frown on their employees getting involved in these things."

"They're worried about liability?"

"The manager threatened to fire her if she testified."

Carl leaned on the jamb and nodded at her papers. "What are you working on?"

Miriam looked feverish and determined. Her hair was pinned up, but several tired strands dangled over her cheeks like Spanish moss. The computer desk where she worked was held together with flimsy metal rods, making the whole thing look like it might collapse.

"I'm trying to make contacts. Legal aid. Child advocacy groups. Whatever I can find." The computer chimed and she checked her e-mail. "This might be it," she said. The first page on screen was Coulton's letterhead. She sent it to the printer and scrolled to the second and third pages, all in legalese and containing the judge's order – it was dated the same day as the hearing. Miriam read the first paragraph. "No change," she said, her voice hard and dour. "Bastard! What the hell kind of judge won't even allow a child to be seen by a doctor?"

Carl took the copy off the printer. "We expected this, Miriam. After that hearing, this was not unexpected."

She leapt up and launched the chair behind her, slamming it into the wall where it made a moon shaped dent in the gypsum board. "Don't tell me what I expected! I didn't expect this. I didn't expect *any* of this." She pointed at his chest. "They took my child away. How can you look at me and tell me this is expected!"

"That's not how I meant it."

"You know what it's like to lose a parent just as well as I do. Now Annaliese has lost her mother for no damn good reason and she's suffering for it." She pushed by him and stormed into the kitchen, walking with a decided bias on her heels. Carl traced a finger along the dent in the wall before following. She threw a bottle cap from her beer at the trash can and missed. "All they do is twist the truth into lies, and they get away with it every time. They assert and assert without a scrap of evidence. They lied about our supposed affair, they lied about my job, they lied about his stalking, they lied to my boss and coworkers. Then I have to spend all my time defending myself instead of getting across all the bullshit he's been doing." She was out of breath, panting like she'd witnessed a violent crime. "All I've done is tell the truth and I've been burned for it."

"We lied about our relationship."

Walking away, she said, "I don't know what our relationship is anymore."

After a moment of searching, Carl conceded, "Neither do I."

"Forget it." She gave her bottle a whoop-de-doo twirl and dropped onto the couch. She muted the baseball game and stared at it absently.

Carl spotted the bottle cap on the floor and kicked it out of sight under the stove. "I need to leave tomorrow."

"That's fine. Just fine."

"Granddad needs me for some work on the farm. His hip is getting pretty bad. He's using a cane now. And next week I have to start on lesson plans for the Fall."

"Go. You've done enough. I'll fight the damn thing by myself."

Carl's anger reared up. "Stop playing the martyr. You're not the only one suffering. You're not the only one sacrificing either."

Still angry, but with less rage in her voice, Miriam admitted, "I know that." Carl was always amazed how her anger could peak and plummet in the space of a heart pulse, which was something he never knew how to deal with. It took him days, even weeks to move past an argument, his own rage subsiding like the waning moon, one night at a time. The room was still and she took a gulp of beer from her bottle. "I appreciate what you've done."

He avoided the subject all weekend, tried to block it from his mind, but it kept bubbling back up like a simmering reflux in his chest. He even considered approaching it in a letter where he might not have to face her, but now that they were talking it needed to come out. The words came hard.

"How long did you work in a strip club?"

She likely knew the question was coming, but was still pale with embarrassment. "I was only a waitress there. I was never on stage."

"When was this?"

"Three or four years ago."

"You were dating him then?"

She stared at some space beyond the walls. "He thought he was really something," she said, clearly disgusted. "I met him there. He was disappointed when I quit. I think he liked the idea – " She drifted off.

"What idea?" Carl asked, thinking Ed was incapable of an idea.

"He would bring in his buddies to show me off. Like they'd never seen tits before."

"You were topless?"

She whispered, "After a few weeks I got used to it. The tips were so good –"

He didn't want to know the specifics of her outfit. What she'd done with her life made his organs swim. It wasn't her exposure that bothered him, but the ways and means of her exposure. Carl painted nudes in college and loved rendering the body's strangeness and sacredness and soft perfection, but he retched at the image of Miriam flaunting her body for sale, wasting it on cold tips from men with liquored breaths and the hands of a man bent on defacing her. He felt she'd been defiled, cheapened by lust, raped with golden showers, and he wanted to somehow resanctify her, to place her properly and put her in a better light. At that moment, he didn't blame her for anything.

"We need to set up the second two-week visitation," he said.

"Ed refused to do it until after the hearing. He was waiting for the judge to say I couldn't take her out-of-state."

Carl went back for the crumpled order. "There's nothing here that changes the original visitation. You can bring her back up next weekend."

"I guess so."

"Let's call him and set it up."

"My God, I can't talk to that man right now."

"I'm afraid you're going to have to get used to it. We're going to have to tangle with him for another sixteen years."

"Fuck." She sat there staring into her half empty bottle before sulking off to the desk. She grabbed the phone and set the recorder. A ring sounded over the earpiece.

"Yes, Miriam?" Ed sounded well and satisfied, with a voice of patronizing concern.

"This conversation is being recorded."

"Whatever."

"We need to set up Annaliese's next two-week visitation."

"It's too late for that."

"I have the judge's order and there's no change. I'm taking her back to Virginia for the second two weeks."

"No you're not. Summer's over."

"The hell it is."

"Labor Day is in two weeks and I have her that holiday. Summer's over."

"Summer isn't over until September 21st. You're the one who kept putting this off."

"Too late now. You can have your regular visitation next weekend, but she's not leaving the state."

"I don't believe this. I —."

"You're not planning on running with her, are you? Maybe *I'm* the one who should be recording this conversation."

Miriam stood, exasperated. "I get another two weeks!" she cried.

"The official school year calendar starts on Labor Day. Same with preschool. You should plan better next year."

"Bastard." She punched a button on the phone, but hit the wrong one and knocked the tape recorder to the floor.

Ed's voice dribbled out of the speaker, dull as a used razor. "I'd like to get a copy of this recording, Miriam."

"Fuck you!" She pounded every button on the keypad until the line went dead. "He'll get away with it. You watch." She kicked the recorder across the room and it smashed into in the same corner where the chair left its impression. Her file folders containing every scrap of legalese she'd collected were on a side table, and she opened one and frantically paged through it. "It says I get *two* two-week *summer* visitations. It doesn't say a thing about Labor Day." Her hands were shaking.

"To hell with him," Carl said. "He's the one in violation here, not you. Bring her up next week anyway."

"He'll use it against me."

"How can he do that? He has to give you the second visitation."

She whipped around to face him. "Because nobody listens to me. Nobody believes me." Her every muscle was taut as she rifled through her papers. Carl leaned against the door jamb, numb and powerless.

Chapter 21

Carl was thankful when the school year began. Having left Miriam in Florida, he was again able to fill his life with routine, though it was a lonely routine, and put some space between himself and this situation that deep down inside he knew was unsustainable. He felt her slipping away again. Something had to give.

Whenever he had time, between working on his house and helping his declining grandfather, Carl drove the back roads of the Piedmont searching for another property he could afford in hope of sparking things forward again. But Miriam had abandoned all ideas of moving forward – she was too wrapped up in settling the past. Though blind to her own infractions, she couldn't move beyond Ed's false accusations, character assassination and twisting of facts. And the child closing down and regressing with each visitation only pulled her down further. By the end of summer Miriam's depression was evident. She wasn't interested in hearing about Carl's plans for a home they would all share, a home that might couple with a marriage license and persuade the judge to reverse custody. Instead she settled into a kind of obsessive self-paralysis.

During the last week of August, Carl prepped his classroom for the school year, taking inventory and placing orders for paper, Prizmacolors and charcoal pencils. Going through the supply room made him feel child-like again and aware that through these mediums was how he best coped with life. And it was not lost to him that since Miriam reentered his life he'd abandoned his art. Not since the afternoon Annaliese pranced into his back yard and made her white powdery explosion had Carl raised his hammer and chisel. The caps on his tubes of paint were crusted dry, and his palette gathered no color but a dull grey skim of dust.

On the first day of class he was confronted with the usual seventh and eighth grader apathy, but now he thought he could better understand them. In a way he welcomed it. He found himself doing what he'd never done before – he watched each student intently, wondering how they were being brought up, what their parents were like and who they were behind their pimply masks. He searched for parallels to his own bouts of apathy, postulating that to better understand his students might allow him to better understand himself.

On the Thursday afternoon after Labor Day he arrived home to a flashing red light on his phone, and he knew his quiet routine wouldn't last. Though it wasn't unusual to find a message of Miriam's latest grievances and spend an hour on the phone calming her down, this time the light was flashing a subliminal code telling him something was horribly wrong. Miriam's shrill and panicked words spilled from the recorder and flooded the room. He grabbed the phone and dialed.

"What's this? What are you saying?" Carl asked.

"There's a hearing tomorrow. *Tomorrow*. Coulton doesn't know anything about it." Carl suspected her attorney wanted to wash his hands of the case, even though they were ahead on the retainer.

"When did you hear about it?"

"Work, Carl. I have to take off work."

"You just got served today?"

"I never *got* served. A secretary at Shank's office left me a *courtesy* call. I can't afford to take another day off work. Friday's one of the best days for tips."

"Call the clerk's office."

"I did. I keep getting put on hold for twenty minutes at a time. No one will talk to me."

"What did Coulton say?"

"He can't go. He's already tied up with other cases."

"He didn't get served on your behalf?"

"No. He doesn't know a thing about it. And I'm going to lose another day's pay. Ed fucking knows that."

Carl felt a tightening under his breast plate. Each of her calls was worse than the last, but he'd never heard her this frantic. "Call the clerk again," he coached her. "Demand to talk to someone."

"All I get is a machine." The line was silent except for her breathing. "I can't do this."

"Yes, you can. Just ask for the hour off. Take a long lunch break."

"The hearings never start on time. And I have to go home and get dressed. I have to get my papers organized. Dammit, my best money comes on that shift, Carl. If I'm not there for lunch, there's no reason to go."

"Can't you trade off with someone?"

"None of the full-timers will give up happy hour for the lunch shift. And besides, I have to pick up Annaliese." Her voice crackled over the receiver. "Can you come down?" she pleaded.

He slid the mouthpiece to his cheek.

"Jesus, Miriam. This is the first week of school."

"Fine then." Some switch was flipped and Miriam's attitude soured. "I'll deal with it myself."

"Look," he said, "I have to make a living too. How do you expect me to help with the apartment and the attorney if I lose my job?"

"I thought you might stand by me, but I guess I was wrong."

"I've wanted to stand by you for years. You don't make it easy."

Her voice thundered over the receiver like some decree of damnation. "I lost my child!"

The room was no more than a stage with Carl standing naked in the center, awaiting verdict from some high character judge. He knew he couldn't use the past on her anymore. She was too busy fighting in her own narrow slice of history to be concerned with Carl's paltry epic. He also knew Annaliese had gotten no better over the past weeks.

He hung up and dialed his school, left a message with the new principal's secretary that he was going to miss the fourth day of classes for personal reasons. This was not a reasonable thing to do on the first week of school. He packed a bag for a long weekend and pointed his truck south.

Late that evening in a truck stop parking lot near Dillon, South Carolina, he sprawled out across his front seat and tried to catch a few hours of sleep. He lay there listening to the footsteps of strangers and the passing rigs grinding their low gears on the way to who knows where. The overcast sky filtered through the bug-splattered windshield and glowed orange and murky from the truck stop lights. A radio sounded from a nearby rig, and he listened to the bass line of an old Johnny Cash tune his grandfather used to play on the phonograph. His thoughts drifted to Annaliese and how she was holding up. He remembered those brief few minutes with her on the beach when he tasted another way of life and how that life appealed to him. Miriam said the girl rarely spoke anymore and had withdrawn from her daycare classmates. The whole last weekend visitation with her mother, she scarcely opened up at all. To Carl this was all the more reason to demand those last two weeks of summer visitation, and he told Miriam so, but she was too terrified of the court to chance it. He watched her paralysis grow, first by anger, then by fear. A part of him understood.

∞

He arrived in town only ten minutes before the scheduled hearing, as he'd dozed off at the rest stop and slept until sunrise. Without enough time to stop at Miriam's apartment, he went straight to the courthouse and waited for her on the brick steps. He stared out across the town green at the commercial strip, with its awnings drawn tight over the storefronts. The corner lunch counter was full of hungry patrons, and a man crossing the street was using a newspaper to fan himself. A nearby flock of birds was tearing apart a pile of trash overflowing from a garbage can. The humidity was offensive, but its haze actually seemed to filter and tame the sun's oppressive rays. Carl sweated badly, so he laid his tweed sport jacket on the steps, revealing a shirt that looked like he'd found it under a seat cushion. With ringed eyes and mussed hair, he resembled a vagrant crapped out on drugs, awaiting a trial of his own. Sheriff's deputies in their brown shirts stepped in and out of the old Georgian courthouse and eyed him like a convict who should never have been granted parole. He wished one of them would question him, try to chip away and uncover his offenses, and he conceived clever comebacks and smart-ass remarks that would make good stories in later years.

Miriam appeared from the side of the courthouse with a fat batch of files under each arm. Carl grabbed his jacket and ran to meet her, offered to carry her load, but she refused. She was too wired to slow down.

"I was afraid you wouldn't show," she said.

"I didn't have time to get to your apartment." He pulled a rolled tie from his pocket and wrapped it around his neck as he walked her into the main hall and down the corridor to the clerk's window. She sat the files on the counter and waved through the inch thick security glass, flagging a mousy secretary who was pecking at a keyboard.

"I'm here for Groeper versus Boyd."

"One moment." She picked up the phone and whispered into it. After hanging up she left the room and closed the door. A second woman was busy reviewing a manifest, placing little checkmarks beside culpable names. Miriam joined Carl on an oak bench across from the window.

"What did Coulton make of all this?" Carl asked.

"He said to go and see. That I'd seen enough to know what to expect from a hearing." She muttered, "I'll be damned if I'll ever learn to expect what I've seen so far."

From the end of the corridor strode a grey haired man in a corduroy jacket and string tie. Carl felt sure he was coming for them, which was confirmed when he stopped at Miriam's feet.

"Miriam Groeper?" he asked with some authority.

"Boyd. I'm not a Groeper anymore."

A manila envelope appeared from under his jacket and he dropped it in her lap. "You've been served."

"What?"

He left from the same direction, and Carl called out to him, "Hold on a minute," but he was through the double-doors before the words reached him. Miriam opened the envelope and read the summons. Her face filled with blood and spite.

"He set me up."

"I don't get it."

"He set me up! This was a ruse. All a ruse."

"There's no hearing?"

"There's a hearing, all right. But not today."

She rose in a rush and knocked over one of her files, sending papers spilling across the floor. Carl bent down to gather them while Miriam rapped on the Plexiglas window. It barely sounded at all. "God dammit, someone talk to me!"

The first woman she spoke to was nowhere in sight, but the second one set down her manifest and marched to the window. "Ma'am, I'm going to ask you to lower your voice."

"You baited me. You bastards baited me."

The woman pushed a button on the phone. "I'm not going to put up with this kind of behavior," she said. "You're going to respect this office."

"Respect? You knew. You *all* knew. I want to know why. You're not paid to take sides." Two deputies approached from either end of the hall, and the first one touched her arm. Miriam whipped around as if he'd put his hand on her ass. She glared into her molester's eyes, but only saw herself in the blackish pool of his sunglasses. "Are you in on it too?" she demanded. "Are you the one who told him I was here? Are you?" Her eyes were capable of shooting flames. The deputies held the ground around her and appeared to be calculating the best way to proceed. All the while, Miriam yielded nothing.

"Ma'am," the deputy said, "I'm here to ensure the safety of everyone in this building. Now you tell me – do I have any reason to be concerned?"

"You're protecting a building. Who's protecting my child?"

"Are you going to calm down?"

"I am calm. It's you people that are stirring everything up. You baited me. You're the ones who gave my baby to a pervert."

A crowd gathered in the central hall to watch. The woman in the clerk's office, forever shielded by a bullet-proof wall, signaled for them to get on with it. The deputy took Miriam's arm.

"Let go of me!"

"I'm going to escort you off the premises."

"I don't fucking believe this," she cried, wincing at the deputy's hold.

"If you have a grievance with the clerk, there are more constructive ways of handling it." He marched her through the main hall, past the throng of onlookers and a bronze plaque of the Ten Commandments, but stopped short of the vestibule. Carl was right behind them with an armload of files, and the deputy turned on him, jostling Miriam.

"Sir, you need to step back."

"I'm with her," Carl said.

The deputy put his free hand on his holster. "I said step back."

Reflected in the officer's lifeless black glasses was Carl cradling Miriam's paper burden. He stared for a moment in disbelief, before slithering back two paces where the other citizens made a space around him. The deputy led Miriam down the courthouse steps to the edge of the green.

"I don't expect to see that kind of behavior in my courthouse again. You can consider this a warning." Miriam was shaking mad and embarrassed. The deputy studied her before changing his tone. He tipped the brim of his hat and said, "You have a pleasant afternoon, Ma'am." For as absurd as the gesture was, it sounded as if he actually meant it. As he climbed the steps, he cut Carl off. "Next time I don't tell you twice. Do you understand?"

Carl didn't have a rehearsed line in his pocket, smart-ass or otherwise. "Perfectly," he said, annoyed and slightly defiant in his humiliation. "May I go now?" The deputy stepped by him, and Carl caught up to Miriam and unloaded the files on a park bench. She was standing there reading the summons.

"What's he suing for?" he asked.

"Spite." She paced into the grass square, arms folded. "Son-of-a-bitch has a new car and he's suing me for child support. And for taking her out-of-state. He's claiming I'm a flight risk."

"You already took her up and brought her back once."

"It doesn't matter."

"Didn't you say they tried that at the last hearing?"

"It doesn't matter. His family has money. He can keep suing forever. He knows he can outlast me."

Carl was getting steamed. "I can pay."

"I don't want your money."

"You don't have a lot of choices."

She lashed out at him, shaking the summons in his face. "I don't have *any* fucking choices!"

"Look, we'll get Coulton for the hearing and we'll make counterclaims. Ed won't gain an inch."

"Bullshit."

"Then we'll take her back to Virginia for that two weeks."

"No." She closed her eyes and her cheeks crimped up.

"Look. Look here," he said. He came up close and took her arms into his hands, but like some battle repressed memory, Miriam flailed away in a rage.

"Don't you touch me!" She was completely unhinged, her eyes showing a terror Carl never imagined. It was the touch of her flesh as she wrenched her arms from his grasp that an old haunted image came back to him, the image of Miriam's bruised wrists from years before on the night she'd shown up on his grandparent's porch.

The deputy was watching from behind a portico column and he was coming down. Fear replaced Carl's compassion as he stared at Miriam's violated shell. Her shoulders were hard and boney, her soft tissue dried up, leaving only a skeletal vestige of the woman he once knew. In as gentle a voice as he could muster, he said her name and it sounded strange to him. "Stay away from me!" she screamed, and ran off across the lawn into town with the summons falling to the ground behind her.

Carl was melting in the intolerable heat, no more than a brown puddle in a strange town. One man was willing to acknowledge his presence, and he was standing behind him. This time it was to Carl the deputy gave a sympathetic stare. Carl asked with his eyes, "What just happened here?"

Chapter 22

Carl knew she wouldn't need long to collect herself, but he still gave her until that evening, well after she had picked up Annaliese, before going to her apartment. He spent the afternoon driving the back roads as if contemplating an escape route. He eventually crossed into Georgia and parked at a private campground and boat launch on the North Prong of the St. Mary's River. On the muddy bank nursing a thirty-two ounce Budweiser, he counted his options. The water before him was infested with mosquitos and cottonmouth, and curled black and deep into the Okefenokee Swamp, a large green blot on his map that looked brooding and untouchable, a place where he might be sucked in and consumed. There was something about being lost in virgin country, be it firm ground or damp marsh that appealed to him. He considered heading for home and being done with it, taking the anonymous winding rural routes where the wilderness might cleanse him and make him a better man on the other side, but the longer he lingered there dirtying his pants and swatting mosquitos, the more he knew he could never leave her like this. He could never leave Annaliese like this. He finished his beer and laid back in the tall grasses, listened to the insects singing and slept away the rest of the afternoon.

∞

Miriam unlatched the door and, without a word, took Carl by the arm and led him to the table in the kitchen. Water off a duck's back, he thought, the woman could shed away the blackest scene in a moment, while he floundered endlessly in darkness. Annaliese sat next to him captive in her high chair. She was fat now and her movements sluggish. Carl didn't need a height-weight chart to know that. Miriam brought him iced tea and a dinner of fried chicken and peas. Annaliese sat there gnawing on a chicken leg. She appeared to regard Carl with suspicion, and he wondered if she regarded all men this way. He sensed anger in her, and that angered him. Her eyes said, "Either be with me or go away, protect me or sacrifice me, nestle me or leave me the hell alone." He wanted to do something for her, but at the moment he was just a stranger taken in by a strange family. He didn't feel a part of them. After dinner, knowing Miriam was sharing the bed with her daughter, he slept on the couch for the evening. Lacking energy and courage, he avoided any serious talk with Miriam, and it was that way all weekend. The beer from the afternoon left a pulsing dent in the back of his head, so he lay down and slept off the night alone.

They spent all day Saturday at the apartment swimming pool, a brackish looking pond shared equally by beetles, frogs and humans. He and Miriam did their best to draw a few words out of Annaliese, which amounted to her favorites: "hungry" and "no." Not once did the girl let Carl hold her. She wouldn't come near him, and he ached at each rejection.

That evening at the computer, wincing from sunburn, he brought up screen after screen, taking notes and printing pages, trying to find the underside of the local hierarchy. The bed behind them where they slept was still unmade and its cotton bedspread was molting little blue tassel tufts all over the floor. He heard them playing together in the next room, though it was mostly Miriam's forced laughter and no more than peeps and murmurs from the child. Annaliese was in a bubble bath where all her toys bobbed under the suds. The child was beginning to accept her mother's physical affection again, her hugs and reassurances, but still she said little. It was as if she feared some horrible retribution where one wrong word might cause her to lose her mother entirely. Words could be a damning thing and silence was a safe substitute.

Miriam stepped to the bedroom door, staying within sight of the bathtub.

"What are you working on?" she asked.

Carl rolled back from the desk and read over his notes. "Elizabeth Shanks and that psychologist who wrote your evaluation both went to Florida State."

"Lots of people down here go to Florida State."

"Same undergraduate class. And that's not all." He reached for the stack of papers in the printer tray and thumbed through them until he found the right document. He handed it to Miriam. "They were both members of the same honor society. It was scholastic and social. It's likely they knew each other."

"That bastard psychologist signed away my baby as a favor to a college drinking buddy?"

"I bet if you go to the courthouse and review her other custody cases, you'll see this doctor's name again and again – all his reports in her clients' favor. And that's not all." Carl took the page from the bottom of the stack. "I found Judge Hawkins and Elizabeth Shanks names on a banquet list for the Dixon Oaks Country Club. It's the only country club in the county."

Miriam looked ill as it all sunk in. "They hire each other. They protect each other." Her mouth was pursed open in disbelief as she kept an eye on Annaliese, whose hands were idle under the bubbles.

"It's not personal, Miriam. To people like Shanks, it's not about justice. It's just business."

"But it's *my* business too."

"You said the judge instructed Shanks to pick out the psychologist?"

"Yeah," she said, over her shoulder.

"This is obviously collusion."

"The appeal deadline is long gone."

"Let's give this to Coulton. Maybe he can figure out a way to use it."

Miriam unfolded a bath towel and opened it wide to receive her child. "It just doesn't matter anymore."

∞

Sunday afternoon Miriam overruled Carl's last-ditch appeal to take the girl back to Virginia for two weeks, as the court order permitted. She justified her decision by adding this to her list of Ed's infractions, though it was doubtful the judge would ever care.

Annaliese's most distinguishable word that weekend was "no." It was one of her favorites and always said with great passion. It was the same cry every time they prepared to take her back to her father, and each time it ripped through Carl's soul like a reminder of his own cry after learning of his parent's deaths – a cry of fear and uncertainty, of knowing beyond a doubt you will never see your parents again. But he sensed his own ancient pain didn't compare to hers.

They agreed to take separate cars to the drop-off where Carl would act as Miriam's muscle – a symbolic gesture likely absurd to both of them – then he would drive all night and be home in time for Monday morning classes. Carl approved since he hated the idea of wasting a Sunday afternoon on the road. Night driving was more of a dream-state, something he could tough his way through and come out on the other side with no memory of the journey. He did wonder how he would appear to his students. Especially in the afternoon classes with another sleepless day behind him, the atmosphere numb, his sense of touch in doubt, everything filtered through a quivering vacuum where people sounded like they were speaking through cardboard tubes.

He tossed his duffel on the floorboard of the S-10 and followed Miriam downtown where the storefronts were dark and desolate. Toe Beard Liquor, Dixon Rental and Choirman's Barbeque all displayed "closed" signs tilting in their windows, all victims of the local blue laws. When they approached the flashing traffic light, Miriam reached back and touched Annaliese's forehead. Instead of pulling into the exchange point, Miriam sped straight out of town, her Beemer straying over the center line whenever she reached back to tend the child. Carl's pulse quickened. He waited for her to check the rearview mirror, and when she did he shrugged in confusion. She replied by extending a skinny arm out the window and waving for him to follow – no questions. They merged onto I-10 heading east toward Jacksonville with the heavy red sun burning the horizon at their backs. She sped up to eighty-five and within twenty minutes the skyline rose before them like a clutter of dormant smoke-stacks glowing orange-red beyond the mess of interchanges. She curled onto a southbound avenue though an upscale neighborhood. At this point, Carl was waving and cursing. He honked his horn several times, but she bolted ahead. He stopped counting the blocks when he saw the St.

John's River glimmering ahead of them. A block shy of the water, she pulled into the parking lot of Saint Bonaventure Hospital's emergency room. She was already taking Annaliese from the car when Carl came up and idled next to them.

"What in God's name are you doing?" he asked.

"She's pointing between her legs and saying it hurts."

"She was fine all weekend."

"That doesn't matter. She said it hurts."

"You'd better be certain about this."

She scanned the hospital grounds. "Don't park here," she said, raising Annaliese into her arms. "This is for emergencies. Park in the visitor lot." She took off with the child.

"Are you sure you know what you're doing?" he called to her.

She stopped at the curb. "I'm not letting him get away with this."

"Do you remember what he did the last time you took her to a doctor without his knowing?"

"I'm not hiding anything. I'm doing it on her health plan. Ed will hear about it soon enough."

"Just be careful what you tell them."

"I'm her mother. I have a right!" With that she marched inside, the child clutching on for a bouncy ride. The wide double door slid aside as if frightened by their approach.

Carl drove into the next lot, took a ticket and soon realized it must have been peak visiting hours. After running the surface lot without success, he spiraled into the parking garage and ended up on the top deck with the darkening sky above him. Being consigned to the visitor lot was appropriate. He could never be more than a visitor to this place, this climate, this straddling between two worlds and the nebulous idea of a bastard family, the world of papers written in threatening legalese and hearings before fools in robes playing God. Miriam was consumed with a depression growing worse by the day. Her skin was tightening over the cheek bones and losing mass under the chin. When Carl first saw her Friday evening he noticed a sprinkle of grey roots at her scalp, proving she'd been dying her hair, but also proving she'd given up dying her hair. Being robbed of her child also robbed her of ten years.

The waiting room was populated with sweaty weekend athletes with blown kneecaps and the usual assortment of elderly with their elderly ailments. But most were simply waiting on others, either knitting, placing phone calls to spread unfortunate news or paging through back issues of Golf Digest. Carl stood there scanning the room when a nurse asked if he was Mr. Rittenhaur and led him through a pair of doors to an endless hallway where she told him to sit down. Examination rooms ran the length of the hall cluttered with IV stands, trays of linen and racks of electronic equipment that looked as lethal as lifesaving. The staff rushed by like he didn't exist. The sterile smell of the place took him back many years. He'd avoided hospitals ever since his grandfather had taken him and his brother to one sixteen years before when there was nothing to do but identify the bodies. His grandfather took care of that while Carl and Vince sat anxiously in a hallway like the one he was sitting in now.

Miriam stuck her head out the nearest door and looked surprised he'd found her.

"They take suspected abuse cases first," she said.

"Miriam, please tell me you didn't tell them that."

"I know he's doing it."

"You said there were no signs when you picked her up."

"Talk to her." She pointed in the exam room where Annaliese sat on a padded table clutching a stuffed dolphin. She was focused on the floor as if in fear of all the gadgets in the room. "She'll tell you."

"She didn't say a word all weekend."

"You see the way she acts when I take her back to him. She won't even warm up to *you* anymore, and she loved you. Now she's terrified of men. What does that tell you?"

He did feel as though Annaliese was repulsed by him, and for no reason he could fathom. "Is she really that bad?"

"She's in pain. She said so. Doctor Ainsberg said I should take her to the ER right away if I ever suspect anything."

A doctor lumbered down the hall trailing a nurse with a clipboard who was in a much bigger hurry. He fumbled for one of a half dozen pens in his coat pocket and she handed him the chart. A black man of fifty, Dr. Clive Williams was nearing the end of a twelve-hour shift, though his weariness appeared to lift when he spoke to them.

"The nurse tells me the two of you have joint custody."

Miriam looked at Carl as if she hardly knew him, her eyes saying, "Who? This man?"

"No. He's just a friend." She acknowledged. "I explained this when I signed in."

"Doctor, the father is on the way," the nurse said.

Miriam stared at her in shock. "No, that's not necessary."

"Ms. Boyd, both parents are always contacted. You gave us Annaliese's card, so we got his contact numbers through the insurance company."

"You called him already?"

"Of course."

Doctor Williams glanced at Miriam's fidgeting hands. "I assume you have custodial rights," he asked.

"No," she said, clearly embarrassed. There was an awkward moment before she added, "We have joint-custody. And he's done this before. Over summer visitation. I picked her up and she had this horrible rash." She waited for Carl to back her up. "The video! I wish I had the video."

"There's a video," Carl said, stupidly.

"He doesn't take care of her, and now she's complaining of hurting between her legs."

The doctor's attention wavered back and forth between the nurse and the clipboard. "Ms. Boyd," he said, prodding around in his pocket for a pen he liked better. He let out a small sigh. "Let's take a look."

"I'll wait out here," Carl said, as the door drifted shut. He didn't sit this time but paced to the end of the hall, glancing through narrow windows into exam rooms where others were tending their own tragedies. The corridor lighting was a brilliant blinding white, as if the bulbs were chosen to intensify the color of blood. The whole building was designed with the highest efficacy to scare the hell out of anyone unfamiliar with medicine.

When he turned back, a man was coming toward him who was not wearing one of the color-coded scrubs. A nurse was right behind him, almost running to keep up. "I said exam room five, sir.

Right back here," she instructed. Carl realized he was coming for him and sidestepped behind an IV stand as if that might lessen the blow. Ed Grouper stopped at the nurse's command and raised a finger at Carl before bursting into the exam room.

"What in the hell is going on here?" Ed bellowed.

Carl stepped down the hall as if approaching a man off his meds. He stood a few paces shy of a right cross. All eyes were on the father, except for Annaliese. She lay on the table with her legs spread, but on sight of her father she clamped them together and tightened her fists to her abdomen. She stared off to the side where she could avoid the faces. The doctor rolled back his chair.

"She was hurting in her private area," Miriam said.

"I know what this is about. Get her dressed."

"He's not done with his exam."

"This exam is over. Get her dressed."

Miriam looked in anguish at the doctor, who was pulling off his gloves. He stuffed them in a contamination dispenser and regarded Miriam over his bifocals. "I don't see anything wrong here, Ms. Boyd. Not even a mild rash." The nurse side-stepped from the room, but not before staring down both the mother and father with disapproval.

"I'll do it," Ed barked, grabbing the girl's shorts off a chair. He stopped by his daughter's side and glared around the room. "Someone get me a diaper." No one responded fast enough. "Never mind," he said, before forcing the shorts over each foot.

"Stop it, Ed," Miriam cried. "The diaper bag is in the car."

"Forget it. I've had enough. We're outta here." He stood the girl on the exam table and hoisted up her shorts, baggy without the usual padding, and snapped them over her bloated belly. He heaved her up high like slinging a coil of rope over his shoulder. Annaliese was going limp and withdrawing from the whole scene, as if retreating into a special place she'd created for herself. Ed pushed out of the room, and Miriam trotted after him.

"Do you see how he is?" she cried. "How he behaves around her? How she reacts to him?"

The doctor followed them out. "The exam was over anyway, Ms. Boyd."

"I need a copy of your report."

"You'll both have your copies," Doctor Williams said.

Ed stopped before reaching the doors to the waiting room. "You're damn right I'll get a copy. Right now."

"We'll have the paperwork ready in a few minutes," Dr. Williams said, finding his reserve energy. "Have a seat outside."

"Not without her." He pointed at Miriam. "I'm not leaving you two back here to talk shit behind my back."

"Then *both* of you wait outside."

A hospital security guard came up behind Ed, who turned to confront him.

"You want to arrest someone?" Ed said with contempt. He took a folded piece of paper from his pocket and shook it open. It was a copy of the original court order, so frayed that he must have carried it wherever he went. "I have custody of this child, and this woman brought her here to smear me. Arrest her."

"He won't even diaper her," she countered. "He doesn't know how to take care of her."

"The hell I don't." He took an aggressive step toward her, but the guard grabbed hold of him.

"Sir," the guard said.

"Sir what?"

"You need to step out. Right now."

With Ed confined, Carl spoke calmly, hoping to settle him down and minimize the damage. "She was just having Annaliese checked out, Ed. She said she was hurting."

He squeezed his daughter tight. "Do you have anything to do with that?"

"No, Ed, I don't."

"Then you keep the God damn hell out of it."

The guard said, "Sir, I'm going to escort you out of the building." He pulled him toward the door, but Ed jerked his arm free and took a step toward Carl, who backed up two.

"You keep the hell away from my daughter!"

He took off through the doors before the guard could grab him again, no doubt pleased to have backed Carl into a tray of linen. Ed seemed to know how far he could push things and when to back off, a careful aggressive dance seen in many predators. The most frightening thing was that it was impossible to tell when he would actually strike. Propped on Ed's shoulder was Annaliese's glazed over face, too shocked and violated to react in any visible way. Her cheeks were white and cold, her gaze forlorn and her mouth hung open in a little 'o.'

"Come on," Carl said, placing a hand on Miriam's back. The child's turmoil was enough for her to break down as they walked back to the waiting room where everyone was waiting to see who would follow the angry asshole who was cursing with a child in his arms. They watched Ed carry her right out the front door to his car parked outside the emergency drop-off with two wheels over the curb. He buckled the girl into her car-seat and she slid in easy, too numb to cry at the separation from her mother.

When the paperwork was ready they called the name Groeper, and Miriam trotted to the counter. Ed was ready, watching the glassed in waiting room from his car for Miriam's first move. Ed abandoned Annaliese in the car and sprinted inside. After each signed the examination report and copies distributed, Ed stormed out as fast as he'd come in. His tires chirped as they sped off into the night.

The city lights washed out the first stars, and the Modis sign shone high amidst the spotted embers of downtown. The relentless heat subsided and the evening air was calm and pleasant coming off the river. Carl followed Miriam to her car where she clutched the steering wheel and wailed. She leaned forward and the horn sounded and she pounded it with her fists again and again, until Carl drew her back.

"Stop. Stop it," he said, holding her.

"He's abusing her. I know it. I just know it."

"You knew it was a risk taking her here."

"You don't believe me either."

"I didn't say that."

"Bastard." She tried to shake him off.

"No. Look. Look at me." He didn't give a damn this time if she screamed bloody murder, and she must have felt it in his hold as she froze and stared wearily through her mussed hair. "I'd have done the same thing, okay?"

She was breathing heavy, taking time. "That bastard," she said, correcting herself.

"But Miriam, if you claim abuse, you have to be able to prove it. No question."

"That's what I was trying to do," she said, as if arguing with a fool. "I'm her mother. It's my job to protect her. Am I supposed to ignore her when she says she's in pain?"

Trying to see it from her side, he said, "No." He looked around the parking lot, halfway expecting they were being watched. He didn't want to say anything more to set her off. "No, you're not supposed to ignore her. Bringing her here is your right. It's every parent's right. He can't use that against you." His hold on her turned affectionate, and he rubbed her arms. He didn't know how to break free. He checked his watch and muttered in frustration, "I have to go."

"Don't."

"I already have to get through classes tomorrow on no sleep. At this rate I'm going to miss first period."

"Don't go. Please, just one more day. I can't go back to that empty apartment alone. I can't."

"I'll be back down in two weeks for the next visitation. You go on home."

"Home? I don't have a home. I have four grimy walls in a shitty apartment project." She popped the wheel one last time and sniffled. "Don't you tell me to go home."

"Drive me up to my car."

"I can't go in that lot without paying. I don't have any money," she said, exasperated at yet another humiliation.

He stepped back and shut the car door, rested two hands on the sill. She had no one else. He was afraid she wouldn't make it back. "Wait for me on the street by the pay booth. I'll follow you back to the apartment."

"You'll stay?"

He knew there was no leaving her, not when she was like this. "Yeah. I'll stay one more night," he relented. Carl couldn't imagine driving all night replaying this scene over and over in his head. He wanted to blot it all out and be in the blackness of sleep. What his principal would say at another unannounced absence from work didn't interest him. He jogged to the parking garage and found the elevators weren't working, so he spiraled up the ramp on foot, crossing and recrossing, losing his orientation as he climbed.

Chapter 23

Miriam took off every Wednesday afternoon from her waitress job for mid-week visitation. She arrived at Palm Kids Daycare after the lunch shift and breezed past the front desk where the usual receptionist failed to wave back or say hi. She walked the hall adorned with *papier mâché* posters and finger art, until she came to Annaliese's classroom just shy of the exit. She peeked through the window in the door and after eyeing Janine Haygood, let herself in.

Ms. Haygood's natural disposition, no matter the circumstances, always involved a tired smile, but this time it looked forced and painful to hold. "She's not here," she said.

"What?"

Ms. Haygood led her back into the hall. "Her father picked her up early. Told the desk he was thinking of pulling her out for good."

"He can't. He cannot and will not do any such thing," Miriam protested.

Ms. Haygood scanned the hall before speaking. "He looked happy," she said in a hushed tone. "And I've never seen him happy."

"Well he won't be happy for long. This is just one more thing I have against him for the judge. He's denying my visitation."

"You go get him. I don't like that man, myself." They nodded together. "And he still doesn't do what needs to be done. On Monday he brought her in without a raincoat and it's been pouring all week."

Miriam opened her purse and dug out a pen. "I want to take this down."

"And he hasn't paid for school supplies. I know that doesn't concern me. That's for management to deal with, but he doesn't pay his bills." Miriam scribbled her notes on the back of an envelope.

"Do you have anything else?"

"Humorless as a chicken count?"

Miriam giggled as she shoved the notes into her purse and thanked her. At the front desk the day school administrator stood behind the receptionist with a file tucked under her arm. She was waiting for Miriam. Tall and middle-aged, she wore a green business suit setting her apart from the rest of the daycare workers, a suit saying she was principal-in-charge. The receptionist crept off to a back room when Miriam approached the desk.

"Did my ex-husband say anything to you about pulling Annaliese out of school?"

Though the two had met before to go over paperwork and insurance forms, the woman appeared to be examining Miriam with renewed interest, as if she might have missed something in their prior meeting. "He said you were to have no further contact with her," she said plaintively.

"He what?"

"Mr. Groeper was in this afternoon with a new court order." She handed Miriam a copy from the file she was holding.

"This can't be." Miriam gripped the pages with both hands, her spirit draining as she read the words. "This can't be," she repeated, her voice rising.

The administrator softened her stance. "I'm afraid we have to ask you to stay off the premises until you work all this out."

"This is all lies. How can he do this? I wasn't even at the hearing."

"I'm sorry, Ms. Boyd, but we have to abide by any court order."

She lowered the page. "Has he pulled her out of school?"

On seeing Miriam's distress, the woman appeared more sympathetic, but the suspicion in her eyes remained. "I'm afraid I can't discuss that with you."

Miriam stepped out in a daze and meandered into the parking lot. The clouds were dense and heavy, making way for the first chill of the new season. She whipped out her cell phone and fingered the buttons. Ed answered on the first ring, as if he'd been looking forward to the call.

"Where is she?" she cried.

"She's with me, right where she's going to stay."

"I have visitation."

"Not anymore. Shanks faxed the order to your attorney, oh . . . about a half hour ago."

"How can there be a hearing without me or my attorney present?"

"Given your little stunt at the hospital Sunday night, the judge was more than happy to grant an emergency *ex parte* hearing."

"What the hell does that mean?"

"It means you lose."

"You can't do this."

"I already did. Goodbye, Miriam."

The line went dead. She clenched the phone, squeezing the life out of it before throwing it to the pavement where it shattered to pieces. She sank to the curb and massaged her face until it hurt. A breeze from the passing front raised the court order and sent it fluttering across the parking lot.

PART THREE

Chapter 24

Carl spent the next two weekends at his grandfather's farm rebuilding one of the lean-to sheds on the hay barn before the last load of timothy came in. His grandfather presided over the project from a lawn chair, hollering orders and raising his cane to point out the obvious. Like Miriam, Malcolm Rittenhaur's age seemed to have accelerated over the long heat of summer. He had slowed down. His hip, which had given him problems before, was now a chronic pain, and Carl was getting used to seeing him limp along with an old hickory cane handed down through the generations. Tinged with the guilt of knowing he'd neglected the old man for too long, Carl was making regular visits without complaint, alternating days with Vince to make sure the old man and his livestock were getting their meals. He was also back to the builder therapy he practiced for so long on his own house, building and rebuilding, though now it was more a continuation of an old bloodline than the aimless avoidance of his own heart. Emotional pain can be masked through labor, so he jumped into the project with zeal, both hiding from the current legal unpleasantness and paying penance for his sins to his family.

Not once all summer did he pick up a brush or chisel. He draped the canvasses leaning on the wall with a blanket and shoved aside his patio workbench and the surrounding boxes of alabaster, visiting his backyard studio only to push the lawn mower back and forth. He'd been through loathsome patches of inactivity in his art before, usually after finishing a major piece or wallowing in black thoughts of the past, but this was wholly different. Miriam and her daughter had somehow erased a piece of his passion, or perhaps only redirected it as they dominated his thoughts.

On a Sunday evening, after another weekend of manual labor, he pulled up to his house and noticed through the first drops of rain the blinds were drawn shut. He knew it had been that way all day, and he was weary. He didn't want to go inside, knowing what was waiting for him.

When he slipped out of the truck, a familiar grey Impala parked down the street bolted forward and bared down on him. He sprung back when the car hurled alongside him and stopped short, wedging him in a one foot space between the two driver's doors. His jacket soaked up the beaded raindrops on the truck. Millie Kilgore sat at the wheel and gave him a big sarcastic smirk.

"God damn, Millie," Carl said, backed up against his pick-up.

"Got some nerve, Carl."

"What the hell's your problem?"

"You are. You done sold-out my family. Called the cops and busted us all up." Her fat face was red and creased deep under each jowl. She looked like she'd been living in her car.

"It wasn't me."

"Like hell. Dale said you were gawking from your front porch."

"I didn't do it, Millie. And I'll give you a tip too. I know the police are looking for you." He zipped his jacket and thrust his hands deep in his pockets. He wondered if the street might be under surveillance. "You shouldn't be hanging out here."

"No shit, Sherlock. Think I've been living the high-life the past two months?"

"I don't know what to tell you, Millie. I'm real sorry."

"The hell you are. Remember, I told you I got friends."

"I said I didn't have anything to do with it," he protested.

"Wouldn't like nothing more than to wreck your dumpy ass."

"Millie."

"Get your grubby hands off my car. God damn snitch."

"I didn't call the police," he said with welling anger, hoping that might back her off.

"Then maybe your lady friend did." Millie closed in on Carl's guilt-ridden face as he glanced at the drawn shades of his house. "I'd watch my back if I was you."

With that she took off, her rear bumper sweeping Carl's pants leg as she tore down the street. He watched the beat up Impala drive from sight and looked around to see if any of her convict friends might be lurking nearby. In a rising fear, he ran for the house.

He found her there again like she'd been every day that week. Ambient light from the candle-lit walls settled on the futon where she slept, corpse-like and pale like some half-devoured ghost. A cotton blanket shroud lay over her body, and her jaw churned, slowly grinding away her teeth. Carl removed his mud-caked shoes and hung his coat on the newel post. In Miriam he recognized a part of himself, an apathy and hopelessness he'd once carried. But now he was functioning and she wasn't. He looked upon her with pity, but he also feared her, feared her temper and mood swings, feared being with her and losing her again.

He crossed the room and flipped on the overhead light in the dining room where a half dozen burning candles flooded the table with red and white wax. One was reduced to a spitting blue flame in the bottom of a fat hollow ring of wax. The wick had burnt off, but the flame was still dancing there, singeing a black circle on the wood table. Carl blew it out and examined it, smelled the burnt maple and the last feathery swirl of smoke. He picked at the charred spot with his fingernail.

"Miriam," he said, agitated. She rolled a little to one side and raised the blanket to her chin. "Miriam, wake up. You set the table on fire." She mumbled in return, as if annoyed at the intrusion. "All these candles," he said. She groaned and sat up, her eyes bewildered, hair matted and tangled. The blanket settled to the floor around her feet. "You can't light these damn things and fall asleep," he said.

She rubbed her face with both hands, her white knuckles mashing and rolling the ball in each eye socket. "I don't care," she mumbled.

"Well I do." Carl went to the kitchen for some aspirin. The counter was cluttered with dirty dishes, dried up leftovers and two spotted bananas. By the sink was an empty prescription bottle, its white cap laying to one side. He picked it up and checked the label, but had no idea what he was reading. He'd never taken anything but over-the-counter. The label said, *Bupropion, 300 milligrams, take once a day with meals.*

"Miriam," he yelled. She was laying down again, though the blanket was still on the floor. "What did you do? How many of these did you take?" He grabbed her shoulder and shook her, but she wrenched away from him.

"Leave me alone."

He held out the bottle. "How many did you take?"

"For Christ sakes." She grabbed the blanket off the floor and balled it up. "I didn't O.D. The prescription ran out. I don't have any money to refill it." She gave a sick laugh like she'd heard it all and stuffed the blanket in the corner of the futon. "I can't even afford to commit suicide."

"If it's helping you, I'll fill it. What is it?" he asked, reading the label again.

"Some anti-depression thing I got at the clinic."

"It doesn't seem to work very well."

"It does some. You wouldn't know."

"I know what I see. You've been wasting away. If you're going to stay here while you're fighting this, then you should get a job."

She recoiled at the suggestion. "I can't work."

"It'll help get your mind off all the crap. You can wait tables or bartend anywhere you want."

"I'm never waiting on anyone else again. I want someone to wait on me for a change."

"So do something else. I'll go get a paper."

"Easy for you. At least you have a degree." She added, with the application of guilt, "All you do is work."

"And you'd prefer I sit around all day and commiserate with you?"

"You're too self-absorbed to care."

"Jesus. I'm paying the rent on the apartment you're not living in. I'm paying for your attorney. I lost count of the number of days I spent in Florida trying to help you. I'm doing everything I can short of losing my job." He studied the burn mark on his table. "You don't know about that, do you? My principal was furious. He informed me after my unannounced four day weekend that if I miss one more class day this term that I'm outta there. Gone, Miriam. Fired."

The rain storm was gaining force and the house creaked from the wild gusts. Miriam scraped together enough energy to look up. "I know what you've done for me," she conceded. "I couldn't have made it through this much without you. At least not without losing my mind. I just need somebody with me."

"I can't be there all the time."

"I know," she said. "I know that. It's not like I planned this."

"I had different plans too," Carl said.

"I'm not going over that again. You need to get over it." The comment stung.

"Don't tell me what I need to get over, Miriam. You of all people."

"There you go again, always so stern, so distant. The angry artist. You're such a cliché."

"I haven't picked up a brush or a chisel since you came back into my life. If I'm stern and distant, it might be because I'm *not* an artist anymore."

She stared at him regretfully, as if just realizing she'd killed something inside him. "I don't want that to happen."

He collapsed next to her, shoulder to shoulder. "I can't paint right now any more than you can get off this couch and get a job. Don't think what you and Annaliese are going through hasn't affected me."

"I'm sorry." Miriam picked up the tv remote and examined it, rubbed her fingers over the buttons before tossing it aside.

"I want to know something," Carl said. "I want you to be truthful."

"What?"

"What happened to you that first night you came to stay at my grandparents' in high school?"

Miriam looked as though that was the last thing she would have ever guessed he would ask. She huffed and said, "Nothing happened."

"Yes, something did. You had bruises on your wrists."

"I did not."

"I don't think it was from your mother."

"Why are you dredging this up?"

"Was it one of your mother's boyfriends?"

She inched away from him. "It was my business and still is. No one else's."

Carl wanted to prove what he'd theorized all along. "Did one of them rape you?"

Miriam covered her face and let out a half sound, catching the rest in her mouth. Her body squeezed itself shut, closing out all the men and machinations and madness in the world. Carl's question was answered.

After a moment, she spoke through her hands. "I read on the internet this morning about a woman who's going through the same shit in the Florida courts. She ran with her child to Georgia and got an attorney there, one licensed in both states. They're in hiding until their attorney can straighten things out."

"What's to stop her from being caught?"

"Attorney-client privilege. He can represent her, but can't be made to turn her in. She could be hiding anywhere. It's easier when the kid's young and not in school."

"I'd say that's a last resort, wouldn't you?"

Her thoughts appeared open to anything, exploring all options. "Or I could run with her and live on a horse farm out west." She gazed into space, seeing the dream. "No one would find us out there."

"And you have this horse farm all picked out?"

She considered him as if she might reveal something in great confidence. "There is an underground for this sort of thing. There are people who are willing to help."

Carl nodded, though not believing. "I remember reading about a doctor that ran off to New Zealand with her kid."

"I don't have a passport. Knowing Ed, he's probably already gotten one for Annaliese and locked it away. But that doesn't mean I can't take her and disappear out west."

This kind of talk worried him and he was conflicted, wondering how it would feel if she disappeared from his life again as quickly as she had come back. He felt both fear and relief in whatever path she choose.

He went to the kitchen to work up dinner. Miriam hadn't been eating well on her own, so Carl had to feed her to keep up her energy. In a half hour they sat silently at the dinner table and ate quick-fry pork chops, a pot of rice and a steamed basket of broccoli. Though he knew no meal would revive her, it might at least maintain her.

From Carl's office that evening came the steady sound of Miriam's fingers clicking on the computer keyboard, surfing the net and sending messages until well past midnight. He stuck his head in the door to see how she was doing, and she diminished the screen she was working on. After he left for bed, she closed the door and locked it.

Chapter 25

They overslept in a hotel outside Darlington, South Carolina, and this time Miriam claimed the wheel of Carl's pickup and was tearing past every car and semi on the interstate. They were on the way to her first hour of supervised visitation, imposed by Judge Hawkins until the Department of Children and Families could ascertain Miriam's "situation and stability," and determine whether or not she was a danger to her child. At the moment she was a danger to every nearby vehicle on I-95.

Carl's legs were growing stiff from pressing the floorboards. He held a road atlas and squinted at the fine print, trying to determine their ETA. "We can be there by noon if you hold this speed," he said, feeling the passing blur of traffic. "You can even let up a bit."

"Why didn't you ask the desk for a wake-up call?" she demanded.

"We'll get there in time," he said, though he wasn't sure if they would. There was no way he was going to tell her that.

They averaged just under ninety miles an hour, which was as much as the little truck could handle without shaking to pieces. The tires whined and the front end wobbled along until a sudden eruption jolted them onto the inner median. Miriam wrestled the wheel back to the right and brought them straight again, but the sound alone terrified them as the front left tire disintegrated and loose bands of rubber lashed the wheel wells, shuddering the vehicle like some broken milling machine from another century. They cried out at the same time, his in fear, hers in dread as their speed rapidly diminished. The parade of vehicles they once blew by were now passing them with the bemused faces of drivers and passengers staring from their windows. The front corner of the old Chevy settled from its convulsions as they came to a rest on the inside median. Miriam cut the ignition and let go of the wheel.

"Shit!" she screamed and pounded the dash.

Carl checked the side-view mirror. "You can't pull off any farther?"

"You're lucky I didn't pull off into a fucking tree."

"Ninety-five will do that to you." He hopped out of the cab. "Lean up," he said. He bent the seat forward and reached for the jack. "Pull it over farther."

She cussed as she turned over the ignition, her cheeks punctuated with anger dimples. The blown tire flopped pathetically as Carl waved her over to the edge of the hard-pack. The mangled strands of rubber no longer resembled a tire, and the steel rim was bent in two places and looked like it had been polished with a wood rasp. He pumped the jack and raised the quarter-panel, strained to turn each lug nut before tossing the wheel aside. He crawled under the chassis for the spare and crawled right back out. He stomped over to the cab and looked under the seat, cursing his stupidity.

"What's wrong?" Miriam asked from a grassy bank where she was waiting.

"The wrench."

"What wrench?"

"The damn wrench. The one to unscrew the spare from the rack."

She didn't seem to comprehend the problem and sat there looking bewildered.

Carl propped himself against the back bumper and wiped his brow with the base of his dirty palm. Though it was a breezy sixty degrees, he was sweating hard and suffused with the shame of making the same mistake twice. "I never replaced it," he said, furious with himself.

"Why would you have to replace something that's supposed to be behind your seat?" she asked rhetorically.

"Because it's not behind my seat. I lost the wrench on the side of the road a few years ago. I never went to the dealer to buy a replacement."

Miriam didn't utter a word. Her skin was bone white at the joints. Under the roar of the traffic, she sat there on the bank with no immediate outlet for her anger.

Carl trotted down the median waving his arms, doing as much to scare people off as plea for help. After a fruitless minute, Miriam pulled off her sweater and tied her t-shirt under her breasts. She adjusted herself, strutted off the grassy knoll and flagged the next truck that roared by. A shiny white Cherokee rolled onto the median and backed up in front of Carl's oxidized S-10. The driver's manner encompassed both charity and opportunity. He climbed down from his cab and sized up the situation, noting the blown tire laying there like a piece of fallen space junk and Miriam in her new baby-doll tee-shirt, making her breasts fuller than they really were.

"Looks like you could use some help," the man said to Miriam.

"I sure could," she said, all perked up for her new savior. It was the first time Carl saw her smile in over a month and he hated the guy for it.

"We need a wrench to get the spare down," Carl said.

The man smiled with confidence, as if he knew exactly what was needed. He lifted the hatch of his Cherokee and stepped aside to show off the two enormous stainless steel tool racks bolted to the side panels. There were drawers of all sizes, cabinet doors, little pad-locked compartments and a single bin large enough to accommodate a body. He stood there for a second admiring his rig, his eyes saying, "So how do you like this?"

"Oh my," Miriam said. Carl worried she might try to feel his biceps.

"Had'er custom made," the man said, his cheeks spread in a beefy smile. "I got any wrench you could need and then some." They all stood there staring at the shiny cabinets. "You should see my wood shop."

Yeah, Carl thought. Some other time. After sliding under the chassis to determine the precise tool required, the man produced the correct wrench and unscrewed the tire bracket himself, perhaps thinking this one act of good will might validate his whole ridiculous setup.

Carl took over once the tire was down. To his amazement, while he worked the lugs over the spare, the tool man was holding court with Miriam on the knoll. They were laughing and carrying on under the din of traffic. For all this guy knew, ring or no ring, he could have been hitting on Carl's wife. He had the tire on in minutes and hurled the ruined wheel into the truck bed with the jack and lug wrench clanging in behind it. By the time he slammed the camper door, Miriam was turning the ignition. The tool man leaned inside, looking for a kiss goodbye.

Carl hopped in the passenger side. "Appreciate the help," he said, leaning in close and extending a hand. The man shook Carl's hand before putting his own to the brim of his baseball cap in a gesture to Miriam. The transmission whined when she backed up to make space. At the first lull in traffic, she punched the gas and jerked into the fast lane, spitting bits of gravel at her savior's feet. The old truck accelerated pitifully. Carl looked back and braced for someone rear-ending them, but there was only the man standing by his rig, smiling wistfully and shaking his head at another missed opportunity.

He folded the map over to Georgia. Miriam settled back into her silent panic and Carl recalculated their arrival time. "We lost about twenty minutes. There's no way we can make that up. The truck will rattle to pieces if you go any faster."

Miriam pushed the pedal to the floor and the speedometer needle inched its way across the dial until a small vibration shook the front end. Carl put his hand on the dash. "You're riding on a spare now, so ease up a little." She did, but only because they nosed up to a silver Lincoln lingering in the fast lane at seventy. The big rigs boxed up the inner lanes and hemmed them in.

"Dammit, old man," she cussed.

"Let's ease up," he said. "We'll get there."

"No, we won't. This is just what they want."

"What?"

"I'm the irresponsible mother. I can't even make an appointment on time."

"That's not going to happen."

"The hell it won't. DCF is keeping a file on me – a god damn dossier. They'll report every slip-up to the judge." She jerked from side-to-side within in the lane. "Move, you old bastard!"

Carl gripped the dash with one hand, but his body faced Miriam. "I'll tell them we got caught in traffic."

"Like they'll believe you anymore than they'll believe me? You're the one I was having *an affair* with. To them you're nothing but a home-wrecker."

"That's bullshit."

"I know that, but you better get it through your head. They'll do and say anything to make me look like a bad mother. Do you know what they said, Carl?" She glared right at him, ignoring the Lincoln whose bumper she was riding. "They said I'm a danger to my child because I gave her a bubble bath. Yeah. Suspected abuse. It's a known fact that some bubble baths are irritating to certain children's genitalia. I guess I intentionally researched for a bubble bath that would make my baby sick. All this because I tried to protect her from him. Him! Never mind the father who calls me 'his little girl' when he licks me!" Two wheels straddled the shoulder before she wove back inside the line. "And I'm the bad mother."

"Miriam, back off a little."

"I'm the *bad mother*." She jerked onto the left shoulder and roared passed the Lincoln. Carl caught the shocked expression of the elderly driver staring back with his mouth gaped open. "*I* abused my *child*," Miriam mocked. "*I need to be supervised.*"

She whipped back into the fast lane, cutting ahead of the bewildered old folks.

"That's enough," Carl said, and put a hand on the wheel.

"Don't you dare," she scolded, her eyes wild. Again Carl felt as if he'd been falsely accused of some heinous crime, but he kept his hand on the wheel.

"Pull it over, Miriam."

"Get your hand off. Get away!" she screamed. The cords in her neck stretched taut and her face burned like the sun. They lurched over two lanes and crossed right back to the inside shoulder before weaving over again. The traffic cleared behind them and a semi blew its horn.

"You're going to get us killed!"

"Let go of the wheel!" she ripped from her throat.

"Pull it over!"

"Get your hands off. Get off!" she raged. "Let go of her!"

They were hurling through space, and time was lost to them. Carl pulled his hand away. "Miriam," he said lightly, still perched at the edge of his seat as they rocketed down the highway. She found her concentration in time to miss the car snailing ahead of them. "Miriam, I am not Ed." She gripped the wheel with both hands like it was the last thing within her control and centered the truck in the fast lane. Carl eased back into his seat, submitting to the gauntlet. He said again, "I am not Ed."

∞

They arrived at the DCF office at 12:40, where Miriam double parked at an odd angle, sprang from the truck and ran inside. She didn't notice Carl grab the keys from the ignition. He sat there afterward shaken and numb, thankful to be alive. Like a distressed bomber pilot after a bad mission, he was tempted to fall to his knees and kiss the ground, but he just slumped out of the cab and stood there, centering on a dull relief and swearing he could feel the steady mass of the earth turning beneath him. It struck him that this was the first time in many years he had been genuinely scared. His legs wobbled and his chest felt tight, a dull black spot festering under the breast bone like the first sign of a heart attack. He leaned over and took a few deep breaths until his blood flowed properly again. He wanted nothing more than to be home, and he was shocked when the first image of home wasn't the house he had been rebuilding for six years, but was the old farmhouse and its mildewy air.

It was the first day of October and though the temperature was more tolerable, the sun's rays were not. Carl stripped off his windbreaker and tossed it on the seat. By his watch there was only fifteen minutes of supervised visitation left. He stepped inside and wandered down a hall lined with meeting rooms until he found them. Miriam was squatting next to her daughter, showing her photos from their trip to the zoo and the day they all went strawberry picking. But Annaliese was far removed, staring away from the pictures. Her mother kept pulling the girl's hand from her mouth and it pained him to see them together like that. And it pained him further to see such a different child than the one he had met a few months before. He took only one step into the room before the guardian appeared from the side and cut him off.

"We follow the letter of the law, sir," she said. Her grey hair was tied up in a bun leaning to one side, making her body appear fragile and off-kilter. "Precisely what's in the judge's order, and no other names are mentioned for visitation. You'll have to wait outside."

He knew by the old biddy's tone that any coaxing would do no good; in fact it would probably make things worse. He spied Annaliese staring down at her inward pointing toes while her mother clapped and smiled helplessly in front of her. He hoped Annaliese would see him, maybe crack a smile and acknowledge in some small way the brief bond they had shared. A look of recognition that would cause the guardian to write something positive in her report, but the girl just sat there without substance.

Carl smiled at the woman and nodded, said "of course" and "thank you," hoping that being overly gracious might score a few points. She turned her humorless demeanor back to the fractured family and took her seat. When he left she was scribbling something on her notepad.

When Carl stepped outside, he saw him across the street in a bank parking lot with the rear half of his car hidden by a cool fountain of palm leaves. The sunglasses welded to his head gave no impression of his eyes. Ed didn't try to hide, but stared right back with all the power of possession. Carl sat in his truck and the two men glared at each other across the highway in a visual game of chicken. He wished he had his sunglasses and he was dying for a smoke.

At one o'clock, Ed fired up his car, revving it loudly, and crossed the road into a nearby parking space, aligning perfectly within the stripes. Before going inside, he took a few steps toward Carl's window. The truck was still double parked where Miriam had left it.

"Haven't you learned not to get involved?" Ed said.

"Guess not."

"She's got you on one tight leash," Ed taunted. Something caught in Carl's throat. He had nothing for him. "Looks to me like you're nothing but an errand boy," he added before turning away.

Carl yanked the door latch and jumped from the cab. Cheap shot coward, he thought. Chicken shit. An old rage welled up inside.

At the last second Ed turned and gave him a mocking smile, and Carl swung at it but caught only air where the smile had been. Before he could recover from his clumsy shot, Ed got him by the throat and slammed his head on the hood of his own truck. After the initial flash of light in his eyes, the lower left side of his back seized in pain. He fell hard in a pile as another shock wave bolted through his body. His limbs were heavy as if pumped full of water. All he could do was wonder how Ed's smug face disappeared so fast.

"Son," Ed said, already walking away. "You ain't got no business down here."

The final humiliation was calling him "son." He figured he'd lain there for only a minute, though he couldn't be relied on to judge time. He pushed himself up and leaned against the front tire, felt his bruised body for blood, but found none. Miriam stepped out and climbed into the passenger seat.

"Please get me out of here," she said.

Carl struggled to his feet, wondering if his back hurt from the fall or whether her ex-husband had kicked him too.

"Did Ed seem more chipper than usual?" he asked.

"I never saw him," she said, staring in disgust at Ed's new car. "They keep us in different rooms for the exchange."

Carl limped around the front bumper with a hand pressed to his back and eased inside. She looked at him as if something might be wrong. "What were you doing on the ground?"

"Just checking the spare."

Miriam flipped down the vanity mirror and pinched the skin under her eyes. "You really should go to the dealer and get that tool."

Chapter 26

By mid-October the river still hadn't recovered from the summer drought, and the water lay a precarious foot below the boat launch. After they finished loading their gear into the hatches, Carl and Mick, dressed in cold-water neoprene, strained to lower themselves into their kayaks without flipping over. The dam below them deadened the flow, so they paddled the first two miles upstream through backwater black and bottomless. Trees lining the way blazed orange and gold, and grew from muddy banks of briars and tangled roots where the water undercut the shoreline. Several weakened trees had toppled over, leaving dead and barren branches reaching like bleached bones to an indifferent sky.

They paddled in long deliberate strokes, hand over hand, pushing the past behind as water split off their bows, rippled out and disappeared in the entanglement. Fallen leaves floated like a million archipelagos, slowing the boats and collecting on the blades of their paddles in a gummy brown rot. Carl's launch was fitted with a deck bag, compass, map, bilge pump, emergency radio, flares, and an assortment of other safety gear that was useless on a mountain stream. Mick Coates kept his deck bare and unencumbered.

They knew they were above the reservoir when the current gathered strength. The passage narrowed and they could see the original cut of the river. A blue heron rustled from the tall grasses and lifted into the air with cumbersome strokes of its wings, and they followed the bird upstream like a good omen. The forest here was dense and tight to the banks, always keeping one side of the river in shade, but it was cool so they tried to navigate in the sun. They paddled hard over two small rapids, cutting up the smoothest channels and being careful not to break their blades on the rocks below the surface. Above each white water they pushed into tide-pools to catch their breath and drink from their water bottles.

Beneath them wandering schools of bluefish glistened when the sun hit just right.

The last rapids were impassable, so they stepped out of their boats and portaged over the rocks on the inside bend, away from the quick waters. They towed their boats by painter lines to the flat water where they awkwardly reentered the cockpits, balancing and wobbling until regaining their equilibrium. A well-fitted kayak embraces its pilot. Half in the water, half out, cutting its silent wake, the best kayaker paddles in stealth, not a splash from the tip and only the faintest rush of water off the bow – a quiet infiltration of nature.

They pushed above the last rapids and were in sight of their landing, a wide sandbar separating the north bank from a dry channel the river had long given up on. With several heavy strokes they ran their boats aground, grinding over the sand, their hulls tipping and looking sad and out of place on the sandbar like mighty fish out of water. In their hatches were camping gear: a gas stove, tents, sleeping bags, lanterns, and fishing tackle. They unloaded it all into a pile before finding their camp chairs, and they set them facing the river where they sank two six-packs, minus two cans, into the current.

Mick popped a beer and cooled his feet in the waters. His build was slim and fit, and he kept his wiry red hair trimmed neatly to his scalp. There was little talk on the river as the journey was a kind of meditation, but arriving at the campsite and finding their chairs allowed their thoughts to organize.

"So what are you doing?" Mick asked. "Are you going to marry her or not?"

Carl took a cold sip and stared into the current. "I don't know. I don't know what I'm doing." He took a pack of cigarettes from his pocket and drew one out.

"I thought you stopped smoking that crap years ago."

"I did," he said, lighting up.

"You want me to tell you what I see?"

"Not really."

"I see a woman who ran off and got herself into trouble. Now she's come home to warm up to an old flame."

"So what if she did? She made a few mistakes. She had an accident."

"An accident? These were choices, Carl. They were all choices. She chose to date the man and she apparently chose not to use birth control. She chose to have the child instead of aborting or putting her up for adoption. She chose to marry a complete stranger, and then chose to divorce the son-of-a-bitch. I don't see any accidents here."

"So she made a few bad choices."

"She always has. Even in high school she was erratic." He watched Carl tense up, obviously getting angry. "I know her parents hold some of the blame," Mick added.

"Some things happened to her back then that you don't know about."

"Like what?"

To answer would be a betrayal. From the first year they dated, Carl had been her one confidant. She used to tell him at length of her grievances with her mother and the comings and goings of strange men and the transient life she led, but the complaints stopped the evening she showed up at the Rittenhaur farm with bruised wrists. A door closed that evening and from there she sought only separation from the past.

"I don't know the whole story," Carl said. "I just know she needs help."

"I think she's using you."

"She lost her kid. I don't expect our old romance to be high on her priority list." The sound of the river was usually a soft silken comfort, but this time Carl didn't feel it. He felt a chill in the air as the sun set on the ravine. "I've learned not to expect much from her."

"What are you getting out of this?"

"She never should have lost her daughter. The whole thing stinks."

"What about you?"

"She's a good mother," Carl continued, ignoring Mick's question. He downed the rest of his beer before reaching into the flow and peeling off another can. The remaining ones he settled back into the sand and weighed them down with a rock. "What about me?" he finally acknowledged, flopping back into his chair.

"Is it the kid?"

"She's really something. I'm still wondering why she isn't mine."

"She's not. She's not your kid. She has a father and you can bet your ass he's going to fight for her. Dirty if need be."

"He's fucking her up."

"Unfortunately, parents have a right to fuck up their children."

"You should see her carry on whenever we drop her off. She's terrified of him. She never acts that way when we pick her up."

Mick leaned forward and hung his head down, as if searching carefully for his words. "If you're not going to marry her, then don't get any deeper into this."

"I told her I would help her, no matter what happened to us."

"What did she say about marriage?"

Carl closed his eyes. "That's all on hold. She refuses to even talk about it."

"Shouldn't she want to? Shouldn't it be easier to get the girl back if you're married?"

"Maybe. I don't know anymore."

"The hell you don't. It makes perfect sense. A two parent household with a stable home will beat out any single father."

"You didn't see what I saw in this court. The judge, the deputies, the attorneys. They don't do things right down there. It's like everyone's been paid off. They even got away with saying we'd been having an affair when we hadn't seen each other in seven years. " He was drinking faster, about to lap Mick. A rush of his old cynicism reemerged. "Besides, if we got married she'd have to stick around this time."

Mick perked up and said, "You're afraid she'll leave you again."

Carl crumpled his can and threw it toward the cockpit of the kayak, where it missed and bounced into the sand. "You don't think that's a valid concern?" he said. "Her leaving? She got it from her father, you know."

"Not if it means losing her kid again."

The sound of the rapids grew sharper as the light dimmed, though the rising surge did nothing to distance Carl from his worries.

"I've got one more question," Mick said. "Since she's been back, have either one of you said 'I love you'?"

In the upper Piedmont, close to the shadows of the lumbering Blue Ridge, Carl usually felt safe from reality, but he could always rely on Mick to keep him grounded in the real world and all its travails. He couldn't answer Mick's question with any confidence. The idea of love and marriage, once the groundswell of his thoughts for her, had become a distant thing. He was sure he and Miriam had said those words, though he couldn't recall the time or place.

They were a week shy of losing daylight savings time, but the evening was still coming on early and the shadows were long and stretched over the ravine where the two friends sat chilling in the gathering dusk. Carl reached down and scooped a handful of river rocks. Marble and bluestone, sandstone and shale – all gathered by chance. He felt their shapes and how they were worn down by time, each with its own personality, its own mood. What force of nature brought them there and how will they be carried away? Which ones will settle in their own place and which ones will erode into nothing but an immeasurable trail of silt to show they had existed at all?

He threw each tiny rock into the current, letting fate carry them.

At last light they set up camp.

Chapter 27

A drawing of an orange jack-o'-lantern was taped into the front window to let the neighborhood know the house was open to trick-or-treaters. Beside the door sat a copper bowl of little candy bars, tarts, and peppermints Carl left for Miriam to hand out in case he didn't return home from the farm in time. But that evening, when kids in costume began wandering door-to-door, his house was dark except for the warm glow of a dozen candles shimmering behind the blinds.

She woke at six-thirty from the first knock on the door. Children outside were giggling and clomping their feet on the porch, but she only rolled over and burrowed her head deep into the pillow. They kept knocking, pounding harder each time until eventually giving up and running off to the next house. Within a few minutes more feet crunched through the leaves followed by an insistent pounding on the door by a small hand. This time Miriam, numb on pills and depression, struggled to the door. Standing before her were two pint-size cowboys, one brandishing a cap gun, and his brother, guns safely holstered, holding up a bag with a dollar sign on it for their booty. Their mother stood on the curb and called out to Miriam, "They're just a couple of showoffs."

"Adorable," Miriam said, and dropped a few candies into their bag. The boys jumped off the porch and, after being admonished by their mother, hollered "thank you" over their shoulders as they ran off. Miriam went back to the futon and curled up, letting the candlelight cleanse the space around her.

Another knock. She stomped to the door and picked up the bowl of candy. This time she found three children on the porch; a boy with a knife through his head and red dye sugar water seeping from the wound, another dressed as either a magician or an undertaker, and behind them, glowing under the porch light, the lightness of a butterfly princess – a girl in a pink tutu with little sagging wings who was dancing on her toes. She waved a star tipped wand, blessing her odd and untamed brothers. Miriam dropped candy into the boy's bags, but her eyes were fixed on the princess. When the brothers bounded off the porch, the littlest one pranced to the threshold and raised her bag in one hand and her magic wand in the other, though she seemed less concerned with receiving treats than with her role of anointer. Miriam stood there holding the copper bowl, staring and shivering. She took a fist full of candy and aimed for the bag, but most of it spilled onto the porch around the girl's slippered feet. The butterfly princess bobbed her wand up and down. She blessed the bowl of candy and blessed her new friend.

"Oh," Miriam said.

They stood there staring at each other, the blesser and the blessed, until the princess took one dainty step at a time off the porch and scurried away into the moonlight, so light and free one might expect her to fly, or wish that she could.

Miriam closed the door. She put her back to it and bent over. After a couple of shuddering breaths, she raised the copper bowl over her head and heaved it across the room where it smashed against the wall in an explosion of silver wrapped disks, fun-size candy bars and sweet-tart hail. The bowl rocked on the floor in a jittery spiral. Miriam shrieked and ripped the pumpkin sign from the front window, tearing it to pieces and leaving it scattered on the floor. She shrieked again, a shriek loud enough to be heard from the street, one to be taken seriously on any other night, but on this haunted evening it was no more than ambiance. She ran upstairs to the bedroom and locked the door. Lingering there on the mattress in a fetal vice, she clamped her body shut, with only the edge of the comforter to soften her image.

Downstairs on the dining room table, in the aftermath of the bombardment of treats, one of the burning candles was leaning in its holder, flirting with a wicker basket full of napkins.

∞

When Carl rolled past the train station onto his street, he thought there was another drug bust. Red and blue lights were twirling and flashing down the lane. It was wishful thinking they finally caught Millie Kilgore, but the notion passed when he focused on the two fire trucks. He parked several houses away where he made out the shadows and silhouettes of costumed children and parents making a strange audience of witnesses. Two hoses pumped up like anacondas were stretched across his yard, one leading into the front door and the other just shutting off its spray into the dining room window, which had been shattered into jagged pieces of wood and glass. Above the window was a ladder propped to the bedroom. Carl's heart raced like he'd been injected with steroids. He pushed through the crowd and broke through the yellow band of police tape, but the cops saw him coming and headed him off, took him by the arm and held him there on the lawn.

"Don't be thinking of running inside," the officer said, studying him as if he might try to break free. "Don't worry, they got her out."

Carl hadn't noticed Lester Kilgore leaning on his usual spot on the fence. With his head cocked forward, the old man called out to him, "Gotta mess on your hands, don'tcha?"

A fireman approached from the house with his yellow turnout coat hanging open, showing a shirt with an embroidered badge on the chest. "The old man's right," he said. "You got yourself a mess." Carl stared at his house as the last wisps of white smoke and steam drifted out the door and windows. The acrid host of his torched possessions made him want to throw up.

The officer guided Carl toward the street. "She's right over here, sir," he said. Carl sidestepped toward the Red Cross volunteer's car where Miriam was draped in a blanket in the back seat. She appeared worn and disheveled, more cold than scared. Under the blanket she wore the same layered sweat clothes she'd been in for the last three days. Her eyes were crimped and distant, lacking even their old color. He opened the car door and bent down to her.

"So you're okay?" he said, seeing she was, or at least seeing she was the same.

"Yeah."

"Did you see Millie Kilgore hanging around? Or any of her red-neck friends?"

"All I saw were a few kids."

"What the hell happened?"

"I don't know. I was asleep."

Two fireman stepped out of Carl's front door, one dragging a hose and the other coming straight toward them. He looked invigorated and happy to be doing what he was doing – a man who loved his job.

"She's structurally sound," the lieutenant said. "We got here just shy of flashover." Carl nodded, but didn't understand what he was talking about. His mind was red from the flashing lights and he wasn't thinking straight. "I can give you a quick look inside."

Carl put an absent hand on Miriam's shoulder. "You stay here." She didn't look interested in going anywhere and drew the blanket up to her neck. When he turned to leave, she clutched his pants leg.

"They called today," she said. "They'll only give me three months."

"What are you talking about?"

"The supervised visitation is funded for only three months. If I don't get her back by then, I won't even get to see her for Christmas."

Carl thought for a second she'd lost her mind. He accompanied the chief and his lieutenant to the porch where he met the bitter smell of burnt carpet and acrylic, charred wood and the wincing stink of loss. The azaleas they had planted with Annaliese that summer had been trampled in the commotion. They stepped on several candies squashed into the porch floorboards as they crossed the threshold. Though the smoke had cleared, it still soaked into his clothes and caused the fabric to stick to his skin. Water dripped from the ceiling and sounded from places he couldn't see. Everything was saturated with a film of poison grime.

The lieutenant pointed his flashlight. "It started back here," he said, working his way to the dining room. "This level is shot, but the fire didn't have time to burn through. You'll have mostly smoke damage upstairs and a few inches of water in your basement." Carl followed the beam of the man's flashlight as it panned over the wreck of his life. "Nothing on this floor is salvageable."

The chief clicked on his own light. "You're lucky this happened when there were so many people out with their cell phones. These old houses go up like kindling." He scanned the floor, lighting several leaking wrappers of melted and smeared chocolate and cream. He examined the charred remains of the dining table. "Here's your combustible." Carl stepped behind him, ducking from the cold drips of water pelting his back. "Does she like candles?"

"Oh, Jesus."

Carl dashed out the door. The crowd was thinning as the neighborhood children were losing interest, perhaps disappointed there hadn't been more damage, and were again wandering the streets and knocking on doors that might have something more to offer. Lester Kilgore was back to his porch stoop holding a cigarette, looking strangely satisfied. One of the fire trucks was pulling away, and a man from the first tanker was rolling up a hose like he was rolling the perfect cigar. A blanket sat crumpled in the back seat of the Red Cross car. The emergency volunteer, a fresh faced young woman recently out of college, met Carl and offered him a coffee from her thermos.

"Where is she?" Carl cried.

"She said she had to get something from her car."

Carl scanned the street where Miriam usually parked her Beemer. The space was vacant.

Chapter 28

The day was a blight of cold rain, a steady pelting downpour swelling the creeks and puddling the yards in a drab preamble to winter. Unsettled masses of grey-white vapor lay frozen in the heavens, unmoving as if it would never again yield to the sun or moon or deep blue sky. Outside the window of the farmhouse the leaves of the mulberry tree still clung green and stubborn to its dripping branches, while others held either random brown clumps of leaves like rotten cabbage or were stripped bare and transparent, bracing for the winter chill to rush through and cleanse them. Except for the sharp green pines lining the ridges, color had gone and left the world in shades of browns and greys.

The attic bedroom smelled of floor wax, old wool suits and leaky sewer pipe. The air was damp and the old plaster walls looked moist, as if they had never properly set. Sloped ceilings ran to the low knee walls, and by one of those walls Carl sat at a small desk that was once his, the one he had used in high school. He hadn't shaved in the week and a half since the fire, and his beard was already dark and full. Receipts and cost estimates and insurance forms covered the desktop, along with a simple lamp and a metal tray full of pens and paperclips. At the back of the desk under the lamp light was Miriam's wedding band he'd stolen, sitting there like a reminder of his circle of failures. He was adding figures on a calculator when his grandfather's awkward combination of footsteps and hickory cane tapped up the stair. The old man opened the door without knocking.

"She's on the phone," he said, winded and leaning heavy on the cane. Carl kept adding numbers and punching buttons on the calculator, figuring the cost of what had happened. The rain pounded the tin roof, a percussive layer awaiting a melody. A rivulet of water trailed down a window pane, making its spidery path.

"I'm done with her," Carl said.

"You act like what she done was intentional. Like she meant to hurt you."

"Maybe she did."

"That's not the case. That's not the case and you know it. Now get yourself on downstairs. She's long distance." The old man began his descent, relying heavily on the hand rail. Carl struggled before remembering he was still paying her phone bill. He tossed the pen to the back of the desk where it took an odd bounce and fell to the floor. Then he set his palms on the desktop and swept everything onto the floor, popping the bulb in the lamp and scattering pens, paperclips, and cost estimates across the softwood planks. The light from the stairwell cast Carl's awkward shadow across the angled wall. The wedding band rolled across the floor and twittered onto its side under the window.

The lone telephone in the house was mounted in the kitchen next to a worn spot on the wood trim that fit the size of his grandfather's palm. The phone cord stretched across the room where the receiver lay on the kitchen table between the coffee pot and a stack of empty margarine tubs the old man couldn't seem to throw away.

"What do you want?" Carl said.

"Please don't be that way."

"What do you want, Miriam?"

Her voice was level and businesslike, without any trace of depression. "I need your help."

"I don't have any more help for you."

"I need you to come down one last time."

"You burned down my house."

"I can get you in to see Annaliese," she said hopefully. "The DCF rep said it would be okay."

Carl didn't want to hear this. He'd had enough, but at the mention of Annaliese he couldn't hang up. "Did you know I had to move back to the farm?"

"I didn't burn the house down. One of the firemen told me it was mostly smoke damage."

"Are you kidding me? The house is an unlivable shell and you act like all you did was redecorate without my permission."

"I'm sorry, Carl. I'm so sorry."

"Do you know the extent of what I lost? All the work I put into that house. And my portfolio, my canvasses . . ."

"Some of those paintings were from college, Carl. You said yourself that no one would ever buy them."

"I wasn't ready to see them destroyed."

"And all your stonework was in the back yard. All your beautiful marble. That was always my favorite stuff, and that's all okay, right?" She waited in silence. "I'm so sorry, Carl, but it was an accident. You know I would never do anything to hurt you."

"Did you know your box in my basement was ruined? All your photos, your birth certificate . . . all that junk from your father."

She paused, as if swallowing the past. "I figured that. Look, I want to come back up and help you rebuild, but right now I have other things to worry about. My daughter is living with an abusive man who's capable of doing God knows what, and I can't even see her without some old hen with a clipboard watching me."

"You're real good at handing out guilt."

"I don't have anywhere else to turn. I can't do this by myself. I don't want to bring you in any deeper, but I still need you for this. Just one last time. And you said you'd help. You said you'd help whether we made it or not – no matter what." And he had once told her just that. "Don't do it for me. Do it for Annaliese. I need her to see you again. You know how much she loved you. If I can get you in there, I know it would help her."

Carl noted the desperation in her voice and searched for a way to endure. He felt like sliding to the floor and shutting down.

"I lost my job, Miriam. I missed classes the day after the fire and I lost my job."

The gravity of his situation finally reached her. "I'm so sorry, Carl."

"I'm homeless and unemployed." He rested his head against the jamb and closed his eyes. He prayed for a way out – out of his ancestral home, out of this town and this life. But his thoughts again wandered back to the girl. "What is it you need me to do?" he asked.

"My car's in the shop and I can't get to visitation this week."

"You can't call a taxi?"

"There are no cabs out here. I'd have to call one in from Jacksonville and that would cost a fortune. I don't even know how I'm going to pay the shop repairs. Ed's still demanding child support and –."

"Okay, fine. I get it." He scuffed his foot on the old linoleum tile, its blurred pattern scarred from the years. "You said I could see Annaliese. How'd you pull it off with DCF?"

"There was a new guardian at the last visitation. A nice one. I just asked and she said okay. Ed doesn't know or else he'd raise a stink."

"You're due to see her tomorrow. It's too late for this week."

She spoke quickly. "It got pushed back. It's going to be this Monday."

"Fine. Monday I can handle."

"Monday afternoon at three-thirty."

Carl laid his palm over the worn spot on the woodwork, comparing the outline of his hand to his grandfather's. "I'll be at your apartment before then. I don't know when, but I'll be there."

She sniffled and her voice cracked. "Thank you. I don't know what –."

He hung up on her. At the back door, he pulled the lacy curtain aside and watched the rain flash lines through the spot light and felt the cold draft on his bare feet. His grandfather hobbled in and put a cup and saucer in the sink, ran water over them. He began rinsing the other dishes that had accumulated on the counter. The sound of running water filled the room.

"What you fixing to do?" the old man asked.

"I'm going down," Carl answered, staring into the foul weather.

"That's not entirely what I meant." Glasses clinked in the drying rack, and for a second Carl believed he could turn around and see his mother and father and grandmother all sitting at the kitchen table, talking over a pot of coffee. The image made him well up.

"I don't know what I'm going to do."

"You're still protecting yourself. Hiding so you don't make a bad decision."

"She's the one who left me."

"And you handled it no better than a fool. You cut yourself off from the world and started acting the way you did before you found her."

Carl turned to him. "You don't understand how I felt about her."

"Then that should make your decision easy."

Carl gazed into his grandfather's crimped up eyes, begging his guidance. "She's changed. I don't know what to make of her anymore."

"Women are made to change. Men ain't. That's something you'll have to learn to deal with." He placed the last glass in the drying rack and shut off the water, writhed a dishtowel with his long shaking fingers. "I know what I'd do," he said.

"What?" Carl asked desperately. He hadn't expected to see such sudden anger in his grandfather's eyes.

"That ex-husband of hers abusing that little girl?"

Carl flinched. "I don't know for sure. But he may be."

Malcolm nodded. "Yep. I know what I'd do."

"What?"

"Don't matter. You're not me. But you remember, no matter what you do, you're a part of me. You have a family and a place in this world. You might not think so much of this old house, but it's going to be half yours one day – one day soon. And just like I remade this place from my granddaddy, you and Vince will be able to remake it into whatever you want – if you're around to remake it." The old man headed for the parlor door, but stopped one last time and thumped his cane. "Whatever you decide, you remember that much. That much is worth remembering."

Chapter 29

People go to Florida for one of two reasons: to fuck or to die. Some people say the mouse and his amusement park are a third reason, but to Carl that was a subset of dying. He didn't have a problem with this, so long as you knew what you were going there for. His lingering problem with Miriam was she went down for one reason and inadvertently did the other. He was astounded how she had thrown away her life. This would be his last trip to The Sunshine State, and along the entire mindless passage down I-95 he agonized over why she'd ever gone there in the first place. But he knew her fantasies and her insecurities, and he boiled it down to easy living; no hassles, few responsibilities, little clothing – it was the perfect fit for the daughter of an alcoholic mother and a runaway father. She was blinded by palm trees and neon and colorful drinks in a place where she could dance to sunrise and sleep until noon in a guiltless tropical splendor. It's easy to forget where you came from when there's sand between your toes.

The south was in the grip of an early cold snap and the wind whipped Carl's truck in sporadic gusts as he crossed the St. Mary's River. A cloud bank was rolling past to the northeast, leaving a chilled and spotless blue sky in its wake. He wore a light windbreaker as it was the last jacket he owned. His winter coat still hung from the newel post in his house where it was gathering mold and stinking of smoke and rotten gym towels. Still, he wouldn't have thought to bring a heavier coat, since he had no image of Florida being a cold weather destination. Miriam once tried to explain not all of Florida was tropical, that she'd once seen snowflakes as far south as Gainesville, but Carl hadn't believed her until now. He kept cracking the window, expecting a rush of warm air, only to roll it back up each time and crank the heater.

When he arrived at her apartment she was pacing back and forth on the sidewalk, but he barely recognized her. She saw his pick-up round the corner and she ran inside. By the time Carl was cutting the ignition, she was struggling down the steps with two suitcases, her purse, and a tote bag bulging with all her legal files, looking about to tear off her arm.

"Wow," he said, staring at her hair. "You've never cut it this short."

"I needed a change," she said, going back to the tailgate.

Carl always loved her hair, but he surprised himself when he didn't mind seeing it mostly gone. He wondered if it helped separate them from the recent unpleasantness.

"What's all this?" he asked.

"Some of Annaliese's clothes. I want her to wear them before they're outgrown." She didn't wait for Carl's help and began heaving the suitcases into the truck bed. "They're just going to waste here."

"Wouldn't you rather stick Ed with buying her a new wardrobe?"

"He's incapable," she said sharply. Her neck turned red whenever she spoke of the man. "These clothes were some of her favorites." She flipped down the glass camper lid and secured the latch. She called out to him, "Where are you going?"

Carl was climbing the steps to the apartment. "I gotta use the can."

"We have to go," she said, tapping her wrist. "We have to go right now."

"It'll just take a second."

"I already locked the door. You can pee when we get there."

He considered her urgency and realized he could better tolerate a little temporary discomfort than Miriam being late for another visitation. Besides, he was anxious to see Annaliese. While they drove toward town, Miriam kept checking the mirrors and tried several times to fold her hands, but they kept fidgeting in her lap.

"Turn here," she said.

"I thought DFC was by the courthouse."

"We're doing the visitation at the daycare now." She stared out the side window at something distant. "It's all worked out."

They pulled into Palm Kids at three-thirty. The high pressure system had pushed the sky clear, leaving them in a crisp blue chill. "Over there," Miriam pointed. "Go to the side entrance." He drove through the main lot and turned into the alley running the depth of the brick school building. "Pull up there and wait."

There were no classroom windows on this end of the building, just an imposing brick wall, a loading dock, and a cooling tower screened by white masonry blocks that had been partially shattered by numerous bumpers. Carl stopped so Miriam was sitting right by the side exit door. She eased from the cab.

"What gives?" he asked. "You said I could go in and see her too."

"You will. I'll be right back."

The passenger door clicked shut, but not all the way, leaving the dome light glowing overhead. Miriam cupped her hands over the wire safety-glass and peered down the corridor before slipping through the door.

Carl knew it wasn't right, but he just sat there. It was not right what she was doing, and he knew damn well what she was doing, but he just sat there waiting, waiting for his life to take off like deep down inside he knew it would, just not how. The hows and whys weren't important, so long as something happened, some magical shift to propel him forward again.

Through the diamond pattern glass was a shadow lurking toward him. He felt the pressure building in his bladder and he almost took off, but saw it was Miriam. He wasn't used to her short hair. The door swung wide and under her extended arm was the girl wearing corduroy pants and a white shirt covered with food stains. She looked uncertain and disoriented.

"Look, sweetie," her mother said in day-glow voice. "It's Carl. You remember Carl." Annaliese stepped out timidly and gazed at the sun as if feeling its warmth for the first time. She stared at Carl's bearded and befuddled face and put her fist in her mouth. Her mother lost patience, scooped her up and plopped her into the seat. She eased the door shut and tugged just hard enough for the latch to click shut. Annaliese whimpered and her mother dug the pacifier out of her purse. Carl had never seen such urgency in a person's eyes.

"Go!" Miriam said.

"What are you doing?"

Miriam yanked the fingers out of the girl's mouth and plugged in the binky. Annaliese stared at the dash, stiff and wide-eyed, bracing like she was about to be struck. Carl took in Miriam's profile as he raised his foot off the brake and the three of them began to drift. Before they rolled far, he sensed a movement over his shoulder. Glancing back he saw the saintly image of Janine Haygood watching them through the exit door.

"They're letting me have her for the afternoon," Miriam said.

"Stop lying. I know damn well what you're doing."

"Just go. I don't care what they do to me. I don't care anymore."

"Do you care what they'll do to me?"

"No, I don't."

At first taken aback at her gross lack of concern, he soon realized he wasn't all that surprised, in fact he almost laughed aloud from a sense of nervous giddiness. Beneath that giddiness was a simmering hatred for her ex-husband. A prickly row of fan palms separated the school grounds from the residential blocks of stucco ranchers and uncut yards. There was no stop sign, but he pressed the brakes anyway, somehow knowing this was the threshold to another life. There was no one in sight. Miriam appeared to be in meditative prayer, waiting for his decision. He studied the girl.

"Hey you. Remember me?" Carl reached over and squeezed Annaliese's knee, but she seized her leg away and stiffened up. Her eyes closed tight, making pained creases at her temples. But it was when her hands shielded her crotch that he sensed the damage done. He said to Miriam, "I don't care either." He popped the clutch and they lurched forward and sped down the first block. Carl sensed a freedom he'd never known, an initial rush that built with each cross-street until they came to the end of the subdivision.

"That way," Miriam said, and Carl made the turn. The distressed child wouldn't come close enough to touch him and was only slightly less repulsed by her mother. He realized he might appear strange to her, so he scratched his beard to show he was under there. Her mother drew her in close and tried snuggling with her. "You'll warm up again, won't you." In her haste she left

Annaliese's coat in the daycare, so she slipped off her own and wrapped it around the girl, who neither protested nor cooperated. "We'll have to stop. I have one of her sweaters in back."

"You have to keep her down," Carl said, shaking his head. "I'm glad I never bought a car-seat."

Miriam drew her own seat belt wide and latched it around the two of them, the buckle making the sound of handcuffs clicking shut. It was a tighter fit than when they buckled in together the prior summer. "Ed's not due to pick her up until five-thirty. The Amber Alert will probably be up before six."

Carl's giddiness dissolved. "Fucking great." The initial rush was over, replaced by a growing sense of fear and paranoia. Instead of running toward something, he was now running away.

"Please don't cuss in front of her. And keep to the speed limit."

"Just great," he said, checking his language. "Just in time for the evening news."

"Hush." She pointed. "Here. Turn here and then take 90 west. Stay off the interstates."

Carl took a deep breath and settled down. He ran the miles like he was sprinting from one existence to another. US90 was a two-lane highway coupled with a railroad smelling of creosote, old warehouses and burnt brush. Billboards for Indian River Fruit made orange, yellow and black spots in his eyes, and the one for the Progressive Baptist Church promised a "breakthrough to blessing" in their next homily. Many of the fields they passed were long ago logged but never replanted, giving the landscape a desolate battle-worn air, with no more than a scattering of crippled trees not worth harvesting. Carl broke several miles of silence.

"You mentioned once getting her to Georgia. That they had more favorable courts for this kind of thing."

"Any state's better than this one." Miriam adjusted the seat belt, giving them more room to breathe. "I found an attorney in Athens who's licensed in both states. He's agreed to work pro-bono. He's filing an appeal in Florida, and in the meantime he's working on an emergency hearing in Georgia for protection while we're in hiding."

"So we're just going to Georgia?"

"We'll be over the state line before Ed finds out. Keep going to Lake City, then take 441 north. And no interstates."

"No interstates," he repeated. "It would have been faster to take Route 1."

"The first place he'd expect to find us is on our way to Virginia. That's I-95 or Route 1. I needed a more discreet option." Annaliese raised her head to see over the dash.

"Keep her out of sight," Carl said, before looking over Miriam. "You too, for that matter." She grabbed her purse off the floorboard and pulled out a pair of old folks' sunglasses that covered half her face. They drove on a while in silence. "You couldn't have let me pee before we did this?"

"I didn't want you to know that I cleared out the apartment. I was afraid you wouldn't do it."

"I haven't peed in five states."

Miriam giggled. "I'm sorry. I can't help it." She burst into laughter.

The tension was broken, and Carl was at least thankful of that. "How did you convince Haygood to go along with this?"

"She's quitting next week and moving back to Texas to be near her relatives. She was really ticked off at management when they threatened to fire her if she testified."

"Are you sure she'll be able to keep this quiet for the rest of the afternoon?"

"Only if her assistant doesn't notice. I'd have done it earlier if it wasn't for her," she said, full of indignation. "She's a nosey bitch."

"But if this nosey assistant is doing her job, then the police have already been called?"

"We don't know anything. Just drive."

Carl checked the gauges. "We have to stop for gas. You couldn't have asked me to gas up either? Before we kidnaped your child?"

"I had to get on with this, Carl. I couldn't sit for another ten seconds without losing my mind."

The speed limit dropped when they rolled into the town of Macintire, past Buzz Barbeque, Preacherman's Liquor, and the Word of Life Ministries. On one corner was a green and white BP station that stood apart from the false front commercial buildings, looking all clean and shiny, though it wore the same dull film of dirt worn by the rest of the town.

Carl nosed the pump into the truck and set the flow. He zipped his jacket and gave Miriam a look that said to be cool, before walking past the little glass booth to the restroom. He was in pain now and slightly crooked over as he walked. He rattled the scarred door knob but it wouldn't turn. The attendant in the glass booth, a wrinkled old black man in a green BP shirt, seemed to be wondering what to make of this clumsy looking white man.

"You gotta have a key," the old man said without offering one.

Carl waited a second longer than appropriate. "Do you *have* the key?"

"Yes, sir."

"Mind if I use it?"

"Don't mind at all."

The key was hooked to a small billy club, and the man put it in the aluminum tray and pushed it under the glass. When Carl finished, he found the gas nozzle had cut itself off at less than a quarter tank. Only a few bucks squirted in. He cursed and pumped it by hand. Miriam knocked on the window.

"I need her sweater out of the small suitcase," she called through the glass.

He unlatched the camper window and pulled the luggage toward him. While he rummaged through the loose clothing, he felt as if they were going on vacation. A half dozen doll size socks tumbled into the truck bed before he found the bright pink sweater tucked under the mess of clothes.

"You couldn't have brought a color that was a little less vocal?" he said, starting the engine.

"It's not like I had much left that she hadn't outgrown."

Back on the road every car was suspicious, every driver and passenger a secret informant in a world plagued by surveillance. After they crossed under I-10, a black Buick nosed up behind them and tail-gated for the next ten miles. Carl kept under the speed limit and watched the car. He couldn't see the driver through the tinted windows. Though there was little traffic, the Buick never tried to pass and was satisfied to trudge along in their wake, until it finally broke south toward Gainesville.

Lake City was a drag of gas stations and repair shops until they met City Hall, which was fronted by a deserted public green and a row of sheriff's cruisers. Carl couldn't understand why this was a better route than the interstate. They turned right at the village green onto US441, Main Street, which was clogged with what little rush hour traffic there was. North of town, after missing every traffic light, they crossed I-10 again and Carl was tempted to catch the west-bound ramp, but sensing Miriam's fragility and in fear of her wrath, he held straight and true to her wishes.

US441 was another two-laner with wide shoulders raised high over land that wasn't much higher than swamp. The map showed the road winding gracefully to the north, but the bone white pavement ran dead ahead and vanished at a point. Hurricane Evacuation Route signs lined the way with their little washing machine symbols, and leaning telephone poles speared the left bank as if thrown down from the Gods. Carl could tell by the thinness of the electric lines that hardly anyone lived there.

It was past five-thirty and closing on dusk when they crossed onto the black Georgia pavement. Carl and Miriam smiled with uneasy confidence, as if passing a first test. The shoulders narrowed as they rolled into heavier logging country, though there was more evidence here of replanting and planning for the future, with grids of baby pines poking their heads out of amber fields. They passed a gathering of buildings with a sign in front advertising camping and hot water. On the side of one of the barns someone had painted "Jesus is Lord" in big clumsy letters.

Carl checked the time. "I don't care if we're in Georgia or Florida. We need to be off the road when that alert goes up." Their road atlas was missing its cover, along with the inner leaf states of Nebraska through New Jersey. Miriam traced a finger over north Florida, and Carl grabbed it from her and flipped it to Georgia. He studied the map and the curve of the road, noted the nearby parkland, and committed to memory what was ahead of them. When he squinted to read the indicated mileage that was in tiny red print, he blew right by the reduced speed sign dropping the limit to twenty-five. The bend in the road came up quick.

"Stop!" Miriam screamed. The S-10 shuddered over the first rack of speed control ripples. Carl dropped the map as the taillights came on fast. He floored the brake and clutch, and Miriam covered Annaliese with both hands. They popped the bumper of the pick-up in front of them, giving it only the slightest jolt.

"Where in the hell did a traffic light come from out here?" he demanded from no one.

"My God, Carl." She checked over her daughter, who appeared numb to it all.

"Son-of-a-bitch."

"Wait. See if he gets out."

A grey hand at the end of a flannelled arm extended from the window and waved for them to follow. When the light turned green, Carl crossed the intersection onto a local road and pulled over with two wheels in the grass. Ahead were a pair of cross-boards and two idle warning lights marking a railroad, and before that a park authority sign telling them they were nearing the Okefenokee Swamp.

"Stay here," Carl said, getting out. "And keep her down."

The man stepped from his cab one heavy foot at a time, walking with an arthritic limp. He was past seventy, with tufts of grey sideburns erupting from under a John Deere cap. He ignored Carl and bent down to inspect his bumper, hovering there for so long Carl thought he might be catching his breath. He rose and applied pressure on the bumper with his toe, probably expecting it to fall off.

"You have a hard time seeing?" the old man asked, acknowledging Carl for the first time.

"No, sir. I was distracted. I apologize for that."

The man noticed Carl's license plate and cinched his jaw. "You should have the courtesy of keeping your eyes open if you're gonna be driving in places strange to you."

Carl bent down and checked the man's bumper. He clutched it with both hands and shook. It was already bent down at one corner and scratched from years of use. "There doesn't appear to be any damage," Carl said hopefully.

"Damned if there ain't. You done marked up my paint."

"Sir, these scratches are already rusty." He ran a hand over it, turning his fingers brown for evidence.

"A jolt like that musta knocked out my alignment."

Carl tried to read the crooked old man. "What would you want to set things right?"

He put a hand on his truck as if it meant something to him. "Hundred might cover the alignment. Then there's my time."

"It won't cost more than forty bucks to get an alignment."

"Then I suppose we should wait for the police so they can fill out a report. Shame to get your insurance company involved. You do have insurance, don'tcha?" The old man waited for Carl's next move.

"Hold on a minute." He went to Miriam's window and signaled her to crank it down. "Look in the glove compartment. There's a metal business card carrier under all the crap." She foraged under the mess of owner's manuals, napkins and repair bills until she found the tarnished box. He flipped the lid and peeled off four twenties from a fold of bills, and strode back to the old man. "Here's eighty bucks for the alignment you're never going to get. That's all I got. We square?"

The man tightened his grip around the bills. Carl wasn't surprised to see a smile creep onto his face as he turned away. He u-turned back toward 441 and motored south. Carl punched the truck over the railroad tracks into the wilderness.

"How much?" Miriam asked.

"Don't worry about it."

"Where are you going?"

"I said we have to get off the road." He checked the clock on the dash. "By now every cop in Dixie is looking for us."

"I can drive tonight if you're too tired."

Even though Carl left at ten-thirty Sunday night and caught only a few hours of sleep at the highway rest stop, he wasn't about to let her take the wheel. "You're never driving my truck again," he said in such a way he didn't have to worry about her asking twice.

The posted speed was back to fifty-five and they blazed ahead into the wilderness. The road was raised higher than before, a causeway over the woodland, with ponding water in deep ditches to each side and a dirty brown line of vegetation marking the most recent flood. Fresh forests of different vintages were laid out in grids, young to the left, more mature to the right, and reversing when they came to a new tract. "Posted" signs were nailed to trees at regular intervals. They'd gone seven miles before passing the first house, and Carl realized they hadn't passed a single vehicle. The light was dimming and the sky was ice blue. He had hoped to find another private campground, but now he had other ideas.

"Look at all these pull-offs," he said. At uneven intervals were driveways without mailboxes, some blocked with wide aluminum gates, others overgrown with weed but still accessible. They all pierced straight into the forest.

"You want to stop here?" she exclaimed.

"This is perfect. No one lives back here."

"We have to eat."

"What did you expect? You want to walk into a restaurant during the evening news?" Miriam appeared angry with herself, and Carl wondered how well she'd planned. She may have an attorney in Athens, but how long could she hide out if she was this reckless? "There's a bag under your seat," he said. She found a column of saltines, a half-liter bottle of water, a warm can of soda and a bag of trail mix. Road food. "There's your dinner," he said.

He checked the mirrors and plunged into the next trail, flushing out a white egret wading in the ditch by the road. They watched it lift high with its prehistoric wings and sail east toward the marsh. The trail ahead ran for no more than twenty yards before it was cut off by an aluminum gate. The differential whined as he backed out. They rode on in the direction the bird had flown and tried the next access. This one was clear of any obstructions and the weeds dawdled out into sandy tire tracks as they ran deeper into the forest. They plunged through the young softwood, the high beams bouncing along and giving the impression they were traveling through a tunnel shored up by spindly sticks, a tunnel that could collapse at any moment. About fifty yards in they crossed a perpendicular trail into a section of older trees, the trunks thicker and the branches higher, making a near full canopy over their heads. Here Carl splayed off axis and plunged into the grid, stopping only when he thought they were deep inside and well hidden. He stepped onto the spongy bed of needles and inspected the timber like he'd been meaning to go there all along. It was much darker under the high branches, with the deepening moonless sky glowing beyond the black treetop silhouettes.

"We'll hole up here for the night," he said, seeing his breath. "I have a drop-cloth and an old blanket behind the seat. You two can bed down in back."

Miriam was still in the cab and had taken a cell phone from her purse. She pushed its blue glowing buttons over and over. "It can't be dead," she pleaded.

"Battery?"

"No signal. We're not covered here." She gazed into the sky as if sensing a gap in the satellites.

"You got a new phone," Carl noticed.

"Yeah." She flipped it closed and slipped it in her purse.

"Who do you have to call?"

"I need to coordinate with someone. The less you know the better."

"You got me in this far."

"I need you for this much, but once we get settled you'll need to go home and pretend you never saw us. You don't know anything about us." She opened the door and slid out.

"I'm not going to give you up to them, Miriam."

"I know you're not, but the less you know the better." She reached for Annaliese, but the girl squirmed away, centering between the two open doors under the dome light. She wasn't going anywhere. "This place is scaring her," Miriam said.

"I don't think it's just the place. I think she's pretty perceptive." He leaned the seat forward enough to pull out the tarp and blanket, and eased it back more gently than needed. He was angry with himself for his earlier cursing in front of the child, and he had a sudden need to tread lightly. The softness of the ground was telling him to be respectful, not to stir, startle, or make things worse for the already traumatized little girl. He felt under the seat for his flashlight, and opened the camper and dropped the tailgate. He triple folded the tarp for a mattress and threw the blanket out like a fishermen tossing his net. When he finished, Annaliese was still under the protection of the dome light with a pacifier pulsing in her mouth, listening to her mother's reassurances.

"You could try the road," Carl said, motioning through the trees from where they'd come. "It leads to a national park. Might have better cell coverage."

Miriam stared through the forest into the coming blackness. "I'm not going out there. Besides, I can't leave her." She brushed an affectionate hand through the girl's locks. "Hey. I just realized, you've never seen mommy's hair this short." She lowered her head so Annaliese could feel her hair, but the child did no more than touch it uncertainly.

"Why don't y'all go back and tell ghost stories or something," Carl said.

"It's too early for her to sleep."

"It's not too early for me. At least take the flashlight and move her back there. Get her used to it." Carl took a swig from the water bottle and recapped it. "Take the food with you." He handed Annaliese the flashlight, remembering the one at the beach and figuring she might feel more in control if she had something to wave in her hand. She placed her palm over the coning and watched her finger bones glow red.

"I have to change her anyway," Miriam said, scooping the girl into her arms and carrying her to the back.

Carl threw on an extra shirt and zipped his jacket to the collar. He balled up in the front seat and tried not to think of the cold. Though he'd slept little in the last thirty-six hours, he was too wired for sleep. He listened to the pensive sound of the branches blowing overhead and watched the changing glow off the cab ceiling from Annaliese's light. Miriam's muffled voice filtered through the window and was full of soothing platitudes that were tinged with fear. The child hadn't spoken since they'd taken her. She hadn't even cried.

Chapter 30

Carl was the first to wake, though he scarcely slept through the chronic pangs of hunger and worry. His throat was sore and his neck was stiff from the cold. The dawn air, crisp and weightless, filtered through the yellow pines that sheltered them. After being preserved overnight, he felt safe and was reluctant to leave, but as the morning sun rose, so did his apprehension.

In a clumsy stretch, he plunged a knee into the horn on the steering wheel, sending a blaring honk as far as the Keys. He sat up with a start, paranoid like the fugitive he was, but calmed himself by fixating on the rearview mirror. He wiped back his thinning hair and squinted like a man whose glasses were just punched off his face. In back all he could make out was a motionless lump under the blanket.

Now with clear eyes, the forest wasn't as dense as the night before. The longleaf pines had regressed and were less mature, didn't feel planted in their rigid grid but dropped randomly by the birds. He walked into the forest to take a leak. He hadn't heard a single car pass all night, but with the sharpening senses that comes with first light, he turned at the sound of something distant. The pitch rose as it approached, and through the vertical bollards of the tree trunks he watched a silver car pass and disappear as fast as it had come. He was shocked at how close they were to the road and he worried they could be seen – at least if someone were looking for them.

He rapped on the camper window. "Time to get up."

Miriam's head rested on a wad of clothes she had bundled for a pillow. She rubbed her eyes hard like she was polishing the inside of a shot glass. The skin around her sockets was stretched and bruised. The only trace of Annaliese was a ball of hair in the crook of her mother's arm.

Carl dropped the tailgate. "You can see us from the road," he said. "We've got to get out of here."

"We're hungry."

"We're all hungry."

Miriam changed Annaliese's diaper and peed behind the largest tree she could find. After buckling in with her daughter, Carl fired up the engine and backed out of the sandy access road, flattening the weeds until Miriam told him to hold up.

"Wait. Stop here." She was fiddling with her new cell phone. The blacktop was in sight, but they were still behind the first line of trees. Miriam hopped out and trotted closer to the road, this time making contact and jabbering excitedly into the mouthpiece. Though she was alone and the dew covered morning was eerily silent, she cupped the phone with both hands as a symbol the call was confidential. Carl was shocked again at how close they had been to the road, and he was nervous about coming out of their shelter. Miriam finished her call and waved him on to pick her up by the pavement. Those first few miles were unnerving since they were retracing their steps, plunging back in the direction of the crime. To Carl it felt like they were taunting those who were pursuing them, but once they turned north on US441, again fleeing and running for their meager reputations, he settled in more comfortably for the chase.

They crossed the Suwannee River, where Spanish moss dripped into its black water from craggy tree branches, and rolled into the town of Fargo. The pumps of the gas station in town were padlocked, and there was no place to eat at this hour, no fast food, diners, or even a convenience store, so they drove on with hungry bellies. One-story homes sitting back from the road were either solid and well manicured, or gutted shells full of age, sad stories and disuse. The few palmettos seemed out of place among the deciduous trees that were unsure of the season, some bare and leafless, other still green, while the maples were amplifying their autumn red glow. Carl cracked open the window for a sobering breath of air as the heater, at Miriam's insistence, blew a hot wind storm at their feet. A mile out of town their speed rose with the posted limit, but they didn't dare surpass it. A sign saying "speed checked by detection devices," reminded them of watching eyes, though another saying "Trees Grow Jobs," gave comfort and told them how far they were from civilization.

They drove by a field of fresh turned earth where a farmer was burning brush at the tree-line. The acrid host of smoke reminded Carl of recent events and soured his mood. A burst of sparks rose from the crackling embers as the old man fed another stick to the fire, and Carl imagined his grandfather doing the same thing at that very moment, or even his own father had he lived so long. He wished he could talk to them, to explain what it was he was doing. He wondered if they would have approved. His mother would have objected and claimed he shouldn't have gotten involved in the first place, but despite the imagined wrath of his mother at going on such a reckless adventure, Carl knew there were times where a little defiance, be it of the written law or a mother's wishes, was a necessary thing, no matter the consequences. As he thought of his family, both the dead and the living, they came to a sight everyone focused on, even Annaliese – they couldn't take their eyes off it. A steel fire tower flanked a long stretch of open road like some life-size erector set, easily bringing to mind a prison watch tower with rifles aimed up and down the lane.

When they rolled into the butt end of Homerville, past the butler buildings, the Dollar General and the Dairy Queen, a grey and brown sheriff's cruiser was coming at them.

"Down! Get down!" Carl put a hand on the girl's head and Miriam pulled her into her lap while trying to stare casually out the window. Annaliese whimpered at the intrusion. The officer at the wheel held a cup of coffee at his lips and was going south in no hurry. He passed without giving them the slightest glance. Carl watched the cruiser in the rear view mirror until it passed from sight. He whipped into a Hardees and parked in the back lot. Only a few cars were angled there in the shade, presumably the employees who had just opened up.

"You two stay put," Carl said.

"No way. We need a rest room."

"Then what do you want to eat?"

Miriam tried to puff some body into her remaining mop of hair as she gave him a long order for the road. She slipped in the back door with Annaliese, while Carl ordered sausage and egg biscuits, a dozen cinnamon rolls, two coffees, cartons of milk and four plastic cups of orange juice. They met in the cab and ate out of white bags with napkins draped over their knees.

Carl sat there chewing and checking his mirrors. "We need a newspaper," he said, stuffing the last bite of greasy sausage and biscuit into his mouth. He climbed out with his coffee and walked to the gas station next door. Both garage bays were open with cars on the racks, but no one was working on them. Carl stepped inside the little office where the coil of a space heater was lit orange. The newspaper rack held *The Atlanta Constitution*, *The Suwannee Democrat*, *The Gainesville Sun*, and *The Florida Times-Union* out of Jacksonville. He jingled the loose change in his pocket, scanning the headlines, and there she was staring back at him from a two inch square photo in the header, smiling in a way he hadn't seen in months. It was strange to see Annaliese's image next to another little girl's name. "Amber Alert in Dixon County," the caption read. He thought it odd that all missing children were associated with the name Amber, and he wondered if anyone would ever name their child Amber again. He picked up *The Florida Times-Union* and folded it under his arm, put the change on the counter and headed for the door, but a middle-age clerk in a hunting jacket told him to hold on. He'd been reading the Atlanta paper when he looked up.

"I need to scan that," the man said.

"It's a quarter."

"It might be."

The bar code was on the bottom of the front page, so Carl put the paper on the counter with Annaliese facing down. The cashier ran a handheld scanner over the paper. Carl checked outside for his S-10 and was relieved to see it was out of sight.

"That'll be twenty-six cents." Carl put a nickel on the counter and didn't wait for the change. He jogged back to the pick-up, dribbling warm coffee through his fingers, and was winded when he handed the paper to Miriam.

"We need to get on," he said. Having little choice, he took them through downtown, which amounted to a few sparsely filled blocks clustered along the railroad. When they rumbled over the tracks, he waited for a report. "So what does it say?"

The front page lay over the dash, angled away so her daughter couldn't see it. Miriam's eyes were fixed on the caption. "It's an old photo," she said, reminiscing. "She's still skinny in this shot." She unfolded the paper to the article on page two and froze. "Oh my," she said, her voice shrinking.

"What?"

She hesitated, frozen on a high ledge. "They have my photo too. 'Miriam Boyd (a.k.a. Miriam Groeper), the victim's mother, is being sought for questioning –'" She choked and trailed off as she read.

"We figured that. What else does it say?"

Her eyes welled up. "It mentions you too." She collapsed the paper into a mangled mess on her lap. Annaliese shoved it away with both hands. "They describe your truck – blue Chevy S-10, white camper. The tag number too. It says you're 'an interested party.'" She shoved the crumpled mess onto the floor and rubbed the bridge of her nose.

A shiver flowed down Carl's neck. He adjusted his mirrors, though they didn't need it. The tips of his fingers tingled, so he gripped the wheel tighter. "Any photo?"

"No," she whispered. "Not yet."

Homerville died out to more intense forestry as logging trucks roared by, smelling of diesel and saw dust. Barren fields were left with enormous piles of brush to be burned like some woodland funeral pyre. A few scattered trees too weak and spindly to harvest were left to mourn on the desolate plain. Mud-tracked side roads splayed off into the threatened stands of trees, and Carl passed several before he knew what to do – he hardly slowed down when he made the turn. For several miles into the Georgia bush the only sign of civilization was a decrepit school bus swallowed in vine and a few abandoned sharecropper shacks, the dried up and abandoned husks of families whose useful lives had passed. By one of these shacks, he drove onto a potted drive that had turned into a community dump. He spun his tires in the red clay and bounced along the ruts. They stopped by a pile of busted concrete, a few tires and a bathtub.

"How do you know no one lives here?" Miriam asked.

"I don't." He backed into a gap in the trees behind the garbage pile and ripped the emergency brake. "Watch out," he said. They scooted forward without questioning, and he retrieved a screwdriver from the toolbox behind the seat. "Start working on the clamps," he called out to Miriam.

The camper was fixed to the side rails by six aluminum clamps, and Miriam strained to loosen them. She yelled back frustrated, "I can't get them. They hurt my hands."

"Give me a minute," he muttered. He'd gotten the first screw off the license plate, which rocked back and forth while he worked out the second. When the plate fell to the ground, he wrapped it in an oily rag and stuffed it under the front seat. He shooed Miriam aside and winced as the first clamp cut into his hand. One by one he threw all six into the woods before he and Miriam raised the aluminum frame and walked it deep into the forest. She sat her side down and massaged her hands. The aluminum underside was dull and lifeless and blended in better than its bright white top, so Carl raised his side and flipped it over, the sheet metal winnowing in thunder until it settled. He planted his hand on his hips and felt liberated. Off with the past, he thought. Miriam was just as invigorated, as if doing anything at all, no matter how desperate or trivial, might help their situation. From the cab, Annaliese was staring into the open hull where her canvas bed still laid unmade. Carl folded the tarp, and Miriam the blanket. "Have you ever stolen a license tag before?" he asked her.

"I'm willing to learn."

They stuffed the makeshift bedding, Carl's duffel and Miriam's tote bag full of legal files behind the seat, but the luggage was too big. They had to leave them exposed in the truck bed.

"What do we do if it rains?" she protested.

He checked the sky where only a few blots of cloud were drifting overhead. "I'll get you to Athens before it rains."

She look worried again, but without any better options she just held on to her daughter. When they hit the main road, Carl scanned his dash. He reached over and popped the glove compartment.

"Look in there for a scraper," Carl said.

She found a plastic handle with a rusty razor blade on the end and stripped off the Virginia inspection sticker from the windshield. Annaliese balled up each curly sliver and threw them on the floor like she was feeding pigeons.

The town of Pearson's two traffic lights signaled the end of the Georgia flats and they climbed into hill country, rising from the planar abyss, past clean picked cotton fields with their crusty shells and leftover white tufts quivering in the morning breeze. Some fields had already been plowed over, their faces turned, exposing the blood red interior left to erode through the winter trials.

The southern fringe of Douglas was a slow commercial burn, on past the municipal airport with its TR132 fighter jet mounted skyward at the gate (no more threatening than a plastic model), past the Pizza Hut, the Waffle King and the Super 8 Motel. The K-Mart was still closed, but a cluster of vehicles belonging to the morning shift was parked to one side. Carl wound the long way through the parking lot, casing the scene of an impending crime. They rolled down the side alley where they found another dumping ground; a wide-screen TV with a bullet hole in one corner, several car batteries leaking acid, and more tires. In back was a loading dock where an idle trailer sat propped on its elbows and a few broken pallets were stacked by the dumpster. Beyond were two cars, and he parked beside them. The screwdriver was still in his pocket. Carl checked the alley and even glanced skyward, expecting K-Mart policemen to be patrolling the roof. He chose an old grey Accord with a line of rust around the wheel wells, since it appeared to be the most abandoned. He crouched between the bumper and the graffiti sprayed wall, working quickly and nervously, his hands shaking. A new motor in him was running, and it ran on equal doses of terror and exhilaration. He turned each screw endlessly and thought they would never come out – he was almost surprised when they did. He tucked the plate in the back of his pants.

"You get it?" she asked.

"Of course I got it," he said. "You never took me for a crook?" He drove to the opposite end of the alley where he backed to a six-foot chain link fence overgrown with honeysuckle. When the new Georgia tag was mounted in back, he wrapped the second Virginia plate with the first and shoved them under the seat. While they drove past the drab storefronts and the looming water tower of downtown Douglas, Carl wondered if he'd ever need those tags again.

The logging died away as they rose further above sea level, through rolling pasture dotted with grazing beef cows and giant spools of hay, past barren fields of cotton husks and giant irrigation machines stretched across the land like lines of copulating insects. Miriam kept raising her hand to point out a cow or tractor to Annaliese, while holding her so close she could barely raise her head to see. Farmers had nailed signs to the trees selling corn cob jelly and vine ripe tomatoes, boiled peanuts, pecan brittle, peach cider and home grown sweet potatoes. Under any other circumstances, Carl would have liked to stop, but they plodded along with their legs and backs stiffening from the long drive. The old downtowns of McRae and Dublin were the only places they saw police cars, and they were usually parked in front of the courthouses. The whole state appeared to be asleep. Carl told Miriam to hold the girl flat across her lap through every town, and she didn't seem to mind – she didn't seem to mind anything. They stopped only when they'd built up equal doses of hunger and confidence, pulling into a Burger King outside Milledgeville. They argued over how to order and ended up in the drive-through, but Miriam made him park anyway so she could use the restroom and change Annaliese's diaper.

On the final thirty-mile stretch, Miriam closed her eyes and Carl had to wake her when they broke over the hills south of Athens. She massaged the skin under her sunglasses. Annaliese was out cold, buried in her mother's warm side.

"We're almost there," he said. "You need to tell me where to go."

Miriam looked disoriented, though not from sleep. She grabbed the atlas and ran a finger along the little square blow up of Athens.

"He's north of town," she said. "There's a bypass. Go all the way around to the east and get back on 441."

They drove on and found the highway heavy with mid-afternoon traffic, the heaviest they'd seen yet, but instead of blending into the masses Carl grew nervous with more eyes around to see them. When they reached US441 on the north end and began putting Athens behind them, Carl questioned her again. "How far out?"

"Just keep going."

Another fifteen minutes passed. "Let me see that map," he said, and she handed it to him with a flip of her wrist. He laid it over the wheel. "We're coming up on I-85. You said Athens. Where are we going?"

Miriam sat up, awake now and more certain of herself. "We're not going to Athens." Annaliese yawned and gave a little stretch.

"You said this would be it for me," he cried.

"I need you to keep going."

"You need to talk to me. Right now. You need to tell me what the hell you're doing."

They crested a hill and bored into a sweep of traffic lights by the interstate where towering gas station signs dominated the horizon.

"I don't want to implicate you any further."

"Implicate me?" The truck was weaving in its lane. "I've kidnapped a child and crossed a state line, stolen a license tag, and littered the great state of Georgia with a rusty camper. You think you can protect me now?"

"There are other people involved, Carl. I need to protect them too. It's bigger than you."

"Then don't tell me about them. Just tell me where we're going."

She hesitated, perhaps realizing her advantage and enjoying it. "I need you to get me to Ohio."

"Ohio," he said, as if hearing of the place for the first time. "Jesus."

"There are people there who can help me."

"And you couldn't have told me this before?"

"You wouldn't have done it."

Carl adjusted his left leg, which had fallen asleep. He felt the child's chubby frame next to his. "You don't know that," he said, but he knew she was right. He would never have gone for this.

"Georgia was realistic," she said. "I knew you would do that much for me."

When they crossed the interstate they noticed for the first time the hazy blue spine of the southern Appalachians. The land reminded Carl of the Virginia Piedmont, and his mind wandered back to his youth and the day he lost his way in the forest. He knew if he followed those mountains north they would lead him home.

"So you're really running?" he said, not willing to accept it. "Going underground?"

"Yeah."

"Out west like you mentioned that time? Some farm?"

"Something like that."

Carl turned at the next service station, which catered mostly to truckers, and stopped at the farthest pump from the attendant booth. He pulled the key from the ignition and steadied himself on the door lever as endless questions filled his head. "Tell me, why couldn't you have waited and taken her yourself when your car was out of the shop?"

"I don't have a car anymore. I sold it for five hundred dollars."

He nodded. It made sense. "And the apartment? All your stuff?"

"Community yard sale last week. The rest went to goodwill. All I have are those two suitcases and my daughter."

Chapter 31

They fled high into the blue toe of the Appalachians where their spirits rose and they felt like free people. From Cornelia to Tallula Falls and on through Clayton, past smatterings of shops selling fake antiques, war memorabilia and chainsaw art, they drove on with excitement as if they'd discovered the passes and passages themselves. The sky clouded and the mountains were sketched in white charcoal hash marks in tight vertical lines, stripped of their foliage except for the ridges of waning red birch. The furry band of horizon where bare trees and grey sky entwined draped around them from peak to peak in an endless strand of garland carrying the weight of the sky. The highway curled right and left, gripping the edge of bottomless valleys where the downgrades smelled of burning brakes and the idea of north no longer existed.

For the first time they let Annaliese sit up, though she could have seen the tops of the mountains from under the crook of her mother's arm. She was more alert than before, but still hadn't spoken, no matter how many cows and cotton fields her mother pointed out that day. But as they climbed and plunged over the mountains the girl's face lost color and a sickness came over her. When her mother wasn't looking, she wavered, and if it hadn't been for the seat belt she would have tumbled to the floorboard. Miriam pulled her in close and put a hand to her forehead. Carl realized what was happening and was relieved when they arrived at the place on the map he had chosen.

The sign said "Welcome to Cherokee, Home of the Lady Braves." The reservation was in a narrow valley bottom lined with businesses selling moccasins and leather goods and ceramics from gift shops named Pow Wow and Dancing Bear. In the middle of town, like a sudden obscenity in a quiet room, sat a fifteen story casino flanked by a parking garage that made all the other buildings in town feel little more than temporary.

"That's enough for today," Carl said, eyeing the motels. Though it was still light, the sun had set on the valley and the thickening clouds made the town feel damp, confined and hidden from the outside world.

"What do you plan on doing?" Miriam asked. "We don't have the camper."

"I plan on getting a room."

"You're going to get us caught."

"I'll pay cash and make up a name."

"You can't do that anymore. They ask for ID."

Carl stared at her in disbelief. "Since when?" He hadn't taken a hotel room since his brief trip to New York seven years before.

"They always ask for ID."

"We've got to do something. I'm burnt out. It's too damn cold to camp and I haven't had a shower in two days. It's also about to rain on your luggage."

Near the west end of town they pulled into a gravel parking lot at a roadside motel. The building was sheathed in vertical boards beaten with chains to make it look vintage frontier, though its oxidized aluminum window frames told them it was probably built in the nineteen-sixties. Standing by the door to the office was an eight foot tall plastic bear with a coy smile as if aware of a gathering surprise. Carl's breath fogged the air as he stepped inside. The bell clanged against the door behind him. The front desk was an enormous piece of timber polished for fifty years by the hands of travelers. A mangled stack of newspapers sat to one side, and Carl was rummaging for an afternoon edition when a man stepped from a back room pinching a wad of tobacco from a shiny bag. He stood flatfooted and denim covered, his stout outline making his baseball cap dainty and foolish. He shoved the black poisonous mass into his mouth with two fingers.

"Help you?" he mumbled.

"I need a room for the night."

"How many?" He folded the bag of chew and put it in a flannel pocket under his jean jacket. Carl found the front page of an Ashville paper and folded it under his arm.

"Two," he said.

The Indian lifted a ledger from someplace hidden and laid it before them. He opened it and wrote a note with a pencil. "Forty dollars. Fill this out." He tore a half-size page from a tablet of preprinted forms and slid it across the timber under Carl's nose. His voice was monotone and uninterested. "I'll need to see a driver's license."

On the form were lines for name, address, make and model of vehicle, and tag number. He glanced out the window, but couldn't see the tired old pick-up and its stolen tag, so he filled out the name, address and vitals of some phantom aberration he found in a deep recess in his head, a place full of lies he hadn't been fully aware of. Since he stole a local license plate he knew he was from Georgia, so he decided to lay on more accent. He didn't know a single Georgian, except for the crooked old man he paid off the day before. He counted forty dollars from his billfold and thumbed another half dozen twenties.

"I'm paying cash," Carl said. "I don't see why you need an ID."

The Indian perked up and regarded him stiffly. "You hiding something?"

"Of course not. I'm just —"

"Some people are a liability. They wreck the rooms, take the keys, steal the linen. That's why we ID." He sucked some juice between his teeth.

"Fine. It's in the truck. Relax," Carl said, turning back out into the evening chill. In the cab he dropped the newspaper in Miriam's lap and pretended to reach for the glove box as he turned the ignition. The Indian watched through the window.

"What happened?" she asked.

"Take a wild guess."

He whipped the truck back with their headlights flashing across the bear's knowing smile and punched into the street where they all wobbled back and forth. Annaliese cried, "wohhh" and held on to the adult knees like she was on some amusement park ride.

"At least someone is having fun," Miriam said, as if heartened her daughter made any sound at all.

"There were a few other motels where we came into town," Carl said. Miriam just sat there stroking her daughter's locks, as if contemplating a new hairstyle.

The next motel was shaped like a warehouse or a cell block. It was a long concrete building with a flat roof running from the street toward a rushing creek that separated the narrow town from the imposing mountain wall to the south. Low wattage lamps snapped on by each door and burned like yellow bug zappers. This time Carl thumbed out sixty dollars and handed his wallet to Miriam. He left the engine running and entered the office, glad there were no smiling bears.

The lobby was finished in bright red carpet and paisley wallpaper, giving the room an uneasy vibration. It could have been decorated with leftover material from the new casino down the road. On a side table was an empty coffee maker and a clear plastic bin for doughnuts and muffins. Carl rang the bell on the counter and waited a few uneasy minutes before the door opened behind him. A dark-skinned teenager walked in carrying a toolbox. His black hair dropped passed his shoulders like a horse's mane, and he wore only jeans and a tee-shirt, seemingly unaffected by the cold. He looked too young to run the place, but he took a seat behind the desk. Carl waited until he was sure.

"I'd like a room, please. A double."

"Thirty-five dollars." The young man didn't need any ledger, just pushed an index card across the counter.

"Somewhere in back, off the road, if you could," Carl requested. "I don't want any traffic noise."

"That's fine."

While Carl invented a new alter ego, he kept glancing at the boy. "So you're a real Cherokee?"

"Yeah," the kid said. "So what's it to you?"

"Well that's really something. I've never met an Indian before."

"Where you from?"

"Georgia."

"You're living on my ancestors' land."

"Well now, I don't know much about all that," Carl said, laying it on as naively as possible. He finished writing his new name and wondered how his accent was going over. "Must be nice having a reservation in such a beautiful place."

"We were forced to hide out here. It's nothing but billy goat land, so nobody cared if we stayed."

Despite Carl's intent and folksy subterfuge, he appreciated the boy's roots and all the generations that had stayed together. "But your tribe's all here. Kinda like a big extended family," he said with unintended earnest.

"Some of us are. Most of us were driven out."

"My people have been in one place a long time too," Carl said, "but they're all either scattered or dead." He began filling out a fake place of residence. He remembered passing through a town called Dublin that reminded him of Compton, and he wrote the name on the card. "I ain't got nothing like a reservation."

The boy was different now, his features softening as if the initial perceived threat had passed. He propped himself on a stool behind the desk and let his shoulders slump. "I'll need some ID too," the boy said.

"So what happened to the people who left here?"

"It was a forced relocation by your government. The Trail of Tears."

"I've heard of that before. What was that all about?"

Carl handed over two twenties while the boy told him about the forced exodus of his ancestors and sister tribes from their homeland, of mothers carrying their children and dying en route to some fraudulent promise of prosperity. The boy spoke with great pride for someone so young. He handed Carl the key to the room and told him about the museum down the road.

"You should see it before you go," the Indian said in all seriousness, as if wanting Carl to understand how things were. When he tried to hand over the change, Carl waived him off.

"I'll stop by there tomorrow. I sure will," he said, taking the key. He motioned to the empty coffee pot. "Looks like I can get breakfast here in the morning?"

"We have coffee and doughnuts."

"That's great. Real good." Carl made his way to the door, but paused on the way out. "Oh. You said you needed some identification or something?"

The boy hopped off his stool. "Don't worry about it," he said, pocketing his tip and disappearing into a back room.

The truck whined as he backed it down the length of the motel and parked in the last space shy of the drop-off to the bubbling creek. The darkening sky sharpened the sound of the water. The dim bulb outside the door lit their breaths as they carried their meager belongings inside where they felt safe and isolated in their own little warren under the mountain.

Carl left on foot to buy food and a smoke, and on his way back he spotted a payphone by the street. No way it works, he thought, but he tried it anyway and was shocked to hear a dial tone. He fed it a handful of quarters and waited, strained to hear the ring-tone over the passing cars. Mick answered.

"What in the hell's going on, man? Your grandfather called here this morning. Said the police were at the farm looking for you."

"What did he tell them?"

"Where are you, Carl? What are you doing?"

"I'm taking care of some things. What did he tell the police?"

"He told them you were living on the farm, but he didn't know where you went. He's worried about you. We all are."

Carl worried for his grandfather. The old man had lied for him, and he was just that – an old man. He didn't need to be dealing with someone else's nonsense. He wondered how he could leave the man in peace.

"I'm going to need some cash, Mick. As soon as things settle down, I can pay you back."

"Things settle down? I know about the Amber Alert. The whole town knows."

Carl hesitated, waited for a few cars to pass that were bottled up at a traffic light. "I don't know what you're talking about. I just took a road trip to New York to see some galleries. Can you PayPal some money in a few days? You know I'm good for it."

"Are you still in Florida?"

He held the receiver with his shoulder and blew into his hands. "The weather's cold where I am." The recorded voice of an operator asked for more quarters. Carl didn't have any left. "Come on, Mick."

"Okay, but don't call this number. Do you have any idea what you're do –"

The line went dead and Carl hung up the phone. A long drag on the cigarette filled his lungs and settled him. He didn't think the police would have moved on him so fast, and he felt bad for his grandfather getting caught up in it all.

A car drove by slowly, as if searching for an address. Carl told himself to keep moving. When he reached the room, Miriam was bathing her daughter, so he lay on one of the double beds with a cheeseburger and rifled through a hundred odd television channels without focusing on any of them. He settled on an old Jeff Bridges movie where he was carrying on with some Aussie woman in the jungle, and they had arrived at some great impasse. They screamed at each other and pleaded and made promises any idiot knew they couldn't keep. To Carl it was all wrong; stilted, tangled and senseless, as if the actors were reciting random lines from an encyclopedia. His head was not in it and it didn't make any sense. By the time the credits rolled, Miriam and her daughter came out wrapped in cheap white towels. Miriam's barely covered her body. Annaliese shivered until her mother clothed her in out-grown pajamas and put her on the next bed with french fries and a soft drink. With little pulsing fingers she grabbed for one of the burgers, and when her mother relented, the girl devoured it like she was starving.

Carl set the shower to near scalding and lingered under the spray, letting it beat two days of grime and worry from his body. His head and shoulders went numb from the pressure. He came out wearing a fresh pair of briefs and a towel around his neck. On the floor was a hand towel covered with curly brown hair clippings – all that was left of Annaliese's meandering locks. The Cartoon Channel was on and the girl sat at the foot of the bed sucking air through her straw, not at all disturbed by her new hair-doo. The curtains were open and he saw Miriam outside, bare-legged and wearing his jacket. She was cupping the cell phone with both hands. As he ran the faucet and examined his beard, she hung up and whisked back inside, shuddering from the cold.

"Don't you dare shave it off," she said, tossing the jacket aside. She was wearing a long tee-shirt with a Cuervo logo settling between her breasts.

"I'm not," he said, feeling the grain.

She sat by her daughter, studying her hair as if she could have done a better job. "The afternoon paper you got from the other motel had your picture in it."

Carl was surprised at how little this affected him. He wasn't even interested in seeing it. He took the shaving cream from his duffel and ran hot water over his fingers. "That so?"

"Don't shave it all," she said.

"I said I'm not."

On a side table dotted with cigarette burns were the scissors Miriam used on her daughter's locks. "They blew up a shot of you working on your porch last spring. It's kinda fuzzy and your hair was longer." She grabbed the scissors and the desk chair. "Sit down," she said, and he resigned himself to it, knowing she was right. She ran her fingers through his wet hair, planning. "I'd have used that picture of us in the restaurant. The lighting was good and you were wearing a tie."

"Maybe they figured I wouldn't be wearing a tie while kidnaping a child." Miriam hummed in agreement. He followed her in the mirror. "Did you cut your own?"

"It's not like I could afford a stylist." She stretched a strand high between two fingers.

"Can't say I like it much. I prefer a woman with long hair."

"So do all men." She snipped off the lock close to the scalp. "I doubt you'll like this much either." She clipped on that way, shearing as close and even as she could. Electric shears would have cut better and easier, but he was glad she didn't have one. He liked her familiar hands going over his scalp, feeling their way around, over and over like a sensual massage as she circled him. Her shirt floated over her breasts and the soft points of her nipples brushed against his shoulders. When she finished, he stood up and looked in the mirror. He ran a hand over his head, working up the fine bit of hair he had left.

"You look so much older," she said. He noted the same about her.

"I feel older." He lathered and cut clean lines down each cheek and under the jaw before turning the razor over to Miriam, who shaved the fuzz from his neck. Then she took a box of hair coloring from her purse and locked herself in the bathroom. A half hour later she stepped out with a bad dye job, her bobbed hair and eyebrows now jet black, which looked painted and unnatural against her fair skin.

"She's asleep," he said. The girl was sprawled out on the bed between stray french fries and hamburger wrappers. Her mother tucked her between the sheets and put her lips to her forehead like it might be the last time. Carl was in the other bed watching CNN with the volume off. She crawled in next to him, and they watched and waited together in the blue lit room.

"There," he said, and pointed the remote. He raised the volume and they watched their old faces from their old lives being broadcast across the country. Most people who are unfortunate enough to have their faces in those little floating captions next to the anchorman are either dead or in big trouble – there weren't many good people on the news. When it was over they lay there on their backs propped on pillows, their arms lightly touching. Carl stared at the splatter of dust on the ceiling caught from the stale air sputtering from the heat pump.

"That was barely a twenty second clip," he said, clicking off the TV. "Tomorrow we'll be back page news."

He watched Miriam reach over and turn off the lamp, and under the fading glow she was a different woman from the one he'd hungered for all those years. She threw a soft leg over him, and he smelled her powdered skin and the stink of the dye and felt her wet hair on his shoulder. He wanted her then, but not out of any sense of love either revived or forgotten, not because she was familiar or unfamiliar, but because she was the last thing he had, the only thing he hadn't lost, and he'd be damned if he'd lose her again. With the slightest gesture of his hand in a familiar place, an old signal they shared, she rolled onto him and he lifted her shirt and seized her body like he owned it, grinding and thrashing and letting her move only when he wanted her to. Miriam buried her face in his chest and gave in completely until there was nothing left but sweat and exhaustion.

The child never made a sound. Miriam rolled off and lay on her back like a corpse to be bled and embalmed. Her breasts splayed out tired and deflated, her bush a lone tangled exclamation mark. Carl lay beside her on the sweat stained sheets and felt the heat bouncing off the ceiling.

"We have to make it all the way tomorrow," she said, still winded. "I can't keep doing this."

"You're going to have to get used to the idea of running and hiding. You're going to be doing it the rest of your life."

"After I get her raised, they can do whatever they want with me."

The blower switched off and the heating unit sounded like a bicycle wheel spinning down as the room slowly quieted.

"Where are these people in Ohio going to take you?"

"I can't tell you."

"You talked about going out west," Carl said, trying to envision such a place. Everything was still now; the room, the valley, the casino neon and the mountains, even the blowing tips of the trees. "I want to go with you," he said.

"Carl."

"I don't have anything left either."

"You do."

"I'm nothing but a worry to my grandfather. I'm out of work. My house is toast. My paintings, my clothes, all my things."

"You still have family. I've never had one of those."

Despite the renewed concern for his grandfather, the idea of his family still eluded him. And now he was a danger to the old man. Better to unburden them of his presence. He rolled toward her. "If there's ever a time to start over, it's now."

"I don't know."

"You're all I thought about for seven years. I'm not going to let you leave me again."

"I'm sorry Carl, but I'm not a replacement for what you lost."

Carl puzzled over this and wondered for the first time if she knew him better than he knew himself. He recognized she'd been a replacement of sorts, but there had been nothing to replace her after she left. Now he was running, not so much with her as keeping up with her, trying not to let her slip away again. In one way or another, Carl had been running since the day his parents died. Miriam rolled toward the other bed where the child was sleeping. Her breasts regained some of their shape between her pinched arms.

"We never had much in common," she said.

A cold draft seeped under the door and engulfed the room. Carl pulled up the bedspread and rested a hand on Miriam's side. "Opposites attract" he said.

After a few sleepless minutes, Miriam asked, "If we made a baby and we didn't work out, would you fight me for custody?"

It was a question he'd considered, since he'd recently seen the extreme sides of her, the sides of both rage and depression. He knew who she had been, but wasn't sure who she was or who she would become. But the answer he truly believed in came to him. "A child belongs with the mother," he said, "so long as the mother's not a danger to the child."

"Do you think I'm a danger to Annaliese?"

With the question framed in this way, he answered no without hesitation. She was a good mother, so long as she was left to mothering. What concerned him about her had nothing to do with rearing a child, and he felt ashamed for having questioned her ability as care-giver. He rolled up behind her and squeezed her shoulder. "You're a wonderful mother," he said. "I would never take our baby away from you."

Chapter 32

They huddled together in the truck and climbed at first light, following the dim cove along the river narrows where the vegetation was lush, almost tropical like a hidden rain forest of giant hemlocks and mountain laurel. The road switched back through moist slopes of rhododendron and gained ground on one of the crooked spines of the Smokies. The upper reaches of the forest were cut from a Japanese wood block print. Below the red spruce ridges were the husks of Fraser fir standing skeletal and dead, white ghosts blighted by some foreign microbe, while the yellow birch collected a spongy green patina over its peeling paper bark, the tips of its branches crimped up like arthritic fingers. The horizon to their backs was growing lighter, but the padded clouds were dense and lingering just over their heads, laying a fine mist on their windshield. They reached the ridge at sunrise.

Earlier that morning, after he picked up their breakfast from a twenty-four hour diner, Carl rummaged through an alley of trash bins and found an old sheet of plastic, which he wrapped around Miriam's luggage and secured with bungee cords. But she was still upset, likely thinking the last of her belongings were doomed to be soaked and grow mold like the last of Carl's possessions in his burnt out house.

They pulled into a parking lot at the pass, and through the two dirty arcs etched by the wipers, Carl read the sign aloud: "North Carolina - Tennessee state line: 5,048 feet."

"This means we're three states away from him," she said.

"And a mile above him."

"I like the idea of looking down on him."

They all stared into the deep recess feeding into the Tennessee Valley, and for a moment again it was like they were on a family vacation. Miriam worried about Annaliese getting sick as the climate grew colder, so she puffed the girl up in multiple layers of shirts and pants, which clearly wasn't appreciated. Annaliese had already outgrown most of the clothes her mother packed, but that didn't stop her from being forcibly bundled like a newborn baby. Miriam went as far as tearing the sleeves and cuffs in order to tug them on. Annaliese wore two pairs of pants, three shirts and the same pink sweater from the day before, all disguised under a blue raincoat. She had trouble bending her limbs, and her feet stuck straight out for the drop into Tennessee.

"Look at the colors here," Miriam said, layered in her own sweaters as they began their descent. "Everything was dead on the south side." Through the hairpin turns into the upper valleys was autumn left behind. Reds and yellows were closer to peak than expired, and the brilliant colors were a benevolent omen for the journey north. Miriam pointed at the vistas and views until her daughter made a small groan. In the time it took her mother to look down, Annaliese vomited like a fire hose, spraying the dash and splashing their legs with orange juice, sausage and scrambled egg.

"Dammit," Carl groaned, shaking the first bits off his sleeve.

"The road!" Miriam yelled. "Watch the road." Carl got them between the lines as Miriam punched open the glove compartment. A wad of napkins spilled into her hand and she began dabbing up the mess.

"Man!" Carl said in disgust.

They passed through a tunnel of fiery red leaves and stopped at the next scenic overlook. Carl climbed out first and cussed some more, tried to shake the puke from his right leg as it dribbled down in little yellow rivulets of chunky orange juice. Miriam was busy cleaning the girl, whose rain coat saved her from the worst of it.

"Give me some of those napkins," Carl said.

"We don't have enough," Miriam said, directing her daughter. "Okay, you scoot out that way. Go to Carl." The driver's seat had the least debris, as Carl's leg took the brunt of the surprise. Annaliese slid by the steering wheel and, for the first time since they had taken her, stretched her arms out to him. Carl stared into her embarrassed eyes as her bile seeped through his jeans.

"Come on," he said, easing her to the ground. "It's okay." The girl looked guilty, but not too guilty, as she surely felt better standing on the side of the road with a beautiful view after a good puke. He bent down and placed a gentle hand on her back. "If you ever feel like you have to throw up again, you just tell me and I'll pull over. Okay?"

Miriam found another pair of shoes in the luggage. "Sit here," she said, and Annaliese plopped down on the curb by a stone wall. Miriam tugged off her shoes and outer pair of pants and rolled them up in a wad. The new shoes didn't fit, and Annaliese winced and kicked.

"Okay, fine." Miriam unwrapped the old shoes and rubbed them in the grass, scrapping off the bitters before putting them back on the girl's little feet. Carl was sitting on the curb dragging his right leg through the grass like a dog trying to satisfy an unreachable itch.

"If we'd taken the interstate this never would have happened," he said.

"If we took the interstate we'd be in jail."

Miriam was dabbing herself off with the last napkin, so Carl found an oily rag behind the seat and rubbed down the splatter on the dash, which only worked it deeper into the cracks like old veins of built-up wax. There was still a puddle on the floorboard.

"This is awful," he said, grimacing.

Miriam stuck her head in the cab. "You're obviously not ready for children." She sniffed and studied the scene, making her calculations. "You need new floor mats anyway." She dragged one out the door and watched it flop to the pavement. Carl did the same on the driver's side before carrying them to a square, bear-proof trash container by the road. He unlatched the lid and dropped them inside, thinking no bear would want these.

As he turned around, a green park service cruiser was coming at him from the valley road. Before he could even panic, the ranger smiled and gave him a nod good morning. Carl grinned like a fool and waved back as his heart raced. Where is she? he thought, his blood going cold. His instinct was to yell for her mother to get her down, a command he'd grown used to, but the girl was sitting in plain view on the stone wall, more like a stuffed animal than a child. But the cruiser slipped right by, penetrating the tunnel of autumn leaves and winding from sight. Carl's heart rate slowed, and he considered how stupid all this was. When he got back to the truck he found Miriam hiding on the floorboard.

"Tell me he didn't stop," she said, her eyes closed.

"He didn't even slow down. Let's get out of here."

They coasted down the mountain, keeping it slow with the windows cracked for fresh air. Carl kept one eye on the chubby little girl.

"Stop worrying. She already lost everything," Miriam said.

Though some of the upper mountain reaches were blighted, the lower slopes were teeming with life. They descended along the Little Pigeon River under the hardwood canopy still leaf-tipped with yellow and burgundy, but further past peak as they dipped deeper into the valley.

Without welcome or warning, they emerged from the forest and plunged into Gatlinburg. It was like they'd woken from a deep sleep and found themselves in a redneck version of Las Vegas. Gatlinburg is where man told nature to fuck off. The road was lined with all makes of invented attractions, cluttered with signs and bogged down with traffic lights. They passed a wax museum with life-size dioramas of biblical sages, indoor championship putt-putt golf with a King Tut motif, Nellie's Fudge n'Taffy and a spindly space needle that might tip over with the slightest gust. There were endless family inns, craft shops, wedding chapels, and sellers of ribs and funnel cakes. Sweet Thelma Lou offered fifty-three scrumptious types of pancakes, Smoky Al's helicopter tours were open sunrise to sunset, and Sid Lachey's Dinner Theater promoted the best of the best. To add to the spectacle, the street lamps and storefronts were decked with wreaths and white Christmas lights, dragging out the holiday shopping season by another month. Everything there clamored for attention and it droned on for miles.

"I've never seen so much crap in my life," Carl said, sitting at about the tenth traffic light.

"This is a family place. It's a place to take the family."

"Is this where we would have ended up on vacation?"

"Sure," Miriam said, perfectly satisfied with the surroundings.

"You could have left me up in the hills."

"It's not that bad. Just a lot of traffic." The signal turned green and they groaned on. "I wish we could take her on one of the go-cart tracks. Even *you'd* like that." Carl conceded the race tracks looked fun. When they passed the biggest pawn shop he'd ever seen, Miriam said, "I wanted to pawn my wedding band, but I couldn't find it. Do you remember packing it?"

"Can't say I do," he said. Annaliese was sitting up again, straining under the layers of clothing and the shared seat belt with her chin raised, peering over the dash at all the excitement. Carl said they were overexposed, so Miriam drew the child in close. The endless strip wouldn't let up. "Is the rest of Tennessee like this?" he grumbled.

"Of course not."

"Dollywood Lane. Good God, you have us going through Dollywood."

"I like Dolly Parton."

"I'm sure she's very nice, but her amusement park is not where we need to be right now."

"I think it's a dinner theater."

"I don't care what it is. Wherever the hell I'm taking us does not go through Dollywood. I'm tired of these damn strips." She gave him a look that said she didn't appreciate the language. The light changed and he punched the gas. Everyone jerked back in the seat.

"You're going to get us caught" she warned.

Carl rolled down his window and leaned his head out for air. Gatlinburg bled into Pigeon Forge with no demarcation at all, no break in the scenery and no lull of concocted amusements, sensations and macadam. Carl felt claustrophobic, as though this painful birth canal was the only path to the promised land. They were past the worst of it by the time they came into Sevierville, where Miriam opened her map to Tennessee.

"Look for Route 321. 321 north." She tilted the map. "Or maybe it's east."

Just off the strip was a small grid of streets centering on an ornate brick courthouse that left the other buildings in town embarrassed in their simplicity. The next traffic light marked a major intersection.

"Here. Turn right here," she said. At the intersection was a post full of road signs that read like a confusing menu, showing multiple routes in seemingly conflicting directions. When the light changed, Carl drove straight ahead. Miriam lurched up and the seat belt squeezed a grunt out of her daughter. "What are you doing?"

"We're following my directions for a while."

Beyond Sevierville the land had not been raped and for the next nine miles they rolled past feed stores, hay fields and wandering cattle. The valley reminded Carl of his grandfather's tract, and he felt exuberant driving through a place of such beauty after the hell he had just endured. He wished he could call the old man and hear his voice, but he knew it wasn't possible. Hopefully Mick talked to him and let him know he was all right.

When they reached I-40 he took the second ramp, west toward Knoxville. Miriam was furious, but holding back, a pulsing vein in her temple giving her mood away. Her cheek bone was sharp, like a sculptor had pinched it from clay.

"I had the route picked out," she protested.

"What? Through every back road in West Virginia? Annaliese won't keep a bite down in those mountains and it'll take another two days to get there."

"I wanted something that's not so obvious."

"I'll have us in Ohio in a few hours."

She leaned against the window and rested a fist on her forehead. "Maybe I don't want to get there so fast." Her voice trembled and she welled up.

"It's a little late to turn this thing around."

"I know that, but I don't know what's going to happen, where we'll end up. I only know these people from on-line and a few phone conversations. I don't know what they're really like."

"How were they on the phone?"

Her lips moved silently, as if mumbling the same question to herself. "They were very nice. Very understanding."

"You mentioned a farm out west. So these folks take people and put them out in the country? Battered women and abused kids?"

"Yeah."

"That doesn't sound so bad," he said truthfully.

"We'll always have to hide."

"We'll home school her."

Carl balanced the speedometer needle on sixty-five. In the valley the foliage was bare and the skeletal trees set off the amber fields and bushy green pastures. They passed a sign that read twenty miles to I-75 – Lexington and Cincinnati.

"You couldn't get a job teaching again without getting caught."

"I don't mind farm labor," he admitted, thinking back. "I actually kind of like it."

"What about your art?"

"I can do that anywhere. A change of scenery will do some good." She looked doubtful, but Carl persisted. "I'm coming too, Miriam. I don't have anything left. I need a change and this is it." He reached over and took her hand. She squeezed his in return as Annaliese stared at their entwined fingers.

"So come then," she said. "I guess I can't stop you."

When they finally hit the northbound ramp onto I-75, Miriam closed her eyes and snuggled with her daughter as the speedometer inched higher. Carl tried again to drop a playful hand on Annaliese's knee, but she squirmed and brushed it off, lilting closer to her mother's side and covering herself. Carl was afraid to imagine what her father had done to change her so. He ached at the possibilities. "What did he do to you?" he said, studying her.

Chapter 33

The four lanes blurred ahead to an abstract place Carl couldn't clearly see, daydreaming as he was to some end where the sky and soil were unfamiliar. He was lost in this nebulous vision with the tires whining and the blower warming his feet, when the truck shuddered and woke them from their uneasy sleep. Miriam and Annaliese roused slowly, but Carl snapped immediately from his hypnosis, his vision numb from tunneling through miles of Kentucky bedrock. The engine leveled, then rattled again and he tightened his grip on the wheel. Miriam was groggy and pallid, her black hair hanging mop-like over her forehead.

"What was that?" she asked.

"I don't know," he answered, scanning the dummy lights in the dash. Something in him died when he noticed the gas gauge. "No."

"What?"

"Oh no."

Miriam craned over, squishing her daughter before pulling back. "My God, how could you?" She drew in her shoulders, as if ashamed of knowing him. The engine's comforting hum was deathly silent as they rolled onto the shoulder and, in accord with their spirits, drifted miserably to a halt. Tractor trailers and flatbeds loaded with tobacco roared by and shook the little S-10, sending an ancient tremble through Carl's soul. He dropped his hands to his lap and Miriam ground her teeth. Annaliese rubbed a knob on the radio with her toe.

"Did you see the last exit?" he asked.

"No, I did not see the last exit."

"It was a while ago. I know we passed Lexington."

There were no highway signs in sight. The shoulder dropped into a deep gully, where a craggy forest with many fallen trees spread out and clogged the land. Carl felt for his wallet.

"Bundle her up and get her down in the hollow until I get back."

"I don't believe this."

"You two have to get off the road."

Though he was furious with himself, he wasn't up to apologizing, nor did he have time. He slammed the door and took off down the shoulder, breaking into a clumsy jog that reminded him how out of shape he was. He hadn't run in years, so he knew he needed to pace himself. Though the sun was glaring, the cold air frosted his lungs and he realized his next mistake – he hadn't layered up. He was dressed only in a shirt and windbreaker, since he hadn't seen the point of bundling up like Annaliese when the heater in the truck worked just fine. Now he was starting to sweat, and the icy cotton shirt clung to his torso. His lungs began to sting so he eased up, taking slow deep breaths and focusing on the fog of his breath and the endless white stripe along the side of the road. After a few hundred yards, he glanced back and saw the truck cab was empty. He sucked air as the cords in his neck strained. Blood pumped hard through his forehead and thighs, and his teeth hurt like someone was squeezing his gums with pliers. In less than a mile he was about to collapse. Each breath iced his lungs, and he imagined his bones shattering with each semi that tore passed. He cursed himself for his recent cigarette habit.

The highway narrowed at a bridge over a local road where the concrete safety rail forced him closer to traffic. From the bridge he could see an intersection a hundred yards away, no more than a crossroads, but he was heartened at any sign of civilization. After the bridge he could see a sign ahead, "exit one mile." He picked up his pace. Ten minutes tops, he thought. A railroad line wound up close to the highway, drawing with it a radio tower, rows of orange trucks and piles of salt and sand. Here he was hitting his stride, acclimating to the burden. Where the highway bent left, an exit ramp dropped in front of him. He couldn't see past the hill as he jogged down the ramp, fearing what he might find. Prayer came to mind, something he couldn't remember last doing, but when he finally cleared the embankment and saw the gas station to the east, he almost dropped to his knees in thanks. He was bent over with his hands on his knees, trying not to pass out when a tractor-trailer gliding down the ramp engaged its air-brakes and almost send him stumbling into the weeds. It rattled to a stop a few feet away as the driver laughed hard through his bearded face. He drove on toward the service station, coughing smoke in each gear, and Carl cussed him and followed.

Though he walked the rest of the way, he was still winded when he reached the cashier. His newly cropped hair stuck straight up from his forehead, and his cheeks gave off a jelly red glow. The girl behind the counter appeared so innocent to him, so out of place in the world he was living. When she tilted her head, she reminded him of one of his less talented students. On her red smock was a badge saying, "Sherry, Happy to Please."

"Gas," he said. "I ran out of gas. Tell me you sell gas cans."

"Right over there, sir." She pointed down an aisle stocked with things that couldn't fit into any one category: shrink-wrapped bundles of firewood, pine tree deodorant hangers, shoe polish, brooms. Stacked at the end cap were bright red, two gallon plastic gas containers. He grabbed one and a deodorant pine tree and went to the men's room where he dropped them on the floor. At the sink he twisted the knobs and adjusted the flow, let the hot water run over his hands to warm the blood. He imagined himself submerged in it. He raised a pool in his hands and splashed it all over him, across his jacket, around the sink and onto the floor. He massaged his eyes with the balls of his palms, and raised another pool to his face, holding it there until it dribbled through his fingers. Through the soap spots and strange fingerprints on the mirror, he didn't recognize himself. Like Miriam, he had picked up more grey hairs, the new buzz-cut exposing more of what was already there. He tried to wipe his hair back, but it stuck up like a wire brush. His two-week beard, now neatly trimmed like some urban hipster, may have helped disguise him, but did little to hide the worry.

He shoved a fist full of paper hand towels in his pocket and picked up his things, along with a bottle of water and a Snickers bar at the register, and had the girl ring it all up with three dollars of gas. By the gas pump he devoured the candy bar like a hunted and starving man. His lungs were primed from the first run and he broke into the same jog as before, though more awkward since he held a sloshing red gas can out to one side. He was feeling good, rehydrated with a fresh blast of sugar in his veins. When the road straightened he assumed he would see the truck in the distance, but there was nothing in sight. There it hit him, a flash of paranoia as he envisioned it knocked off the road by a snoozing long-haul driver, or seized by a state trooper with a wide brim hat and an attitude. He worried until he caught a glimmer of the empty S-10 in the distance. The harder he ran, the smaller the blue dot of the truck seemed to be.

The railing at the bridge again nudged him closer to oncoming traffic, making the perceived speed of the passing rigs and minivans increase. One of the big trucks coming at him was an unreal sight – a semi with two low hips protruding from each side, and it was riding over the white line, running fast. By the time Carl could read the "wide load" banner on the front bumper, the air horn blew and it was on him. In a blink, he made out the profile of the wing where it had been dismantled from the fuselage. The plane's propellers had sheared off in a crash, leaving nothing but twisted metal shards on its mud-caked nose. The fuselage was strapped down to the flatbed and the bruised wings were stacked behind it. When the severed wing flew past him over the white line, Carl jumped aside at the last second and smashed his knee into the bridge's concrete safety rail. He let out a cry and the plastic gas container tumbled down the shoulder, coming to a rest on its side a few yards away.

"Fuck!" he screamed, dropping to the ground clutching his knee. He lunged for the gas can to set it upright. A little fluid dribbled from the air valve, but the container held. By the time he looked back at the wrecked airplane and its ride, they were nearly out of sight – the driver never even slowed down. Carl winced as he pushed his kneecap from side-to-side with the tips of his fingers. It was already beginning to swell. He forced himself up but could no longer run. Instead he settled into a clumsy hobble where he barely bent the joint. His truck was still over a half mile away, but he could make out enough detail to see the cab was still empty. There was no one in sight. Just let me get there, he now openly prayed. Almost home.

When he came to the pick-up, he screamed Miriam's name over the embankment. He opened the cab and popped the gas cap release.

"Miriam!" he cried, leaning against the side-rail, his face flush and in full realization of his pain. When he uncapped the tank and began pouring the gasoline, a nightmare fantasy of flashing blue lights made spots in his eyes. A light grey Crown Victoria stopped fast behind him and angled its nose into traffic. A state trooper stepped out wearing a blue-grey shirt with KPS insignia shining on each collar. Carl waved to him and smiled.

"Just ran out of gas," he hollered.

The trooper stood there behind his door and watched him empty the can before setting it in the truck bed. He inspected Carl like he was a fool. "You might want to keep an eye on your gauges."

"Yes, sir. After that walk, I can't argue with that."

Carl climbed into the cab and turned the ignition. The engine cranked a while before the gas flowed again. His hands were shaking. He checked the mirror and the officer was still watching him, maybe running his tags. Should have stolen new ones in Gatlinburg. Glancing into the woods as he accelerated, Carl merged into traffic and the cop kept right on him, following down the ramp and right into the same gas station parking lot where the cruiser broke off toward the convenience store as the S-10 pulled under the canopy. Carl flinched when he grabbed the pump handle and steadied himself on the rail. The pump didn't work and he noticed the "pay first" sign. In line at the register, he found himself right behind the man in uniform, who was stirring a Styrofoam cup of coffee.

"Looks like you needed some refueling too," Carl said, thinking to himself, "just shut up."

"Looks that way," the trooper said, paying and pushing out the door.

After prepaying and setting the pump, Carl seized his map from the front seat. The last exit was ten miles back down US25 before he could jump back on the northbound lanes to find them. Since he'd left the spot both times in a hurry, he hadn't taken good mental notes of the highway – he wasn't even sure if he would recognize where they had been. And what if the same cop found him there again?

But he knew it was about two miles south, give or take, so he punched out of the lot and sped south on US25. He watched his odometer and groaned in pain every time he pushed the clutch. After a mile he crossed the road running under the interstate bridge where he'd busted his knee. The road he was on gradually split off from the interstate, and he fell into near panic, driving over the line and looking frantically as if the woman and child might appear anywhere at any time, or as if they might never appear again. He clocked three miles and whipped around. The only thing of note he passed was a small nursery run out of a trailer. It appeared to be more of a backyard hobby than a business, but it was in about the right place so he stopped there and parked behind a stand of young Douglas fir, all with burlaped root-balls the size of beanbag chairs. He limped into the forest, climbing over downed trees and slipping on wet leaves as he descended the hill toward the interstate. Cars and rigs streaked through the mesh of bare branches as he struggled to the barb wire fence in the hollow. The fence was in far worse shape than his grandfather's had been. He seized the rusty wire strands for balance, making brown lines across his gas smelling palms. He breathed heavy and looked up and down the gully, then back toward the woods.

"Miriam!"

From the depression where he was standing the thunder of the traffic blew over him like the haunted cry of a million lost souls screaming past at eighty miles an hour, all in search of better places and times. He called her name again, but his voice was lost in the howling. His knee was stiff as he gutted his way back up the hill, using one hand on the ground for balance. He fashioned a cane out of a stick, but it broke under his weight and he fell and slid in the damp leaves. He struggled to his feet, riddled with guilt, and forced himself on. By the time he neared the nursery, the traffic noise had faded to a distant hum and he could again hear his feet kicking through the autumn droppings. Through the branches he could make out a clump of people standing near his truck: one stocky, two thin, the fourth a child holding a plant. They were all looking his way when he emerged from the woods like some homeless man dragging an unwanted appendage.

"I told you he'd come looking here," the older woman said. She was a greying hippie in her sixties, her gaunt hair collecting on shoulders padded with a wintery sweater she had probably knitted herself. She stood between Miriam and Annaliese, and together they made an earthy looking family. But to Miriam's other side, standing too close, was a man about her age, and Carl could tell he was not right. Though he wasn't overweight, a severe double-chin lopped under his open mouth that was chewing a red delicious apple. They all stared at Carl, windblown and red faced, dragging himself across the gravel parking lot. He just nodded, too tired and relieved to say anything.

Miriam broke in first. "I was afraid you got lost," she said with a flighty nervousness only he could detect. Annaliese was holding a geranium in a foil wrapped pot.

"I was worried," was all Carl could manage to say in one breath.

The older woman chimed in. "It's a good thing Marvin found them out there. Too cold for a child her age with only that little jacket," she said, obviously unaware of the layers under it. Marvin smiled at the sound of his own name. He was clean shaven down to a wreath of body hair around his neck.

"I didn't want them sitting there on the interstate," Carl said. "People come by not looking."

"No place is safe," the woman said in support.

Marvin stepped forward. "Wanna bite of apple?" He held out the half-eaten fruit while his mouth hung open, showing a triangle of red skin between his teeth.

"No thanks," Carl said, coming no nearer.

Miriam touched the woman on her arm. "Thank you so much," she said, and whisked the girl into the cab as she clutched her geranium. Marvin lumbered behind them and offered to help.

"No, no. We're fine," Miriam said over her shoulder. He was too close.

The woman peered into the truck from the driver's window. "You don't have a child seat?"

"Stolen," Carl piped up. "We're gonna buy another when we get to Cincinnati."

She looked frightened for the girl. "People will steal anything, won't they? You're lucky they didn't run off with her in it."

"I imagine so." It took some effort for Carl to raise himself into his seat. "Appreciate you taking care of them."

"No trouble. You got a full tank now?"

"I sure do," he said, clenching his teeth as his toe pressed the clutch. Miriam closed the other door and tugged over the seat belt. Marvin stood an inch from the window, chewing and longing, hypnotized on Miriam like she were some brilliant fire. They rode off in silence and were soon speeding north again in the droning malaise.

"I thought we could make Cincinnati on the tank," Carl said.

"That nut was in the woods."

"He was obviously harmless."

"We could have been caught."

"Well, we weren't caught. At least you found a warm place to wait. I wasn't off on some picnic. Aren't you at least wondering what happened to my leg?"

After calming herself, she said with some contrition, "What happened?"

He didn't answer right away, because he didn't know how to explain. "I almost got hit by an airplane."

Miriam shook her head and stared at the passing water tower and butler buildings, the farthest outskirts of the city chewing up the land. "You're crazy," she said quietly.

Carl shifted in his seat and tried to straighten his leg.

"You may be right."

Chapter 34

It was not until they passed Dayton, where the hill country around the Ohio River receded, that Carl felt they were truly out of the south and felt the reality of the miles they had traveled. North of Springfield and on past Mechanicsburg the hills leveled to fallow fields of severed corn stalks and freshly turned soil, black and rich as if churned up from some compost deep within the earth. The horizon opened wide as a purple cloud bank slewed over from the west, a dark front of wind and chill unfurling over the farmland spread out flat and endless like nothing Carl had ever seen. The fields were interrupted only by distant creeping boxcars, red cedar windbreaks and isolated graveyards on the gentlest of rises. It was easy to picture snow coming on.

Carl contemplated the many farms they passed and couldn't help but to envy them. Each was monumental, anchored by an ancient barn standing proud and dignified. Around it were lean-tos, sties, dairy barns, and clusters of shiny aluminum storage buildings for grain and corn, whose conical tops were all connected like some massive high-tech tinker toy. He imagined what he and Vince could do with his grandfather's farm if they had the money to modernize and adapt to the day's economy. His mind tore down the mess of sheds and decrepit outbuildings that had multiplied over the generations of Rittenhaurs, and he planned and replanned the entire complex with each mighty Ohio farm they passed. He also wondered about the supposed farm where he and Miriam and the girl might settle for a time.

The smaller towns were like islands in the fields, each an archipelago with its requisite water tower, dairy bar and Sears bungalows, always with pasture lapping at its edges. "Welcome to Marysville, Where the Grass is Greener," one town proclaimed, though its roads were potholed and broken. "Ohi-grow," another sign boasted. The town of Marion came on with a sad industrial malaise, its idle trains resting indefinitely on endless sidings. In Bucyrus a man stood atop a cherry picker hanging Christmas wreaths on the lamp posts, but like in Gatlinburg, Carl and Miriam couldn't see celebrating anything.

They rolled out of Bucyrus in late afternoon with a bucket of fried chicken. The sky was heavy and bloated like it had rained for many days, but the road looked dry, even as a light mist settled on the windshield. Carl flipped on the wipers to clear his tired eyes. They passed a flatbed trailer hauling a large motor boat inland for the season. This was surreal to see after so many miles of mountains, hills and ranges. Miriam excitedly pointed out the boat to Annaliese, but the girl just sat there devouring her drum stick.

They drove by a crossroad sign Carl didn't chance to read. Miriam shouted, "Here. Turn here!" He let his foot off the gas and the sound of the engine wound down to a murmur. They missed the turn, but Miriam was emphatic, as if she'd dropped her baby out the window. "Go back," she said. The fields were open and he spotted another road cutting back to the first, so he made the turn and they crept along like locals. It was strange to be driving so slowly, so far into these unknown fields. They were used to the hum of the engine putting miles between them and the past, but to be puttering along only a few miles an hour in the middle of a field of severed corn stalks gradually settled them into this fresh landscape as if it were their destination all along. Perhaps it was the distance they had come or the odds they had so far beaten, but Carl felt curiously comfortable in these new surroundings.

After a few hundred yards they read a sign written in blocky letters saying, "The Prayerful Mother's Temple." Without Miriam having to ask, Carl motored down its tree-lined avenue.

"Is this it?" he asked. "This is where we're going?"

"I don't know," she murmured. There was a yearning in her voice, a desire for something she couldn't place. A grey brick church was settled into a grove before them, with parking lots on either side. She pointed to the most abandoned lot and unlatched her buckle. Carl sat there staring while she got out with her child.

"What are we doing here, Miriam?"

Her face was uncertain. She didn't answer, nor did she wait for him as she trailed off with her daughter to a tiny chapel on the lawn. It was circular in plan with glass block walls arcing up to form an awkward dome, so the whole room glowed around them. Their footsteps echoed on the black granite floor in a timeless inquiry, the tap of each toe a note in a sacred dance. Under the dome was a statue of a mother extending her baby toward a priest, though it wasn't clear if she was handing the baby over or taking back what was rightfully hers. The sculpted priest was bland and spiritless with only his collar giving him any priestly authority. He held out his plastic hands as if uncertain how to proceed. A spider's web entwined their fingers, freezing them in indecision.

Carl limped inside and found them at the altar.

"I thought you were Episcopalian." he said.

"It's practically the same thing."

 Miriam grabbed the chicken leg Annaliese was sucking on and flung it outside into the grass. Together they knelt in front of a rack of electric candles. The sign on the collection box said $2.00, and next to it was a button. Carl pushed some bills into the slot and watched Miriam instruct the girl to push the button two times. With the altar two candles brighter than before, Carl stepped out and waited for them in the late greying afternoon, letting the mist bead in his hair. When Miriam and the child stepped outside, he turned with a start.

"If this isn't where we're going, then we need to get on." he said. "We're running out of daylight."

"I want to see what else is here," Miriam said, as if guided by some invisible force.

It wouldn't do any good arguing, and with his leg swollen, he didn't have any fight left in him. The three of them explored a herringbone brick path that eventually broke in two directions, one to the main church, the other plunging deep into the forest where family altars, shrines and chapels lined the trail, each dedicated to a favored saint. Miriam led the way, pausing at her favorites until they reached a small plaza in the woods displaying, among other more elaborate edifices, a large whitewashed crucifix made of reinforced concrete. Half of Christ's left arm was sheared off, so he hung on the cross by steel rebar and a tether of masonry flesh. Miriam kneeled again to pray, while Carl sat on a bench feeling the swollen tissue around his kneecap.

At the sound of rubber tires on gravel, he saw a priest in a golf cart approaching from another trail. His down coat was unzipped, exposing his black garb and collar. At first Carl figured he was fresh from the seminary since his face was boyish, but as he rolled closer his sandy-haired comb-over became apparent. He didn't have the haggard cloak of older priests Carl had known, but the lines extending from his eyes suggested he was older than he first appeared. The priest parked the cart between them and rested his hands on the wheel.

"The main chapel is open," he said. "You're welcome to stop in on the way out." He smiled like a friendly tour guide and examined Annaliese for a long uncomfortable moment. A change came over him. He concentrated on Miriam as though recognizing something in her. "I saw your truck when you pulled in. All the way from Georgia."

"We're just passing through," Carl cut in, hobbling toward him. The priest acknowledged Carl with a glancing eye, before turning back to the mother.

"We've had visitors from every state in the union."

"Is that so?" Miriam said, fingering her turquoise cross.

"Maine to California, Alaska . . . Florida." He smiled at Annaliese as if she were burdened with some special handicap, though it was clear he wanted Miriam's attention. "Have you come for confession?"

"We're running short on time." She pulled Annaliese under her wing.

The priest dragged his hair over the top of his head and gave a troubling stare through the shaggy trunks of the silver maples. "Remember the sanctity of the confessional," he said. He popped the brake and the little white cart rolled away with scarcely a sound.

Carl stepped into the space where the priest had been. "He knows, Miriam."

"I can see that."

"Let's just get out of here."

"No. I need to talk to him."

"Are you nuts?"

"I need this. I need to tell someone." She looked like she was about to run screaming into the forest. "He can't report us if I tell him in confession. That's what he meant."

She took the girl into her arms and marched down the long path to the old brick chapel. Carl limped behind and had a hard time keeping pace. By the door to the sanctuary they found the priest's golf cart sitting idle next to a hose bib with a plaque saying "holy water." They pushed on the heavy doors and stepped inside. The dank grey afternoon gloamed through the stain glass and bathed the whitewashed walls in placid tones. Several old women sat in the pews, spaced out evenly so their prayers might not bump into each other. Carl was always afraid to breath in these places. Each step sounded like a carpenter's hammer on wood. Miriam spotted the confessional and sat Annaliese down in the adjacent pew.

"You wait here with Carl. Okay?" Even her whisper echoed through the hallow chamber.

The girl welled up and she released a small shrill cry that arrived as a musical note in the vaulted nave. One woman looked over, but the others were either too engrossed in prayer or too wise in age to take notice of a fussy child. Carl sat by her and patted her knee.

"You can wait here with me."

The girl hopped up and attached herself to her mother's leg.

"Okay. You come too," her mother said, taken with her daughter's renewed affection. "It might be better if you did."

She opened the paneled door to the confessional and guided the girl inside. Carl felt a brief glimmer of desperation that he was watching them disappear forever. The sound of the door tapping shut resonated through the lofty space, the echo settling like sand falling from the heavens.

Carl had never grown comfortable in churches large or small, perhaps because he sensed his mother dwelling in the pews, reciting aloud as she often did from the Book of Psalms or a favored passage from Exodus. He could still hear her rigid inflection, "Thou shalt not," as he eased outside into the mist.

Though common sense told him to keep off his leg, his nervous energy said to keep walking, so he forced his way back to the edge of the forest, trying to limber it up and burn off his worries. The sky was dense and growing darker, waiting for the right moment to drop its load. The trail splintered off in multiple directions, each going from point to point, door to chapel, altar to cross, grotto to shrine, every axis with a tangible destination. Just choose a direction and some end would be waiting for you. Carl studied the plan and the lines of sight like a painter, searching for order, when he caught a glimpse of something in the distance behind his truck, a pale flash of grey. It was over a hundred yards away, and he squinted and waited, but saw nothing more. A moment later, one of the cars in the back of the lot pulled away and wound from sight.

Miriam and the girl were shepherded outside by the priest, and Carl met them by the parking lot where they all stared gravely at each other. The priest scrutinized him like he was some reckless boy about to take his teenage daughter to the dance. His tone was both of protection and determination.

"You're less than a half hour from the bay," the priest said. "You'll still have some daylight to find where you're going."

Carl still didn't know where they were going, but thought it best to leave it alone. He couldn't comprehend the idea of a bay, since he only knew the shape of Lake Erie as having a smooth oval bottom. He never pictured bays and inlets and places of refuge. This priest knew more about where they were going than he did, and it annoyed him.

"I can find my way in the dark just fine," Carl said.

"Keep under the speed limit."

"I've been driving the speed limit for the last eight hundred miles," he said, though it wasn't true. He'd drifted up to eighty-five on the interstate while Miriam was napping, and he'd easily pushed it over the limit when they crossed dead-straight over the Ohio plain. He'd done fine getting her this far, he stewed, as his knee ached and throbbed.

The priest regarded Carl as a soul already lost. He focused on Annaliese and squatted in front of her, bouncing in the knees, which also annoyed Carl since that was something he could no longer do. The priest reached out to the girl who stood there treelike, dead branches for arms, shy and uncertain. She faced away, but watched him from the corners of her eyes. When he took her reluctant hand and wrapped a strand of red rosary beads around her wrist, her mouth made a big "O" and she played with the beads between her fingers.

"What do you say?" Miriam asked her, but the child just stood there examining the strand of reddish rocks. Her mother coaxed her again and tried to hide her own embarrassment. Annaliese dropped the beads on the wet pavement, and her mother bent down awkwardly and picked them up for her.

"She's hardly said a word since –."

"I see," the priest said nodding firmly, apparently putting this together with what he'd been told in confession. "I see." He rose, and Miriam gazed into his soft boyish face.

"Thank you," she said.

The priest laid his hands on Miriam's head and blessed her and then the girl before walking back to the chapel, carrying his new burden.

When they made for the S-10, Carl noticed the crumpled sheet of plastic used to wrap the luggage laying on the pavement behind the truck. His insides knotted up. He tried to run, but only limped horribly since the bad leg worked no better than one long post. He clasped the side board.

"What? What's wrong?" Miriam called to him.

He bowed his head. "Shit."

"What?"

"I saw the son-of-a-bitch."

She trotted up closer while her daughter was occupied with her shiny new beads.

"No," Miriam gasped when she peered into the empty truck bed. "Oh God damn!" She looked desperately into the cab and tried the door, but it was locked. She pounded the window with both fists. "Do you know what was in those suitcases?"

Carl leaned on the side-rail and buried his head in his forearms. "Clothes?"

"All her baby pictures. Every damn one. Oh God. Her Christening dress." She roamed in circles in a manic frenzy. "Her first shoes. Her pjs from the hospital."

"I thought you would have packed a little more practical. Packed what she needed."

"Practical? I'm never going back there, Carl. Never. Those are the closest things I have to a family history. I can leave everything else in my life behind, including my drunken mother, but not my baby's possessions." She stopped at the passenger door and pounded the glass again. "Oh damn." She broke down.

"I'm sorry Miriam."

Her voice lacked any hope. "You said you saw him."

"I was waiting for you out back. I thought I saw something behind the truck. Then some car drove away. Even if I knew what he was doing, there's no way I could have chased him down." Miriam leaned into the door, her tears flowing. "Come on now," Carl said. "It's getting dark." He unlocked the door and helped her inside. They circled both lots, checking behind the few parked cars in hope the suitcases had been ransacked and left behind in a mess, before turning down the alley of trees leading away from the shrine.

"My God," she whimpered, staring back at the temple. "If we only hadn't ditched the camper."

"We had to, Miriam. You know that."

"I know," she whimpered.

The seat belt was hanging idle over Miriam's shoulder, and for the first time the girl sat away from her mother, leaning nearer to Carl's hard frame. Annaliese was showing signs of opening up, but unknown to her it coincided with the loss of her own past. Perhaps a clean break was a good thing, Carl surmised. They would all start over together.

They turned north again on Route 4, their destination close but uncertain, a new silence raining down on them.

Chapter 35

In the lap of Sandusky lies a bay of grey flat water that on a rainy day in mid-November is as dull as a winter puddle. Route 4 spills into the bay from the heart of downtown, where a tree stands alone in the sparse and sterile city park, waiting to be decorated for the season. Across the bay the roller coasters of Cedar Point whip above the horizon like doodles on a napkin. The park was out-of-season and the coasters idle with only a few security lights shining ghostly from its shore. Between the curling loops and the distant Marblehead lighthouse lies open water, where the horizon is benign and infinite, where the great lake merges with the sky.

They drove into town alongside an industrial plant glowing acid orange from the spotlights. The complex was fenced high with chain link and barb wire, and had its own water tower and trails of steam rising from strange places on the roof. They crossed a commercial strip, past the high school and hospital before plunging under the railroad tracks and finding themselves on a street lined with ugly brown bungalows. Eventually the road broke left onto Columbus Avenue and put the bay in front of them. They crept down the street, taking in the strangeness of the houses and businesses, all aged beyond their prime.

Miriam held a note written in her own hand, and she read it as the first street lights flickered on. "Look for Washington Street," she said, peering through the dying daylight. Annaliese perked her head up in quiet interest, straining against the seat belt her mother had eventually buckled. Here the road was populated with larger houses, old brick and stone Victorians, some still lived in but most converted to shops and offices. A symbolic contraction occurred where the avenue ran between two flanking churches, one Gothic, the other Romanesque, making a threshold to downtown where the safety of the bay lay dark and quiet beyond. "Here it is," she said, but Carl drifted through the traffic light. "What are you doing?" she said, exasperated as he again ignored her directions.

"We'll go right back," he said, calming her. "I just want to see the water. We came all this way."

The last two blocks of downtown were mostly darkened storefronts. Only the corner sports bar showed any sign of life, with "Go Browns," "Miller High Life," and "Proud to Serve" banners glowing in the windows. Many of the upper stories were boarded, which contrasted with the brilliant marquee of the State Street Theater, announcing ticket sales for "The Nutcracker." At the base of the street they circled the block to the water and Carl rolled down his window to get a better feel for the place. They all peered out at the long ferry terminal stretching along the wharf. He was surprised to see there were no boats in the harbor. The only movement on the bay was a lone sea gull swooping down and lapping at the bitter water, squawking as it rose out of each dive. Along the shore were a few old brick warehouses with abandoned smoke stacks, shattered windows and spidery fire escapes crawling up the walls. Signs bolted to the warehouses said, "No Trespassing" and "No Parking Anytime." There was a tinge of sewage in the air.

"It's not Florida, is it?" Miriam said.

Carl gazed longingly over the water toward the dimming shores of Marblehead, somehow knowing he'd come to the end of something. He felt an overwhelming urge to stay there, to keep them all in that one sacred ugly place and let the heater blow on their feet and warm them. But he knew it was time.

He circled back to Washington Street and turned east, following Miriam's instructions. In a few blocks she told him to turn before parallel parking on a tree-lined street. They could walk from there, she told him. When Carl shut the door, Miriam pulled out her cell phone and dialed. He wanted to give her space, so he buried his hands in his pockets and decided to work his leg. Lights were coming on in the houses, and he peered into them while he strolled to the end of the block, sampling the lives of other families he couldn't before imagine. At the end of the street was a grassy park, and beyond a sliver of shimmering water from an inland canal. On closer inspection, he noticed the canal was lined with boat garages. It was something he'd never seen before and he thought they were terribly ugly, all with cheap siding and tin roofs, some with apartments and awkward decks thrown on top as afterthoughts. He hadn't seen a single boat in the slips at the end of Columbus Avenue or on the open water, and the bay was empty of traffic. He assumed all the boats were in dry dock, or had been taken inland similar to the one they'd passed near Bucyrus, but now he realized they were all right here, hidden behind suburban garage doors like the family sedan – ready for any occasion.

By the time he made it back to the truck it was raining, and Annaliese was standing on the sidewalk with the little blue hood over her head. Her mother reached behind the seat and pulled out her tote bag full of legal papers and slung it over her shoulder.

"Why don't you leave all that here?" Carl asked.

"I've had enough stolen for one day."

They walked a half block to a corner tavern. It was originally a two-story house, but someone shuttered the downstairs windows and built a heavy boxlike addition that came right to the corner. The whole place was covered in aluminum siding, and since there were so few windows it looked like a monolithic wreck on the street like a beached freighter. The only thing indicating it was a tavern was the orange neon "open" sign glowing in the transom.

Miriam and the girl stepped under Carl's extended arm where they met the cracking of billiards and the stale smell of nicotine and pine cones. A horseshoe shaped bar took up the right side of the room, and three pool tables sat in a row on the left. The walls were heavily textured stucco with boards nailed to them at odd angles in a sad attempt to simulate the half-timbered construction favored by their ancestors. Behind the bar was a Miller Lite clock and over each pool table was a Budweiser Lamp in a Tiffany style knock-off. The couple by the nearest pool table tended their beers and smokes between shots, while a second pair kept conversation with the bartender, a sturdy woman with a foot propped on an empty keg smoking a Virginia Slim. The cigarette pack sat by one of a dozen ash trays ringing the bar. Carl figured all the men were war veterans, each with buzz-cut grey hair and grimacing faces, as though recalling long ago battles. The women, hardened on the home-front, looked apt to give as well as they got. They were all getting on in years, and they were all friends.

When Carl, Miriam and the child stepped inside everyone but the woman taking her shot at the pool table paused to take in their presence. No one said hello. Carl felt he was barging into a stranger's living room, though a part of him did feel safe, knowing they couldn't be seen from the street. There were no tables, so they took the three bar stools nearest the front door. One of the men on the other side of the bar forced himself up and strode down a corridor under a sign saying "gals/gents." When the bartender faced Annaliese, Carl immediately thought this was no good. This was the wrong place, the wrong people. You can't bring a kid into a bar. She made brief eye contact with Miriam before easing back into small talk with her friends.

Carl checked his watch. "When are we meeting them?" he asked Miriam.

"They should be here any time."

Miriam never sat down. She rested the legal papers on a stool and balanced Annaliese on the next one, guarding her closely while she fiddled with her rosary. Carl stretched his stiff leg to one side and rested its heel on the brass rail near the floor. It felt good to be sitting still, planted in one spot, at least for a while.

The telephone behind the bar rang like a fire alarm and jolted all three of them, but no one else in the tavern took notice. It rang only once and stopped without anyone answering.

Miriam stared at Carl's profile, looking tired and regretful. "I have to change her." she said.

He sensed her eyes on his cheek and he turned to her. "What's wrong?"

She was welling up. "Nothing." She gazed at him for a long thoughtful moment before gathering Annaliese and the files into her arms. When she passed behind Carl, she brushed his back with her shoulder, leaning into him in a long nudging caress. Though she was layered in sweaters, it was a warm nudge giving him comfort and reminding him of the night before. He watched them circle the bar, watched Annaliese's cheek safely tucked in the hope of her mother's neck as they passed from sight down the narrow corridor.

The bartender wandered over in her own good time and asked what he wanted.

"What do you have on draft?"

"Bottles," she responded. She was the youngest one in the tavern, but no less than fifty and looking like she'd seen at least as much in life as the vets.

"Just give me a light beer," Carl said. "A glass of white wine and a coke too." He watched her reach under the counter, grab a brown bottle and pop its top. A foam mushroom grew from the neck as she set it on a napkin. "You have a menu?"

She let out a chuckle, though it was more of a gasp that devolved into a hacking cough. She reached for her cigarette.

"No food here," she said, still hacking as she waddled to the other side of the bar and returned with a bowl of salted nuts. Carl took a sip and the beer stung his throat. His body wanted to heave it back up, but he held it as it burned past his frost-bitten lungs. He ran a hand through his hair, still getting used to it. He coughed and wondered if he was getting sick.

Ten minutes passed before Carl ordered a second beer. The bartender never brought the wine or coke, but he didn't mind. White wine needed to be chilled, he knew that much, and the coke would just get watered down as the ice melted. Miriam must be having a time changing the girl, all layered up like she was.

When the bartender placed another sweating bottle in front of him, the woman shooting pool howled. She had obviously beaten her partner, who sat on a nearby stool shaking his head. She gave the man a kiss on the lips that wasn't returned.

"Go on," she told her friends. "I'm played out." As the man racked the balls, the game's winner walked over and sat next to Carl. The bartender motioned for the cooler, but the woman waved her off. "Make it a coffee," she said, thumping a cigarette from her pack. Her hair was dyed jet black and done up in a hairdo giving it twice the body she should have for her age. Carl could see the Budweiser lamp glowing right through it. A pea green sweater stretched over her breasts and kept the same shape over her mid-section.

"I see you put your husband in his place," Carl joked.

She snorted and was pleased as a steaming cup of coffee was set before her.

"I wouldn't have that old loser for my husband," she said, loud enough for all of them to hear. The man rifled his cue and the balls cracked across the room. She brought the cup to her lips as if the taste might recover a memory. "Actually, he's as good a man as I've ever known. I'm just past ever marrying again."

Carl nodded, not completely understanding, but accepting. He glanced down the corridor again, and the woman checked her watch.

"Don't worry about them," she said.

"Excuse me?"

"They're on the bay by now." She examined him more closely, surveyed his poorly cut hair and blighted eyes. "You look awful."

"What are you talking about?"

"I'm not supposed to say, but she said you were all right." She wrapped her hands around the coffee cup, savoring its warmth. Carl felt the cold air drafting from the hallway. He lurched up and limped hurriedly toward the restrooms, knocked on the door under the "gals" sign and called to her. The door creaked open under the weight of his hand. A lone scabbed sink hung off the wall next to the toilet – the room was empty. He rushed into the men's room and it was the same. He burst open the last door and met a rush of cold wet air. From the stoop overlooking the rear parking lot, he heard water dripping through the downspout and the spray of a distant passing car. He stormed back inside where the bartender was refreshing the woman's coffee.

"Strong," she said. "I like it strong, like my men."

"Where are they?" Carl demanded.

"They're fine. They'll make Pelee Island in a few hours." Carl stared at her blankly, still wondering if they were talking about the same thing. She wouldn't look at him. "You're not going to cause problems are you?"

Carl tore out the front door, forgetting his knee and its swollen ligaments, and sprinted down the street through the rain and across the park to the depressing alley of boat garages backing the bay. He ran without thinking about pacing or fatigue, pain or police. He ran down the narrow alley between the garages and their cheap siding and sterile windowless fronts to the end where he stumbled into the bulkhead, sucking air and panting like a dying dog, crippled up and bearing his whole weight on one good leg. Before him was a narrow breakwater and beyond the darkened bay and shadowy loops of Cedar Point. He was searching for something else and he found it – a single distant light tracking slowly toward the inlet. He bent down and rested, rested there and breathed, heard the drops of rain on tin rooftops and the grey water lapping the shore.

Shaking and soaked, dragging the extra weight of his leg, he plodded back to the tavern and sat down again next to the woman. The bartender had taken away his bottle. Carl and the woman concentrated on what was in front of them, as if it was better not to have any memory of the other's face.

"They're safe, Carl. They'll be over the lake tomorrow. That's all I can tell you."

He gripped the edge of the bar, needing something to hold on to.

"The police are looking for me," he said.

"So?" She finished her coffee and picked up her purse. In it lay the same type of cell phone Miriam had been using.

"They know I'm in on this," he said.

"How so?"

Carl had no answer. He tried to think it out. "They'll look in my truck. They'll find things there."

"Had Miriam and her baby ever been in your truck before this week?"

"Of course."

"Well then, a stray hair or fingernail won't prove a thing."

She pulled a few bills from her purse and put them under the saucer. Coming back from the coat rack, she handed Carl a folded page torn from a spiral notebook. "This is for you." The woman called out goodbye to her friends and walked out the door, leaving Carl with the sound of cracking billiard balls. He laid the piece of paper on the bar. It was folded three times and he spread it open. The note was in Miriam's loopy script and it was scrawled hastily across the page. All it said was, "Thank you."

He dug out his wallet and put some cash on the counter. No longer aware of his knee, he limped through the door to the sidewalk where it was raining hard. The street lamps glowed yellow, leaving the world used and abandoned, left without purpose. A parked car down the street flashed on its headlights and roared his way. Carl stood there as the frigid drops of rain pierced through him. He was blinded, hypnotized by the lights and the space and the emptiness of it all. Soon the car was on him and he stepped off the curb into its glare. The driver slammed on the brakes and skidded to a stop just shy of his knees. Carl dropped his hands on the hood and stared at the woman through the arc of the wipers. He stumbled to the window and she rolled it halfway down as rain splattered inside. He rested his fingers on the edge of the glass.

"What do I do?" he pleaded. "What do I do now?"

She lilted her head to one side and gave him a strained expression. "Go home." She rolled up the window and he watched her drive away.

Darkness settled on the town, but Carl no longer stared into the warm lit houses as he limped back to his truck. When he crawled into the cab and shut the door the windows fogged, obscuring his vision, making the world harder to see. He started the motor and flipped on the defogger and sat there listening to the surging fan, but it did no good. He cracked the window to breath fresh air into his lungs, get oxygen to his brain. Laying down across the seat he was overcome with exhaustion. A numbness radiated from his knee. His cheek pressed against the cold vinyl where they had sat for so many miles. He smelled the odd mix of bile and musk and the rich top soil rising from the girl's geranium laying on its side on the floorboard. Something reflected from the dash, something out of place, and he reached out to it. It was his grandmother's turquoise crucifix hanging from the radio knob, jiggling from the vibration of the motor.

Carl hungered for his illusion for so many years he was blind to the reality in front of him all along. Laying there fingering the old heirloom and sensing Miriam's lost wedding band burning white hot in his pocket, he found himself with no regrets, his old void nearly filled, but this time it was not with the illusory vestige of Miriam. Betting on her instincts, and his own, he trusted the girl would soon be in a better place, a place where she might find her own way less impeded. It was in the safe delivery of the child where he found solace. And though he'd crossed from warm coast to cold, water to water, finding dead ends at each shore, he had only wandered off like a child straying into and out of a fool's paradise. But he'd come to an end here; a safe barrier, a place of reference he could use and follow and find his way home.

He would rest a while now. Get some sleep. At first light he would drive.